ALSO BY BRAD THOR

Path of the Assassin
The Lions of Lucerne
State of the Union
Blowback
Takedown

Visit www.BradThor.com

THE FIRST COMMANDMENT

Brad Thor

POCKET
BOOKS

LONDON • SYDNEY • NEW YORK • TORONTO

First published in the United States of America by Pocket Books, 2008
An imprint of Simon & Schuster Inc.
First published in Great Britain by Pocket Books UK, 2009
An imprint of Simon & Schuster UK Ltd
A CBS COMPANY

Copyright © Brad Thor, 2007

1 3 5 7 9 10 8 6 4 2

Simon & Schuster UK Ltd
Africa House
64-78 Kingsway
London WC2B 6AH

www.simonsays.co.uk

Simon & Schuster Australia
Sydney

A CIP catalogue record for this book
is available from the British Library

ISBN 978-1-84739-194-0

Printed and bound in Great Britain by
Cox & Wyman Ltd, Reading, Berks

For Scott F. Hill, Ph.D.—
a dedicated patriot who has put love of country
and love of family above all else

De inimico non loquaris male, sed cogites.

Do not wish ill for your enemy, plan it.

CHAPTER 1

When it was hot and humid, life in Cuba hovered somewhere between absolute misery and "the bath is ready does anyone have a razor blade?" But when it was cold and raining, Cuba was downright unbearable. Tonight was one of those nights.

When the guards arrived at the isolation cells of Delta's "Camp 5," where the most dangerous and highest-intelligence-value detainees resided, they were in a worse mood than usual. And it wasn't because of the weather. Something was wrong. It was written all over their faces as they pulled five prisoners from their cells and ordered them at gunpoint to strip.

Philippe Roussard hadn't been at Guantanamo the longest, but he had definitely been interrogated the hardest. A European of Arab descent, he was a sniper of extraordinary ability whose exploits were legendary. Videos of his kills played on continuous loops on jihadist websites across the internet. To his Muslim brothers he was nothing short of a superhero in the radical Islamist pantheon. To the United States, he was a horrific killing machine responsible for the deaths of over one hundred U.S. soldiers.

As Roussard looked into the eyes of his jailers, though, he saw more than the usual pure hatred. Tonight it was coupled with absolute disgust. Whatever middle-of-the-night interrogation tactic the Joint Task Force Guantanamo soldiers had in store for Roussard and his four colleagues, something told him it wasn't going to be like anything they had experienced before. The guards appeared on the verge of losing control.

Had an attack been successfully executed against the United States? What else could have put the soldiers in such a state?

If so, Roussard felt certain that the Americans would make the prisoners pay. Undoubtedly, they had devised yet another humiliating exercise designed to insult their prisoners' Muslim sensibilities. Privately, Roussard hoped the torture involved the attractive blond soldier and that she would disrobe down to her lacy, black lingerie and rub herself against him. Though he knew it was wrong, his fantasies of what he wanted to do to that woman were what kept him nicely occupied during the long, lonely hours of isolation he endured.

He was still speculating about his fate when he heard the door at the far end of the cell block shut. Roussard looked up, hoping it was the blond, but it wasn't. Another soldier had entered carrying five paper shopping bags. As he passed, he threw each of the prisoners a bag.

"Get dressed!" he ordered in awkward Arabic.

Confused, all of the prisoners, including Roussard, removed the civilian clothing from their bags and began to get dressed. The men cast furtive glances at one another as they tried to figure out what was happening. Roussard was reminded of stories he'd heard about Jewish concentration camp prisoners who were told they were being taken for showers when they were actually on their way to the gas chambers.

He doubted the Americans were dressing them in new clothes only to execute them, but nevertheless the uncertainty of what they were about to face filled him with more than a little trepidation.

"Why don't they try to make a run for it?" one of the guards whispered to his comrade as he stroked the trigger guard of his M-16. "I just want one of these fuckers to rabbit on us."

"This is bullshit," replied the other. "What the hell are we doing?"

"You two, shut up!" barked their commander, who then called in a series of commands over his radio.

Something definitely wasn't right.

Once they were completely clothed, shackles were placed around their wrists and ankles and they were lined up against the far wall.

This is it, thought Roussard as he held the stare of the soldier who had been hoping for one of the prisoners to make a run for it.

The soldier's finger went from his weapon's trigger guard to its actual trigger and he seemed about to say something when a series of vehicles ground to a halt just outside.

"That's us," shouted the Task Force commander. "Let's mount up."

The prisoners were shoved toward the door. Roussard hoped that once they got outside and he could see where they were going, things would make more sense.

That plan was dashed as one by one, black hoods were placed over each man's head before he was taken outside to a waiting column of green Humvees.

Ten minutes later, the convoy came to a stop. Before Roussard's heavy hood was removed, he could make out the distinct, high-pitched whine of idling jet engines.

On the rain-soaked tarmac, the prisoners stared up at an enormous Boeing 727 as their shackles were removed. A metal staircase had been rolled up against the side of the aircraft and its door stood wide open.

No one said a word, but based on the demeanor of the soldiers—who seemed to have been ordered to keep their distance from the plane—Roussard came to a stunning conclusion. Without being directed to do so, he took a step forward. When none of the soldiers tried to stop him, he took another and another until his feet touched the first metal step and he began climbing upward two at a time. His salvation was at hand! Just as he had known it eventually would be.

With the sound of the other prisoners pounding up the gangway behind him, Roussard stepped cautiously into the cabin. He was met by the plane's first officer, who compared his likeness to a photo on his clipboard, removed a heavy black envelope, and said, "We were told to give you this."

Roussard had received envelopes like this before. Without even opening it, he knew who it was from.

"If you wouldn't mind taking a seat," continued the first officer. "The captain is eager to be underway."

Roussard found an empty place near the window and buckled himself in. As the main cabin door was closed, several members of the flight crew disappeared into the rear of the aircraft and returned lugging odd-looking pieces of medical equipment, along with an equal number of large, plastic coolers.

None of it made any sense to Roussard until he opened the envelope and read its contents. A slow smile then began to spread across his face. It was done. Not only was he free, but the Americans would not be able to come after him. He was going to have his revenge—and much sooner than he would have thought.

Opening his window shade, Roussard could see the soldiers climbing back into their Humvees and driving away from their airstrip, several with their hands hanging out the windows and their middle fingers raised in mock salute.

As the aircraft's engines roared to life and the heavy beast began to roll forward, cheers of "Allahu Akbar," *God is great,* erupted from the front of the plane.

Allah was indeed great, but Roussard knew it

wasn't He who had arranged for their release. As he stared at the black envelope, he knew their gratitude was owed to someone much less benevolent.

Turning his attention back to the window as the soldiers quickly disappeared from view, Roussard cocked thumb and forefinger, took aim, and pulled an imaginary trigger.

Now that he was free, he knew that it was only a matter of time before his handler turned him loose inside America to exact his revenge.

CHAPTER 2

FAIRFAX COUNTY, VIRGINIA
SIX MONTHS LATER

A crack of thunder shook the walls and the bed-room windows exploded in a hailstorm of broken glass. Powered completely by instinct, Scot Harvath reached for his girlfriend, Tracy, and rolled off the bed.

He landed hard on his bad shoulder. Shifting his weight, he reached up and yanked the drawer free of his nightstand. It came down with a crash. Foreign coins, a bottle of painkillers, a set of keys to locks he had yet to locate on the property, pens, and a pad of paper from the Ritz in Paris all spilled onto the wood floor.

Everything was there, except what he desperately needed to find—his gun.

Harvath rolled onto his stomach and breaststroked wildly beneath the bed. All he came up with was an empty box of hollow-point ammunition and an equally empty holster.

His instincts screamed at him to find a weapon while his conscience screamed at him for going to bed without one. But he *had* gone to bed with a weapon. He *always* did. He had placed it in the drawer right next to him. *He was sure of it.*

Maybe Tracy had gotten to it first. He turned to her, but she wasn't there. In fact, in his groggy grab and roll, he wasn't quite sure if she'd even been in the bed at all. *Nothing was making sense.*

Getting to his feet, Harvath stayed low and made for the hallway and the stairs at the far end. With every step, his trepidation mounted. His gut was trying to tell him something. Then, on the final landing, he saw the blood. The floors, the walls, the ceiling . . . they were all covered with it.

There was so much of it everywhere. Where had it come from? *Who* had it come from?

Despite the adrenaline pumping through his body, his legs felt like two blocks of solid granite. It took all of his willpower to inch forward toward his entryway and the open front door.

When he stepped outside, what he saw came in quick, sharp stabs of vision—bloody brushstrokes painted above the doorway, an upturned picnic hamper, and collapsed upon the threshold next to a small white dog was the body of the woman he had been falling in love with.

Harvath thought he saw movement somewhere along the tree line at the edge of the property. He was looking for anything he could use as a weapon when a long, black knife swung over his shoulder from behind and the blade was pressed against his throat.

CHAPTER 3

FAIRFAX HOSPITAL
FALLS CHURCH, VIRGINIA

Harvath's head snapped back so suddenly that the shock startled him awake. It took several seconds for his heart rate to slow and for him to recognize where he was.

He looked around the hospital room and saw that everything was just as he'd left it before he'd drifted off to sleep. The bedrail he'd intended only to rest his forehead against was still there, as was the bed's occupant, Tracy Hastings.

Harvath's eyes scanned the length of her body, searching for any sign that she'd moved during his nap, but Tracy remained in her coma. She was the victim of an anonymous assassin's bullet five days ago, and she hadn't moved since; not even a fraction of an inch.

The ventilator continued its rhythmic cycle of *woosh, pop . . . woosh, pop.* Harvath couldn't bear to see her like this. She had already suffered so many traumas. But the worst part was knowing that her current suffering was his fault.

In spite of what the world had thrown at her—in particular an IED in Iraq that had exploded in her face, taking one of her beautiful blue eyes and her career as a top Naval Explosive Ordnance Disposal tech—she had managed to maintain an incredible sense of humor. Though it had taken him a while to admit it, Harvath had fallen for Tracy the minute he first saw her.

They had been thrown together quite by accident just under a month ago in Manhattan. Harvath had traveled to the Big Apple to spend the Fourth of July weekend with his good friend, Robert Herrington. Robert, or "Bullet Bob" as he was known to his buddies, was a storied Delta Force operative who'd recently been medically discharged from the Army due to an injury he'd suffered in Afghanistan.

Harvath and Herrington had a jam-packed weekend of drinking and carousing planned when New York City came under a horrific terrorist attack. Little did either of them know that Bob would be killed later that night.

With the island of Manhattan completely sealed off and police, fire, and EMS units stretched to the breaking point, Bob had helped Scot assemble his own team to hunt down the perpetrators.

The team was composed of special operations

personnel from the Manhattan VA facility who, like
Bob, had all been recently discharged for various
injuries suffered overseas. Harvath had been standing
on top of the VA building along the East River when
Tracy and two other pals of Bob's had stepped onto
the roof.

At twenty-six, Tracy was ten years younger than
Harvath, but there was a wisdom and worldliness
about her that made their ages irrelevant. When Harvath later shared this observation with her, she joked
that deactivating deadly explosive devices for a living
had a way of aging a person, fast.

She might have carried herself like a woman older
than her twenty-six years, but she certainly didn't look
it. She was the picture of fitness. In fact, she had the
most sculpted body of any woman Harvath had ever
known. Tracy joked she had a body to die for and a
face to protect it. It was her way of dealing with the
scarring she had suffered as a result of the IED detona-
tion in Iraq. The plastic surgeons had done a fabulous
job in matching the pale blue of her surviving eye to a
replacement, but no matter how Tracy applied her
makeup, she still couldn't completely hide the thin
facial scars.

None of that mattered to Harvath. He thought
she was gorgeous. In particular, he loved how she wore
her blond hair in pigtails. Pigtails were for little girls,
but there was something decidedly sexy about them
when worn by a woman.

That was Tracy in a nutshell. There was nothing
ordinary about her. Her wit, her compassion, her per-

sistence in the face of injury were all traits Harvath admired deeply, but those weren't what had made him fall in love with her. His reason for falling in love was much more selfish.

The reason Harvath cared for her so deeply was that for the first time in his life, he'd found someone who truly understood him for who he was. She saw beyond the waves of constant wisecracks, through the never-ending stream of jokes, and over the pile of rocks that Harvath had stacked to wall himself off from the rest of the world. He didn't need to play games with her and she didn't need to play games with him. From the moment they met, they could each be themselves. It was a feeling Harvath had never thought he would experience.

As he looked down at Tracy in her hospital bed, he knew it was a feeling he would never experience again.

Gently, he untwined his hand from hers and stood.

CHAPTER 4

In the hospital room's private bath were a tooth-brush, toothpaste, razor, deodorant, and shaving cream. Laverna, the night nurse, had dropped them off shortly after Harvath had arrived on the morning of Tracy's shooting. It had been quite obvious that he had no intention of leaving. He was ready to stay for as long as it took to get her better.

Closing the door, Harvath took off his clothes and turned on the shower. When the water was good and hot, he climbed inside and let it pound against his body. When he closed his eyes, pieces of his nightmare came back and he fought to banish them to the far reaches of his psyche. Scrubbing himself with a tiny bar of courtesy soap, he tried to think of something else.

It was working, but he knew the demons would be back. They'd been hovering over him every day and night since Tracy had been shot.

One of the doctors who'd been standing in the room when Harvath came out of a particularly bad version of the dream suggested that he seek some therapy, but Harvath politely laughed him off. The doctor obviously didn't know who he was talking to. Men in Scot's line of work didn't seek therapy. Who in the world could ever begin to comprehend the life he led, much less the incredible toll it had taken on him over the years?

Throwing the temperature selector all the way to cold, Harvath shocked his body awake and climbed out.

Wrapping a towel around his waist, he leaned against the sink and wiped a patch of fog from the mirror. For once in his life, he actually looked the way he felt—horrible. His normally bright blue eyes were dull and bloodshot, his handsome face drawn and haggard. His sandy brown hair, though not long by any stretch, was in need of a haircut. And though his taut, muscular five-foot-ten frame would have been the envy of men half his age, he'd barely eaten in the last five days and it was sadly undernourished.

Only once before had Harvath ever been filled with as much doubt and self-loathing as he was now.

Eighteen years ago, he had defied his father, a SEAL instructor at the Naval Special Warfare School near their home in Coronado, California. He had tried out for and been accepted to the U.S. Freestyle Ski Team. Though his father knew his son was an exceptional skier, he had wanted him to go to college after high school, not enter the world of professional athletics. Father and son were equally stubborn, and neither talked to the other for a long time afterward. It was Scot's mother, Maureen, who managed to keep the family together. And though there was some communication between the two men, things were never really the same again. Father and son were more alike than either cared to admit, which was what made the tragedy of the elder Harvath's death even more unbearable.

When Michael Harvath was killed in a training accident, Scot was never the same again. No matter how hard he tried, he couldn't get his head back into competitive skiing. As much as he loved the sport, it didn't seem that important to him anymore.

With a portion of his substantial winnings, he bought a backpack and traveled through Europe, eventually settling in Greece on a small island called Paros. There he found a job as a bartender, working for two mismatched, expat Brits. One was a former driver for a south London crime family, the other a disgruntled ex-SAS soldier. After a year, Harvath knew what he wanted to do.

He returned home and enrolled at the University of Southern California, where he studied political science and military history. Upon graduating three years later, cum laude, he joined the Navy, eventually trying out for and being accepted to Basic Underwater Demolition SEAL school (BUD/S) and a specialized program known as SQT or SEAL Qualification Training. Though the selection process and subsequent training were grueling beyond measure, his mental and physical conditioning as a world-class athlete, his refusal to ever give up on anything, and the belief that he had finally found his true calling in life propelled him forward and earned him the honor of being counted as one of the world's most elite warriors—a U.S. Navy SEAL.

With his exceptional skiing ability, Harvath was tasked to the SEALs' cold-weather experts, SEAL Team Two. There, despite a tragic loss on one of his first assignments, Harvath had excelled.

Eventually, he caught the attention of the members of the Navy's famed SEAL Team Six, who helped hone his skills not only as a warrior, but also as a linguist, improving upon his rudimentary knowledge of French and teaching him Arabic.

It was while he was with Team Six that Harvath assisted a presidential security detail in Maine and caught the eye of the Secret Service. Wanting to bolster their antiterrorism expertise at the White House, they eventually succeeded in wooing him away from the Navy and up to D.C. Harvath soon distinguished himself even further, and after a short time was recommended for an above-top-secret program at the Department of Homeland Security being spearheaded by an old family friend and former deputy director of the FBI named Gary Lawlor.

The program was called the Apex Project. It was buried in a little-known branch of DHS called the Office of International Investigative Assistance, or OIIA for short. The OIIA's overt mission was to assist foreign police, military, and intelligence agencies in helping prevent attacks against Americans and American interests abroad. In that sense, Harvath's mission was partly in step with the official OIIA mandate. In reality, he was a very secretive dog of war enlisted post–9/11 to be unleashed by the president upon the enemies of the United States to help prevent any future terrorist attacks on America.

The rationale was that if the terrorists weren't playing by any rules, then neither would the U.S. But because of sensitive PC biases that existed in America, which seemed to suggest our nation was the only one that should abide by the rules, the president realized that Harvath's true mission could only be known by a key few, namely the president himself and Harvath's boss, Gary Lawlor.

Harvath was to be backed by the full weight of the Oval Office, as well as the collective might of the U.S. military and the combined assets of the U.S. intelligence community. The program sounded fantastic on paper, but reality, especially in bureaucratic Washington, often turned out to be something else entirely.

Harvath didn't want to think about his job now. It was because of it, because of *him,* that Tracy had been shot. He didn't need the results of any investigation to tell him that. He knew it as surely as he knew that the woman lying in that hospital bed didn't deserve any of what had happened to her.

The FBI had been able to piece together some of what had happened. They had discovered the hiding spot the shooter had used in the woods at the edge of his property. Their assessment was that whoever the assassin was, he'd dug himself in sometime during the evening, probably several hours before daylight.

The killer had left behind a shell casing with the message—*That which has been taken in blood, can only be answered in blood.*

There had also been the bizarre act of painting his doorframe with blood. The first run of analyses ruled out its being Tracy's. It had been painted there sometime during the night and had already dried before Tracy was shot.

Then there was the dog that had been placed on the doorstep as a gift in a picnic basket. Harvath had only to take one look at the thank-you note that had been left with it to know who it was from. But if someone was going to target him or Tracy, why leave such a blatant calling card?

Weeks earlier, on a covert operation in Gibraltar, Harvath had saved the life of an enormous dog known as a Caucasian Ovcharka—the same breed as the one that had been left on his doorstep. The owner of the dog in Gibraltar was a contemptible little man—a dwarf, actually—who dealt in the purchase and sale of highly classified information. He had also helped plan the attack on New York. He was known simply as the Troll.

But how had the Troll found him? Only a handful of people knew about the historic church and grounds named Bishop's Gate that Harvath now called home. He found it hard to believe that the Troll would be so careless or stupid as to announce that he was behind Tracy's shooting.

The timing, though, stank, and Harvath wasn't a person who believed in coincidences. There had to be a connection, and he was determined to find out what it was.

CHAPTER 5

When Harvath came back into the hospital room, Tracy's parents, Bill and Barbara Hastings, were sitting on either side of her bed.

Bill Hastings was a large man, about six-foot-four and over two hundred pounds. He'd played football at Yale and looked like he could still play. His hair was gray and Harvath put him in his mid to late sixties. Seeing Harvath enter the room, he looked up and asked, "Any change?"

"No, sir," replied Harvath.

Barbara smiled at him. "You were here all night again, weren't you?"

Harvath didn't reply. He simply nodded. Having to deal with Tracy's parents was one of the more difficult aspects of keeping vigil at her bedside. He felt so damn responsible for what had happened to her. He couldn't believe how kind they were to him. If they blamed him at all for what had happened to their daughter, they didn't show it.

"How's the hotel?" Harvath managed. The silences in the room could be unbearable, and he knew he had to start carrying some of the conversational weight.

"It's fine," replied Barbara as she reached for Tracy's hand and began stroking her forearm. Tracy's mother was a stunningly elegant woman. Her deep red hair was perfectly coifed and her fingernails were perfectly manicured. She wore a silk blouse, an Armani skirt cut just above the knee, stockings, and expensive pumps.

Though Harvath would never have uttered such a trite line, it was obvious where Tracy got her good looks.

The Hastings made a very attractive pair. With the fortune that Bill Hastings had amassed in the hedge fund arena, it was no surprise that they were almost permanent fixtures on the Manhattan society pages.

After the July 3 attack on New York City, they had debated cutting their summer in the south of France short, but Tracy had convinced them to stay. Manhattan was going to be a nightmare to get back to and to get around in for some time to come, so the longer they could delay their return, the better. Their plans had changed the minute Tracy had been shot. They had chartered a private plane and rushed to Washington to be by their daughter's side.

Harvath was struggling to come up with something else to say when a nurse stuck her head in the door and said, "Agent Harvath? There is a gentleman here to see you. He's waiting in the lounge."

"Okay, I'll be right out," replied Harvath. He was happy to give the Hastingses some time alone with their daughter.

Stepping around Mr. Hastings, Harvath bent down and whispered in Tracy's ear that he'd be back in a little bit. He gave her hand a loving squeeze, then headed for the door.

Just as he was reaching for the handle, Bill Hastings said, "If that's the fellow from the Bureau again, make sure you tell him that we never did find Tracy's ID in her personal effects."

Harvath nodded and exited. Outside the room, he slid Tracy's driver's license from his pocket and looked at it. *God she was beautiful.* He didn't have the heart to tell Bill Hastings that he was the reason her ID was missing. In the short amount of time he and Tracy had been together, they'd never stopped to take any photos.

Though he felt guilty for deceiving her parents, Harvath had no intention of giving it up. It was one of the few reminders he had of the way she was, the way *they* were, before they had been torn apart.

Entering the lounge, Harvath found his longtime friend and boss, Gary Lawlor, waiting for him. "How's she doing?" he asked.

"Still the same," replied Harvath. "Anything new on the investigation?"

Gary motioned for him to sit down. It was a windowless room with a television mounted on a wall bracket in the corner. Harvath took a seat and waited for the man who had become like a second father to him to close the door and sit down.

When Gary took his seat, his expression was all business. "We may have gotten a break in the case."

Harvath leaned forward in his chair. "What kind of break?"

"It has to do with the blood that was painted above your doorframe."

"What about it?"

"The forensics people now know it wasn't human."

"What was it?"

"Lamb's blood."

Harvath was confused. *"Lamb's blood?* That's doesn't make any sense."

"No," replied Gary, "but it's what they found *mixed with* the blood that I want to talk to you about."

Harvath didn't say anything. He just waited.

Leaning forward, Lawlor lowered his voice and said, "After Bob Herrington's funeral, the secretary of defense took you for a ride and asked if you were up to taking out his killer. Do you remember him telling you that they were planning on letting him escape so that they could track him back to the people he was working with?"

"Yes, so?"

"So, do you remember *how* they planned on tracking him?" asked Lawlor.

Harvath thought about it a moment. "They spiked his blood with some sort of radioisotope that created a signature they could follow via satellite."

Lawlor leaned back in his chair and watched as Harvath processed the information.

"The lamb's blood contained a radioisotope."

Lawlor nodded.

"That's impossible. I took care of Bob's killer myself." Harvath was about to add *and I watched him die* when he realized he hadn't actually witnessed the terrorist check out.

Though Harvath doubted anyone could have survived what he had done to Mohammed bin Mohammed, the fact remained that he hadn't actually confirmed that the man was dead.

"They don't believe it was Mohammed," said Lawlor. "From what I have been able to gather, this is a completely different radioisotope."

"Purposely put into the lamb's blood and painted over the front door of my house?" asked Harvath.

Once again, Lawlor nodded.

"Why?"

"Somebody is sending you a message."

"Obviously, but who? If it's a radioisotope, even if

it's a different one than what was used on Mohammed, it shouldn't be that hard to figure out where it came from. We'll start there."

"It's not going to be that easy," said Lawlor.

"Why not? The whole thing is a DOD program. They keep records like anyone else. Contact the Def Sec's office and let him know we need access."

"I already tried."

"And?" Harvath asked impatiently.

"No go."

"*No go?* You've got to be kidding me."

Lawlor shook his head. "Unfortunately, I'm not kidding."

"Then we'll go to the president. Even the defense secretary answers to someone. If President Rutledge tells him to open his files, believe me, he'll open his files," said Harvath.

"I already spoke with President Rutledge. It's a no go."

Harvath couldn't believe what he was hearing. "I want to talk to the president myself."

"He knew you'd say that," said Lawlor. "And he feels he owes it to you. There's a car waiting for us downstairs."

CHAPTER 6

When Harvath and Lawlor were shown into the Oval Office, President Rutledge stood up and came around his desk to greet them.

He shook Gary's hand and then as he shook hands with Harvath inquired, "How's she doing?"

"Still no change, sir," replied Harvath as the president ushered him and Lawlor to one of the sofas perpendicular to the Oval Office fireplace.

As they took their seats, Rutledge got right to the point. "Scot, I know I speak for all Americans when I say that I am very sorry for what happened to Tracy. This nation owes your entire team a great debt for what you did in New York."

Harvath had never been comfortable with praise, especially when it came from the president, but he was even less comfortable now. The operation in New York City had essentially been a failure. So many people had died, including one of his best friends. Though Harvath and his team had managed to take down most of the terrorists involved with the plot, they had been playing catch-up the entire way. It was not something he was at all proud of.

He acknowledged the president's remarks with a quiet "thank you" and listened as the man continued.

"Scot, you have been one of this nation's greatest

assets in the war on terror. I don't want you for a moment to doubt how much your service has been appreciated. I know too well that yours can often be a thankless job and that is why I am thanking you once again."

Harvath had a bad feeling about where this was going. He could sense the other shoe was about to drop. He didn't have to wait long.

Jack Rutledge looked him right in the eye and stated, "We've known each other for several years and I've always been straight with you."

Harvath nodded. "Yes, you have, sir."

"Often against the advice of my advisors, I have filled you in on the big picture because I wanted you to understand your role in it and why you were being asked to do certain things.

"What's more, I filled you in because I knew I could trust you. Now, I am asking you to trust me."

The president paused as he tried to get a read on Harvath. The counterterrorism operative's face was inscrutable, forcing Rutledge to ask, "Can you do that? Can you trust me?"

Harvath knew the correct answer was, *Of course, I can trust you, Mr. President,* but those were not the words that came out of his mouth. Instead, he replied, "Trust you regarding what, sir?"

It was not the answer the president wanted to hear, but it didn't come as a surprise. There was a reason Scot Harvath was so good at what he did. He wasn't a pushover, not by a long shot.

"I'm going to ask you to do something. I know

you're not going to like it, but this is where I need you to stay with me."

Harvath's alarm bells began ringing. He nodded slowly, encouraging the president to continue.

"I want you to let us track down the gunman who shot Tracy."

The president wasn't offering him a yes or no proposition. Even so, Harvath had no intention of being sidelined. Being careful of his word choice and his tone, he stated, "I'm sorry, Mr. President, I don't understand."

Rutledge didn't mince words. "Yes, you do. I'm asking you to sit this one out."

Too often, the fine art of diplomacy eluded Harvath. Looking the president right in the eyes he said, "Why?"

As president of the United States, Jack Rutledge didn't have to explain himself to anyone, much less Scot Harvath. He didn't even have to have this meeting with him, but as he'd stated, the president felt the nation owed Harvath a great debt—not only for what he'd done in New York and then afterward in Gibraltar, but on many other occasions.

What's more, Harvath had once saved the president's life, as well as his daughter's. He deserved a better explanation and Rutledge knew it. The president just couldn't give him one. "There are forces at play here I am not at liberty to discuss, even with you," he said.

"I can appreciate that, Mr. President, but this isn't a random act of terrorism. Whoever did this did it because it's personal. The blood above my door, the shell casing, the note—somebody is calling me out."

"And I've assembled a team to take care of it."

Harvath tried to keep his cool as he replied, "Mr. President, I know you've got the FBI working overtime, but as good as they are, they're not the right agency for this job."

"Scot, listen—" began the president.

"I don't mean any disrespect, but from everything we've seen this guy is a professional assassin who's probably affiliated with a major terrorist organization. If we're going to catch him, the people hunting him have to understand his mind-set. They need to be able to think like him, and the FBI just can't do that."

"The people I've put on this job can. They'll find him, I promise you."

"Mr. President, this guy shot Tracy in the head. The doctors say it's a miracle she wasn't killed. She's lying in a coma she may never come out of and it's my fault—all of it. I owe it to her to find who did this. You have to bring me onboard."

Rutledge had worried things would go this way. "Scot, I can't stress enough how important it is that you trust me on this."

"And I need you to trust *me,* Mr. President. Don't sideline me. Whoever is on this team you've put together, I can help them."

"No you can't," said Rutledge as he rose from his chair. It was a clear signal that their meeting was over.

Forced to stand, Harvath repeated, "Don't shut me out of this, sir."

"I'm sorry," replied the president, extending his hand.

Reflexively, Harvath took it. Rutledge covered their clasped hands with his left and said, "The best thing you can do for Tracy right now is to be with her. We are going to get to the bottom of this, I promise you."

Harvath's shock was slowly being shoved aside by a surge of anger. But before he could say anything, Gary Lawlor thanked the president and steered Harvath out of the Oval Office.

As the door behind his visitors closed, the door to the president's study opened and the tall, gray-haired, fifty-something director of the Central Intelligence Agency, James Vaile, stepped into the Oval Office.

Rutledge looked at him. "What do you think? Will he cooperate?"

Vaile fixed his eyes on the door Scot Harvath had just exited through and thought about the president's question. Finally, he said, "If he doesn't, we're going to have a lot more trouble on our hands."

"Well, I just promised him that your people were going to handle this."

"And they will. They've got plenty of experience dealing with this kind of thing overseas. They know what they're doing."

"They'd better," replied the president as he readied himself for a briefing in the Situation Room. "We can't afford to have Harvath involved in this. The stakes are just too damn high."

CHAPTER 7

Harvath and Lawlor rode back to the hospital in silence. Harvath didn't like being hamstrung, especially when they were facing a problem he was more than qualified to handle.

Lawlor didn't push him to talk. He'd known before they even got to the White House how the meeting was going to unfold. The president had made it absolutely clear that he didn't want Harvath or anyone else poking around in this investigation. What he didn't say was *why*.

Though Lawlor wasn't happy with the president's decision either, he had to give Rutledge credit for telling Scot in person. He was right—it was the very least he owed him.

At the hospital's entrance, the driver pulled the car to the curb and Harvath climbed out. There were a million things Lawlor wanted to say to him, but none of them seemed appropriate at this point. Instead, it was Harvath who broke their silence. "He has put together a special team to hunt Tracy's shooter, yet I can't have anything to do with it? That doesn't make any sense. There's a lot more to this than he's telling us, Gary, and it pisses me off."

Lawlor knew he was right, but there was nothing either of them could do about it. The president had given them a direct order. Though he was just as bewildered as Scot was, Lawlor only nodded and replied, "Let me know if anything changes with Tracy."

Disgusted, Harvath closed the car door and walked into the hospital.

Upstairs in Tracy's room, her parents were eating lunch. As he entered the room, Bill Hastings asked, "Any news on the investigation?"

Harvath had no desire to burden Tracy's parents with his problems, so he told them a half truth. "They're working it from all sides. The president has taken a personal interest in the investigation and is doing everything he can."

The ventilator continued its rhythmic *hiss, pop, hiss, pop,* and Harvath tried to ignore it. Pulling a chair up alongside the bed, he took Tracy's hand and whispered in her ear that he was back.

If only the president could see her like this, he might not be so quick to pull him off the investigation. All the way back to the hospital, Harvath had tried to figure out why Rutledge was doing this. No matter how many angles he came at it from, none of them made any sense.

The president knew better than anyone else what an asset Scot could be in a case like this. For a moment, he thought maybe Rutledge was concerned about the task being too emotional for him, but Harvath had more than proven himself capable of separating his work from his emotions.

The more Harvath thought about it, the more he realized he actually took everything about his job personally, and that was one of the things that made him so good at what he did.

No, the fact that he had a personal stake in the outcome of this investigation didn't have anything to do with why the president was boxing him out. It had to be something else.

Harvath gently stroked his fingers up and down Tracy's arm as his mind ran through yet more possibilities. The more scenarios he constructed, the further away he felt he was getting from the truth. He thought he knew the president pretty well, but this time he couldn't figure him out.

Harvath replayed the meeting in his mind's eye. He'd been taught through vigorous Secret Service training how to spot microexpressions, the subtle subconscious clues a subject gives out when he is lying or preparing to do something dishonest. Even the best of Washington's doublespeak politicians couldn't hide their intentions or the truth from a seasoned Secret Service agent who knew what to look for. And Scot Harvath knew what to look for.

For whatever reason, President Jack Rutledge had been lying to him. Harvath was certain of it.

He was still deliberating this when his BlackBerry rang. He ignored the call and let it go to voicemail. Nothing was more important than being with Tracy right now.

When the phone rang two more times, Harvath figured it might be urgent and pulled the device from the holster clipped at his hip. The caller ID showed a Colorado area code.

He depressed the button to answer the call, raised the device to his ear, and said, "Harvath."

"Are you alone?" came a voice from the other end.

Harvath glanced at Bill Hastings, who was reading a copy of the *New York Times* as he ate his lunch. Turning his attention back to his phone he said, "Yeah, go ahead."

"Are you still interested in midget wrestling?"

Harvath sat up straighter in his chair. "You've got something?"

"Affirmative," said the voice.

"What is it?"

"Not over the phone. I've got a plane waiting for you. Don't bother packing a bag. You need to get out here ASAP."

Harvath looked at Tracy and was silent.

"ASAP," repeated the voice.

Though Harvath was certain he must have imagined it, he thought for a moment he had felt Tracy return his grasp.

"Are you still there?" asked the voice after several seconds of silence.

Harvath snapped himself out of it. "Yeah, I'm still here," he replied.

"Reagan National, now," ordered the voice. Then the line went dead.

CHAPTER 8

Mark Sheppard was a big fan of zombie movies. *Dawn of the Dead, 28 Days Later*—you name it and chances were that Sheppard had not only seen it, but owned it. There was something about death that had always fascinated him.

It was a strange preoccupation, but one that had served the tall, sandy-haired twenty-seven-year-old reporter well. He had begun his career at the *Baltimore Sun* writing obituaries. It was a probationary assignment designed to allow editors to evaluate the writing and copyediting skills of their cub reporters. Most young journalists hated their time on the obit desk, but Sheppard had reveled in it.

From there he moved to the crime beat. Legendary crime reporter Edna Buchanan had once said that the crime beat "has it all: greed, sex, violence, comedy, and tragedy," and she was right. Though it was a high-turnover, sink-or-swim position where editors continued to test their journalists' mettle before promoting them to more glamorous beats, Sheppard fell in love with it and made it known that he had no intention of ever doing any other sort of reporting.

To his credit, Sheppard was an exceptional crime reporter. He had an eye for detail and a propensity for sourcing, and he knew how to tell one hell of a story.

Over his years on the beat he had developed a wide array of contacts—on both sides of the law. Both police captains and mob captains respected him for his integrity. His sources always knew that he never went to press unless he had gotten all of his facts straight.

Because of his reputation for being a straight shooter and always protecting the anonymity of his sources, news tips flowed in Sheppard's direction on a regular basis. They rarely proved newsworthy. The key was to know which ones were worth running down. Hemingway had once said that a writer needs to have a "shockproof bullshit detector," and Sheppard couldn't have agreed with him more. He found that the amount of energy he put into investigating a tip was often commensurate with how solid its source was. Of course, for every rule there was always an exception.

For Sheppard, the more outrageous the claim, the more his interest was piqued. At the moment, his interest was quite high.

Driving toward the Thomas J. Gosse funeral home on the outskirts of the city, headlines were already forming in his mind. There was no question he was putting the cart way before the horse, but Sheppard's gut told him that if this story panned out, it was going to be huge.

That meant the headline had to be huge as well. And it had to be sensational. This had the potential to be a front-page story. Hell, it might even be an explosive investigative series.

As Sheppard pulled into the funeral home's parking lot, he settled on his headline. It was campy, but once people began to read his reporting the title would take on a whole new meaning. It would be shocking—not only because of the crime itself, but because of its alleged perpetrators.

Locking his car, Sheppard ran the headline through his mind one more time. *Invasion of the Body Snatchers.*

It was one hell of an attention-grabber. He just hoped the man who'd called him with the tip wasn't wasting his time.

CHAPTER 9

MONTROSE, COLORADO

Though it wasn't yet fall, there was a chill in the night air as Harvath stepped onto the pavement outside the small, one-building airport.

Leaning against a white Hummer H2 emblazoned with the logo of his Elk Mountain Resort was one of the biggest and toughest men Harvath had ever known in his life. Called the Warlord in his past career, Tim Finney had been the Pacific Division Shoot Fighting Champion. Adept at annihilating other men, most notably with his hands, head, knees, or elbows, Finney was one of the few people Harvath knew he probably couldn't beat in an all-out street fight.

Finney towered over him by at least seven inches, was nearly twice as wide, and rang in at an amazing 250 pounds of solid muscle. Not bad for a guy in his early fifties. He had intense green eyes and his head was completely shaved. Despite his size and his reputation as an absolutely ruthless, no-holds-barred fighter in the ring, Tim Finney was a happy-go-lucky guy. And he had a lot to be happy about.

Nobody rode for free in the Finney family. Old man Finney, the family patriarch, was a tough SOB, and all of his kids had paid their own way through college. Tim had done it by bouncing at a string of nightclubs in Los Angeles, before his talents as a fighter were recognized and a private coach took him under his wing and steered Finney to the Pacific Division Championship of Shoot Fighting, the sport that would go on to give birth to the popular Ultimate Fighting series.

Tim Finney always had his eyes on the next mountain he wanted to climb, and if the mountain proved too difficult, he had a backup plan and another way of tackling it. He was the consummate, always-prepared Boy Scout.

He had worked in the family hotel business for several years and then set out to conquer another dream—establishing his own exclusive five-star resort nestled on more than five hundred extremely private acres in Colorado's San Juan mountains a half hour outside Telluride. But his dream didn't end there.

At the resort, Finney created a cutting-edge tactical training facility like no other in the world. It was called Valhalla, after the warrior heaven of Norse mythology.

Finney brought in the best set, sound, and lighting designers from Hollywood to create the most realistic threat scenario mock-ups ever seen. And then he did something extremely revolutionary; he opened it up not only to high-end military and law enforcement units, but also to civilians. He even advertised in the Robb Report, and that advertising, as well as the incredible word of mouth from his customers, had paid off, big time. His closely guarded guest registry read like a *Who's Who* of corporate America, and of the sports and entertainment worlds to boot.

The success allowed Finney to take Valhalla to a completely different level—a level that was only whispered about in the most secure conference rooms of places like the Central Intelligence Agency, the Delta Force compound at Fort Bragg, and many off-the-books, black ops intelligence units throughout northern Virginia and places farther afield.

Those in the know referred to Valhalla's spin-off as the *dark side of the moon*. Hidden well beyond the boundaries of Elk Mountain and Valhalla proper, the spin-off was benignly referred to as *Site Six*.

It had been called Hogan's Alley on crack—a reference to the FBI's mock town at their training academy in Quantico where they staged everything from bank robberies to high-stakes hostage standoffs.

Finney kept a small army of carpenters and engineers on staff around the clock year-round. Many of them were ex-Hollywood people looking to get out of show business and put their skills to use somewhere else. The legend was that if you could get Tim Finney satellite imagery of your target, he could have a working mock-up built to train on within forty-eight hours, fourteen if time was absolutely crucial and nobody cared about wet paint.

In a low valley secluded by mountains on all sides, Finney's Site Six team had replicated everything from Iraqi villages to foreign airports, embassies, and terrorist training camps. The detail and scope were limited only by a client's budget and depth of intelligence regarding the target. And to Finney's credit, he never allowed budget to dictate the training experience his client's people would gain at Site Six. Finney was a true patriot and did everything in his power to make sure American military and intelligence personnel had the most detailed and realistic training experiences possible before they went to take down the real thing.

At the end of the day, Finney wasn't in business to make more money. He already had plenty of it. He was in business to make sure his clients—whether they be guests at his Elk Mountain Resort, shooters who came to sharpen their skills at his Valhalla Training Facility, or real-life warriors who came to practice taking down mocked-up targets at Site Six before going overseas to do the real thing—got the best experience possible.

It was in that last capacity that Harvath had come to be acquainted with Timothy Finney and Valhalla's Site Six.

Based on a series of aerial photographs taken by a Predator drone aircraft, as well as some covert video shot from the ground, Finney and his team had mocked up a chemical weapons facility in Afghanistan that Harvath had been put in charge of taking out.

Every single member of Harvath's team credited the training they engaged in at Valhalla and Site Six as having given them the edge that allowed their mission to be successful.

That training, along with Finney's irreverent sense of humor, had cemented a friendship between them that had garnered Harvath not only a standing invitation to join the Valhalla/Site Six instructor team, but also a standing invitation to stay at the resort if he ever needed to get away from D.C. and his life as an overworked counterterrorism operative for the U.S. government.

Though Harvath probably could have used a five-star vacation right now, that was not the reason he was standing on the sidewalk outside the Montrose, Colorado, airport. He was here because in Timothy Finney's never-ending quest to create more thorough experiences for the warriors who trained at Valhalla and Site Six, he'd recently developed an entirely new program that was once again making him the talk of the American intelligence community.

CHAPTER 10

As he drove, Finney reached behind his seat, pulled a cold beer from a cooler in back, and offered it to his guest.

Harvath shook his head *no*.

"I guess I'll cancel the dancing girls too, then," said Finney as he put the beer back.

Harvath didn't respond. His mind was a million miles away as he pulled his BlackBerry from its holster and checked it again for messages. He'd given Tracy's father and her nurses his number in case anything changed. He'd also explained to Bill Hastings, as best he could, why he had to leave.

Remembering that cell phone reception at the resort was notoriously spotty, Harvath was wondering if he should have given them that number too when Finney asked, "Do you want to eat when we get in, or do you want to get right down to business?"

"Let's eat after," said Harvath as he tucked his BlackBerry away. "Then nobody will have to stay late on my account."

Finney chuckled. His laugh, like his voice, was in keeping with the rest of his massive stature—a rich basso profundo. "We work the Sargasso staff in three shifts around the clock."

"Business is that good, huh?"

Finney laughed again. "I keep saying heaven forbid peace should break out any time soon."

"Don't worry," Harvath replied as he stared at the reflection of himself cast against the passenger window and the ever-darkening sky. "It won't."

They made small talk the rest of the way to the resort. Finney knew Harvath well enough to know that if he wanted to talk about what had happened to Tracy he'd be the one to bring it up.

Harvath didn't, so they talked about everything else but.

Approaching the main gates for Elk Mountain, Finney radioed ahead to the guardhouse that he was coming in "plus one."

Though the guards knew their boss and his vehicle by sight, they still stopped the Hummer, recorded its arrival, checked it over thoroughly, and then waved it on through. Harvath had always been impressed with the level of security at Elk Mountain.

At the main lodge, Finney stopped to pick up his director of operations, Ron Parker. He was a lean man with a goatee, in his late thirties, who stood about five-foot-ten.

Climbing into the backseat, Parker removed a Coors from the cooler, reached around, and punched Harvath in the left arm. "Good to see you," he said.

Looking up, he could see Finney's raised eyebrows in the rearview mirror. "What?" he asked.

"Do you think that behavior is appropriate?" replied Finney.

Parker leaned between the front seats as he popped the top from his beer and asked, "It's your other shoulder that got messed up, right?"

Harvath nodded. "My left's fine. Don't worry about it."

Parker smiled, sat back, and took a long pull from his beer.

"You know that's not what I'm talking about," replied Finney. "Right?"

"Listen," said Parker, "as of ten minutes ago I'm off-duty. And what I do on my personal time is my business."

"Then you're fired. I'll have the pink slip on your desk in the morning."

Parker took another swig of beer. "Super, I'll place it on the spike with all the rest of them."

Both Finney and Parker were notorious for their professionalism, but as Harvath had gotten to know them he realized that they made an important distinction. They took their careers and what they did at Elk Mountain very seriously, but they never took *themselves* too seriously, especially when in the quiet company of good friends.

Finney looked over and saw Harvath smile. "It's good to have you back."

"Not much has changed, has it?" said Harvath.

Finney thrust his beefy hand into the backseat and motioned to Parker to hand him a beer. "We doubled all the locks on the wine cellar after your last visit, but other than that, no."

Parker and Finney limited themselves to one beer each. Finney had his finished in two swallows, just as they arrived at yet another checkpoint. This time, they were all required to present photo identification. The guards were dressed in Blackhawk tactical gear, like the ones at the main gate, but in addition, these guards had been issued body armor and were openly carrying weapons.

Harvath knew that the men at the front gate were also strapped; they just kept their iron out of sight. Here, though, Finney's people were making a very clear show of force. Two men carried H&K 416s, while a third held a highly modified Benelli twelve-gauge and never once took his eyes off the passengers in the Hummer. Harvath had no idea where Finney was getting his guards, but he seemed to be doing a damn good job.

As they pulled away from the checkpoint and drove toward the Sargasso facility, Harvath asked, "Ex SWAT?"

"Special Forces, actually," replied Parker.

Harvath laughed dismissively. "C'mon."

"He's one hundred percent serious," said Finney.

"Doing guard duty?"

"Guard duty is only one of the things they do here," answered Parker. "They're on a rotation, so it's a shift everyone has to pull each month."

"I know what those guys make in the private sector. You've got some very expensive gatekeepers."

Finney smiled. "And worth every penny of it."

"But make no mistake," added Parker. "They've got it pretty good here. We've got an excellent bonus and compensation package that far outpaces what these guys would be pulling in anywhere else."

Harvath looked at Finney, who added, "We don't even advertise for them anymore. They come to us."

The SUV came to a stop in front of the poorly lit entrance of what looked like an old mineshaft.

Harvath was about to ask where they were when he saw a faded sign hanging over the opening that proclaimed *Sargasso Mining Company*. He was looking at the understated entrance to Finney's hot new intelligence venture.

CHAPTER 11

One hundred feet down the sloping tunnel that led into the Sargasso shaft, Harvath half-expected a tour guide with an authentic miner's head-lamp or a bearded, dust-covered, suspender-wearing actor to appear and regale them with stories of the Old Lucky Seven Mine. At 101 feet, Harvath's attitude changed.

He had to give Tim Finney credit. They weren't greeted by a stainless-steel, pneumatically sealed, hi-tech, James Bond–style door. Instead, it was a door composed of five aged wooden planks with splintered crosspieces that looked ready to fall off its hinges.

A rather unremarkable sign was nailed to it that stated *Danger. Keep Out.*

Finney produced a set of keys and unlocked a rusted padlock that kept a heavy iron chain in place

across the door. He continued to lead down a wide,
rough-hewn passageway. The trio followed a set of
tracks that Harvath figured must have once been used
to haul supplies in and gold out.

The large tunnel continued sloping gently downward. After another hundred feet the tunnel widened
and a series of lights could be seen up ahead.

When they got there they were greeted by another brace of guards. Though they looked just as serious
as the last set of guards, these men simply waved them
along.

"They get a couple hundred feet below ground
and your guys start to slack off, don't they?" Harvath
joked.

Finney and Parker both smiled. "You have no idea
how many passive security checks you have gone
through on the way down here," said Parker. "Not
only have your body temperature and heart rate been
monitored since entering the mine, but we know if
you're carrying any sort of weapon, explosives, pow-
ders, liquids, or gels on your person as well."

"Everything except whether I'm wearing boxers
or briefs," stated Harvath.

"We've got that too," replied Finney as he pretended to consult the earpiece attached to his radio.
"Apparently, it's a blue thong with the words *Go Navy*
embroidered in sequins."

Harvath grinned and gave him the finger. They
kept walking until they arrived at a miners-style elevator. Finney raised the grate and they all stepped inside.
Removing a keycard from his pocket, Finney swept it

through a magnetic reader and then presented his right thumb and pupil for biometric verification. Once he had been approved, the elevator began to descend.

It came to a stop at the bottom of the shaft, where they were met by a low-exhaust Dodge Ram pickup specifically designed for subterranean driving.

As the truck's driver took them deeper into the mine, Finney explained the purpose of the Sargasso program. "We've had teams visit us from Fort Bragg, Camp Perry with the CIA, as well as Fort Story with the SEALs, and they all love the training here, but at the end of the day, no matter how good their people are, their success or failure comes down to one critical component—intelligence.

"That gave me an idea, and I started making a few phone calls to people I know back east. We hear a lot about the high attrition rates in the special operations community as operators leave the armed forces and go to work for groups like Blackwater or Triple Canopy where they can make a hell of a lot more money. What you don't hear about are the attrition rates in the intelligence community.

"I never had any desire to run a private military company, per se. But a private intelligence company, now that's something completely different, and it seemed to dovetail well with what we were already doing here."

Harvath held on to the headrest in front of him as they hit a series of potholes. Once the surface had smoothed out, he asked, "I understand how Valhalla and Site Six make money for you, but how do you make money with your own intelligence company?"

"We do it in two ways," replied Finney. "First, I don't have to focus on the entire world. I focus solely on the sweet spots where the most action is happening. All the terrorism and terrorist-related intelligence that we gather and analyze is from areas where the U.S. government is backlogged and overloaded.

"Second, there's no congressional oversight of what we do. We have a lot more latitude in our operations. There are agencies willing to pay a lot of money for us to gather intel for them. As far as our ops tempo is concerned, we're double the volume of where Ron and I projected we'd be by this time. We can't get guys out of the CIA, NSA, FBI, and the like fast enough to come work here."

Harvath shook his head. Finney was amazing.

The truck came to a stop before a final checkpoint in front of what looked like a pair of heavy blast doors. Once they had been waved through, Finney led the way into the heart of the Sargasso Program's Operations Center.

It wasn't at all what Harvath had expected. The minute they stepped inside, they left the feeling of being in a mine hundreds of feet beneath the surface behind them. If Harvath hadn't known better, he would have sworn he was in some cutting-edge development think tank on the Microsoft campus.

Gone were the caged bulbs strung along the rough-hewn walls. They had been replaced with sophisticated fixtures recessed at the edges of the ceiling that replicated bright, outdoor light. The floors were polished granite and the offices were walled in with sheets of soundproofed glass, the opacity of which could be dialed up or down based on the occupant's desired level of privacy.

Impossibly slim, high-definition monitors suspended on the glass acted like windows to the outside world. As they passed scenes of Alpine Switzerland, the Bolivian rainforest, and a spit of rocky coastline from Maine, Finney explained that employees were allowed to choose their own "view" from a database of digital backdrops from around the world. It was just one of the many small touches Finney had created to make his employees' time below ground as pleasant as possible.

At the end of the next hallway, the group turned left and arrived at an office where the virtual window displayed a river with jagged mountains in the background. In the midground a man in waders was fly-fishing. The sound of river water gently moving by played from a hidden speaker somewhere in the room.

"Tom should be right back," Finney said in regard to the office's absent occupant. "We can wait in here for him."

On top of the polished chrome desk was a neatly arranged stack of files, a lone silver pen, and a pad of Post-it notes. Whoever this guy was, he either didn't have a lot to do or was extremely well organized. Based on what Finney had told him, Harvath figured it had to be the latter.

He had turned his attention to the virtual window and was admiring the scene when Tom Morgan entered the office. "That's the Snake River," said Morgan as he set a paper coffee cup and his laptop down on his desk. "One of the finest dry fly rivers in the world."

"This particular spot is just outside Jackson Hole, Wyoming. Island Park, isn't it?" asked Harvath as he turned around.

"You've fished the Snake, then."

Harvath nodded. "Both the Henry's and the South Fork. In fact I think I've fished that exact spot," he added as he pointed over his shoulder at the screen. It was a scene he recognized immediately.

He'd been planning to take Tracy there that fall to teach her how to fish. The summer crowds would be gone, the leaves would be turning, and the mountains would be gorgeous. He'd already reserved a small cabin at a place called Dornans just inside Grand Teton National Park. He wondered now if they'd ever be able to go anywhere together again.

"I love the Snake, but there's some pretty good fishing around here in Colorado. That's part of the reason I took this job," said Morgan, pulling Harvath's mind back to the here and now.

Harvath acknowledged the remark with a knowing smile as Tim Finney made formal introductions. Tom Morgan was ex-NSA and somewhere in his late sixties. He wore glasses, had a mustache, and walked with a limp—the result of a field operation gone bad, which he never discussed.

After a lifetime of suits and ties at NSA headquarters in Fort Meade, Maryland, Morgan had embraced

Elk Mountain's somewhat casual dress code. Tonight, he was wearing jeans, a plaid shirt, and a tweed sport coat. He appeared very fit for his age. When he spoke, there was a slight New England accent to his words, and Harvath placed him as a native of Rhode Island or New Hampshire.

"Tom's the reason I asked you to come out," said Finney as they all sat down.

This was the part Harvath had been waiting for. "What have you got?"

Morgan didn't mince words. "I think we've located the Troll's lockbox."

Harvath looked at him, his eyebrows arching. "Everything?" he asked.

Morgan looked at him and replied, "Bank accounts, data deposits, *everything.*"

CHAPTER 12

So the way we see it," said Finney as Tom Morgan wrapped up his presentation and closed his laptop, "we've got this little runt's nuts in a vise. The only question is how hard do you want to squeeze?"

Harvath was impressed. Finney and his Sargasso Intelligence Program had been able to do what the United States government wouldn't or couldn't do. They had located the Troll's stock-in-trade, his highly classified data.

It wasn't a tough decision for Harvath to make. The Troll had helped Al Qaeda carry out the attacks on New York City.

Then there was the whole matter of Tracy.

Looking at Finney, Harvath said, "I want you to squeeze so hard his eyes roll back into his fucking head."

The Warlord nodded at Morgan, and the former NSA employee picked up his phone and dialed. The Troll's field of play was about to be dramatically upended.

CHAPTER 13

ANGRA DOS REIS, BRAZIL

Three hours southwest of Rio de Janeiro by car, or forty-five minutes by helicopter, was the hottest getaway in Brazil, the bay of Angra dos Reis.

Known for its warm waters, white-sand beaches, and lush vegetation, Angra dos Reis, or simply Angra as it was called by those in the know, boasted 365 islands—one for every day of the year. Angra was a mystical place, its breezes laden with the scent of exotic tropical flowers that intoxicated its visitors.

Upon its discovery by Portuguese naval officers in 1502, one of the officers wrote home saying that they had discovered *paradise*.

Angra was indeed a paradise. The kind of paradise one could easily get lost in. And lost was exactly what the Troll had wanted to be, though not without certain creature comforts.

The private island he'd leased was a half mile long and a quarter mile wide. It was known as Algodão. It boasted a helipad, speedboat, and accommodations rivaling the greatest luxury hotels in the world. Though it could easily sleep eighteen, at present there were only three souls ashore—the Troll and his two snow-white Caucasian Ovcharkas, Argos and Draco.

Weighing close to two hundred pounds each and standing over forty-one inches at the shoulder, these giant animals were the dogs of choice for the Russian military and former East German border patrol. They were exceedingly fast and absolutely vicious when it came to protecting their territory. They made the perfect guardians for a man who stood just under three feet tall and had very powerful enemies—many of whom were his clients.

The Troll lived by the motto that knowledge didn't equal power; it was the precise *application* of knowledge that equaled power. He had also learned very quickly that it could also equal incredible wealth.

It was in following this motto that the Troll had made a substantial living for himself dealing in the purchase, sale, and trade of highly classified information. Each piece on its own had a certain value, but the skill—the art if you will—was in knowing how to join together just the right tidbits to create a true masterpiece. That was where the Troll excelled in his profession. It was quite amazing, especially for someone whose prospects in life had been seen as so dismal that even his parents had given up on him.

When it became obvious the Troll was not going to grow any further, his godless Georgian parents made no attempt to find a suitable loving home for their son, nor did they try to find even a half-decent orphanage. Instead, they abandoned the boy, selling him as if he were chattel to a brothel on the outskirts of the Black Sea resort of Sochi. There, the boy was starved, beaten, and made to perform unutterable sex acts that would have shamed even the Marquis de Sade himself.

It was in the brothel that the Troll learned the true value of information. The loose-lipped pillow talk of the powerful clients proved a goldmine once he had learned what to listen for and how to turn it to his advantage.

The whores, most of them life's castoffs as well, felt a kinship with the dwarf and treated him well. In fact, they became the only family he ever knew, and he repaid that kindness by one day buying their freedom. He had the madam and her husband tortured and then killed for the inhuman cruelty he had spent years suffering at their hands.

From the ashes of his youth, the Troll rose a fiery phoenix armed with a cutthroat business acumen and a gluttonous appetite for the best of everything in life.

In his palm-thatched living room, he cradled a glass of Château Quercy St. Emilion Bordeaux between his two small hands as he stared through the villa's glass floor at the colorful starfish and vibrant sea life playing in the illuminated water below. He had indeed come a long way since the brothel in Sochi. But was it far enough?

Draco looked up as his master slid off his chair and padded across the room in his handmade Stubbs & Wootton Sisal Pajas. Argos remained in a deep sleep, still recovering from the wound he had suffered in Gibraltar. It was good for all of them to get away from his estate in the rainy Scottish Highlands. The weather was much more agreeable in Brazil. It was also a safer place.

Though few knew of Eilenaigas House, he would not feel safe there for some time. After what his clients had done in New York City, he knew the Americans were quite literally out for blood. He'd seen it for himself firsthand in Gibraltar. If he lived to be a thousand, he would never forget the horrifically macabre death the American operative Scot Harvath had visited upon Mohammed bin Mohammed. It was something no sane man could have ever devised. Yet it was perfect. Mohammed had deserved it a million times over, especially for the sadistic acts he had visited upon the Troll as a young boy in that brothel near the Black Sea.

Harvath had been incredibly cruel in meting out the punishment to Mohammed, but in almost the same breath he had shown himself to be incredibly compassionate. Argos would have surely died if Harvath had not given him medical attention himself and found him an able veterinarian. Harvath had even gone so far as to pay the doctor out of his own pocket for the animal's surgery. Though the Troll had never been very fond of Americans, this was a man he respected. He was a ruthless, cold-blooded killer, who also possessed a marked degree of humanity.

Turning his mind to dinner, the Troll removed several large Kobe steaks from the refrigerator, part of a special shipment he'd had flown in from Japan.

The Japanese were famous for the beer-and-sake-laced diet they fed their premium cattle—and of course for the massages the cows received. Nothing was too good for Kobe cattle, and the painstaking efforts showered upon the animals yielded an incredible meat. It was finely marbled with fat that was less saturated than the fat in other beef, was significantly lower in cholesterol, and was without rival in flavor and tenderness.

As he set the steaks up on the counter, both of the dogs appeared by his side, their nostrils flaring at the scent of the beef. They both asked so little from him and yet gave so much in return. They were his ever-present companions, truer and more loyal than almost any human being he had ever known.

The Troll plated a steak for each of the dogs and set them down on the floor. Immediately, they fell upon them and the beef disappeared.

When his food was prepared, the Troll set it upon the dining table, uncorked another bottle of Château Quercy, and climbed into his chair to eat.

His steak was perfect. Cutting into it was like slicing into a piece of soft, ripened Brie.

He savored every bite of his meal, and when his plate was clean and his wine glass empty, he removed his dinnerware to the kitchen.

Pouring himself a snifter of Germain-Robin XO, he took a long sip and closed his eyes. For all of his accomplishments, the Troll's life was a lonely place.

CHAPTER 14

The living-room windows were on sliding tracks and had been pulled back to open the room onto the sea. A light breeze carried the smell of the ocean mixed with the tiny island's exotic flowers. *Only the Brazilians could create a night so perfect,* mused the Troll as he climbed up to the table he used as a desk and opened his rugged General Dynamics XR-1 GoBook laptop. Via a small, inflatable satellite dish positioned outside, he was soon connected with his rack of dedicated servers secretly housed in a bunker deep within the eastern Pyrenees Mountains.

A British entrepreneur had rolled the dice on an idea that the Swiss approach to banking could be replicated in the digital realm.

The Brit's facility in the European principality of Andorra boasted redundant power supplies, redundant network feeds, FM200 fire suppression, redundant air-conditioning, and multistage security identification processes. His servers were connected to generous bandwidth allocations, fully burstable, with multiple aggregated providers, ensuring 100 percent availability for maximum uptime.

It had all been music to the Troll's ears. Relying on the servers at his estate was out of the question. Eilenaigas House was beyond dangerous, at least for now. If he kept a low-enough profile, the U.S. intelligence services would give up on him eventually, but until they did, he'd have to stay far away from his home in Scotland.

When it was all said and done, there were much worse places to pass one's time than a private island in Brazil. And he would know. He'd been to them.

Listening to the music of the waves as they gently washed against the rocks outside, the Troll logged on to his primary server and began the authentication process to gain access to his data. He still had not sifted through the windfall of intelligence he had gleaned from raiding the NSA's top-secret files in New York during the Al Qaeda attack. The amount of data he'd stolen from the Americans had been beyond his wildest dreams.

The NSA program had been named Athena, after the Greek goddess of wisdom. Apparently the Greeks didn't have a goddess of blackmail.

It had been a *deep black* data-mining operation. Using both the Echelon and Carnivore systems, the NSA had been gathering intelligence that could be used as leverage against various foreign concerns—governments, heads of state, and influential foreign businesspeople.

In short, the Athena Program had been created to collect and sort extremely dirty laundry. Once they had their teeth into something particularly juicy, such as the Princess Diana crash, TWA 800, or the true cause of Yassir Arafat's death, they assigned teams of operatives to flesh out the big picture and uncover as much supporting data as possible. That way, when it came time to use it, they had the victim pinned against the wall so tightly, there was absolutely no room for him or her to wiggle free.

And when they uncovered a conspiracy involving several powerful foreign figures, it was like hitting the jackpot.

The Troll had to smile. It was devious, deceitful, and utterly un-American. And now, all of the NSA's data belonged to him. *The gift that will keep on giving.* There was enough in there to keep him busy for three lifetimes. The biggest risk was jumping the gun and selling off the pieces of information too quickly. He would have to study all of it and understand how it interrelated before he began assigning values. Fortunately, the Athena analysts had already done a lot of his work for him.

The Troll clicked on the subgroup folder he'd been working in and waited for its contents sheet to appear. It didn't.

He clicked on the icon again and waited, but still nothing happened. He checked his uplink status. Everything appeared to be okay. So why then wasn't his data coming up?

He tried another file and then another. They were all the same—*empty.* The Troll's heart caught in his throat. This couldn't be happening. This *wasn't* happening.

He quaffed the balance of the brandy in his snifter, wiped his bearded lips with the sleeve of his linen shirt, and went through every single file on every single server.

All empty.

As he neared the end, he saw an animated icon that didn't belong there. It was a little bearded man with a horned helmet, a sword in one hand, and a shield in the other. The figure hopped from one foot to the other and on every fourth hop banged his sword against his shield.

It looked like a little Viking, but the Troll knew better. This was no Viking. It was a Norseman—the codename of American counterterrorism operative Scot Harvath.

CHAPTER 15

Enraged, the Troll clicked on the icon and opened the folder. It took a maddeningly long time for the file to load. For a moment, he thought it might be a trick—a way to purposely keep him online so that American intelligence could pinpoint his location.

Finally, the file loaded. It was a series of screen captures for all of his bank accounts. Every single balance reflected the same amount—*zero*.

A scream welled up from deep inside his tiny body as he hurled his brandy snifter against the wall. The dogs leaped up and began barking.

His entire life's work was gone. *Everything.* The only thing that was still his was the estate in the Scottish Highlands, but if the Americans had been this thorough, the Troll had little reason to doubt that they had found a way to tie that up and keep him from doing anything with it as well. British antiterrorism laws were quite severe. It wouldn't take much for the Americans to convince the U.K. authorities to play ball.

The dogs were still barking. The Troll grabbed a pewter dish filled with pistachios and was about to launch it when he thought better of it. "Silence," he ordered, and the barking dogs fell quiet.

He needed to think. There had to be some way out of this.

He spent the next two hours going through his servers, remotely connecting to his various bank accounts scattered around the globe. Then began a series of angry phone calls, during which he suffered through excuse after excuse from each of his bankers. They plied him with empty promises to get to the bottom of what had happened, but the Troll knew it was no use. The Americans had done it. They had gotten everything. He was ruined.

While the Troll had no idea what he was going to do next, he knew one thing for certain. Scot Harvath was responsible, and he was going to make him pay.

He went back to the lone computer file that had

been left behind. The dancing Norseman mocked him as it hopped from one foot to the other. Slowly, the Troll scrolled through the data. On his third pass he found it.

Now the Troll understood why the file had taken so long to load. Embedded within that annoying, hopping Norseman icon was a message.

It was an invitation to a private chat room from none other than Scot Harvath. The Troll shut down his computer.

This was going to take some brainpower. He resisted the urge to pour another brandy. Instead, he brewed a small copper pot of potent Turkish coffee and returned to the living room.

As he watched the brightly colored fish below the glass floor, he considered his options. This would be a fight for his very survival, and though he guessed himself to be far beyond Harvath in the brains department, there was no telling what kind of resources the American had at his disposal. The gravest error he could make here would be to underestimate the man.

Since there was no clock ticking on the offer to enter the chat room, the Troll decided to take his time and research his adversary first.

CHAPTER 16

Y ou're positive he saw the link?" asked Harvath.

Morgan nodded. "We loaded the icon with a program designed to ping us back once he clicked on it and then erase itself. He saw it. Believe me."

"I still don't like how long this is taking," said Ron Parker as he paced along one side of the long table. They had all gathered in the Sargasso Intelligence Program's conference room, which also doubled as its War Room when sensitive operations required monitoring. "We should have set a time limit on him."

Tim Finney held up his hand. "Gentlemen, he'll come. Don't worry. He doesn't have a choice. He's taking his time because he can. Making us wait is the only power he has at this point, and he knows it."

Parker stopped pacing and poured himself a cup of coffee from the machine on top of a low-slung credenza. Above it was a large oil painting of a bugling elk in a lush mountain valley. "He could also walk away."

Harvath had always appreciated Parker's keen, tactical mind. Only fools refused to consider retreat when it was the best option. But in this case, Harvath knew his opponent better than Parker did. The Troll might try to double-cross them, but he wasn't going to simply disappear.

"There's too much at stake for him here," said Harvath, signaling to Parker that he wanted a cup of coffee too. "He can't afford to walk away. He'll want to get back what we took from him."

"Fat chance of that happening," replied Parker as he handed Harvath a mug and sat down next to him. "Have you got any idea what you're going to say when he does appear in that chat room?"

"How about, *In addition to your data and your bank accounts, we also revoked your membership in the lollipop guild, asshole?*" offered Finney as he bellied up to the credenza.

Though he didn't much feel like it, Harvath smiled. "I hadn't thought of that one. I'll throw it in the pot and see what moves me when the time comes."

"It's come," said Tom Morgan as he punched a button on his laptop and pushed it across the table to Harvath.

Flat-panel monitors at the front of the conference room sprang to life with a real-time view of the chat room. A message indicated that a new chatter had entered. As this was a private chat room that had been created solely for this exchange, they all knew they were looking at the digital presence of the man known only as the Troll.

Harvath's fingers hovered above the keyboard, but Finney shook his head *no.* "He made us wait. Now let's return the favor. We've got the upper hand here. Let's make it clear."

Though he wasn't sure he agreed with his friend,

Harvath waited. Moments later, the Troll fired the opening shot.

You have taken things that do not belong to you, he typed.

Harvath didn't need any coaching. So have you, he replied.

I want my bank accounts and my data restored, immediately.

And I want to know who shot Tracy Hastings, Harvath responded.

There was a long pause. Finally, the Troll responded, So that is what this is all about? There was another pause before the dwarf added, Perhaps we can come to an arrangement.

Finney looked ready to make a suggestion, but Harvath held up his hand to stop him. He knew what he was doing. If you cooperate, I'll let you live.

The Troll typed :) followed by, I have been threatened by more powerful men than you and yet here I am. You will have to offer me something more.

You killed a very good friend of mine in New York, replied Harvath. You are lucky that I am offering as much as I am.

You are referring to Master Sergeant Robert Herrington. His death was most regrettable, but it should be noted that it was Al Qaeda who killed him. I was nowhere near New York when the attack took place.

The Troll knew way too much about Harvath, and it made him very uncomfortable. How did you find out where I lived?

It was not difficult.

Humor me, Harvath fired back.

I conducted a simple credit check.

My name is not on my new house. None of the utilities are in my name. I don't even receive mail there.

I know you don't, answered the Troll. It all goes to a local pack-and-ship store in Alexandria. Your last known address before you got smart and switched to the pack-and-ship was an apartment several blocks away. I hired someone to ascertain whether you still lived there. The day my source showed up you were moving to the house. He simply followed you to your new domicile. From what he tells me, Bishop's Gate is quite lovely.

Harvath was done dancing. Did you order the hit on Tracy Hastings?

The Troll took his time. Finally he typed, No. I did not.

Do you know who did?

Maybe.

It took everything Harvath had to keep his temper in check.

CHAPTER 17

Moments later, the Troll responded, Agent Harvath, you have taken everything I have. Unless you put something more than threats against my life on the table, there really isn't anything in this for me and I don't see any point in continuing our conversation.

Harvath had expected this and was prepared to bargain. I'm prepared to purchase the information from you.

Using my own money, of course.

Of course.

I want it all, stated the Troll. Half as a show of good faith now, the rest upon delivery of the information.

Harvath typed slowly and deliberately. You'll get one million *if* and *when* you provide me proof of the shooter's identity. And as far as good faith goes, you're going to demonstrate yours by giving me the name of the person who followed me to Bishop's Gate.

I never reveal my sources, replied the Troll. Not even for one million dollars, which by the way is a mere pittance considering what you took from me.

Then there is no deal.

Agent Harvath, what happened to Ms. Hastings was indeed unfortunate. When I heard about it, I questioned my source, in detail, but he neither saw nor heard anything that could be of value to you. He followed you and early the next morning he placed my gift upon your doorstep.

Harvath had figured whoever it was had been nothing more than a courier, probably some cut-rate private eye the Troll had hired on the cheap. It was a concession he was willing to make, and he let it drop.

Before he could type a response, the Troll added, I heard they found lamb's blood above your front door.

The man's sources were scarily good. It sickened Harvath that such a person could worm his tentacles in wherever he pleased, even a highly sensitive federal investigation. So what?

So, very biblical, wouldn't you say?

Can you help me or not? asked Harvath.

I want a show of good faith from you first.

I already told you I'll let you live.

A rather empty threat considering that you have no idea where I am.

Harvath nodded to Tom Morgan and then typed, Just so you know, I don't make empty threats.

A fraction of a second later, an infrared surveillance image appeared on the screen and Harvath narrated. This satellite footage was taken over your location in Angra dos Reis less than ten minutes ago. From what I can tell, that's you near the front of the structure, and the two hot spots on your left would be the dogs. Am I correct?

The Troll didn't respond. Harvath figured he had to be shocked. Having an adversary discover where you live is an incredibly unsettling violation. It was nice to be able to dish out a little of the Troll's own medicine.

So now you have my show of good faith, added Harvath. I'm a man of my word. If I had wanted you dead, you'd be dead.

Minutes passed as the Troll tried to piece together how they had tracked him down. Finally, he typed, It was the wire transfer to the property management company.

Now it was Harvath's turn to post a smiley face. :) With Finney's help, he had stripped the Troll of everything and had knocked him completely off-balance.

A few minutes later, as he finished his instructions to the newly acquiescent Troll, Harvath left the man with one final warning, You are not to leave the island. If you do, I will hunt you down and kill you myself.

CHAPTER 18

SOUTHERN CALIFORNIA

The call from Philippe Roussard's handler came in the middle of the night. "Do you have everything in place?"

Roussard sat up in bed and propped a thin pillow between his head and the cheap stucco wall. "Yes," he responded, sliding a Gitanes from the pack on the nightstand and lighting it up.

"Those things will kill you," warned his handler as he heard Roussard's Zippo clank shut and the operative took a deep drag.

Philippe swept his dark hair back from his face and replied, "Your concern for my well-being is quite touching."

The caller refused to rise to the bait. Their relationship had been much too contentious of late. They needed to work together if they were going to succeed. Taking a deep breath, the handler said, "When you are finished, the boat will be waiting. Make sure no one sees you get on it."

Roussard snorted in response. No one was going to see him. No one ever did. He was like a phantom, a shadow. In fact, he was so elusive that many people didn't even believe he existed. The U.S. government, though, was a different matter.

Until his capture, no one had ever seen him. No one knew his name or nationality. The American soldiers in Iraq called him *Juba* and had lived in abject terror of being his next victim.

All of his shots came from at least two hundred meters and as far away as thirteen hundred. Almost every one was perfect. He had an intimate understanding of body armor and knew right where to place his shots—the lower spine, the ribs, or just above the chest.

Sometimes, as in the case of the four-strong Marine scout sniper team in Ramadi, he dispatched his targets with absolutely pristine shots to the head. With well over a hundred kills to his credit, Roussard was a hero to those Iraqis who resented the American occupation and an avenging angel to his brethren among the insurgency.

The Americans had hunted him relentlessly and eventually they caught him. He was shipped to Guantanamo where he endured months of torture. Then, just over six months ago, he had been miraculously delivered out of captivity. He and four other prisoners had been loaded aboard a plane and flown back to their homes. Only Roussard knew why it had happened or who their benefactor was.

Now, as he slipped his powerful, six-foot frame into a pair of Servpro coveralls, the irony of his situation wasn't lost on him. America had secretly agreed to his release along with the four others in order to protect its citizens against further terrorism. Yet here he was, inside America itself, ready to carry out his next attack.

CHAPTER 19

Regardless of the distasteful habits Roussard had cultivated in order to blend into Western society, he was still a true mujahideen at heart. His nature ran quite contrary to that of his handler, who was all too comfortable with Western excesses, especially rich food and expensive spirits.

The French boarding school in which Roussard

had been raised had had little influence on him
beyond teaching him how to comfortably blend in
among his Western enemies. His true education had
come from years spent at a nearby mosque and then
later at several secret camps throughout Pakistan and
Afghanistan.

It was there that he learned that "Al Qaeda" didn't
translate to "the base," as most Western media outlets
had so ignorantly reported, but rather, "the database."
It referred to the original computer file of the thousands of mujahideen who were recruited and trained
with the help of the CIA to defeat the Russians in
Afghanistan.

To this file, said to be one of the most closely
guarded secrets of the Al Qaeda leadership, had been
added thousands upon thousands of more names since
the 1990s. These mujahideen were from all walks of
life and were drawn from more ethnic and socioeco-
nomic backgrounds than any Western government
would ever admit. They had been recruited, indoctri-
nated, trained, and dispersed around the world to wait
until they were called to battle.

As Roussard drove his van across the San Diego-
Coronado Bridge he reflected on what might happen
to him if he was apprehended. This was America, after
all, and it had already done its worst to him in Guantanamo. Catching him here on their own soil, they
would do even less. That's how easy they were to
exploit. They passed convoluted laws that served to
protect their enemies better than their own people.

When America caught its so-called terrorist enemies, it lacked the courage to put them to death. Zacarias Moussaoui, the blind cleric Sheik Omar Abdel-Rahman, and even Ramzi Yousef were all given life sentences. They were a testament to America's cowardice and weakness, and the fact that it would inevitably fall to the true followers of Islam.

Merging onto Third Street, Roussard made several turns and doubled back twice to make sure he wasn't being followed. When he got to the address on Encino Lane, he parked the van at the base of the driveway and placed an orange cone both in front of and behind the vehicle. While he doubted anyone was going to notice anything at this time of night, a home disaster restoration truck might pique a neighbor's interest, but it wouldn't warrant a call to police.

As he approached the front door, Roussard removed a lockpick gun from his pocket and hid it beneath his box-style metal notebook. As he reached the door, he pretended to ring the bell. Quietly, he worked the lock, knowing the woman inside did not have a home alarm system.

When the lock released, he stepped inside and closed the door behind him. Roussard paused in the entryway until his eyes grew accustomed to the darkness. The house smelled like furniture polish, mixed with the scent of the nearby sea.

Once his night vision was established, he moved quietly down the hallway toward the master bedroom. The hall was lined with family photographs, most of them from many years ago.

At the bedroom, Roussard found the door wide open and his victim fast asleep upon her bed. Crossing over to her, he tucked the metal folder beneath his left arm and unzipped his coveralls.

For a moment, he thought he might have dropped it, but then his hand closed around the object he was searching for.

When he looked back down at his victim, he received the shock of his life. Her eyes were wide open and she was staring up at him. Her bedroom windows were open, and if she screamed, he could be done for.

Roussard's instincts took over. He grabbed his notebook with both hands and swung—hard. He hit the woman across the left side of her head.

Her mouth opened as if to scream and Roussard hit her again. The woman's eyes closed and she lay motionless atop her bed.

Blood ran from her nose and her ear. It matted her long gray hair and stained her nightgown. She was unconscious, but still very much alive, which was how he wanted her.

Dropping his notebook on the bed, Roussard scooped the woman up into his arms and carried her into the bathroom. There he placed her in the tub, stripped off her nightgown, and covered her body with a moist paste. Next he sealed all the bathroom vents with duct tape.

He walked back outside to the van and retrieved two sealed plastic buckets and a tool belt.

Back in the bathroom, Roussard set the buckets

down next to the tub and removed an atomizer from inside his coveralls.

He opened the woman's right eye first and then the left, liberally applying the substance and making sure each eye had been completely covered. His job was almost finished.

Roussard removed a screwdriver from his tool belt and pried the lids loose on each of the buckets. He grabbed a towel from above the toilet and tossed it just outside the bathroom door. It was time.

Prying the lids off both buckets, he emptied their contents over his victim, still lying unconscious in her bath, and then hurried from the bathroom, making sure to close the door firmly behind him.

Roussard wedged the towel beneath the door and fixed it in place with more duct tape. He then removed the cordless drill from his tool belt along with a handful of screws and secured the door firmly to its frame.

He walked back outside, replaced the orange cones in the van, and slowly drove back the way he had come.

At the San Diego Marriott Hotel and Marina, Roussard changed out of his coveralls, rubbed the van down for fingerprints, and headed for his dock. The boat was right where his handler had told him it would be.

Once he had navigated his way out into the open, inky-black water, he took out a clean cell phone, dialed 911, and gave the address of a woman in need of assistance on Coronado's Encino Lane.

When asked for his name, Roussard smiled and threw the phone overboard. They would piece together who was responsible soon enough.

CHAPTER 20

Tom Gosse, the funeral home's director and namesake, had told Sheppard that he'd rather not have their conversation tape-recorded. That meant that the reporter had been forced to take notes, and he was the world's shittiest note taker.

He couldn't blame Gosse for not wanting to be on tape. If the story he was telling was true, someone had already been killed to keep it quiet.

Sheppard sat at his kitchen counter nursing a Fosters as he flipped through his notes. The funeral director was a solid guy. Several times during the interview, Sheppard backtracked and pretended to mess up the facts in order to trip him up, but Gosse was unflappable. There was no question in Sheppard's mind that the man was telling him the truth.

According to his story, about six months ago he'd been at the chief medical examiner's office doing a pickup. While waiting for the body, he had hung out with a pal of his, an assistant ME named Frank Aposhian. According to Gosse, they were pretty good friends. Their boys attended the same high school and the men played cards together a couple of times a month.

During Gosse's pickup, his conversation with Aposhian was interrupted by two men who identified themselves as FBI agents and requested to speak to the assistant ME in private. As Frank was in charge of the office that night, the request didn't strike Gosse as odd at all. Law enforcement officers came and went all the time in the ME's office, and it definitely wasn't for the coffee.

One of the agents followed Aposhian into his office while the other began examining corpses. But not just any corpses—he only seemed interested in unclaimed bodies, more commonly referred to as John Does. Many of them were found in parks, under bridges, or in abandoned buildings, often half-eaten by rats or stray dogs by the time they were discovered.

Their fingerprints were run through local and national databases and investigators were assigned to try to uncover their identities, but more often than not they went unidentified. Mortuary science students practiced their embalming techniques upon them, and the John and Jane Does were then placed in plywood coffins to be interred in the nearest potter's field.

What struck Gosse as odd was that the agent didn't appear to know what he was looking for. He didn't carry any photos with him. He simply moved from corpse to corpse checking them over as if he were shopping for a new set of golf clubs.

When Aposhian appeared moments later with the man's partner, the agent pointed at one of the bodies, and the assistant ME wrote down the number from the toe tag and went back to his office to process the paperwork.

The body was bagged and loaded into a nondescript van, and the G-men disappeared.

When Gosse asked his friend what the deal was, Aposhian told him that he'd been instructed not to speak about it. Apparently, the corpse wasn't a John Doe at all, but rather a person who had been involved in a serious felony case.

That's where the story should have ended, but it didn't. The FBI agents had presented the proper paperwork to claim the body, but had insisted that Aposhian hand over the ME file on it as well. They explained that the Bureau was involved in a complicated sting operation that would be jeopardized if the man's death became public. It was an unusual request, but the men were polite and had all their paperwork in order, so Aposhian had no reason to get into a pissing match with them. It wasn't until months later that the assistant ME realized his mistake.

One of the mortuary science students working with him that night had retrieved the wrong file for him. When Aposhian called the local FBI field office to try to correct his mistake they told him they had no record of an Agent Stan Weston or Joe Maxwell ever being assigned there. He next contacted FBI headquarters in Washington, D.C., but they informed him that they didn't have any agents by those names in the entire Federal Bureau of Investigation and that maybe he had made a mistake.

Aposhian checked his notes. There was no mistake. None of this was making any sense.

He handed the John Doe's fingerprint card to a woman named Sally Rutherford. Rutherford was one of the office investigators and Aposhian's girlfriend of eleven months. The next day, there was an email printed out and waiting for Aposhian on his desk.

According to Rutherford, there was some sort of mix-up. The prints came back as belonging to a man who had been killed in a shoot-out with police in Charleston, South Carolina, days after the FBI agents had taken the John Doe from their facility. The investigator had a call in to the Charleston Police Department and was waiting to hear back.

Aposhian figured it was all just another bureaucratic screwup, but changed his mind the night his FBI agents paid him a return visit.

Gosse, who was at his friend's apartment for poker night, didn't recognize the men at first. After all, it had been six months since he had first seen them at the ME's office.

They asked to speak to Aposhian outside, and when he returned, he was visibly shaken. Whatever these guys told him, it wasn't good.

Gosse asked his friend what was going on, but Aposhian didn't want to talk about it. In fact, saying he didn't feel well, the assistant ME cut their game short and sent his poker buddies home.

When Gosse was back at the ME's office for a pickup the next day, he was about to knock on Aposhian's door when he heard an argument coming from within. He stepped away from the door just as it opened and Sally Rutherford stormed out. Gosse wasn't one to pry, but his friend looked tremendously upset.

It was obvious Aposhian needed to talk, but the man didn't want to do it at the office. They decided to meet at the funeral home later that night.

When his friend got there, Gosse transferred the phones to the answering service and broke out a bottle of Maker's Mark. He set two glasses on his desk and poured a couple of ounces in each. Gosse was a born listener. He didn't force the conversation. He waited for his friend to speak, and when he did, the man shared with him an incredible story.

CHAPTER 21

MONTROSE, COLORADO

It had been several hours since Harvath had arrived at the resort. With the Sargasso staff monitoring the private chat room for any communication from the Troll, Harvath's hosts decided to take him back down to the resort for dinner.

Elk Mountain's main building resembled a majestic hunting lodge from the nineteenth century. The trio sat outside on the heated terrace near an outdoor stone fireplace overlooking the resort's lake.

Finney's penchant for perfection was evident everywhere, even down to how well his fires burned. When a staff member quietly appeared with a basket of logs, Finney explained that they used a precise mixture of walnut, beech, and eucalyptus, with just the right amount of seasoned pine for its aroma.

Finney's attention to detail was just as sharp, if not more so, when it came to Elk Mountain's food. He had spared no expense snapping up one of the best chefs in the country. The man was a culinary powerhouse who had pioneered American Alpine cuisine and held more James Beard, Zagat, and Wine Spectator awards than the resort had wall space to display. It was the first time since Tracy's shooting that Harvath had actually finished a meal.

He even allowed himself an after-dinner drink. Like it or not, he knew that he had to relax. He was wound way too tight and wasn't doing Tracy or himself any good in this state.

After the plates were cleared, two waiters appeared at Finney's side—one with a bottle of B&B and three snifters, the other with an elegantly carved humidor. Finney instructed the men to set everything down on the table and then they silently disappeared.

"You know a bartender at the '21' club in New York invented this?" queried Parker as he pulled the cork from the bottle. "Benedictine liqueur and cognac. It became so popular that the French started bottling the combination themselves. The guy never saw a dime of the profits. God, I hate the French."

Harvath smiled. Ron Parker had harbored a passionate dislike of the French for as long as he'd known him. Parker liked to say that they were the only army in the world with sunburned armpits.

Finney offered Harvath a cigar but he shook his head. The after-dinner drink would be enough.

When Parker handed it to him, Harvath raised the snifter to his nose and closed his eyes as he breathed in the spicy fragrance. For a moment, he almost forgot his problems.

As he sipped his liquor, he listened while Finney and Parker discussed the things they normally did—the state of world affairs, plans for improving the resort, Site Six, and Sargasso, as well as Parker's predatory practices with the female guests of Elk Mountain—an amusing but necessary concession Finney had made when asking Parker to give up a great position back east and move to their minimally populated corner of Colorado.

It was nice for Harvath to listen to the banter between his old friends. As his mind wandered, his thoughts were drawn to Tracy. He pulled his BlackBerry from its holster and checked its signal status. The terrace was usually the best place in the entire resort to get a signal, but he wasn't getting anything.

Finney asked him if he wanted to use one of the resort's cordless phones, and when Harvath said yes, Parker used his radio to ask a staff member to bring one to the terrace.

Harvath called the nurse's station at the hospital back in D.C. and asked to speak with Laverna, Tracy's night nurse.

When the woman came on the line, she said, "Am I glad you called."

Immediately, Harvath feared the worst, and his entire body stiffened. "Why? What happened? Is Tracy okay?"

"Tracy's fine, but a Mr. Gary Lawlor is looking for you. He says it's an emergency. I tried your cell phone, but all I got was your voicemail."

"I know," replied Harvath. "I'm in an area that doesn't have good coverage. Did Mr. Lawlor say what the emergency was?"

"No. He just said that if I saw you or heard from you to have you call him right away."

Harvath thanked Laverna and gave her Tim Finney's direct number at the resort before ringing off. His next call was to Gary, who picked up on the first ring.

"Gary, it's Scot. What's going on?"

"Where the hell are you?" demanded Lawlor. "I've been trying to get hold of you for hours."

"I'm at Tim Finney's place in Colorado."

"*Colorado?* Why didn't you tell me you were leaving town?"

"It all happened kind of last-minute," said Harvath. "What's going on back there?"

"Don't bullshit me," replied Lawlor. "You've got him working Tracy's shooting, don't you? You're using his Sargasso group. Were you not listening to the president when he *specifically* told you to stay out of it?"

"Finney's people got a lead and I came out here to check up on it. Period. Now, what's going on back

in D.C. that's so important you left an urgent message
with Tracy's nurse?"

Lawlor was quiet for a moment as he tried to
decide how to break the news. The minute Harvath
heard what he had to say, there'd be absolutely no
controlling him. Realizing there was no good way to
say it, Lawlor just came out with it. "Your mother was
attacked in Coronado tonight."

CHAPTER 22

Harvath felt like throwing up as he listened to the
details of his mother's assault. When the police
arrived at her home on Encino Lane they could hear
her screaming.

They kicked in the front door and followed the
sound of her voice to the bathroom at the back of the
house. It took two officers several minutes to break
down the door, which had been screwed shut.

They found her in her bathtub, naked and covered
with locusts. The insects, most of them several inches
in length, appeared to have been feeding off her. One
of the forensics people at the scene later identified the
substance Maureen Harvath had been covered with as
"bug grub," a product available in many pet stores for
feeding locusts.

She had no idea what the objects swarming over
her body were, because she couldn't see them. She had

been blinded. Her eyes had been painted over with black ink, and the doctors at the hospital still were not sure if she would ever fully regain her eyesight. She had been incredibly traumatized and was under heavy sedation.

With the last piece of information from the crime scene, Harvath's feelings of anguish turned to rage. A note had been found scribbled in red on the bottom of one of the buckets they believed the attacker had used to carry the locusts into the house. The note read: *That which has been taken in blood, can only be answered in blood.*

From watching Harvath's face and hearing only his side of the conversation, Finney and Parker assumed Tracy had taken a turn for the worst. When they heard that Harvath's mother had been attacked, they said the only thing that good friends can and should say in such a situation, "What do you need?"

What Harvath needed was the resort's jet, and Finney was on his radio arranging it before he even finished asking.

Parker had friends in the San Diego Police Department who could liaise with the Coronado cops, so he headed for Sargasso to get the intel ball rolling.

They had every reason to believe that the man who had attacked Maureen Harvath was the same person who had shot Tracy.

Harvath had been right. This *was* personal.

CHAPTER 23

Something the Troll had said during their chat room session kept replaying in Harvath's mind as the Elk Mountain Cessna Citation X raced toward Coronado.

He had pointed out that the lamb's blood above Harvath's door was very "biblical." Harvath didn't disagree, but ever since it had happened, he couldn't connect it to anything—at least in a way that made sense. Now his mother had been attacked and subjected to a veritable "plague" of locusts. Also biblical.

Harvath fired up Finney's onboard laptop and accessed the internet. He entered *lamb's blood* and *locusts* as his search terms. Over half a million results came back. The first was from Wikipedia, and the summary line said it all. The lamb's blood and locusts were from the ten plagues of Egypt. Harvath opened the link.

The plagues were recounted in the book of Exodus. They were the ten calamities visited upon Egypt by God in order to convince Pharaoh to release the Israelite slaves.

The first plague was the rivers of Egypt and other water sources turning to blood. It was followed by reptiles, or more specifically frogs, overrunning the land. Then there were lice, flies, and a disease on livestock. Next came a plague of unhealable boils, followed by hail mixed with fire. There were locusts, then darkness, and finally the death of every first-born male, except those of Israelites whose doorposts were painted with the blood of the Paschal lamb.

Whoever had shot Tracy and attacked his mother was definitely using the ten plagues as a bizarre kind of playbook, but in reverse order.

The tenth plague was the killing of all the first-born males in Egypt. Only the Israelite houses with the blood of a sacrificial lamb smeared on their lintels and doorposts were spared. God literally "passed over" their houses, and from this the festival of Passover had been born. It marked the release of the Israelites from their bondage under Pharaoh and the birth of the Jewish Nation. How it applied to Harvath and the shooting of Tracy Hastings was beginning to seem a little clearer.

The shooter apparently saw himself as the angel of death. He had passed over Harvath's house and spared him, but had tried to take Tracy instead.

The ninth plague dealt with darkness, hence the deliberate blinding of his mother. God had instructed Moses to stretch his hand over Egypt, and it brought about a plague of "complete and utter" darkness lasting for three days.

The eighth plague, meant to "harden Pharaoh's heart," was the plague of locusts. Neither Harvath's heart nor his resolve needed any further hardening at this point. Targeting both Tracy and his mother was enough. Regardless of what the president or anyone else said, his mind was made up. Whoever was behind these attacks had to not only be stopped, but killed, and that was exactly what he was going to do.

Harvath continued reading. The rest of the plagues were equally unpalatable, and he had no desire to imagine what their modern-day equivalents would look like. His only hope was to stop whoever was behind them before he could strike again.

That led Harvath to an even worse thought. Whom would this nutbag target next? First it was Tracy. Then it was his mother. Was this guy only targeting women who were close to him, or would he target men too? Should Harvath warn all of his friends? Even if he wanted to, what would he say? *There's a plague of biblical proportions with your name on it?* No, the key here was to stop this guy before he could strike again. But to do that, they were going to need a break—a big one.

CHAPTER 24

When Harvath walked into the hospital room and saw his mother lying there he was overcome with rage. Her face was badly battered and bruised. Who the hell would do something like this?

Though he wanted to go to his mother, he couldn't. The emotion of it all—the guilt he felt for being the reason she'd been targeted and the primal anger he felt in reaction to such an audacious violation—was crushing. Harvath found himself choking up. When the tears came, he did nothing to wipe them away.

Finally, he forced himself to walk over to the side of her bed. As he stared at his mother's swollen face, Harvath gently took one of her hands in his and said, "Mom, I'm so sorry."

He stood there like that for several minutes and finally pulled a chair alongside the bed and sat down. As he smoothed his mother's hair, an unwelcome twinge of déjà vu surged through him. It was almost like being in Tracy's hospital room.

Why the hell was this going on? Why, when he was finally getting his life together, was someone trying to rip it apart?

It was a good question and one that he'd asked himself many times since Tracy's shooting.

Out of everything Harvath had mastered in his life, relationships with women wasn't one of them. For a long time, he blamed his occupation and the demands his career placed on him. But when he met Tracy, he swore he wouldn't let his job be an excuse for another failed relationship.

He also blamed his commitment phobia on the stress his father's career had placed on his mother. In truth, though, they'd had an excellent marriage in spite of his dangerous profession and the all-too-frequent occasions when he had to disappear for weeks, sometimes even months at a time.

Finally, one night as Tracy lay sleeping next to him, Harvath looked deep inside himself for a reason—the real reason he had used to push every good woman who had ever come into his life away from him.

He saw the face of Meg Cassidy hover before his

mind's eye. As with Tracy, they had met under extraordinary circumstances. In Meg's case it had been a hijacking. Afterward, they'd been assigned to an incredibly difficult operation. For all intents and purposes they should have been perfect together—*maybe even as perfect as he and Tracy were.* But things just hadn't worked out. She was an incredible woman and someone Harvath regretted deeply having lost.

Nonetheless, it was an odd image to fixate on. Meg had moved on with her life. She had met someone new and was going to marry him soon.

His mind then went to a very dark corner that he usually worked hard to stay away from. He was in the right place. He knew it by the gut-wrenching feeling he experienced as he began to explore one of the darkest days of his life.

It was his second assignment with SEAL Team Two. They'd been sent into Finland in the middle of one of the worst winters on record. The blinding wind-driven snow made it nearly impossible to see or hear anything. His team split up into pairs as they closed in on their target.

Somehow, the men they were hunting had turned the tables and had snuck up on them from behind. How they knew that the SEAL team was there, Harvath never could determine.

By the time the confrontation was over, he had taken a round through the shoulder and his dead teammate had taken one through the head.

Though he managed to take out all the shooters, he found little satisfaction in it. The guilt he carried was immense. His teammate had a wife and two little kids.

Harvath had insisted that he be the one to inform the man's wife. Though she'd been a good, strong Navy spouse, the look on her face when she got the news broke Harvath's heart wide open. He vowed to never cause another wife that kind of pain ever again.

For years Harvath thought that meant making sure all of his men came back alive. It was a noble goal, but in their line of work people sometimes died. It was the biggest downside to what they did for a living. It was also one of the reasons that Harvath preferred working alone whenever he could.

Lying there next to Tracy, Harvath had finally understood why he'd pushed all the good women from his life. And at that moment he made a new vow to himself. If Tracy turned out to be the one for him, he would never let her go.

Harvath's chain of thought was broken as the BlackBerry at his hip vibrated with an incoming call. "Harvath," he said as he raised the device to his ear.

"Scot, it's Ron Parker. We've got something you should see."

"What is it?"

"How quickly can you get over to the San Diego Marriott?"

"The one on the bay?" asked Harvath as he looked at his mother. The doctors had told him that though she was stable, they planned on keeping her sedated for at least the rest of the evening. "Probably about fifteen minutes. Why?"

"You'll see when you get there. One of my contacts from the SDPD will be waiting for you. Ask for
Detective Gold."

CHAPTER 25

In the dead of night, the San Diego Marriott Hotel
& Marina was an eerily beautiful composition
of metal and curving glass. The slashes of red and
blue from the strobes atop the various police vehicles parked at its base only added to its dramatic
façade.

After having to flash his creds and get in the face
of a rather obstinate patrol officer who didn't want to
let him by, Harvath eventually found the detective
named Gold. For some reason, Parker had failed to
mention the detective's first name, which was Alison.
Not that Harvath had any problem with female detec-
tives, it just seemed an odd detail to leave out.

Knowing Ron as well as he did, Harvath figured
Gold had been a guest at Valhalla and that she and
Parker had probably had some sort of affair. Not mentioning that she was a woman was probably Ron's way
of trying too hard to paint her as a competent cop and
one whom Harvath could trust. It wasn't necessary.
The fact that Gold was all right with Parker made her
all right with Harvath. Very quickly, the tall, attractive
redhead, whom Harvath placed somewhere in her late

thirties, proved that she was very worthy of both Parker's and Harvath's respect.

After introducing herself and apologizing for the patrol officer, Alison Gold led Harvath to a windowless, white Chevy Express cargo van. The rear doors were open and inside a team of specialists from the department's Forensic Science Field Services Unit was collecting evidence.

"According to a witness who was walking her dogs near your mother's home shortly before the attack, there was a white commercial van parked on the street. We've already found magnetic signs in the van that come pretty close to matching the witness's description of the lettering she saw."

Gold rapped on the side of the van to get the attention of one of the techs and had him show Harvath what she was talking about. "Anyone who saw the van would assume your mother had a pipe burst or something and that it was being repaired. Coronado police have already checked with all of the Servpro franchises in the area, and none of them had any requests for service even remotely near your mother's home."

Harvath wasn't surprised. "And the van?"

"It was rented from a fleet leasing company in Los Angeles. We're checking into that now, but don't expect to come up with much."

Harvath didn't either.

"As far as prints and fibers, the vehicle is cleaner than clean. The Coronado PD hasn't found anything in her house either."

"And I doubt they will," replied Harvath.

"Why is that?" asked Gold.

"This guy's a professional."

The detective raised her eyebrows in response.

"I don't know how much Ron told you, but a friend of mine was shot outside my home in D.C. a few days ago, and we believe it's the same person who attacked my mother," said Harvath.

"Yeah, Ron explained that much. He also told me not to ask what you did to piss somebody off so bad that he'd attacked people you know on both coasts."

Harvath looked at her, but didn't say anything.

"That's okay," replied Gold, acknowledging his silence. "I've been to Elk Mountain. I understand."

She didn't know the half of what went on there, but Harvath let it slide. Parker was every bit the patriot Finney was and would never spill items of national security just to create engaging pillow talk. Changing the subject, Harvath asked, "How'd you find the van?"

"Based on our witness's description, we rolled back the footage from the cameras on the bridge. We saw the van going over and coming back from Coronado. Using our traffic cams, we were able to track the vehicle here."

It was good police work, but all Harvath had to do was gaze out toward the marina and the hundreds of boats parked along the docks to know that this guy was already long gone. He had a good idea how, but he still had to ask. "So he dumped the van here, and then what?"

Gold tilted her head in the direction of a hotel surveillance camera. "We've already pulled the footage. Like you said, this guy is a professional. He knew we were going to pull the tapes. He never looks directly into the camera. I'll make sure you get a copy of everything, but I don't think it'll do much good. He's wearing a baseball cap pulled down so tight you can't see his face. He's also wearing baggy clothes and is walking hunched over so that we couldn't get a good gauge of his height or his weight either."

"Did he have a car waiting for him or did he go down to the docks?"

"He went down to the docks," replied the detective. "The marina people are pretty strict about logging what boats are in what slips, registration numbers and all of that, but—"

"But by now he's probably already in Mexico."

Gold agreed. "If it was me I'd have a car waiting in Ensenada, if not someplace farther up the coast, and from there I'd just disappear."

She was right. It was exactly what Harvath would do, and it pissed him off. They were only hours behind the man who had shot Tracy and had attacked his mother, but it might as well have been days. With a boat and nearly two thousand miles of coastline on the Baja Peninsula, this guy could be anywhere.

The only thing Harvath knew for sure was that he had not disappeared for good. He'd turn up again, and when he did, it wasn't going to be over a cup of Constant Comment and a sob story about how he was misunderstood as a child.

At some point the two of them were going to have to square off, and when they did, only one of them was going to walk away from it alive.

CHAPTER 26

ANGRA DOS REIS, BRAZIL

The Troll looked at the list again and then pushed the pad of paper away. In a word, he was *stunned*.

Getting hold of the list had been as close to impossible as he had ever come. The Troll had precious little to bargain with and was forced to call in the favor of a lifetime from someone extremely well placed whom he knew was sitting on a piece of information so hot, it was practically radioactive.

Once he had that information, he had enough currency to go after what he was really looking for. Though Harvath had taken almost everything from him, the Troll still had a couple of aces up his short sleeve, and he played them masterfully.

Picking up his empty coffee cup, he slid down from his chair and padded into the kitchen. A cold breeze moved through the house carrying upon it the promise of rain. That had been one of the few drawbacks of this private island paradise. On the infrequent occasions when it rained, it poured. This meant that all of his satellite transmissions had to be suspended until after the storm had passed.

The pots of sobering Turkish coffee were burning a hole in his stomach. Removing the remnants of a half-eaten baguette, a wedge of Camembert, and a bottle of mineral water, he set them on a tray and returned to the table, where he looked at the list once more.

A million different things were floating around his mind, and he found it hard to stay focused. With each piece he uncovered, the puzzle only grew bigger.

One of the most interesting items he had discovered was that a little over six months ago, the Americans had secretly released five of the most dangerous prisoners they held at Guantanamo Bay. They had used a radioactive isotope to taint their blood in order to track them, but it had failed, and the Americans had lost track of them.

That all formed the *what* of the equation. What the Troll couldn't put together was the *why*.

Had it been some kind of a hush-hush trade? If so, who was it with and why track the men? Were they hoping to get them back, and if so, from whom? Who wanted them in the first place?

As far as the Troll could see, the prisoners were in no way connected. They all came from different organizations—even different countries. It didn't make any sense.

He supposed an Al Qaeda connection probably could be established among the five, but not in such a

way that the release en masse made any sense. And
they certainly hadn't been released because they had
been model detainees or had been wrongly incarcerat-
ed in the first place. No, these were very rough, very
dangerous men.

Their dossiers listed multiple escape attempts and
multiple attacks on the Joint Task Force Guantanamo
guards. While it was probably a relief to some of their
captors to see them gone, the United States must have
commanded a heavy price in return.

That had been the Troll's theory, but no matter
how hard he tried to find a link, he couldn't. There
was an absolute black hole of information—a very rare
intelligence phenomenon, especially by his standards.
Information could be hidden, but it never simply
evaporated. The fact that he had to drill down so hard
to get what was sitting in front of him right now told
him one thing—the United States didn't want word of
the release of these five men ever getting out.

The soldiers who had been involved with releasing
the prisoners that rainy night nearly six months ago had
all been promoted and transferred out of Guantanamo.
The United States had done a very good job tying up all
its loose ends, but why? What were they hiding?

The Troll let that question spin in his brain for a
bit while he focused on another piece that didn't seem
to fit—Agent Scot Harvath.

Over the last several hours, it had become quite
apparent that Harvath had some exceptional resources
at his disposal, but they weren't resources that
belonged to the U.S. government per se.

On the contrary, for some reason the United States regarded him as a liability and, according to the Troll's sources, wasn't allowing Harvath to pursue the investigation into who'd shot Tracy Hastings. Harvath was working alone.

Be that as it may, the man obviously had friends— and quite talented ones at that. The Troll was still chiding himself for having lost everything. His data, his fortune, all of it.

At first, he had entertained the idea of putting a contract out on Harvath, but not only would it have been prohibitively expensive, if anything happened to Harvath, the Troll might very well never see his money or his data again. He had no choice, at least for the time being, but to let things play out. If an opportunity presented itself at some point in the future, and one always did, then he would make his move. But for now, he was going to have to give every appearance that he was playing ball.

Reaching across the table, he pulled the thin pad of paper back toward him and studied the list of five names again. What should his next move be?

As a clap of thunder roared from somewhere out over the bay, the Troll lifted his pen, crossed the top name off the list, and then logged back into the chat room. What Harvath didn't know wouldn't kill him.

CHAPTER 27

After talking with her doctors, Harvath had sat with his mother again and had watched her sleep. It was still too early to tell if the damage to her vision would be permanent, but they were hopeful that her eyesight would begin to return soon. The blows she had taken to her head during the attack were what concerned them the most at this point, and they wanted to hold on to her for at least the next several days for more testing and observation.

After a little while longer, Harvath had stood. He loved his mother dearly, but no matter how much he wanted to, he couldn't just sit there by her bedside and wait for someone else to be attacked. He needed to act. So with a group of her friends on deck ready to sit vigil, he had climbed back aboard Tim Finney's Citation X and had flown back to Colorado.

Though the trip was smooth and uneventful, Harvath couldn't get any sleep. Tracy lay near death and his mother had been assaulted and tortured. He would have to live with the horrors of what had happened to them for the rest of his life. For a moment, he wondered if that was a part of the plan. The thought of it turned his stomach sour and once again he tasted the bile rising in his throat.

Harvath was coming unglued and he knew it. He was not one to let his emotions get the better of him, but this was different. The victims were people he knew and loved who were getting attacked. Would there be others? Probably. Would the attacker become more emboldened and potentially kill? That was a possibility—one so big that Harvath didn't even like to think about it, but he had to count on it.

Everyone, no matter how good, left clues. This guy was dropping pretty obvious ones, but none that helped Harvath figure out who he was or how he could be stopped.

Harvath wracked his brain all the way through the plane's touching down and the ride up into the mountains to the resort.

When he got there, Finney and Parker were waiting for him.

"Did you get any sleep on the way back?" asked Finney.

Harvath shook his head *no*.

His friend handed him a key card in a small folder with a room number on it. "Why don't you knock off for a bit?"

"What about the Boy from Ipanema down there in Brazil?"

"We heard from him right before a storm front moved in. His comms are down for the time being. We'll keep an eye on things. When the weather starts to break, we'll come get you."

Harvath thanked his friends and headed for his room. At the door, he made a conscious decision to shut his mind off and try to leave all his problems outside. Sleep was a weapon. It kept you sharp, and right now Scot Harvath needed it badly.

Opening the door, he kicked his shoes off and fell onto the bed. The resort was famous for its insanely high-thread-count sheets, down duvets, and feather-beds, but Harvath didn't care about any of that. All he wanted was sleep.

In a matter of moments his prayers were answered and he stepped off the cliff of consciousness into one of the deepest, darkest sleeps he had ever known.

CHAPTER 28

It was midmorning when Ron Parker called Harvath and told him to meet him in the dining room.

Harvath grabbed a quick shower, throwing the temperature control all the way to cold at the end to help wake him up and shake off the remnants of the horrible nightmare that had visited him every night without fail since Tracy's shooting.

He dressed in the spare clothes Finney had arranged for him and then called both hospitals to check on how his mother and Tracy were doing.

In the restaurant, Parker already had breakfast

waiting for them. Harvath poured himself a cup of coffee and asked, "Where's Tim?"

"He's glued to the markets this morning. There's a stock in South America he has his eye on."

Harvath got the picture and didn't ask any more questions. Once he had gulped down his breakfast, Parker drove him out to Sargasso.

When they entered the conference room, Tim Finney and Tom Morgan were waiting for them.

"The weather's almost cleared," said Morgan as Harvath poured himself a cup of coffee and sat down. "We should be hearing from our friend shortly."

"How's your mom doing?" asked Finney as he took the chair next to Harvath.

"Awful."

"I'm sorry to hear that. How about Tracy?"

"No change," he replied. Wanting to steer the questions away from his series of misfortunes, he posed one of his own. "Has that sawed-off little shit bag moved at all?"

"Nope," replied Parker as he stood in front of his laptop and took a sip of coffee.

"Has anyone been out to the island to see him?"

"Negative."

Harvath leaned back in his chair and massaged his face with his hands. "So we're back to waiting."

Finney tapped his pen against the conference table. "Yep."

The screens around the room were all illuminated and showed the chat room with the last message from the Troll indicating that he had information for Harvath but that it would have to wait until the rain had passed.

"How's Alison look?" asked Parker, breaking the silence that had fallen upon the room. "Good?"

Harvath smiled. No matter how luxurious the surroundings, lying in wait was still lying in wait, and cops as well as soldiers always talked about the same thing. "Yeah," Harvath replied. "She looks very good."

"If I could convince her to move here full-time, maybe we could have something."

Finney snorted derisively. "And deprive all the resort's female guests of your attention? Not on your life."

Parker laughed. "It doesn't matter. San Diego is where her career is. She's not going to leave that. Not even for me."

Harvath was going to respond when Tom Morgan snapped his fingers and pointed to one of the screens. The Troll was back.

CHAPTER 29

It seemed an odd request at first, but Harvath wasn't the world's fastest typist either, and Morgan had assured him that they wouldn't be putting themselves at risk.

With his headset on and a nod from Morgan that it was safe to proceed, Harvath said, "Okay, I'm here."

"Agent Harvath, how nice to hear your voice," replied the Troll over their encrypted voice-chat link.

"Yours too. It's a lot deeper than I expected."

The Troll laughed. "All the better to prevent you from building an accurate voiceprint of me. That Echelon listening program your government has is quite good, you know."

Harvath tried to place the man's accent. He spoke the Queen's English with an exceptional British accent, but there was something beneath it. *Czech, maybe?* Or was it Russian? Harvath spoke passable Russian and knew many native Russian speakers. This man sounded more like he came from outside mother Russia proper. Perhaps Georgia.

That fact notwithstanding, Harvath still had no desire to make small talk, so he got to the point. "Your last transmission said you had something for me. What is it?"

"Through a couple of sources I still have access to, I was able to secure a list of names. Four, to be exact," lied the Troll. "All released en masse from the U.S. naval detention facility at Guantanamo Bay."

"And why would I be interested in them?" asked Harvath.

The Troll paused for effect and then said, "Because one of those men is the person you're looking for."

Harvath looked at Finney, Parker, and Morgan, who were all quietly listening in on the exchange. "What are you talking about?" he asked.

The Troll laughed. "As it turns out, Agent Harvath, there is quite a bit your government is keeping from you. Quite a bit they do not wish for you, or anyone else, for that matter, to find out."

"Like what?" asked Harvath.

"Like the fact that these four men released from Guantanamo were very nefarious characters. All of them bona fide terrorists with multiple confirmed kills against American soldiers, as well as intelligence operatives and private contractors."

A million questions raced through Harvath's mind, not the least of which was why the hell four bona fide terrorists would have been released. It didn't make any sense. "Your information must be off."

"I thought so too at first," replied the Troll. "But there's more. The four men had their blood tainted with a radioactive isotope shortly before they were released. It was part of a top-secret project your government uses occasionally to track operatives who are going into dangerous areas, as well as prisoners it wants to release back into the wild."

At that moment, a series of realizations began crashing down upon Harvath.

"The only problem," continued the Troll, "was that whoever sent the plane to pick the men up knew about the top-secret program. The aircraft had been outfitted with equipment capable of conducting full blood transfusions."

As Harvath tried to focus his mind, he asked, "How do you know all this?"

"It was part of a report filed after your government lost track of these four men when the plane landed overseas. Containers with their tainted blood were taken in four different directions and discarded. They were eventually recovered by the Central Intelligence Agency."

"I still don't see what this has to do with—"

"The blood painted above your doorway," interrupted the Troll with impatience, "it contained the same unique radioisotope used on the four men released from Guantanamo."

CHAPTER 30

We don't have much choice," offered Finney, trying to be the voice of reason in the group. "If you say no, or if you miss his deadline, he'll bolt. I know it."

"So what?" replied Parker. "If he runs, we'll find him. It may take a while, but we'll track him down eventually. Besides, he's got zero bank balances across the board. Maybe he's got some hard currency stashed here and there, but how long is that going to last him? Not long."

"And if he decides to use the money to take out a contract on Scot?"

It was a scenario Parker had considered, but didn't deem plausible. "Then he'd really be in trouble. If he killed Scot he'd never get his data or his money back."

"But he could start over," said Finney. "Maybe he could even extort protection money from the four men on his list. He could offer to get rid of Harvath for them."

"He'd have to find them first, and based on what we've been told," countered Parker, "that's not something even the United States government has been able to do. Right?"

Parker was speaking to him, but Harvath had only half heard him. His mind was still replaying the conversation he'd had with Gary Lawlor shortly after hanging up with the Troll.

Everything the dwarf had told him made sense. He had been right about the radioisotope program and the fact that the blood over Harvath's doorframe had been tainted with it. He had little reason to suspect the information about the men released from Guantanamo was anything but accurate as well.

That was what really bothered him. If these four detainees were as bad as the Troll claimed, they never should have seen the light of day again. So why were they free? What possible reason could there have been for letting them go?

This line of questioning led Harvath to something even more disturbing. These men could never have been released from Gitmo without the president's knowledge. Suddenly, he knew why the president had wanted to sideline him. For some reason, Rutledge was protecting these men. *But why?*

Protecting them made about as much sense as releasing them. Harvath shared his shock and disap-

pointment at the president with Lawlor, but his boss
had little sympathy for him. He reminded Harvath
that he was under direct orders from Rutledge to back
off and let the president and his people handle it.
Lawlor then demanded that he come home.

If anyone knew that there were times not to play
by the rules, it was Lawlor. His refusal to acknowledge
that now was definitely one of those times not only
pissed Harvath off, but left him feeling strangely abandoned.

Parker snapped his fingers in front of Harvath's
face to get his attention. "Am I talking solely for my
own benefit here?" he asked.

"I'm sorry," replied Harvath, bringing himself
back to the present. "What were we talking about?"

Parker rolled his eyes. *The Troll*. Are we going to
agree to his deal or not?"

Harvath thought about it a moment and then
replied, "I'm inclined to pay him."

"You gotta be kidding me," moaned Parker as he
threw his hands into the air. "Jesus, Harvath."

"Tim's right. He knows better than to put a hit
on me. If he does, he'll never get back any of what
we took from him."

"But—" attempted Parker.

"And I know if anything does happen to me,"
continued Harvath, "I've got two friends who will
make sure he pays."

Finney looked over both of his shoulders trying to
spot the friends Harvath was referring to, then
exclaimed, "Oh! You mean us."

Harvath ignored them both and rattled off a list of instructions to Tom Morgan.

Forty-five minutes later, the Troll posted his list of four names, along with their nationalities and some other info, to the private chat room. The list made no sense at all. The nationalities were all across the board. Harvath had no idea what they could possibly have in common, but it didn't matter. He was convinced he had his man. It was the third entry on the list—*Ronaldo Palmera, Mexico*. Mexico was only a short boat ride from San Diego.

Harvath typed the name on his computer and hit *send*.

While the Troll went to work tracking down anything he could about the target, Parker and Morgan got started on their own research. Finney and Harvath were left alone to talk.

"Any of the names ring a bell with you?" asked Finney.

"No," he replied.

"Syria, Morocco, Australia, and Mexico? I don't know about this. I think your pal the Troll is pulling our legs."

Harvath shook his head. "If he plays us, he'll be the one who loses. He knows that."

"But what kind of a list is that? It sounds like a judging panel for an international figure-skating competition. We're talking about four of the worst of the worst released from Gitmo."

"So?"

"So, what's the link? What do these guys have in

common that they'd all be released at the same time? And who'd care enough about these assholes to send a plane to pick them up and change out their blood as part of the in-flight entertainment?"

Harvath couldn't argue with him. "Maybe Ronaldo Palmera will be able to tell us."

"Maybe," replied Finney. "But first we'll have to find him. Mexico is a big place."

"We're talking about the guy who attacked my mother and almost killed Tracy," replied Harvath. "I don't care if we have to tear the whole country apart. He's ours."

CHAPTER 31

BALTIMORE, MARYLAND

Since interviewing Tom Gosse, *Baltimore Sun* reporter Mark Sheppard hadn't slept much. The first thing he had done was verify Gosse's claims that his friend, State of Maryland Medical Examiner Frank Aposhian, and his girlfriend/investigator, Sally Rutherford, had actually been killed in a traffic accident. They had, but the circumstances around it weren't as cut and dried as Gosse made them out to be.

According to Gosse, Aposhian said that the night the supposed FBI agents had returned to his home, they had threatened him. They had told him to cease any fur-

ther inquiries into the John Doe that had been removed
from the ME's office. Aposhian didn't want any trouble
and agreed not to ask any more questions. The problem,
as it turned out, wasn't with Aposhian asking questions,
it was with his girlfriend, Rutherford.

The woman smelled something funny and
refused to throw in the towel. As far as she was concerned, there was nothing to compel her to obey a
pair of fake FBI agents—no matter how convincing
they were. What's more, they had no idea she and
Aposhian were an item. All they knew was that she
was an investigator in the ME's office and had run a
set of prints for him. As long as she was careful,
whoever these clowns were, they'd have no idea
what she was up to.

So Rutherford continued to dig. But what she
found was far from comforting.

She avoided contacting the police department in
Charleston. Rutherford had already reached out to them
once and couldn't help but wonder if they had tipped off
the men who had shown up at Frank's apartment.
Instead, she contacted the Charleston coroner's office.

Based on the backup copy of the ME file she'd made
after Aposhian had been visited again by the so-called
FBI agents, she had no doubt that her John Doe and the
police shoot-out victim in Charleston were one and the
same. What was different, though, was that her stiff had
died from a drug overdose—not gunshot wounds.

Deepening the mystery was the fact that an application for exhumation could not be filed for the
corpse, as it had already been cremated. When asked

who had authorized the cremation, the coroner's office told her that they didn't have that information and would have to get back to her.

They never had the chance. Later that night, Rutherford and Aposhian were both killed when they ran a red light and were T-boned by another vehicle.

The fight Gosse had overheard that day sprang from Aposhian's telling Rutherford to just let the John Doe situation go. Rutherford had uncovered something on the internet, but Aposhian didn't want to hear about it. He just wanted it all to go away. That was when she had stormed out of her office.

That night at the funeral home, the assistant ME had turned down his friend's offer of a second tumbler of Maker's Mark and had called Rutherford on her cell phone. He said he felt terrible about their fight. He agreed to go pick her up, and that was the last time Tom Gosse ever saw him alive.

Gosse was convinced that whoever wanted Aposhian to stop asking questions about the missing John Doe had somehow caused the fatal accident.

Sheppard, though, wasn't so sure. Using his network of contacts in the Baltimore PD, he spoke to all of the personnel involved in investigating Aposhian's crash. None of them had any doubt that the accident was anything other than the assistant ME tragically running a red light. There was nothing wrong with the vehicle and Aposhian hadn't been using his cell phone at the time of impact, but he did have a minor blood alcohol level—something Tom Gosse probably blamed himself for. But at the end of the day, the accident seemed to be Aposhian's fault. As one of the officers put it, *The poor guy simply fucked up.*

Be that as it may, Aposhian and Rutherford had both apparently been on to something when they were killed. Throw in a couple of shadowy figures posing as FBI agents and even the biggest cynic would have a hard time ignoring the possibility that some sort of conspiracy might be afoot.

Why use a John Doe from Baltimore to fake a shoot-out with police in South Carolina?

Sheppard found the beginning of an answer to the question in less than two minutes. Charleston was a small town, especially by metropolitan Baltimore standards, and even more helpful was the fact that their citizens didn't often get into police shoot-outs.

He was only halfway through the first newspaper article he'd pulled up on Google when he knew what his next move would be. Mark Sheppard was going to have to go to South Carolina.

CHAPTER 32

MEXICO

It was a crappy little café in a crappy little Mexican town, but it had halfway decent sandwiches, cold beer, and, unbelievably, a high-speed internet connection.

"Progress," Philippe Roussard mumbled to himself as he wiped the lip of his bottle of Negro Modelo with his shirt and entered his password.

The setup was quite simple and had been around for quite some time, but with all their technology the Americans had yet to find a way to crack it. Which was why it was perfect.

Roussard and his handler shared a free, web-based email account. Instead of posting cryptic messages on an electronic bulletin board, or risking being undone by sending emails back and forth, they simply left brief notes for each other in the account's *draft* folder. As soon as the other read the message, it was deleted. No trail, no trace, and no chance of anyone monitoring their conversations.

Roussard did what he had to do, logged off, and then dragged the cold bottle of beer across his forehead. *What a country,* he thought to himself. *High-speed internet, but no air-conditioning.*

The bottle felt good across his face and along the back of his neck. Earlier this morning he had stopped for gas, found the men's room, and shaved. It was one habit he practiced religiously each day. He could thank his mother for his dark features. Stubble only made it worse. While some had told him over the years he looked Italian, that wasn't how the majority of the world saw him. Roussard couldn't escape his breeding. He looked like what he was—a Palestinian.

For all diplomatic intents and purposes, he was French. He spoke the language and carried a French passport. He even harbored a strong dislike of Americans, which meant he fit in perfectly when he was in France. But the reality of the situation was that he hadn't been there for years. The war in Iraq had kept him quite busy.

Being Juba, being everywhere and nowhere, striking down Western imperialist soldiers one by one with a crack from his rifle was an all-consuming affair. Then he had gotten caught.

Between intensive interrogations, Roussard had had time to think—lots of it. And in that time, certain things had become clear to him. America's time was drawing near.

It wouldn't happen in months or even years, but in a matter of decades, America would fall. It was already happening. It was happening right before the eyes of each and every American, yet they were too fat and happy with their Big Gulps and satellite television to see it.

Roussard was amazed at how a nation once so proud could fall so far so quickly. The fabric of American society was in tatters. All one had to do was to pull at any one of the threads and it disintegrated even faster. If it wasn't so arrogant, America might have been worth pitying. It had achieved much, but like Rome, its gluttony for power and world domination was already hastening its drumbeat to the grave.

Roussard was anxious to get back to work. The plagues were a brilliant idea. It added an extra element of torment to what Scot Harvath would be made to suffer. And after he was finally done with Harvath, Roussard planned to return to his work in Iraq. Though the Islamic Army of Iraq had trained and deployed excellent sniper teams, the fear they struck into the hearts and minds of their enemies was not as profound as that which Juba had been able to create.

Juba was a nightmare. Juba the sniper who struck without warning kept American troops awake in their beds at night wondering if they would be next. Juba was the angel of death who decided who would live and who would die. *As soon as this assignment is complete,* he told himself, *I can return to my brothers in Iraq. Then once more I will be home.*

CHAPTER 33

Sargasso Intelligence Program
Elk Mountain Resort
Montrose, Colorado

It was late afternoon when Scot Harvath reconvened in the Sargasso conference room with Tim Finney, Ron Parker, and Tom Morgan. The resort's chef had prepared a late lunch and the men made small talk as they ate.

Once the meal was finished, Morgan began the presentation. "I want to do a brief overall primer and then get to specifics. Agent Harvath, I am assuming you may know a lot of this, but I think Mr. Finney and Mr. Parker will benefit."

Harvath politely signaled for Morgan to proceed.

"In the wake of 9/11, a lot of people got rolled up in Afghanistan, Iraq, and elsewhere. According to my sources, detainees come from more than fifty countries, only forty-one of which have actually been released to the press.

"The largest number of detainees come from Saudi Arabia, followed by Afghanistan and then Yemen."

"No surprise there," responded Finney.

"Indeed," agreed Morgan as he activated his laptop and the screens throughout the room glowed to life with the first slide of a hastily assembled PowerPoint presentation.

"How does Mexico tie in?"

"For some time, both American and Mexican intelligence agencies have been aware of highly specialized, paramilitary training camps throughout Mexico, a number of which are located within a day's drive of our southern border.

"The camps are operated by a group of former Mexican military special forces troops, known as the Zetas, who deserted in the mid-1990s to work as enforcers for high-paying drug cartels."

Morgan advanced to the next slide—a collage of surveillance photos. "The camps are frequented by a variety of Arab as well as Asian nationals, including Thais, Indonesians, and Filipinos."

"Representatives of all the world's Islamic radical hot spots," remarked Finney. "It's a regular terrorist Disneyland down there."

Morgan nodded and advanced to his next slide. "I have a colleague in D.C. who has said for years that via the Zetas, terrorists are exploiting the ability of the drug cartels to smuggle men, weapons, and explosives across our porous border with Mexico. As investigations continue, I think someday in the future we will be able to prove that men and materials involved in the attacks on Manhattan over the Fourth of July weekend came into this country via our southern border."

"If we knew about all of this before, why didn't we do anything? Build a fence, take out the camps, anything but just sit here while we were being invaded?"

Morgan grimaced and said, "For that kind of question you need a political analyst. As far as American intel people and a few enlightened members of Congress are concerned, the barbarians aren't at the gates, they've already blasted their way through. In addition to Al Qaeda cells in northern Mexico, we've seen activity by Hezbollah and Islamic Jihad, among others. They're all down there."

The former NSA man advanced to his next slide. "Not only are they down there, but they have absolutely no fear of anyone moving against them. Their balls are so big they've actually begun building mosques like this one outside Matamoros, Mexico—only a few miles across the Rio Grande from Brownsville, Texas."

Harvath had heard all of this before and had seen the evidence. The congenitally corrupt Mexican government had neither the desire nor the guts to take a stand against the Zetas and the drug cartels. They couldn't care less about the clear and present danger the two groups posed to American security.

Finney was aghast. "What the fuck, Scot? Is this for real?"

It was one of the few things about his country Harvath was ashamed of, and his failure to respond spoke volumes.

"Why doesn't the president or Congress do anything about this?"

"It's complicated," replied Harvath.

"So is prostate surgery, but you do it regardless of how much of a pain in the ass it is. The alternative is unacceptable."

"Listen, I agree. The terrorists, the drugs, the tidal wave of illegal immigrants. I've got friends on the Border Patrol. This is criminal, and we've only got ourselves to blame. As far as I'm concerned, how can we call America the most powerful nation on earth when we can't even secure our own borders? We're being overrun, and if we don't get a handle on it immediately, we're going to wake up real soon to a very different America—one that even the most liberal among us isn't going to enjoy very much."

"So what are we going to do about it?"

Harvath loved Finney, but now wasn't exactly the time to be solving this particular problem. "Short of loading up your Hummer with cinder blocks, mortar, and gas money to get to the border," he said, "there isn't much we can do."

"Actually," said Morgan, focusing his attention on Harvath, "that's not exactly true."

CHAPTER 34

So now we get to the specifics of the presentation," replied Harvath.

"Precisely," replied Morgan as he advanced to the next slide—a grainy surveillance photo. "Ronaldo Palmera, forty-three, born two hours outside Mexico City in Querétaro.

"A Zeta and visiting instructor at several of the camps, Palmera was known for his expertise in paramilitary warfare and exotic explosives. According to Mexican law enforcement officials, he was also known as one of the most ruthless of the cartel enforcers. In particular, he was known for the horrific ways he invented to torture and kill his victims."

The more Harvath listened, the more he was certain that this was the right guy.

"At some point, Al Qaeda was impressed enough with Palmera to offer him a boatload of money to come to Afghanistan and work in their training camps. He was already somewhat conversational in Arabic, but added Dari and Pashto as well. Soon after, he converted to Islam."

"The Troll said that all of the men on the list had multiple confirmed kills against American soldiers, intelligence operatives, and private contractors, so I'm guessing Palmera wasn't brought to Gitmo just for his involvement with the Al Qaeda camps," said Harvath.

"No," replied Morgan as he advanced to another slide, "he wasn't. After 9/11 the United States launched Operation Enduring Freedom. In advance of putting ground forces into Afghanistan, highly specialized CIA and Special Operations teams were sent in to collect intelligence, help form alliances, and so forth. Without question, it was one of the most dangerous and important missions immediately after 9/11. It was also one of the most successful. It would have been even more successful if it hadn't been for Palmera.

"With bin Laden's blessing, Palmera assembled his own teams to track down the Americans that Al Qaeda knew were going to be slipped in in advance of the ground campaign. The five U.S. teams you see in this photo were taken out by Palmera, many in ways that are so gruesome, they don't even bear mentioning.

"Suffice it to say that Palmera did most of the wet work himself—torturing and killing his American captives after they had been disarmed and could no longer fight or defend themselves. It's said that he liked to keep trophies from his kills. In the case of the American advance teams, it was their tongues. He cut them out while the soldiers and CIA operatives were still alive and then had a shoemaker in Kandahar cobble a pair of boots from them."

Harvath thought of his friend Bob Herrington,

who had been wounded in Afghanistan while helping another wounded Delta Force operative and had seen his career come to an end because of it. Although he had been forced out of a job he loved, he hadn't hesitated to step up once again when his country needed him. Harvath knew what kind of men those soldiers and CIA operatives Palmera had killed were. They were incredibly brave, incredibly capable, and put their love for their country above all—just as Bob had.

Harvath knew that when he located Ronaldo Palmera, he was going to make him pay for a lot more than what he had done to his mother and Tracy Hastings.

Harvath was about to say as much when Ron Parker looked up from his laptop and interrupting his thoughts by saying, "We've got activity in the chat room."

CHAPTER 35

Santiago de Querétaro, Mexico

The city of Querétaro was hot, dirty, and crowded. Though its population was just under 1.5 million, most of them seemed to crowd into the historic downtown—a UNESCO World Heritage Site, so recognized for its well-preserved Colonial-era architecture.

Depending upon whether you were a Mexican or a Spanish historian, Querétaro was known as the cradle of Mexican independence or as a hotbed of revolutionary activity. It was in this city that the plot to overthrow the Spanish and push them back to Spain was born. It was also where the peace treaty known as the Treaty of Guadalupe Hidalgo was signed, ending the Mexican-American War and ceding parts of the modern-day U.S. states of Arizona, New Mexico, Colorado, and Wyoming, as well as all of California, Nevada, and Utah. In return, the United States agreed to take over $3.25 million in debts owed by Mexico to American citizens.

With both radical Islamic fundamentalists and a good majority of the Mexican government intent upon bringing down the United States, Querétaro seemed a perfect place for Ronaldo Palmera to call home.

When word came from the Troll of Palmera's whereabouts, Ron Parker was actually disappointed that he wasn't holed up in one of the training camps. With all of the ex–Special Operations people on the Elk Mountain payroll, he had hoped they could assemble their own strike team, slip across the border, and take out an entire camp.

Harvath would have liked that too, but grabbing Palmera in Querétaro had some distinct advantages. Foremost among them was that the city was at the crossroads of Mexico and had one of the most dynamic economies in the entire country. This meant that large amounts of American and European capital as well as large numbers of businessmen moved through Querétaro on a regular basis. With their shaved heads, Parker and Finney weren't exactly going to blend—not the two of them together and especially not Finney. He was so big that he stood out everywhere he went, but Harvath had a good idea of how they could turn that to their advantage.

Operationally, Parker and Finney had enough tactical knowledge and experience to pull off what Harvath wanted to do. What's more, a three-man team was as big as they dared put together for this operation. As good as the guys from Valhalla and Site Six were, the crew for this kind of assignment was best kept small.

When their jet touched down at Querétaro International Airport, a well-dressed Finney and Parker took up bodyguard positions around an even-better-dressed Harvath.

Once through customs and passport control, Finney and Parker unpacked radios from their bags, affixed them beneath their sport coats, and placed Secret Service–style ear buds into their ears. The policemen guarding the terminal studied their movements, but no more intensely than they did those of any other wealthy foreign businessman who came through the airport. Americans and Europeans were still a thing of both wonder and envy in Querétaro.

Halfway along the main road into the city, Finney instructed Parker to pull off. They followed a poorly paved road for about seven miles into one of the worst Mexican slums any of them had ever seen. Rental car or not, this wasn't a good place to be driving a shiny, new American luxury four-door.

After doubling back twice, they finally found what they were looking for. As they pulled up in front of the tiny auto parts store with its hand-painted signs and rusted bars across its windows, Finney looked at Parker and said, "Keep it running."

Climbing out of the car, Finney spotted an old man in a T-shirt and sandals sitting in a lawn chair propped up against the front of the building. When the old man smiled, he showed a row of gold teeth.

Finney approached him and asked a question about the road into Querétaro. When the old man gave him the predetermined response, Finney then asked him if he had a spare tire that would fit their car. The old man raised himself from the wobbly lawn chair and motioned for Finney to follow him inside.

Harvath and Parker watched from the car. This wasn't part of the agreement, and neither of them liked it, but they had little choice but to sit and wait.

Moments later, Finney re-emerged with what they assumed was their tire wrapped in a large garbage bag. The old man came around the back of the car and knocked twice with his gnarled knuckles on the trunk. Parker depressed the trunk release, and Finney carefully laid the tire inside.

Ten minutes later, they pulled the car off to the side of the road and got out. Popping the trunk, they removed the plastic bag from around the "spare tire." Duct-taped inside the tire was everything Harvath had asked for. The Troll had charged them dearly for the weapons, but seeing as how they had no sources in Mexico and Harvath couldn't tap any of his D.C. connections for fear the president would find out what he was up to, they'd had little choice but to agree to buy what they needed from the Troll and his extensive network.

Harvath was glad to have the weapons. If Ronaldo Palmera was as dangerous as everyone said he was, they were going to need them.

CHAPTER 36

Though Palmera could have lived anywhere in Querétaro, he preferred the hardscrabble El Tepe neighborhood where people minded their own business and didn't ask a lot of questions.

He kept an unassuming two-story house not far from the main market square. In the rear was a patio of sorts where he had planted an extensive garden, the highlight of which was neat rows of dwarf fruit trees.

Gardening was a pastime Palmera had come to late in life and it had become a reliable way to soothe his nerves and take his mind off all he had seen and all he had done.

To represent the five pillars of Islam, he had planted five different types of trees: apple for the testimony of faith; apricot for the ritual of daily prayer; cherry for the obligatory almsgiving; nectarine for fasting, and peach for the pilgrimage to Mecca—a journey Palmera had yet to undertake.

As he tended to each type of tree, he was reminded of his commitment to Allah and focused his mind on what that particular pillar of Islam meant to him. In the midst of an all-too-secular world, Palmera's garden was his sanctuary, his earthly Paradise. It was also the weakest link in the defense of his home.

Early on, Harvath had abandoned the idea of snatching Palmera off the street—too many witnesses and too many things that could go wrong. Their best chance was to take him at his house.

From what the intel revealed, Palmera lived alone and didn't travel with any bodyguards—his reputation being all the protection he needed. The one thing that Harvath was worried about, though, was how extensively Palmera had the neighborhood wired. Spreading your money around to local charities, churches, and families in need was a great way to purchase loyalty and eyeballs that would alert you to any indication someone had come looking for you.

In the end, there simply was no way for Harvath and his team to know. Therefore, they had to adopt the attitude that every single person within a four-block radius of Palmera's house was on his payroll and ready to drop a dime at a moment's notice. Trying to sneak into the neighborhood was out of the question. They would have to go in bold as brass.

And that's exactly what they did.

They parked the rental car a block away from Palmera's house and paid a couple of shopkeepers a hundred bucks apiece to keep an eye on it. Though Finney spoke very little Spanish, it was clear what would happen to the shopkeepers if they returned and something had happened to their vehicle.

He took up his position behind Harvath and Parker and they walked to the corner and turned onto Palmera's street. Harvath talked animatedly and pointed at different buildings, a roll of blueprints under his arm.

Three-quarters of the way down the block, Harvath spotted the narrow gangway that led to the rear of Palmera's house, and he stopped. Removing the blueprints from underneath his arm, he unrolled them across the hood of a parked car and appeared to study them intently. Taking a small digital camera from his pocket, he handed it to Parker and ordered him to start taking pictures.

The neighborhood people had no idea who the man with the blueprints was, but based on the size of his bodyguard he had to be somebody very important. If he was visiting El Tepe, that could only mean one thing—redevelopment. And redevelopment meant money, lots of money.

They watched as the man studied his plans and his assistant took photographs of their shops and buildings, while the dutiful bodyguard stood by, ready to discourage any unbidden approach.

Eager to look worthy of the businessman's interest in their neighborhood, several of the shopkeepers along the street shuffled inside to get brooms and began sweeping off their sidewalks.

Harvath continued to gesture, using his pen to point out how the power cables entered several different structures. Satisfied that they had garnered the right kind of attention, Harvath studied his blueprints for a few minutes more, then pointed at the gangway just ahead of them. Tucking the drawings for Tim Finney's new riding arena at Elk Mountain under his arm, he began walking. This would be one of the most dangerous moments of their entry plan.

Tom Morgan had covertly piggybacked onto an NSA satellite that allowed him to monitor everything that was going on from back in Colorado. As of this moment, Ronaldo Palmera's home was empty. If they were going to get inside, now was the time to do it.

Receiving the "all clear" over his earpiece, Ron Parker relayed the message to Harvath, and they casually turned into the narrow gangway. It was strewn with garbage and smelled like urine. Harvath had smelled worse.

He ignored the smell and even a rat that looked as if it could have been a contender at Churchill Downs and made his way to the end of the passageway.

He had his lockpick gun halfway out of his pocket when he arrived at a heavy wooden door laced with black iron bands and realized they'd have to think of something else. The door looked as if it had been pulled from a medieval castle or fortified Spanish mission, and its thick iron lock was just as forbidding. They'd have to go over the high stone wall.

Fortunately, they were fairly well concealed from the street, and Harvath got right to work.

Taking two steps backward, he counted to three and then leaped for the top of the wall. He latched on and gave a silent thanks that it wasn't capped with broken glass—a common security measure in third world countries. He pulled himself up, swung his legs over, and dropped into the garden below.

As he did, he heard something that turned his blood to ice.

CHAPTER 37

The animals tore out of their makeshift doghouse and barreled down on Harvath with amazing speed. His vision narrowed. All he could see were their contorted, hideous faces with their grisly teeth and pitch-black eyes.

In an instant, they were airborne—their mouths wide open, ready to tear at his flesh. Harvath had time neither to draw his weapon nor to get out of the way. His only reaction was one of pure instinct. He raised both his arms to protect his face.

There was the sound of two quick pops as the animals slammed into Harvath and knocked him back against the wall. Quickly, he spun away from them, surprised to have his arms free.

Harvath readied for the dogs to launch their next assault and then realized it wouldn't be coming. He looked up and saw Ron Parker straddling the wall, his silenced pistol clasped in both hands. His eyes quickly scanned the garden for any other threats. Seeing none, he hopped down and joined Harvath.

"Tom Morgan sends his apologies," said Parker as he made sure the animals were dead. "He never noticed the dogs."

Harvath looked down at the two bodies on the ground. The animals were absolutely vile. They appeared to be some sort of pit bull–Doberman cross that had gone horribly wrong. They were revolting to look at. All the same, Harvath regretted having to kill them. He loved dogs.

But there was no question that these boys would have torn him apart. He was lucky Ron Parker was such an exceptional shot.

"Thank you," said Harvath as he pulled his weapon.

"That's one you owe me," replied Parker as Finney came over the wall and landed just a few feet away.

"Those are the ugliest dogs I've ever seen," said Finney as he grabbed them by their hind legs and pulled them toward the corrugated metal doghouse.

While Finney hid the carcasses, Parker scanned the adjacent windows for any sign they'd been discovered, and Harvath worked the locks on Palmera's back door.

When he had the door open, he signaled Finney and Parker and they slipped inside behind him.

Just as the Troll had said, Palmera didn't have an alarm system. But somehow the Troll had overlooked the dogs. Harvath made a note to take it up with him later.

With their weapons drawn, the men quickly swept through the house, clearing each room as they went. There was no sign of Palmera or anyone else. That gave Harvath a few extra minutes to look for something.

With Finney watching the front door and Parker the back, Harvath started searching. He began with the downstairs closets, and when those turned up empty, he headed upstairs.

He looked through all the closets, under the bed, and was pulling up a chair to gain access to a hidden attic space when Finney called for him to come back down.

"What's up?" whispered Harvath from the top of the stairs.

Finney tapped his ear bud. "Morgan's got a car inbound that matches the description we've got for Palmera."

"How long?"

"Forty-five seconds, tops," replied Finney. "We need to get in place."

Harvath glanced over his shoulder toward the bedroom where he'd found the tiny attic space and decided it could wait.

Harvath was halfway down the stairs when he heard his friend say, "Guys, we've got a little problem here."

Harvath hurried down the rest of the stairs and joined Finney near the windows at the front of the house. He was right. They did have a problem. Ronaldo Palmera wasn't alone.

CHAPTER 38

Palmera climbed out of his Toyota Land Cruiser accompanied by two additional men—neither of whom looked Mexican.

The pair were both just a hair shorter than the six-foot-tall Palmera, and had obviously been spending a lot of time out of doors. Their skin had been darkened by the sun, and while they might have been able to pass for South Americans with some people, their facial features immediately gave them away to Harvath. These two were Arabs; most likely connected to one of Palmera's training camps.

If that was true, they posed a very serious threat. Harvath had to think fast.

One of the most popular covert methods of subduing a dangerous suspect was to hand him a ticket for a five-second ride via a TASER X26. When the electricity began coursing through the subject's body, his neuromuscular system was impaired and he collapsed to the ground. Some screamed, but most were so locked up they just fell to the ground where their hands and feet could be Flexicuffed and a strip of duct tape could be placed across their mouth.

That was how a TASER was used against a single suspect. Three men was something else entirely.

Harvath checked the secondary cartridge holder below the TASER's handgrip. He wasn't surprised to find it empty. The weapon had probably been used before it had made its way into his hands. For what, he didn't want to know.

The absence of a secondary cartridge left Harvath and his team with very few options.

Finney and Parker would do what it took to get the job done. They weren't afraid of getting their hands dirty, but they couldn't just pop Palmera's buddies because they looked Arab. Though they probably were a couple of dirt bags involved in some very bad things, there were still some things Harvath wouldn't do, and killing men who hadn't given him a reason was one of them.

That said, when it came time to do the deed, Harvath didn't often need a lot of convincing. He could tell just by looking at most people what kind of men or women they were. Maybe it was his Secret Service training. Maybe it was the years he'd spent in dangerous professions, but the bottom line was that having killed on numerous occasions, he recognized that ability in others instantly—the hard, implacable face, the ever-watchful eyes, it was always there. A person familiar with killing wore it like a hundred-dollar haircut—it was unmistakable.

Harvath had no doubt that Palmera and his companions were going to be trouble. The trick was to take them down before any of them could react. Harvath, Finney, and Parker had the element of surprise on their side. The only question was, with this sudden addition of two new players, could they still use it to their advantage? They didn't have much choice. They had to.

Harvath indicated to Finney and Parker what he wanted them to do, and the men took their places.

With his hand wrapped around the TASER, he prayed his plan would work.

CHAPTER 39

From his vantage point at the windows, Finney watched as the men walked up the sidewalk. Suddenly, he exclaimed, "Oh, shit!"

Harvath raced from his hiding place just in time to see Palmera and his accomplices turn down the gangway and head toward the rear of the building.

The entire plan had been predicated on their coming through the front door. Now they were going to come in through the back, and to do that, they were going to have to come through the garden. The moment the dogs didn't respond to their entry, Palmera would know something was up.

The only thing Harvath hated more than coming up with a hastily formed plan was coming up with a second hastily formed plan because the first one tanked. Each time they changed their tack the odds were more heavily stacked against them.

Even so, Harvath had been trained to adapt and overcome—to think quickly on his feet and to succeed no matter what the odds. The plan that now sprang to his mind was pure military instinct born from years of practice.

Since Parker was the best shooter in their group, he got the hardest job. Leaving him at the front door, Harvath and Finney raced toward the back of the house.

The back door with its multiple deadbolts was still open, and they raced through it and into the garden. They took their places just as Palmera slid his key into the heavy iron lock of the garden door.

The key began to turn and then stopped. Harvath knew why. Palmera had expected to hear something. Undoubtedly, the dogs normally went nuts when they heard Palmera's key in the lock.

Harvath shot Finney a look. They might be able to take Palmera and his pals in the gangway, but with the element of surprise no longer on their side, something very bad could easily happen.

Finney got the message. Reaching over to the lean-to doghouse he rattled the sheets of corrugated metal.

The two men stared at the door, their ears straining for any sound from the lock that would signal Palmera's intent. Nothing happened. Obviously, the sound they had created was not what Palmera was looking for. Harvath changed his focus from the door to the top of the wall, certain that at any moment Palmera or one of his cronies was going to pop his head over to see what was going on.

The moment never came. Instead, Palmera

provocatively rattled his key in the lock. He was toying with the dogs—trying to get them worked up. Perhaps they were even better trained than Harvath had imagined. After all, they hadn't sprung until he was already over the fence and in the garden. This could have been a game Palmera played with them, getting them all worked up before he revealed himself as being the "perceived danger" on the other side of the door. Harvath knew plenty of people who liked to tease their dogs good-naturedly from time to time. Maybe his plan would work.

As the key turned and the heavy lock *thunked* open, a small smile crept across Harvath's face. It was definitely going to work.

Palmera's face was the first thing he saw. It was pockmarked from years of horrible acne and barely covered by a lousy excuse for a beard he had grown in reverence to his Muslim faith. His black hair was unkempt and his dark, narrow eyes told Harvath everything he needed to know about him. After Harvath was finished with Palmera, he would kill him. But first, they had a little talking to do.

When the Mexican terrorist had stepped all the way into the garden, Harvath sprang from his hiding place and let the barbed probes of his TASER rip. They tore through Palmera's thin cotton shirt and lodged in his chest. Instantly, the electricity began flowing, and the assassin was treated to something American law enforcement officers referred to as "riding the buffalo."

As his muscles locked up and his six-foot frame

raced face-first toward the ground, Tim Finney put all of his weight behind the garden door. It slammed shut with a deafening crack that sounded like a rifle shot and sent both of Palmera's cohorts tumbling into the gangway—leaving one of them unconscious.

Before the other man realized what had happened, Finney had reopened the door and was on top of him. With one well-placed blow to the head, the man had joined his friend in the realm of the unconscious.

Parker had been charged with kneecapping the Arabs if things had turned sour, but now that they'd been both knocked cold, he jogged down the gangway and helped Finney drag their bodies into the garden.

With Palmera's hands Flexicuffed behind his back and a piece of duct tape across his mouth, Harvath relieved him of a semiautomatic pistol, two knives, a can of pepper spray, and a Keating Stinger. This guy was a real sweetheart, and Harvath couldn't wait to go to work on him. If he was lucky, Palmera would be difficult and require a very lengthy interrogation.

Harvath kept his knee pressed into the back of the man's skull as Parker and Finney duct-taped and hog-tied his amigos with Flexicuffs and pitched them into the corrugated lean-to to sleep it off on top of the dead dogs.

Once they were done, Harvath stood up and yanked the just-reviving Palmera to his feet. With the cold tube of his sound suppressor pressed against the killer's ribs, Harvath didn't need to articulate what would happen if he did anything stupid. Palmera was a smart man and knew all too well what was in store for him.

CHAPTER 40

Ron Parker drew the living-room curtains as Harvath tore the piece of duct tape from Palmera's mouth and shoved him into a chair.

When the man opened his yapper to curse the three of them, Harvath kicked him in the *maracas* so hard it knocked the wind out of his lungs.

As Palmera lay on the floor gasping for air, Harvath yanked him up by his shirt and placed him back in his chair. "I ask questions and you answer them. That's how this works. Any deviation from that program and I am going to get nasty. Do we understand each other?"

Palmera didn't respond. He simply glowered at Harvath.

Removing the TASER from the holster at the small of his back, Harvath pressed the device against Palmera's neck and pulled the trigger. Even without an additional cartridge that could be fired from a distance, up close the TASER could still be used as an effective touch-stun weapon.

Instantly, Palmera's body locked up, and he fell

forward out of the chair. When he hit the floor, his nose bore the brunt of the impact and shattered.

As Harvath helped him back into his seat, he leaned in toward his ear and said, "You know every one of those cases of people dying in America via a TASER are bullshit. Ninety-nine percent of the time they have an underlying heart condition. How's your heart, Ronaldo?"

"Fuck you," the man spat as he fought to fully regain his breath.

Harvath placed the TASER on the other side of his neck and said, "We can do this all night. I brought lots of extra batteries."

Palmera began to spit in his face, so Harvath let him ride the buffalo again.

Harvath placed the man back in his chair and waited until his breathing had stabilized. "If this isn't getting your attention, we can prepare a footbath for you and get the battery out of your truck. It's up to you."

Instead of English, this time Palmera cursed at him in Spanish. It was a subtle indication that they were beginning to wear him down.

Palmera's broken nose was bleeding, so Harvath signaled for Finney to bring them a towel from the kitchen.

When Finney returned and handed him the towel, Harvath wrapped his hand with it, grabbed Palmera's nose as hard as he could, and pulled the man toward him.

The assassin roared in pain. Harvath made sure he

spoke loud enough to be heard. "What were you doing in D.C.? How'd you find my house? How'd you find my mother's house?"

Palmera didn't answer. He was on the verge of passing out from the pain. "Why are you targeting the people around me?" demanded Harvath. "Are you working alone or did someone send you? Answer me!"

Harvath was ready to give the scumbag another ride for five with the TASER when Finney put a hand on his shoulder. He didn't need to say anything. The gesture was enough. They had all night if they needed to work on him. Beating him unconscious would only serve to hinder what they had come to do. They were here to get information, and if Harvath didn't get control of his emotions, he was going to blow it.

He let go of Palmera's broken nose and tried to push the images of what had happened to Tracy and his mother from his mind. There'd be plenty of time to take out his full anger on Palmera, but not yet.

Harvath stepped away from his prisoner and watched as the man's chin slumped against his chest. It was a good thing Finney had stopped him when he had. Palmera's eyes were unfocused and half-closed.

Just as Harvath was about to slap him around a bit to bring him to, Palmera began mumbling. It was faint and neither Harvath, Finney, nor Parker could understand what he was saying. He was probably just reciting verses from the Koran. They all did that when they were scared. No matter how tough Palmera thought he was, he was no match for Harvath. It was very like-

ly that the man saw in Harvath what Harvath had
seen in him—the ability *and* the willingness to kill.

Until Harvath knew exactly what Palmera was
saying, he knew he needed to treat every utterance as
potentially important. Placing the TASER up against
the man's groin, Harvath sent the unmistakable message that Palmera could keep playing the tough guy,
but that it would be at his own peril.

As Harvath leaned forward to try to decipher
what the man was saying, there was what sounded like
an enormous oak tree being split down the center by
a white-hot bolt of lightning. Harvath's vision
dimmed and he stumbled backward.

Bumping into the coffee table, he lost his balance.
From somewhere behind where Palmera had been sit-
ting, Harvath heard the sound of breaking glass and
Finney and Parker desperately shouting at each other.

Seconds later there came the sound of squealing
tires from outside on the street. It was followed by a
sickening thud, and even in his haze Harvath knew that
a car had hit someone. He prayed it wasn't Palmera.

Shaking off the stars that were clouding his vision,
along with his self-contempt for being suckered into
such a powerful headbutt, Harvath forced himself to
his feet and struggled out the door and into the street.

Finney looked up from where Ronaldo Palmera's
mangled body lay beneath the bumper of a dented
green taxi cab and shook his head.

Harvath moved toward the corpse and Ron Parker grabbed his arm. "He's dead," said Parker. "Let's get
out of here."

"Not yet," replied Harvath, as he slipped out of his friend's grasp and walked over to Palmera.

A crowd was beginning to form, but Harvath ignored them. Bending down, he slid the digital camera from his pocket, snapped a picture, and removed the man's disgusting boots.

Joining Finney and Parker back on the sidewalk, Harvath said, "Now we can go."

CHAPTER 41

CHARLESTON, SOUTH CAROLINA

Mark Sheppard's police contacts warned him to mind his Ps and Qs in Charleston. Since 1995 it had been consistently recognized as the "best-mannered" city in America and they didn't take well to rude or boorish behavior. Sheppard didn't know whether to say thank you or be insulted. Either way, he didn't plan on being in town long enough to make an impression.

Police shootings were very rare in Charleston, and Sheppard had no problem finding what he was looking for. According to the newspaper articles he'd read, the main tactical response group on site for the John Doe police "shoot out" was the Charleston County Sheriff's Office SWAT team. The SWAT community was a relatively small one, and Sheppard was able to parlay his influence with a high-ranking Baltimore SWAT member into an introduction with SWAT chief Mac Mangan in Charleston.

Though normally a smooth operator with the media, Mangan had never cared much for reporters. As far as he was concerned, they had one goal and one goal only—to make him and other law enforcement officers look bad.

Dealing with those from his own backyard was bad enough, but having to indulge a Yankee journalist who was undoubtedly on his way down here to second-guess his team and paint them as a bunch of trigger-happy hicks did not sit well with him. If he and his wife hadn't been such good friends with Richard and Cindy Moss up in Maryland, he never would have agreed to this meeting.

Sheppard met Mangan—a big bull of a man in his late forties—at the Wild Wing café on Market Street, where they ordered lunch.

By the time their food arrived, Sheppard felt confident that he had exchanged enough cop talk to put his subject at ease and transitioned into what he really wanted to discuss. "I assume Dick Moss told you why I'm here?"

Mangan nodded and took a bite out of his sandwich.

"What can you tell me about what happened?"

The SWAT team leader thoughtfully chewed his food and then dabbed his mouth with his napkin. "Bad guy barricades himself inside house. SWAT team goes in. Bang. Bang. No more bad guy."

Sheppard smiled. "I get it. Charleston County is not a place that takes kindly to bad guys."

Mangan raised his thumb and forefinger in a pantomimed pistol and shot Sheppard a wink as he dropped the hammer.

The reporter laughed good-naturedly. "The *Post and Courier* article went into a little more detail, but it sounds to me like they got it pretty much right."

The SWAT team leader opened his mouth and took another large bite of his sandwich.

"I'm beginning to think that maybe I should have started asking my questions before we got our lunch."

Once again, Mangan raised his pretend pistol and pulled the trigger as he shot Sheppard another wink.

The reporter was getting pissed off. "You know, Dick told me to be prepared for the *aw shucks* dipshit redneck routine, I just didn't expect it to start so quickly."

Mangan stopped chewing.

"Don't let me interrupt your lunch," Sheppard continued. "As long as I'm paying for your hillbilly happy meal, I want to make sure you enjoy every bite. By the way, what kind of kiddy toy comes with barbeque and a draft? A pack of Marlboros?"

The SWAT team leader wiped his mouth with his napkin and dropped it on his plate.

Sheppard watched him, not caring at all if the man was pissed off. He hadn't come all the way down to South Carolina to get jerked around by Stonewall Jackson here.

Slowly, a smile began to spread across Mangan's face. "Dick said you could be a bit touchy."

"He did, did he?" replied Sheppard.

Mangan nodded.

"What else did he say?"

"He said that after I got done fucking around I should try to answer your questions."

Sheppard noticed that his left hand had curled into a death grip around his Coke. With a laugh, he allowed himself to relax. "So does that mean you're done fucking around?"

"That depends," answered Mangan. "Are you done being sensitive?"

Typical cop ball-busting. Sheppard should have seen it coming. Cops were no different in Charleston than they were back in Baltimore. In response to the man's question, the reporter nodded.

Mangan smiled. "Good. Now what do you want to know about the shooting?"

"Everything."

Mangan shook his head back and forth. "Let's just cut through all the crap."

"Okay," said Sheppard, playing along, "Dick said you were the first guy in the house. What did you see?"

"That's the first thing we need to get straight," he replied. "I wasn't the first guy in."

"What do you mean?"

Mangan signaled for Sheppard to turn off his mini tape recorder. When he did, the SWAT man looked over his shoulder and then, turned back to the reporter and said, "The only way I'm going to tell you anything is if you agree that it's all off the record."

CHAPTER 42

Philippe Roussard was fit and athletic, but he had never considered himself much of a sportsman. How an entire culture could be so obsessed with such a wide array of sports was beyond him. Surely, it was a luxury only a Western nation like America could afford.

Roussard sat and watched the young aerialists of the U.S. Freestyle Ski Team practice. It was a bright, cloudless day. The temperature was perfect—upper seventies and not much wind, excellent conditions in which to train.

The setting reminded him of the many villages where his family would rent chalets for their holidays. Of course, they were much more remote than this. The need for security in his family was such that the few times a year they did get together, it was always somewhere where they ran little risk of being seen, or worse, targeted.

The 389-acre Utah Olympic Park had been the site of the 2002 Olympic bobsled, luge, and ski-jumping events and was also a year-round training site for members of the U.S. Ski Team.

From his surveillance, he had learned that the aerialists were required to "water qualify" all new jumps before they'd be allowed to actually try them on the snow once the winter season arrived. Three plastic-covered ramps, or "kickers," as they were called, mimicked the actual ramps the skiers performed their aerial acrobatics off during the regular season. The difference here was that instead of landing at the bottom of a snow-covered hill, they landed in a pool of water.

Roussard had been anxious to see how it was done, and on his first visit to the park he had been greeted with some exceptional stunts. The aerialists, in their neoprene "shorty" wetsuits, ski boots, and helmets, would clomp up a set of stairs to the top of whatever ramp they were going to use, unsling their skis from over their shoulders, and then click into the bindings. The plastic ramps were continually sprayed down with water and the athletes skied down them exactly as they would on snow.

Racing straight down the plastic-covered hill, the skiers hit the ramp at the end and were launched into the air where their bodies conducted twists, flips, and contortions that defied gravity and sheer belief.

The surface of the splash pool was broken with roiling bubbles put in via a series of jets to help soften the skiers' landings. Coupled with the bungee cord harnesses and trampoline jump simulators there was quite a bit of science at work here. It was a fascinating series of images that Roussard would carry with him for the rest of his life. He was thankful that he would be long gone before his plan took effect.

Sitting on the hill that overlooked the pool, the green valley below, and the snow-capped mountains beyond, Roussard closed his eyes and allowed himself to feel the sun against his face. Every day during his captivity, he'd wondered if he would ever breathe free air again. He had traveled the world and had visited few places as peaceful and serene as Park City, Utah. But that peace and serenity was about to change.

When his handler had contacted him on the disposable cell phone he'd purchased in Mexico there'd been an argument. Roussard wanted to finish his assignment. Maneuvering through this intricate list of persons in Scot Harvath's life was not only dangerous, it was superfluous. Not that Roussard was worried about getting caught; he knew he had the advantage over everyone in this assignment as none of them knew where or whom he would strike next.

Even so, he was smart enough to realize that with every attack he carried out, the odds of his being captured or killed were increasing.

Roussard wanted to skip to the end of the list, but his handler wouldn't hear of it. Their relationship was growing strained. Their last conversation in Mexico had ended with the normally calm and collected Roussard shouting and hanging up.

When they spoke a couple of hours later, Roussard's temper had cooled but he was still angry. He wanted Harvath to pay for what he had done, but there were other ways to do it. Vengeance should be bigger and more extreme. No survivors should be left behind. The people close to Harvath should die, and he should feel and see their blood upon his hands for the rest of his life.

Finally, his handler had relented.

Roussard watched as the last aerialists of the day climbed the stairs for their final jumps. It was time.

Carefully, he slung his backpack over his shoulder and walked down to the edge of the pool. The lack of security at the park amazed him. Spectators and staff smiled and said hello to him as he passed, none of them suspecting at all the horror he would shortly unleash.

The first device was packed inside a long sandwich roll and then wrapped in a Subway foods wrapper. It went into a trash receptacle near the main gate to the pool.

From there, Roussard calmly let himself in through the unlocked gate and headed toward the locker room. He was a chameleon, and 99 percent of his disguise came from his attitude. He had nailed the mountain casual, resort-town look perfectly. The ubiquitous iPod, T-shirt, jeans, and Keens—they all came together with his air of purpose in such a way that anyone who looked at him assumed that he either was a skier or worked for the park. In short, no one bothered Philippe Roussard because he looked like he belonged there.

In the locker room, Roussard quickly and carefully placed the rest of the devices. When he was done, he let himself out an unalarmed emergency exit and headed for the parking lot.

He placed the buds of the iPod into his ears,

donned his silver helmet, and left the glass bottle with his calling card note where investigators should find it.

Firing up the 2005 Yamaha Yzf R6 sportbike he had stolen across the border in Wyoming, Roussard pulled out of the parking lot and slowly wound his way down the mountain.

Nearing the bottom, he pulled over and waited.

When the first of his explosions detonated, Roussard scrolled through his iPod, selected the music he wanted, revved his engine, and headed for the highway.

CHAPTER 43

SOMEWHERE OVER THE SOUTHWEST

Getting out of Mexico had been Harvath's greatest concern. But once they were safely away, he traded one concern for another. After Finney's jet had reached its cruising altitude and passed into U.S. airspace, a phone call came through.

Harvath and Parker listened as Finney chatted with Tom Morgan. He ended the call by telling his intel chief to send everything the Sargasso people had.

Finney then looked over at Harvath and said, "Scot, I've got some bad news."

Harvath's heart seized in his chest. *Was it his mother? Tracy?* He didn't need to ask as Finney picked up a remote, activated the flat-panel monitor at the rear of the cabin, and tuned to one of the cable news programs.

Helicopter footage showed a raging fire with countless emergency vehicles gathered around one of the main buildings of the Utah Olympic Park that Harvath knew all too well. "What's going on?" he asked.

"Someone placed several pipe bombs packed with ball bearings throughout the U.S. Freestyle Ski Team training area. At least two went off in the locker room while the team was there."

"Jesus," replied Parker. "Do they have casualty estimates yet?"

"Morgan's emailing them now," said Finney. "But it's not good. So far they haven't found any survivors."

Harvath turned away from the television. He couldn't watch any more. "What about the coaches?" he asked.

"Morgan's sending everything he has," responded Finney as he powered up his laptop and avoided Harvath's gaze.

Harvath reached out and pulled the laptop away from Finney. "There's a reason Morgan contacted you with this. What about the coaches?"

"You think this is connected?" asked Parker.

Harvath kept his eyes glued to Finney as he said, "The seventh plague of Egypt was hail mixed with fire."

Parker was at a loss for what to say.

"Two of the coaches were my teammates," said Harvath. "They were like family to me. I don't want to wait for Morgan's email. I want you to tell me what he said."

Finney held Harvath's gaze and replied, "Brian Peterson and Kelly Cook were pronounced dead at the scene along with nine other U.S. Ski Team members."

Harvath felt as if he had been hit in the chest with a lead pipe. Part of him wanted to scream out *Why?* But he knew why. It was about *him*.

The more pressing question was, when was it going to stop? That, too, had an equally simple answer—when he put a bullet between the eyes of whoever was responsible for all of this.

He regretted losing Palmera. The idiot had run right out into the street and had gotten himself killed.

Not that it made much difference. They could have been there all night. If and when Palmera had cracked, his information wouldn't have been worth anything, because he obviously wasn't the man they were after. Someone else on that list was, and Harvath was determined to track him down before he could strike again. But time was obviously running out.

CHAPTER 44

Tom Morgan finished his presentation by playing the CCTV footage from the San Diego Marriott and the Utah Olympic Sports Park in a split screen on a monitor at the front of the Sargasso conference room. "Though we don't have a shot of his face, the cops found a note with the same message as the other two crime scenes—*That which has been taken in blood, can only be answered in blood.* Everything here tells me we're dealing with the same guy."

Harvath agreed. "Let's get that footage to both hospitals. Even though we don't have his face, I'd feel better about my mother and Tracy knowing their security people were keeping an eye peeled for this guy."

"We're going to send some of our guys out too," replied Finney.

"What do you mean?" asked Harvath.

"We've handpicked two teams to cover your mom and Tracy," answered Parker.

Harvath looked at him. "That would cost a fortune. I can't ask you guys to do that."

"It's already done," replied Finney with a smile. "The sooner you catch the asshole who's responsible for all of this, the sooner I can bring my guys back and put them on a gig that actually pays."

"I owe you," said Harvath.

"Yeah, you do, but we'll take that up later. For right now, we need to figure out what our next move is going to be."

It was a word Harvath didn't want to hear, much less acknowledge. This was not *our* move, as Finney had put it. It was his move—Harvath's. He loved Finney and Parker like brothers, but he preferred working alone. He could move faster and there was less to worry about. While Finney and Parker had been a big help to him in Mexico, he couldn't put them at risk anymore.

He was already struggling under a mountain of guilt. He needed to start compartmentalizing his life— firewalling off everyone he could from danger, and that included Tim Finney and Ron Parker.

Turning to Tom Morgan, Harvath asked, "What do we know about the three remaining names on the list?"

Morgan handed folders to everyone and then opened a file on his computer. The CCTV footage on the monitor disappeared and was replaced with three head-and-shoulder silhouettes, with names and nationalities underneath. "Not much. Scattered intelligence references. A smattering of aliases. Little to no known contacts. What I could find is in the folder. I'm afraid it looks like we're going to be at the mercy of the Troll for running these three down."

"Have you put them through our domestic databases?" asked Harvath as he studied the screen and set his folder on the table.

"Yes," replied Morgan, "but I can't find any visas, visa applications, airline tickets, or anything else that suggests any of them have recently entered the United States."

Harvath wasn't surprised. "This guy isn't going to leave a trail."

Morgan nodded.

"Then do you think Mexico was a red herring?" asked Finney.

"I think we wanted Mexico to equal two plus two," said Harvath, "but it wasn't that easy."

"So is the Troll playing us?"

Harvath shook his head. "I think we jumped the gun. We have no idea which way our guy went after he left the San Diego Harbor. He might even have stayed within the U.S. But in our minds, Mexico made the most sense, and when the Troll handed us Palmera, we jumped."

"So?"

"So maybe we shouldn't jump anymore."

"You went with your gut," clarified Parker. "You didn't *jump*. Instinct is part of good investigative technique."

"Yeah? So is evidence," replied Harvath.

"Well, this guy doesn't leave a lot of evidence behind."

"Let's face it," said Finney, "we're not being left with anything."

Harvath studied the countries of origin of the

remaining three men on their list: Syria, Morocco, and Australia. According to the Troll, one of those men was responsible for three horrific attacks, and there was every reason to believe there'd be more. Since whoever was preying upon the people close to Harvath was tying the attacks to the ten plagues of Egypt, Harvath wondered if maybe the answer lay within the plagues themselves.

Then again, maybe it didn't. Maybe it all had something to do with Egypt as a country. Still, there was no making sense out of any of it. And what terrified him was that there were six plagues left. Would this nut job combine them as he had with his mother? Or would they each be loosed individually? And behind all of it, what did the president have to do with releasing the four from Gitmo in the first place? Surely a release of this magnitude couldn't have happened without his knowledge.

Gathering up the folder and his notes, Harvath excused himself from the conference room and went to Tom Morgan's office.

He needed to check on his mother and Tracy. He dialed his mother's hospital first. She was awake and he spent twenty minutes talking with her, reassuring her that everything was going to be all right and that he'd be back out to see her as soon as he could. As he was preparing to say good-bye, another of his mother's friends arrived at her room, and he was heartened by the fact that she wasn't alone. It would have been better if he could be there, but he couldn't be in two places at once.

He clicked over to a new line and called the hospital in Falls Church, Virginia. Tracy's parents had already gone back to their hotel for the night. Her nurse, Laverna, was on duty, and she gave Harvath a full update on her condition. It wasn't good. While her overall condition had not changed, small signs were materializing that suggested her situation was beginning to deteriorate.

Glancing at the fly-fishing scene on Tom Morgan's wall, Harvath asked Laverna for a favor. When she held the phone up to Tracy's ear, he began to tell her about the wonderful vacation the two of them were going to take as soon as she got better.

CHAPTER 45

Leaning back in Morgan's desk chair, Harvath closed his eyes. There had to be something he wasn't seeing, some sort of thread strung just beneath the surface of everything.

At this point, he knew of only one man who could answer his questions. Though already rebuffed by him once, Harvath decided enough had changed to warrant trying again. Picking up the phone, Harvath dialed the White House.

He knew better than to ask for the president directly. No matter how much Rutledge liked him, he had multiple layers in place to prevent direct access.

The best Harvath could hope for would be to reach the president's chief of staff, and even then there was no knowing when or if Charles Anderson would pass the message along to the president.

He needed someone he could trust and someone who would get the president on the line right away. That someone was Carolyn Leonard, head of Jack Rutledge's Secret Service detail.

Getting to an agent while she was working, much less getting her to step away from active protection to take a phone call, was a near impossible task. When Carolyn Leonard picked up the phone, she wasn't happy. "You've got five seconds, Scot."

"Carolyn, I need to speak with the president."

"He's not available."

"Where is he?"

"He's in the cement mixer," replied Leonard, using the Secret Service codename for the Situation Room.

"Carolyn, please. This is important. I know who carried out the attack on the U.S. Olympic facility in Park City today."

"Give it to me and I'll have it run down."

Harvath took a deep breath. "I can't do that. Listen, I need you to tell the president that you have me on the line and that I have important information for him regarding today's attack. He'll want to hear what I have to say. Trust me."

"The last time I let a man slip that one past me I ended up pregnant with twins."

"I'm being serious. People's lives are at stake here."

Carolyn thought for a moment. Harvath was

clearly violating the chain of command. He had come to her as a shortcut, which meant that either time was of the essence or other avenues were unavailable.

He was a legend in the Secret Service, and his heroism and patriotism were above reproach, but Harvath was also known as a shoot-from-the-hip maverick who often chucked the rule book in favor of expediency. His "ends justifies the means" way of doing business had also become legendary in the Secret Service and was always held up as an example of what not to do.

Often, Harvath was characterized as having more balls then brains, and agents were admonished not to follow his example. It had been made crystal clear throughout the organization that Harvath's success as a U.S. Secret Service agent had been due more to luck than anything else.

Leonard's ass was on the line. Her job was to protect the president, not to decide what phone calls should get passed through to him. Going to the president with this would clearly be overstepping her bounds and could very well lead to a demotion, transfer, or worse.

"Scot, I could get fired for this," she said.

"Carolyn, the president is not going to fire you. He loves you."

"As did, supposedly, my ex-husband who left me with said twins, a mortgage, and over twenty-five thousand in credit card debt."

"For all I know, Jack Rutledge may be on this whackjob's list as well. Please, Carolyn, this guy is a killer and he needs to be stopped. I need your help."

Leonard had always liked and admired Harvath. Regardless of what the powers that be said about him, he was a man who got things done, and never once had his motives been questioned. Everyone at the Secret Service knew that he put his country before all else. If there was ever someone more deserving of a favor, Leonard had never met him. "Hold on. I'll see what I can do."

CHAPTER 46

WHITE HOUSE SITUATION ROOM

Four and a half minutes later, Jack Rutledge picked up the phone. "Scot, I heard about your mother and I want to let you know how incredibly sorry I am."

Harvath let his silence speak for him.

"Agent Leonard tells me you have information about today's bombing that I should know about," continued the president. "She says you know who's behind it."

"It's the same person who shot Tracy Hastings and who put my mother in the hospital."

Rutledge's blood began to boil. "I told you to stay out of this."

Harvath was incredulous. "While this guy continues to prey upon the people I care about? Two are in the hospital, two more are dead, and plenty of others who were just in the wrong place at the wrong time have been killed or injured. I'm sorry, Mr. President, I can't just *stay out of this.* I'm right in the middle of it."

Rutledge struggled to remain calm. "Scot, you have no idea what you're doing."

"Why don't you help me? Let's start with that group of detainees you released from Guantanamo Bay a little over six months ago."

Now it was the president's turn to be silent. After a long pause, he spoke very carefully. "Agent Harvath, you're treading on extremely thin ice."

"Mr. President, I know about the radioisotope that was supposed to track them and I know it was found in the blood above my doorway. One of those men is sending a message by targeting the people close to me."

"And my word that the people I have on this are doing all they can isn't good enough for you?"

"No, Mr. President. It isn't," replied Harvath. "You can't shut me out any more."

Rutledge bowed his head and pinched the bridge of his nose with his thumb and forefinger. "I don't have any choice."

Harvath didn't believe him. "You're the president. How's that possible?"

"I'm not at liberty to discuss any of this with you. You need to obey my orders or else you and I are going to have a very big problem."

"Then it looks like we've got a very big problem, because there've already been three attacks and they're going to keep coming unless *I* do something."

The president paused as his chief of staff slid him a note. When he was done reading it he said, "Scot, I need to put you on hold for a minute."

Clicking over to the line where the director of Central Intelligence, James Vaile, was waiting, Rutledge said, "You'd better be calling me with some good news, Jim."

"I'm sorry, Mr. President, I'm not. Actually, we've got a bit of a problem."

"That seems to be par for the course today. What is it?"

"Are you alone?"

"No, why?"

"This has to do with Operation Blackboard."

Blackboard was a codename the president had hoped never to hear uttered again, but ever since Tracy Hastings's shooting it seemed to be all he and the DCI talked about.

Placing the receiver against his chest, Rutledge asked his chief of staff to clear the room and close the door behind him.

Once everyone was out, the president said, "Now I'm alone."

CHAPTER 47

The CIA director got right to the point. "Mr. President, you'll recall that one of the Gitmo detainees exchanged in Operation Blackboard was a former Mexican Special Forces soldier turned Muslim convert who was helping to train Al Qaeda operatives. His name was Ronaldo Palmera."

Though the president normally remembered only the most significant names in the war on terror, the names of the five men released from Guantanamo had all stayed with him. At the time, it was because he harbored a fear in the deepest recesses of his soul that the names would one day come back to haunt him. Suddenly it looked as if that fear was about to become reality. "What about him?"

"Palmera was struck and killed by a taxi cab in Querétaro, Mexico."

"Good."

"His wrists were Flexicuffed behind his back when it happened," replied Vaile.

"Not so good, but from what I recall the man had a lot of enemies. He was an enforcer for some of the big drug cartels down there, correct?"

"Yes, Mr. President, but that's not the problem. Apparently, Palmera jumped through a window and then ran out into the street. Three men, *three white men,*" Vaile added for emphasis, "were seen coming out of Palmera's residence immediately afterward. One of

them removed Palmera's boots and then they disappeared."

"Removed his boots?"

"Yes, sir. You'll recall that Palmera was rumored to
have made a pair of boots from the tongues of the
Special Forces and CIA agents he killed in
Afghanistan. When he was captured, we looked but
never found the boots. He obviously had them stashed
somewhere and picked them up after he was released
from Guantanamo."

"Obviously," replied the president, who could feel
an intense headache coming on. He looked down and
saw the blinking light of the line where Harvath was
sitting on hold. "So according to your information,
three gringos were responsible for Palmera exiting his
home, *through a window,* with his arms Flexicuffed
behind his back, at which point he ran into traffic and
was run down by a taxi cab."

"Yes, Mr. President."

"Then one of these men removed Palmera's boots
and the trio fled the scene?"

"Exactly," replied Vaile. "We think they may have
come in via Querétaro's international airport, and
we're working on getting hold of the aviation logs as
well as customs information and security tape
footage now. I don't need to tell you what this is
starting to look like."

"I know exactly what it looks like. It looks like we
broke our word. None of those men from Gitmo were
supposed to be touched. Ever."

"In all fairness, Mr. President, if we'd been able to

track them, we might have been able to prevent this from happening."

"I'm not going to rehash that, Jim," replied the president, growing angrier. "Secretary Hilliman and the folks at DOD had every reason to believe the isotope tracking system would work. We still don't know how the terrorists found out about it."

"Well, they did. The blood transfusions probably began the minute that plane left Cuban airspace."

They'd had this argument ad nauseam. The DOD blamed the CIA for losing the five terrorists released from Gitmo, and the CIA blamed the DOD for betting the farm on the isotope tracking system. Each was sure the other was where the leak about the ultrasecret tracking system had come from. The whole plan had been based upon being able to track the five men, and it had fallen apart. Now, it was coming back to haunt them all.

Switching gears, the president said, "How come I haven't had any updates on your progress locating the terrorist stalking Harvath?"

"Because unfortunately there hasn't been much progress. Not yet, at least."

"Damn it, Jim. How the hell is that possible? You've got every available resource at your disposal. You told me the people you put on this were seasoned counterterrorism operatives. You promised me, and I promised Harvath, that this would be taken care of."

"And it will be, Mr. President. We're doing everything we can to hunt this guy down. We'll get him, I assure you."

Vaile was sounding like a broken record, but Rutledge let it go for the moment. He had other problems to deal with. "So how do we fix this problem in Mexico?"

"It's going to take a lot of work. We'll have to create a pretty damn convincing deception and even then I don't know if it will fly. We were warned what would happen if anything befell any one of the five."

The president didn't need to be reminded of the penalty terms of their agreement. He'd been forced to make a deal with the devil, and he'd agonized over violating the nation's first commandment in the war on terror. "Let's just get to the bottom line here."

"For starters," replied the DCI, "we need to figure out who was chasing Palmera."

The president once more looked down at the flashing light on his phone. "And then?"

"Then we make sure that person can in no way, shape, or form be associated with you, this administration, or the United States government," replied Vaile.

"And then?"

"Then we pray to God the people we had to deal with six months ago don't see right through us and make good on their threats."

CHAPTER 48

Harvath hung up the phone in utter disbelief. He had no idea who the president had spoken to while he'd had him on hold, but when Jack Rutledge got back on the line he was beyond angry, and their conversation went from bad to worse.

The president told him point-blank to back off the investigation, and when Harvath refused, the president said he had no choice but to order his arrest on grounds of treason.

Treason? Harvath was shocked. How could trying to save the lives of people who were important to him, people who were American citizens, be an act of treason?

The president gave him twenty-four hours to get back to D.C. and turn himself in. "And if I don't?" Harvath had asked.

"Then I cannot and will not be responsible for your well-being," Rutledge had answered.

And there it was. The cards were all on the table and Harvath now knew exactly where he stood.

He ended his conversation with the president by saying, "I guess we've each got to do what we feel is right," and hung up the phone.

It was a moment Harvath could never have foreseen. The president of the United States had actually threatened his life. It was incomprehensible—just as incomprehensible as being labeled a traitor. For a moment, Harvath wondered if this was all some sort of bad dream, but the stark reality of the situation was too much to be anything but real.

His standing was now clear. In spite of years of selfless service to his country, he was disposable. His expertise, his track record, even his loyalty, were nothing more than items on a balance sheet to be weighed and disposed of at will.

Though Harvath wanted to give the president the benefit of the doubt, he could not bring himself to; not now. Not after having been taken into the president's confidence so many times in the past. Never once had Harvath betrayed that confidence. His loyalty and his discretion were above reproach, but those apparently mattered little if at all anymore to Jack Rutledge.

Harvath felt betrayed and abandoned. The president had actually chosen the terrorists over him. It was absolutely surreal.

Be that as it might, the one thing Harvath didn't feel was hopeless. The president could threaten him with arrest for treason, or worse, but the threats carried weight only if he got caught. And with a twenty-four-hour head start, the last thing he planned on doing was being apprehended.

Looking down at the folder he'd put on Tom Morgan's desk, he pulled out the latest smattering of data he'd been given before leaving the conference room.

As he studied the list of aliases used by the released detainees, he came across one that he actually knew from his past, but it had belonged to a man he had killed and whom he had most definitely watched die. There was no way he could still be alive. The discovery could only mean one thing. Somebody was using his alias.

CHAPTER 49

Three and a half hours later, Harvath spoke into his headset and said, "You're positive?"

"Yes," replied the Troll, who went over the information again. "Abdel Salam Najib is a Syrian intelligence operative who has been known to use the alias Abdel Rafiq Suleiman."

Najib was the third name on the list, and the Suleiman alias had originally belonged to the man Harvath had killed. "What about Tammam Al-Tal?" he asked.

"Also Syrian intelligence and Najib's handler. That's the connection you were looking for, isn't it?" asked the Troll.

"Maybe," said Harvath, not wanting to give anything away to the Troll. "I want you to forward us everything you pulled on both Najib and his handler, Al-Tal."

"I'll send it now."

Harvath logged off his computer, removed his headset, and turned to face his colleagues.

"You want to explain this to me?" asked Finney as he interlaced his thick fingers behind his head and stared at Harvath.

"On October 23, 1983, a yellow Mercedes-Benz delivery truck packed with explosives drove out to the Beirut International Airport. The First Battalion Eighth Marines of the U.S. Second Marine Division had established their headquarters there as part of a multinational peacekeeping force sent to oversee the withdrawal of the PLO from Lebanon.

"The driver of the truck circled the parking lot just outside the Marine compound and then stepped on the gas. He plowed through the barbed wire fence on the perimeter of the parking lot, flew between two sentry posts, went through a gate, and rammed his vehicle into the lobby of the Marine HQ."

"Why didn't the sentries shoot this idiot?" asked Finney.

"They weren't allowed to use live ammo," replied Parker, who had lost a good friend that day. "The politicians were afraid an accidental discharge might kill a civilian."

When Parker didn't add any more, Harvath continued. "According to one Marine who survived the attack, the driver was smiling as he slammed his truck into the building.

"When he detonated his explosives the force was equivalent to over twelve thousand pounds of TNT.

The rescue effort took days and was hampered by continual sniper fire. In the end, 220 Marines, eighteen Navy personnel, and three Army soldiers were killed. Sixty additional Americans were wounded. It was the highest single-day death toll for Marines since World War II and the battle of Iwo Jima. It's also the deadliest attack on U.S. forces overseas post–World War II, but what's most interesting from a counterterrorism viewpoint is that, kamikaze pilots notwithstanding, the attack on the Marine compound was the first real suicide bombing in history."

Finney was speechless. He was familiar with the story, but not in such detail.

"We never knew exactly who was responsible, so aside from a few shells we lobbed at Syria, there never was any concrete response," stated Harvath. "Now fast forward to about five years ago and a man named Asef Khashan.

"Khashan was extremely adept at guerrilla warfare and the use of high explosives courtesy of training he had received from Syrian intelligence.

"He was a driving force within the Lebanon-based Hezbollah terrorist organization and reported directly to Damascus. When the United States uncovered information that Khashan had been directly involved in the planning and staging of the 1983 bombing, it was decided it was time for him to take an early retirement."

Parker looked at Harvath from across the table and said, "And you were sent in to give him his pink slip."

Harvath nodded.

Finney unclasped his hands and removed the pen he had tucked behind his ear. Pointing at the screen in the front of the room he said, "So this guy Najib is after you for what you did to Khashan?"

"If I'm right," said Harvath, "then sort of."

"What do you mean *sort of?*"

"The actual connection between Najib and Khashan is via their handler, Tammam Al-Tal. Khashan was one of his best operatives. Some say that he was like a son to Al-Tal. When Khashan was killed, Al-Tal placed a bounty on my head."

"If this was a covert operation, how'd he know you were involved?"

"We used a Syrian military officer the U.S. had on its payroll to help track down Khashan," replied Harvath. "I never gave him my real name, but he had compiled a dossier on me with surveillance photos and other pieces of information from our meetings. When he was indicted for embezzlement not long after, he tried to use the dossier as a bargaining chip. The dossier eventually made its way to Al-Tal, who used all of his resources to connect a name to my photos. The rest is history."

"Did Al-Tal have anything to do with the attack?" asked Parker.

"We could never uncover enough evidence to prove whether he was directly involved. There is a mounting pile of evidence, though, that Al-Tal has been helping coordinate the sell-off of the weapons of mass destruction Saddam Hussein stashed in their country shortly before we invaded."

"How much is the bounty he put on you?"

"Somewhere around $150,000 U.S.," answered Harvath. "Allegedly, it represents the bulk of Al-Tal's life savings, and due to his willingness to expend said life savings to fund my demise, the powers that be in Washington removed Syria and Lebanon from my area of operations."

"It would seem that we've got more than enough to believe that Al-Tal is behind the attacks on Tracy, your mom, and the ski team," said Finney. "Do you have any idea where he is?"

"He's undergoing treatments in Jordan for stage-four lung cancer."

"With the end drawing near," stated Parker, "he's probably even more determined to take you out."

Harvath tilted his head in response as if to say, *Maybe.*

"But what does Najib's alias have to do with Al-Tal?"

Harvath looked across the table at Parker. "Abdel Rafiq Suleiman was the alias Khashan was using when I tracked him down to a Hezbollah safe house just outside Beirut."

"So?"

"Al-Tal had given Khashan that alias."

"It's not uncommon for aliases to be recycled," offered Morgan. "In some instances, a lot of time and money goes into building them. If a previous operative wasn't too high profile, an agency or a handler might decide to pass the alias on to another operative."

At that moment, Harvath knew exactly how he was going to take down Abdel Salam Najib.

He was going to make his handler give him up on a silver platter.

CHAPTER 50

Mark Sheppard had returned home with the makings of an absolute bombshell. Mac Mangan, the Charleston County SWAT team leader, had turned out to be a better resource than he ever could have imagined.

Though Mangan had asked that their discussion after the tape recorder was turned off be "off the record," Sheppard knew there would be no story without it. It had taken him a major chunk of the afternoon, but he had finally gotten the SWAT team leader to agree to be quoted as an anonymous source.

Something was very wrong about that shooting, and Mangan had no desire to increase his complicity in it any further than he already had. The fact that a reporter from the *Baltimore Sun* had come all the way down to Charleston to talk to him about it told him he needed to start making things right.

Sheppard listened as the SWAT team leader recounted the events surrounding the takedown. It had all supposedly been coordinated via the FBI in D.C. But no one from the FBI's Columbia, South Carolina, field office had been involved. The two agents who arrived to work with the SWAT team explained that the Columbia office was being purposely shut out. There was a concern that their fugitive had access to a person inside, and pending a full internal investigation, Charleston law enforcement was supposed to remain mum on the Bureau's involvement in this takedown.

Sheppard had asked Mangan to describe the two FBI agents who had magically shown up from out of town with information leading to the subject's location. They were the same men whom Tom Gosse had seen take the body from the ME's office in Baltimore and who had threatened Frank Aposhian. The SWAT leader had described them to a tee, right down to the names they were using—Stan Weston and Joe Maxwell.

The "agents" were very convincing. They were polite, professional, and had all the right credentials. What's more, they had come to apprehend a criminal who had threatened to kill a bunch of kids and whom the whole state was anxious to see brought to justice.

Mangan and his Charleston County SWAT team were called out, but were relegated to providing cover as Weston and Maxwell took the lead. The pair claimed they wanted to talk to the suspect in hopes of bringing him out alive. Shortly after they entered the house where he was holed up a brief, but fierce gun battle ensued.

Before the smoke had even cleared, Maxwell was at the door letting Mangan and his men know that the suspect had been killed and that they were going to need a meat wagon.

As the lead tactical officer on site, Mangan approached the house to survey the scene for his after-action report. Weston met him at the threshold and bodily blocked his entrance. The agent stated that he and his partner needed to collect evidence and that until they were done, the fewer people trampling the crime scene the better. Mangan didn't like it. These guys were being a little too overprotective, and he made his feelings known loudly enough that Maxwell came to the door and told Weston to let the SWAT leader inside.

The first thing he wanted to look at was the corpse. It was in a back bedroom, a machine pistol still clasped in his hand and a sawed-off shotgun lying on the floor next to him. As Mangan studied the body, something struck him as funny. In spite of all the bullet wounds the subject had suffered, he wasn't bleeding very much.

As Mangan bent for a closer look, Agent Weston swooped in and said he needed him to back up so he could get on with his job. Regardless of the voice in the back of his head telling him he had every right to examine the corpse, Mangan did as he was told.

Moments later, Agent Maxwell gently hooked him under the elbow and led him back toward the front of the house. As they walked, Maxwell explained that the FBI had decided to give the Charleston County

SWAT team credit for the takedown. This had been a local problem and the citizens of South Carolina would feel much better knowing their own people had put this animal out of commission.

Though it was going to make his guys look good, there was something about all of this that just didn't sit right with Mangan—especially the body. He'd been around enough stiffs in his time to know that the only kind that didn't spill blood when shot or stabbed was the kind that was already dead.

There was something else he didn't feel right about. Maxwell and Weston looked and acted like the real deal, but there was something off about them that Mangan just couldn't put his finger on.

Leaving the house, Mangan walked quickly back to the SWAT van and climbed inside. Grabbing one of the team's small, black surveillance cases, he had his men switch radio frequencies and instructed them to keep their eyes on the house. If either of the FBI agents appeared at a window or was preparing to exit via the front or back door, he wanted to know about it. With that, Mangan exited the truck.

Crouching low so he wouldn't be seen from inside, Mangan slipped around the side of the house, being careful to stay beneath the window line. When he arrived at the back bedroom where the body was, he unpacked a special fiberoptic stethoscope. He would have loved to have had a camera as well, but there was no way he could have drilled through the wall without being detected.

The fiberoptic stethoscope, or FOS for short, was

an exceptionally sensitive instrument that enabled tactical teams to listen through doors, windows, and even concrete walls. Mangan powered up the FOS, put on a pair of headphones, and began listening to what was going on inside.

Considering that Maxwell and Weston had shot up a dead body, Mangan wasn't surprised that they were busily planting evidence. What did surprise him was why they were doing it *and* on whose orders.

Once the SWAT team leader had finished recounting his tale, Sheppard understood why he had chosen to keep his mouth shut and go along with the charade. Now the ball was in Sheppard's court, and he needed to plan his next move very carefully. He was about to accuse the president of the United States of several extremely serious crimes all tied together by a disgustingly elaborate cover-up.

CHAPTER 51

AMMAN, JORDAN

The two men sat inside the blue BMW 7 series on a quiet side street near the center of town. Most of the shops were closed for the afternoon prayer. "After this we're even," said the man in the driver's seat as he retrieved a small duffel bag from the backseat and handed it to his passenger.

Harvath unzipped the bag and looked inside. Everything was there. "As soon as I am safely out of your country," he replied with a smile, *"then"* we'll be even."

Omar Faris, a high-ranking officer of Jordan's General Intelligence Department, or GID for short, nodded his heavy, round head. The six-foot-two Jordanian was used to making deals. In the world in which he operated, deals were de rigueur—especially when it came to keeping the swelling tide of Islamic radicalism in check.

What's more, he had always liked Scot Harvath, even with his unorthodox tactical decisions. No matter how he carried out his operations, Harvath was a man of his word and could be trusted.

The two had been paired together in Harvath's early days with the Apex Project. A cell of Jordanians had killed two American diplomats and was plotting to overthrow King Abdullah II. Though officially the GID had no idea that Harvath was operating inside their country, Faris had served as his partner and a direct conduit to the king.

Abdullah had asked only one thing of Harvath— that he do his utmost to bring the cell members in alive. It was an incredibly complicated and dangerous assignment. It would have been much easier to kill the terrorists and be done with the entire operation. Nevertheless, at great risk to himself, Harvath honored the king's request.

In doing so, Harvath not only earned the sovereign's respect but also earned a couple of points with

Faris, who was promoted as a result of the mission's success.

"Of course if your presence here becomes known, His Majesty will disavow any knowledge of you or your operation. If the Syrians, or anyone else for that matter, discovered that we were allowing you to stalk an operative of theirs who was in our country undergoing cancer treatment, it would be devastating for Jordan's image—not to mention the diplomatic fallout," said the GID officer.

"Don't bullshit me, Omar," replied Harvath. "You know as well as I do that Al-Tal's a threat to you too. A lot of the weapons he's been helping the Syrians unload are going to groups like Al Qaeda who could very well use them here."

"We are aware of that, but it doesn't change the fact that our image is of paramount importance to us. Our credibility with our neighbors and allies would be significantly eroded if our involvement in your operation became known."

"What involvement?" asked Harvath as he zipped up the duffel.

Faris smiled, removed a manila envelope from beneath his seat, and handed it to his friend. "Per your request, we have compiled a complete dossier."

Harvath wasn't surprised at how much was in there. The GID was usually very thorough. "Surveillance logs, photos, layout of the building—this is a pretty impressive dossier for less than twenty-four-hour notice."

"Al-Tal has been on our radar screen for some

time. When it was discovered he had entered the country under an assumed identity to begin his treatment, we began around-the-clock surveillance."

"Any listening or video devices in the apartment?" asked Harvath.

"Of course," replied Faris. "We were very concerned about the weapons sales. Any information we could have collected would have proven quite helpful."

"But?"

"But the man has proven quite cautious. He speaks often on the telephone, but none of what we have picked up is of any direct use. We suspect someone else is running the operation for him while he seeks his medical treatment."

"You said he doesn't have much longer."

"This is what his physicians have said. Weeks. A month tops."

"And his family?" asked Harvath.

"It's all in the dossier."

"I don't want any record of me being in that apartment. I want all of your listening and video devices removed."

"I'm afraid we can't do that," said Faris.

"Why not?"

"When he first arrived, he and his family traveled to the hospital on an almost daily basis. Now he is resigned to his bed at home full-time. There is always someone with him. It would be impossible for any of my people to get in there and remove those devices."

"Then I'll remove them for you," stated Harvath.

"I'll need a detailed schematic of where they've all been placed."

Faris reached into his breast pocket. "I thought you might ask for that."

"What about the surveillance teams?" asked Harvath as he slid the piece of paper into the dossier.

"They'll be pulled off as soon as you enter the building."

"Then it looks like we're all done here."

Faris handed Harvath the keys for the nondescript, gray Mitsubishi Lancer he'd organized and then shook his hand. "Be careful, Scot. Al-Tal may be dying, but it's when an animal is sick and cornered that it is the most dangerous."

Harvath climbed out of the car, and as he prepared to close the door, said, "Tell your men to get ready to drop their surveillance."

Faris was slightly taken aback. "Don't you want to study the dossier first?"

"I've seen all I need to see. The sooner I get in there and get control of Al-Tal, the sooner I can bait the hook and start chumming the waters for Najib."

Faris watched as Harvath unlocked the Lancer, threw the bag in, and pulled away from the curb. Though he knew Harvath was a professional, he didn't like what the American was headed into.

CHAPTER 52

When Al-Tal's wife and twenty-year-old son returned from the mosque, Harvath was waiting for them. Wearing a thin, black ski mask, he slipped out of the stairwell into the dimly lit corridor and placed his silenced, .45 caliber Taurus 24/7 OSS pistol against the back of the son's head.

When the mother opened her mouth to cry out, Harvath grabbed her by the throat. "If you make any sound," he told her in Arabic, "I will kill you both."

With the mother and son Flexicuffed and pieces of duct tape across their mouths, he relieved them of their house keys and let himself into the apartment. Before entering the building, Harvath had gone through the dossier, committing pertinent facts about Al-Tal's residence and its occupants to memory.

He'd read enough about Al-Tal's bodyguard to know that he was extremely dangerous. A former interrogator for the Syrian Secret Police, the man had routinely brutalized subjects by submitting them to horrific beatings and making them watch as he raped and sodomized their wives and children.

When Harvath crept into the apartment, he found the hulking bodyguard wearing a leather shoulder holster over a sweat-stained T-shirt. He was focused on a pan of greasy lamb's meat he was heating over the stove in the kitchen. He looked up just as Harvath's pistol spat two rounds into his forehead.

The hot pan clattered to the floor and Harvath made it into a short hallway just as Al-Tal's nurse appeared. Undoubtedly, Al-Tal had chosen him because of his size. If push came to shove, the cagey intelligence operative had probably figured he could use the nurse as extra muscle.

Harvath struck him full in the face with the butt of his weapon, and the man folded like a cheap wallet.

Stepping over the nurse, Harvath swung into the rear bedroom. He found Al-Tal propped up in bed and affixed to an IV with a PCA, or patient-controlled anesthesia. It allowed him to regulate the flow of morphine for his cancer pain via a small device in his clawlike hand.

"Who are you?" the man demanded in Arabic as Harvath entered the room.

Before Harvath could answer, he noticed the gray-haired man's right hand slip beneath his blanket. Harvath put three rounds into the bed, and Al-Tal immediately drew back his hand.

Harvath walked over to the bed and pulled back the blankets. He found both a pistol and a modified AK-47.

"Who are you?" Al-Tal spat again as Harvath removed the weapons. His eyes were narrow and dark, his voice arrogant.

"You'll discover who I am soon enough," said Harvath, knowing the man spoke flawless English.

Binding his hands and feet to the bed, Harvath gagged him and left the room.

CHAPTER 53

Harvath secured the nurse, fetched his bag from the stairwell, and then brought Al-Tal's wife and son inside. After he was certain they had gotten a good look at the bodyguard and knew that Harvath meant business, he dragged the corpse into the bathroom. Removing the plastic shower curtain and liner, he wrapped the body, sealed it with duct tape, and dumped it into the tub.

Using Omar's schematic, he tore out all of the video and listening devices. Though he believed the GID operative had been straight with him, he decided to leave the ski mask on. Now he had to deal with the rest of the mess he had made.

Harvath hated taking hostages. Not only were they a liability, they were a downright pain in the ass. They needed to be fed, given bathroom breaks, and kept from escaping. On such short notice, though, and considering the time constraints and the fact that Al-Tal was at the stage where he never left his apartment, it was the best that Harvath could do.

Cutting Al-Tal free of his restraints, Harvath pulled the IV out of his arm and dragged him into the bathroom so he could see what had become of his bodyguard. Once he'd gotten a good look, Harvath dragged him into the dining room where his nurse and family were being kept.

Harvath jerked a chair from the table and shoved

Al-Tal down into it. After he had Flexicuffed the Syrian to it as tightly as he could, he removed the man's
gag.

"You will die. I promise you," sputtered Al-Tal.

"An interesting threat," replied Harvath as he
removed another chair and sat down, their faces nose
to nose, "especially since you already placed a
$150,000 price on my head."

"It's you. The one who killed Asef."

"Don't you mean Suleiman?" asked Harvath.
"That was the name you had given him, wasn't it?
Abdel Rafiq Suleiman?"

Al-Tal didn't answer.

It made no difference to Harvath. He could read
everything he needed to in the man's face. Al-Tal was
furious and terrified all at the same time.

"I know a lot more about you than you think,
Tammam."

"What do you want?" demanded the Syrian spy-
master.

"I want information."

Al-Tal laughed derisively. "I will never give you
anything."

Harvath hated everything about him. It wasn't
often that he took pleasure in killing, but this would
be different. "I'm going to give you one chance.
Where is Abdel Salam Najib?"

Al-Tal stopped laughing.

Harvath looked at him. "If you prefer, we can call
him Suleiman. After all, you gave him that alias after
Khashan died."

"You mean after *you* killed him."

"Neither of us has much time, Tammam. Let's not bicker over semantics."

"Let my family go and I'll tell you anything you want to know."

Now it was Harvath who laughed.

"At least let the nurse go. He has nothing to do with this."

Harvath wasn't going to do anything for this monster. "Where is Najib?" he repeated.

When Al-Tal refused to answer, Harvath leaped up and grabbed Al-Tal's wife. He didn't like doing it, but she knew well enough who her husband was, and this had to be done.

Harvath dragged her within two feet of Al-Tal, keeping his eyes locked with the man's own the entire time.

"What are you going to do to her?"

"It's up to you," replied Harvath as he removed the pistol from beneath his jacket and used it to comb the woman's hair over her left ear.

"In our line of work, we don't target each other's families," snapped Al-Tal. "You know that."

"The old intelligence agent's credo. How amusing, especially considering what you have done to my family."

"What are you talking about?"

"My mother, my girlfriend—don't act like you don't know."

"Your *mother?*" said Al-Tal. "How could I have done anything to your mother? I don't even know who you are. You say you are the man who killed Asef, but I don't even know your name."

Harvath didn't believe him. The man was lying. "This is your last chance."

"Or else what? You will shoot my wife?"

"You saw what I did to your bodyguard."

"Yes, but it is something entirely different to shoot a man's wife, a mother."

The Syrian was right. Harvath had absolutely no intention of shooting her. But he was willing to torture the hell out of her to save his own family and loved ones from going through any more pain.

Harvath slowly holstered his weapon. He watched a smile creep across Al-Tal's sharp face. The man's overconfidence was sickening. He thought he had Harvath all figured out. He was about to learn how wrong he was.

"Some things are worse than being killed," said Harvath as he removed a small can of Guardian Protective Devices OC from his jacket pocket. Attached to the nozzle was a long, clear plastic tube.

Grabbing a tight handful of Al-Tal's wife's hair, Harvath immobilized her head and shoved the tube into her ear. "Have you ever been exposed to pepper spray, Tammam?" he asked as the woman screamed from behind the duct tape across her mouth.

"Leave her alone," demanded Al-Tal.

Harvath ignored him. "The way it burns in your eyes, your nose, your throat?"

"I said leave her alone!"

"Going in through the ear canal is another experience altogether. When I depress this button, a fine, aerosolized mist will rush through this tube and it will feel to your wife as if someone has coated the entire inside of her skull with flaming gasoline."

"You are obscene!"

"I'm nothing compared to you. And the fear you feel flowing through your body right now is nothing compared to the guilt you will feel from what else I have in store for your family."

When Al-Tal didn't respond, Harvath pulled his wife's chair right alongside his and said, "Take a good look at her face. What's going to happen now is because of you."

The woman's eyes were wide with fear, as were those of Al-Tal's son and the male nurse.

Wrenching the man's hand open, Harvath forced all his fingers closed around the can of OC. Lifting Al-Tal's index finger, he slid it onto the release switch.

Al-Tal's wife had never stopped screaming and now she screamed with even more force. Her body writhed against its restraints and she violently threw her head from side to side trying to dislodge the tube that had been shoved into her ear canal.

"Yes!" shouted Al-Tal, unable to bear his wife's being tortured any further. "I will tell you how to contact Najib, you bastard. Just leave my family alone."

CHAPTER 54

Tell him the imam is not well. He must come quickly so that they may read from the Koran one last time together."

When Tammam Al-Tal's wife finished delivering the carefully scripted message, Harvath pulled the phone away from her ear and hung up. Now, all they had to do was wait.

Fifteen minutes later, the phone rang. Mrs. Al-Tal didn't need to be reminded about what would happen if she didn't do and say everything exactly as they had rehearsed.

Harvath lifted the phone back up to her ear and leaned in to listen.

Abdel Salam Najib had a deep, penetrating voice. He spoke in quick, authoritative clips and was every bit as arrogant as his mentor. "Why did the imam not call himself?"

"He is too weak," Al-Tal's wife responded in Arabic. Her words were thick with panic and fear.

"He is dying, then."

"Yes," she replied.

"How much longer does he have?" asked the man.

"We have been told he will probably not live through the night."

"You are still at the apartment?"

"Yes. The doctors wanted to move him to the hospital, but Tammam refused."

Najib scolded her. "You should know better than to use his name over the phone."

Harvath tensed. Was she trying to tip Najib or was it an honest mistake? Harvath had no way of knowing. Pulling a tactical MOD fighting knife from his pocket, he opened the blade and pressed it against the woman's throat. Harvath agreed with Najib. She should know better, much better.

Al-Tal's wife choked back a terrified sob. "He wishes to be taken back to Syria, but the doctors have told us the journey would only hasten his passing."

"The doctors are right," said the operative. "The imam should not be moved. Who is in the house with you?"

The woman spoke slowly, careful not to phrase the information in any way that might get her into trouble. "Our son is here, of course, as is the imam's nurse. There is also another friend who came with us from home and attends to the imam's safety and comfort."

Najib knew both the bodyguard and the son. They could be trusted. The nurse, though, he didn't know. "Have you learned how to administer your husband's medications?"

The question took her by surprise. "His *medications?*"

"Yes. His morphine."

She had no idea how to answer. It wasn't a question she had been expecting. She looked to Harvath, who firmly shook his head *no.*

"I don't know anything about that," she answered.

"Well, you must learn," replied Najib. "There will not be much to do, not if the imam is actively dying. Command the nurse to teach you what to do and then let him go. The imam and I have important things to discuss before he leaves to see the Prophet, may peace be upon Him. I do not want the nurse in the apartment when we speak."

Harvath nodded and Mrs. Al-Tal's voice cracked, "It will be done."

Najib was silent for several moments. Harvath began to worry that he might suspect something. He'd come too far to lose him. *What the hell was he waiting for?*

Finally, Najib said, "I will be there by the evening prayer service. Is there anything special the imam would like me to bring to him?"

Unsure of how to respond, the woman looked at Harvath, who shook his head. "Nothing," she answered. "Just come quickly."

"Tell the imam that he must wait for me."

"I will," responded the woman, the tears welling up in her eyes.

The conversation over, Harvath took the phone and replaced it in its cradle. Najib had taken the bait and the hook was set. All that was left to do was to reel him in. But Harvath knew all too well that you never celebrated until the fish was actually in the boat.

CHAPTER 55

Harvath offered each of his captives a bathroom break, but only the male nurse had the guts to take him up on it. He relieved himself right next to the tub with its plastic-wrapped occupant.

Having the nurse ambulatory made it a lot easier to move him to the spare bedroom. Harvath then brought in Al-Tal's wife and son, and once they were all secure, made his way back out to the dining room.

Al-Tal was sweating, his gray-and-blue-striped pajamas clinging to his wet body. He needed his morphine.

Harvath released Al-Tal from his chair and, with one arm slung around the man's waist, helped him back to the bedroom. After doing a thorough search of the pillows and bedclothes, Harvath helped the man up and eased him beneath his blankets. Al-Tal was so frail it was like handling a doll made from papier-mâché.

Once he was in bed, Harvath reinserted Al-Tal's IV and placed a fresh piece of tape over the needle on the back of his left hand. Like Pavlov's dog, the Syrian's dry mouth began to water with anticipation of the warm wave about to rush through his beleaguered body.

Harvath laid the PCA trigger on the bed, but just out of Al-Tal's reach. When the man bent forward to pick it up, Harvath pushed him back. "Not so fast. I still have a few more questions for you."

Al-Tal was angry. "I did everything you asked."

"And now you're going to do more."

"Is it not enough that I have turned on one of my own agents? A man who trusts me implicitly?"

Harvath ignored him. "Who arranged for Najib's release from Guantanamo?"

"I don't know."

"How about I get your son and bring him in here? How about I go to work on him? Would you like that?" asked Harvath as he removed his knife from his pocket and flicked it open. "I'll start by peeling back the skin from the fingertips of his left hand. I'll keep going until I am at the wrist and the hand has been completely degloved. Just when he starts to become numb to the pain, I'll prepare a bowl full of juice from the lemons in your kitchen and soak his hand in it. It'll be a pain like no other he's experienced in his life."

Al-Tal's eyes closed. "I will answer your questions."

Harvath repeated his inquiry. "Who arranged Najib's release?"

"I told you, I don't know."

"I'll make sure to let your son know how cooperative you've been before I start in on him," replied Harvath as he stood up.

"I'm telling the truth," sputtered Al-Tal. "I don't know exactly who it is."

"But you do know something."

The Syrian nodded and then let his eyes wander to the morphine pump.

"No dice," said Harvath, comprehending the unspoken request. "You tell me what I want to know and then you get your morphine."

Al-Tal's shoulders sagged as he expelled a *woosh* of air and settled into the pillows that were propping him up. "I was contacted with an offer."

"What kind of offer?"

"For the right price, this person claimed he could get Najib released from American custody."

"And you believed him?"

"Of course not, not at first. Our government had already lobbied for Najib's release. We claimed that they had captured an innocent man, a man whose family desperately needed him back home."

"But the U.S. didn't buy that, did they?" asked Harvath.

"No, they didn't. So we tried another approach. We admitted that Najib was a very dangerous criminal who was wanted for a string of grave offenses in Syria. We promised to put him on trial and to even allow the United States to monitor the proceedings, but they still wouldn't agree."

"And along comes this mystery person who claims he can get Najib out if the price is right."

"More or less."

"So what was the price?" asked Harvath.

"I had to agree to nullify the bounty I had placed on *you*."

Harvath was dumbfounded. "What are you talking about?"

"We struck a bargain," replied Al-Tal. "I canceled the contract and Najib was released from American custody."

Harvath was beginning to believe that the man

was playing him. "How is that possible if you didn't even know who I was?"

"I still don't know who you are," responded Al-Tal as he drew a circle around his face—an allusion to Harvath's ski mask. "Normally, hostage-takers only keep their identities hidden because they know at some point they will release their hostages. Is that why you haven't shown us your face?"

"I've kept my word and will continue to do so. The outcome of this situation is completely in your hands. If you cooperate with me, I'll let your wife and your son go."

"What about my nurse?"

"Him too."

"And me?" asked Al-Tal as if he already knew the answer.

"That, I am going to leave up to Najib," said Harvath.

CHAPTER 56

THE WHITE HOUSE

President Rutledge was angry. "I don't want any more excuses, Jim," he said to his director of Central Intelligence as he balanced the phone on his shoulder and bent over to tie his running shoes. "You should have had this guy by now. If you can't start showing me results, I'll replace you with somebody who can."

"I understand sir," replied James Vaile. He deserved the admonishment. The team he had fielded to apprehend the terrorist stalking Scot Harvath was more than qualified to do the job. The problem was that the hunted was outsmarting his hunters at every turn. The only evidence he left behind was what he wanted his pursuers to find. While Vaile had no intention of admitting defeat, certainly not while American lives were at stake, everyone—including the president—knew that they were chasing a formidable quarry.

"Now what about the alert?" demanded Rutledge as his mind turned to the people behind the killer and the threats they had made against America.

"I don't think it's necessary," replied the DCI, "not yet."

"Explain."

"Even if the terrorists can ID Harvath from the closed-circuit footage from the airport in Mexico, we still have complete deniability. He's gone off the reservation and we're doing everything we can to apprehend him. And at the end of the day, *they're* the ones who provoked him."

"And *we're* the ones who couldn't control him," stated the president. "Frankly, I'm having trouble seeing any downside here. We quietly send the alert out to state and local law enforcement agencies and ask them to keep their eyes open. We don't have to say we have specific intelligence of an imminent terrorist action, because we don't. We won't raise the national threat level. We'll just leave it at that."

The DCI was silent as he composed his response.

"With that many cops and state troopers on the lookout, we might get lucky and thwart any potential attack," added Rutledge.

"We might," said Vaile, conceding the point. "We might also get a lot of questions, and I guarantee you someone is going to connect it to what happened in Charleston."

"You don't know that for sure."

"Mr. President, cops talk to each other, and they're very good at connecting dots. Lots of them are going to draw the same conclusion. And the press is going to pick up the thread eventually too. Once word starts circulating about this alert, we won't be able to put the genie back in the bottle."

"So your plan is to do nothing?"

"Absolutely, if for no other reason than if the terrorists get wind of the alert, they could take it as an admission of guilt on our part. If they saw us girding for the exact type of attack that they had threatened, they'd know we were behind Palmera's death."

That was an angle Rutledge hadn't considered. "But what if they do attack and we did nothing to prevent it? Could you live with the consequences—especially in this case? I know I couldn't."

"I probably couldn't either," replied the DCI. "But, we're not at that point yet. This is about one man out of five. A man who, I might add, had a lot of enemies and who probably would have died a violent death sooner rather than later."

Vaile's reasoning made sense. Though the president's gut was telling him not to go along with the DCI's plan, he decided to trust his intellect. "What about Harvath, though? He's the wild card in this that could push everything into all-out chaos."

"That's where we have some good news," Vaile assured the president. "We've already got a line on him. If he doesn't turn himself in by your deadline, we'll have him in custody soon after."

"Good," said Rutledge as he prepared to leave for his run. "I just hope we get him before he puts the nation any further at risk."

CHAPTER 57

AMMAN, JORDAN

Harvath had spent the next hour and a half interrogating Tammam Al-Tal, allowing only an occasional small dose of morphine to be pumped into the man's cancer-ridden body.

As good as Harvath was, Al-Tal was a tough read. Undoubtedly, the man had a lot of experience in interrogation, as well as counterinterrogation, and that made Harvath question everything he was able to extract from him.

Harvath kept the questions coming—doubling and tripling back to try to snag the man in a lie, but it never happened. Al-Tal appeared to be telling the truth. He had no idea who had targeted Tracy or Scot's mother or the ski team.

Harvath was preparing to go at Al-Tal again when, his body wracked with fatigue and the mind-numbing pain that even morphine couldn't assuage, the man drifted off into unconsciousness.

Al-Tal was beyond the point of any usefulness.

It was now time to focus on Najib.

The distance from Damascus to Amman as the crow flies was about 110 miles. With only light traffic and a speedy entrance at the border crossing from Syria into Jordan, Harvath had at least another hour before Najib showed up at the apartment. It would be more than enough time for him to get ready.

Harvath used Al-Tal's wife to answer the intercom downstairs, and when Abdel Salam Najib entered the apartment, he was greeted by the butt of Harvath's Taurus 24/7 OSS pistol as it slammed into the bridge of his nose.

The man was taken completely by surprise. There was a spray of blood as he collapsed to his knees. Harvath drew the pistol back and swung again hard. It connected with a sickening crack alongside Najib's jaw. His head snapped back and he fell the rest of the way to the floor unconscious.

Harvath relieved the operative of all his weapons,

which included a 9mm Beretta pistol, a stiletto knife, and a razor in his left shoe.

He stripped him all the way down to his shorts and duct-taped him to one of the dining-room chairs. He wasn't going to repeat any of the mistakes he had made with Palmera.

After spending several moments peering through the curtains to make sure there was no one outside waiting for Najib, Harvath headed into the kitchen where he located a bucket and filled it with cold water.

Back in the dining room, he hit Najib in the face with the water full force. The man came to almost instantly.

He began coughing as his head instinctively swung from side to side to get away from the water. When his eyes popped open, it took his brain a moment to process everything that had happened, but he soon put it together.

Working his jaw back and forth to see if it was broken, Najib looked up at the masked man standing in front of him and spat a gob of blood at his feet.

Harvath smiled. Spitting to Middle Easterners was like giving someone the finger in the West. It was a macho show of bravado meant to exhibit a person's fearlessness.

Harvath didn't move a muscle. He stood there like a statue as Najib's eyes scanned the room. Harvath counted silently to himself, *one one-thousand, two one-thousand* . . . and then Najib saw it.

The body of Tammam's bodyguard lay on top of the dining-room table—just to Najib's right. It had been laid out as if part of some horrific banquet. Horrible things had been done to it. Skin had been flayed off the arms and legs, the chest cavity was wide open and gaping, black holes were the only remnants of where vital human organs used to be.

Najib was a hard man, but he was clearly shaken by what he saw.

"Let's talk about your release from Guantanamo," said Harvath, breaking the silence.

Najib spat at him again and cursed him in Arabic, *"Khara beek!"*

Al-Tal had told Harvath that Najib was one of the best operatives he had ever had, better even than Asef Khashan. He promised that Harvath would have a very hard time breaking him. As far as Al-Tal knew, the man wasn't afraid of anything or anyone. He had been sent into Iraq to assist in coordinating the insurgency. His reputation was known far and wide. Those who resisted his commands or, worse yet, failed him in their assignments, were dealt unspeakable punishments that Najib carried out personally.

He was one of the most feared men in Iraq. His skill on the battlefield was rivaled only by his skill in a torture chamber. It was said that the use of short knives, purposely dulled, for videotaped beheadings of Westerners was his idea. To him, the scimitar was too efficient a tool. Victims needed to be shown being slaughtered like animals. One or two whacks with a long sword weren't enough. They needed to suffer righteous agony at the hands of the brave warriors of the Prophet, and Najib was a master of agony.

Harvath knew his type all too well. The only way to get a psychological advantage over him was to shock him so hard that he was thrown completely off balance. The body on the table was a good start, but Harvath knew it wouldn't be enough.

Still, he asked his question again, and this time more specifically in Arabic. "The night you were freed from Guantanamo you boarded an airplane. Tell me about it."

"Fuck you," Najib replied in English. "I will tell you nothing." His voice was even more unsettling in person.

The man was well over six feet tall and twice as wide as Harvath. His arms were enormous and he looked like one of those people who was naturally muscular and didn't need to work out in a gym. He had dark hair, dark eyes, and a thin scar running beneath his chin from one ear to another, which Harvath figured he didn't get from tying his neckties too tight.

All and all, Najib was a very nasty character and Harvath was glad to have gotten the jump on him. No matter how good a fighter you were, this was not somebody you would ever want to meet on an equal footing.

Harvath stepped to the table and withdrew a cordless drill from his duffel bag. He fitted it with a thick, Carbide-tipped masonry bit and gave the drill's trigger a squeeze to make sure the bit rotated properly.

Next, Harvath took a gauze pad he had found in the nurse's supply and coated it with Betadine antiseptic solution. Knowing that having an area prepped for injection was often more frightening to most people than the actual injection, Harvath bent and took his time in cleaning Najib's right kneecap.

Harvath didn't need to take the man's pulse to know that his heart was racing. He had only to look at his throbbing carotid artery and the sweat forming on his forehead and upper lip to see that he was scared shitless.

But being scared didn't mean he was going to cooperate. Harvath decided to give him one last chance. "Tell me about the plane. Who was on it with you?"

Najib focused his eyes on an object across the room and began reciting verses from the Koran. Harvath had his answer.

He shoved a gag in the man's mouth to prevent his screams from being heard outside the apartment and then snugged his chair sideways up against the wall and pinned him there to keep him from flipping over once the pain began.

Harvath wrapped his arm around the inside of Najib's thigh, placed the masonry bit at the side of his kneecap and squeezed the drill's trigger.

The operative's entire body went stiff. Tears welled in his eyes and as the fluted bit tore into his flesh he began to scream from behind his gag.

He writhed against his restraints, but the duct tape and Harvath's weight pinning him to the wall allowed him little room to move, much less escape from the incredible pain he was experiencing.

Harvath continued, slowly. When he hit bone, the drill bit created a sickening cloud of smoke, which poured forth from the bloody entrance wound. Najib's body shuddered, every fiber in his being straining to escape the madman whose drill bit was laying waste to his knee.

Suddenly, there was a *pop* as Najib's kneecap exploded in a mass of shattered bone and the man finally passed out from the pain.

CHAPTER 58

Harvath opened an ammonia inhalant and waved the pad beneath the man's nose. In a matter of seconds, Najib was coughing and rearing his head.

Harvath held up a syringe and tried to get the operative to focus on it. "This is morphine," he said. "All you have to do is talk to me and you can have all you want."

His head spinning, Najib looked down and saw his knee swollen to twice its normal size. Averting his eyes, he then saw that his other knee had recently been swabbed with Betadine. It was too much. His head began to wobble as he once again started to pass out.

"Stay with me," ordered Harvath as he grabbed

Najib's face and forced another ammonia inhalant pad
under his nose.

The man's head reared backward once more and
he shook it back and forth to escape the fumes irritat-
ing the membranes of his nose and lungs.

Harvath knew that the fumes also triggered a
reflex, causing the muscles that control breathing to
work faster, and he waited a moment for the operative
to catch his breath.

Holding up the syringe again he said, "It's up to
you."

With pain etched across his battered, furious face,
Najib slowly nodded *yes*.

Harvath inserted the needle into the man's thigh.
He depressed the plunger, but stopped before all the
drug had been injected. "When you tell me everything I want to know, I'll give you the rest."

He reached for the gag and added, "If you stall me
or try to call out, I will go to work on your other
knee. Then I will do your elbows and then I will move
on to the individual vertebrae in your back and your
neck. Are we clear?"

Najib nodded and Harvath removed the gag.

He fully expected some sort of tough guy pro-
nouncement—a promise to hunt him and everyone he
cared about to the ends of the earth or some such
thing, but instead Najib surprised him. He stammered
a question, "Is Al-Tal still alive?"

The question was all too human and Harvath
didn't like it, not one single bit. It made things difficult. It made them complicated.

It was much easier when scum like Najib spewed their hatred about America and asserted their unequivocal belief that it was only a matter of time before they would be victorious and all the nonbelievers would see Muslims tap dancing atop the White House.

Though it helped to dehumanize the enemy, Harvath could still do what he had come here to do. All he needed to do was think about the atrocities Najib had orchestrated in Iraq against American soldiers and Marines to know that there was nothing human about this animal.

And the thought that he might never be able to hold Tracy again and feel her hold him back steeled his heart and filled his soul with rage.

"Al-Tal's fate is up to you."

"So he's alive?" demanded Najib. "Prove it. I want to see him."

"That's not part of our deal."

"You show me Al-Tal or I will tell you nothing."

So much for our deal, thought Harvath as he left the dining room and walked into the kitchen. He came back a moment later with the bowl filled with lemons, removed his knife from his pocket and sliced one in half.

He walked over to Najib, held the lemon above the entry wound in his knee and squeezed. As the citric acid seared his torn flesh, a howl built up in Najib's throat. Harvath covered the operative's mouth with the gag just in time.

Once the pain had somewhat receded and the

man had settled back down, Harvath removed his gag and said, "I will not warn you again. Now, tell me about the plane."

Najib didn't look as if he had any intention of complying, but when Harvath picked the drill back up, placed it against his left knee, and squeezed the trigger, the man started to talk. "It was a commercial airliner. A 737."

"Who was on it?" asked Harvath, releasing the trigger.

"Two pilots and a medical crew dressed like flight attendants."

"Had you ever seen any of them before?"

Najib shook his head *no.* "Never."

"What language did they speak?"

"English mostly."

"Mostly?" asked Harvath.

"And some Arabic."

"What was the medical crew for?"

"We were told that our blood had been polluted. Some sort of radioactive material had been introduced into our systems so the United States could track us. Once the planes reached a certain altitude, we received transfusions."

"Who told you your blood had been tainted?" asked Harvath, his rock-steady hand holding the drill in place.

"The medical personnel."

"And how did they know?"

"I have no idea," replied Najib. "They were getting us out. That's all I cared about."

"And you just went along with it? What if it was a trick?"

"We thought of that. They had two devices that looked like radiation detectors. When they passed them over our bodies, the devices registered the presence of radiation. When passed over the bodies of the crew, there was no indication. We all had been feeling nauseated for a day or two leading up to leaving Guantanamo. We thought it was food poisoning, but the medical crew said it was a side effect of the radiation that had been introduced into our bodies."

Harvath watched for any cues that Najib was lying to him, but he didn't see any. "Who arranged for your release?"

"Al-Tal."

"Someone came to Al-Tal," clarified Harvath, "and offered to help arrange your release. Who was that person?"

"I never knew. Neither did Al-Tal."

"Why would someone have wanted to help get you released?"

"I don't know."

"Who was powerful enough to do that for you?" demanded Harvath.

"I don't know," replied Najib.

"Of all the prisoners at Guantanamo, why did this magical benefactor choose you?"

Najib felt the drill bit pushing against his kneecap. He watched as the tip broke the skin. "I swear I don't know," he screamed. "I don't know. I don't know!"

Harvath pulled the drill bit back. "The other men

who were released with you that night, tell me about them. Had you ever seen them before?"

"No," answered Najib. "I had been kept in isolation. When I was allowed to exercise, it was in an enclosed area. I never saw any of the other prisoners."

"I know about your time in Iraq," replied Harvath, tempted to shove the drill bit through the man's throat to avenge every U.S. serviceperson he'd been responsible for killing. "Were these men affiliated with people you knew in Iraq?"

"We were all concerned that the plane might be bugged, so we did not speak of associates or what we had done prior to being imprisoned at Guantanamo."

"What did you talk about, then?"

"Besides our hatred of America?"

Once again, Harvath was tempted to ram the drill bit through the man's throat, but he kept his rage under control. "Don't push me."

Najib glowered at Harvath. Finally he said, "We talked about home."

"Home?"

"Home. Where we lived. Syria, Morocco, Australia, Mexico, France."

"Wait a second," interrupted Harvath. "Syria, Morocco, Australia, Mexico, and *France?"*

Najib nodded.

Harvath couldn't believe it. "I thought there were only four of you on that flight out of Guantanamo that night. Are you telling me there was a fifth prisoner released with you?"

Once more, Najib slowly nodded.

CHAPTER 59

There was a storm of emotion raging inside Harvath. Instead of being able to climb out of the blackness of the mystery he'd been dumped in, he found the hole getting deeper.

There weren't four men released from Guantanamo that night, there were five. Could the Troll have not known about the fifth prisoner? Harvath doubted it. The Troll was like no one he'd ever seen when it came to getting his hands on the most sensitive of intelligence. No, Harvath was certain he knew all about the fifth passenger that night.

Harvath wrung as much information about the flight as he could from Najib and then proceeded to the close of his plan.

He dragged Najib into the spare bedroom and showed him Al-Tal's nurse, wife, and son bound, but still very much alive. He then dragged him to Al-Tal's bedroom, where he pulled back the blankets and showed that the man hadn't been harmed and was sleeping peacefully.

"I have one more question for you," said Harvath.

Najib looked at him. "What is it?"

"The bombing of the Marine compound in Beirut in 1983. Asef Khashan was one of Al-Tal's operatives. We know Khashan was involved in planning and helping to carry out the bombing."

"That was a long time ago," said Najib, his suspicion that the man in the mask holding him captive was an American agent now confirmed.

Harvath ignored the remark. "Did Al-Tal have direct knowledge in advance of the attack? Did he help Khashan plan and carry it out?"

Najib had no desire to help the hangman fit his noose around his mentor's neck. After more than twenty years of trying to identify those involved, the Americans still had no evidence on Al-Tal. If they had, he would have been taken out just like Asef.

"I want an answer," stated Harvath, sick of the sight of this monster who had butchered so many American troops.

"No," said Najib. "Asef had been free to plan and coordinate Hezbollah actions in Lebanon as he saw fit."

Then Harvath saw it—the tell, a small cue that indicated Najib wasn't telling the truth. "I'm going to ask you one more time," he said. "Think very carefully before you answer. Did Al-Tal know of, or was he involved with the 1983 attack on the Marine compound in Beirut?"

Najib paused for several moments, and then smiled. He knew the American knew he was lying and he knew that he was going to die. "No," he stated, "Tammam Al-Tal was not involved and he had no advance knowledge whatsoever of the glorious attack upon your two hundred twenty precious Marines."

There it was again—the tell. There was no question in Harvath's mind. Najib was definitely lying.

Harvath drew his silenced Taurus pistol and shot

him point-blank in the forehead. "You forgot the eighteen Navy personnel and three Army soldiers who were also killed there that day, asshole."

He then turned the pistol on Al-Tal and shot him once in the head and four times in the chest. It was overkill, but it felt good.

Repacking his duffel, Harvath took the stairs down to the lobby, removed his mask, and left the building.

CHAPTER 60

McLean, Virginia

Though Secret Service agents were supposed to eschew predictability and routine, in their off-time Kate Palmer and Carolyn Leonard were dedicated creatures of habit.

As residents of the same northern Virginia neighborhood and two of the few women on President Jack Rutledge's protective detail, Kate and Carolyn had become good friends early on. While Carolyn was technically Kate's boss, their professional roles made no difference when they were away from work.

Unless the president was traveling, Saturday was a day off for them. Carolyn's children visited their grandmother every Saturday, so the women always had the day to themselves to do whatever they wanted.

Their Saturdays started with a group cycle class at Regency Sport & Health Club on Old Meadow Road, and then they did an hour in the club's strength-training center. By then they were spent. After a lengthy steam followed by a quick shower, the friends were ready for their next favorite Saturday activity, shopping.

In a career world that demanded they compete at the same physical level and be judged by the same performance standards as men, Kate and Carolyn enjoyed their weekend opportunities to reaffirm their femininity. Shopping might have been viewed as a stereotypical female pursuit, but neither of them cared. It was refreshing to be out with a girlfriend and not have to worry for the entire day about being one of the boys.

Though Leonard was still working off her husband's debts, she was a smart saver and an even smarter investor. All work and no play could make Jill a dull girl, so she made sure to keep a little extra money squirreled away for her outings with Kate.

Their routine at Tysons Galleria was always the same. They surfed shops like Salvatore Ferragamo, Chanel, and Versace first, looking for any sales or bargains. Then it was off to Nicole Miller, Ralph Lauren, and Burberry, where they seldom left without at least a shopping bag each.

Lunch was at one of three spots—Legal Sea Foods of Boston, P.F. Chang's, or the Cheesecake Factory. Today it was P.F. Chang's.

After a lunch of lettuce wraps, crab wonton, lemon scallops, and Cantonese roasted duck, the women paid the check, emptied their wineglasses, and headed for the parking lot.

Cutting through Macy's, they were approached by one of the most gorgeous men either of them had ever seen. He was at least six feet tall with dark hair and piercing blue eyes. He looked Italian and was wearing an impeccably tailored gray suit.

Despite being an accomplished sniper, Philippe Roussard also enjoyed engaging his targets up close. He liked to take his time, to listen to them beg for their lives and then watch them die. Sometimes, though, he didn't get his way. In this case, he would have to read about the women's deaths in the paper— if the news was ever published at all.

"Che bella donna," he said as he approached, and he meant it. The ladies were both very attractive; much more so than in their surveillance photos.

Italian, Carolyn Leonard thought to herself. *I knew it.*

While she didn't normally engage strangers, she'd had a little wine with lunch, and today, after all, was her day off. Besides, how much trouble could the guy be? He worked for Macy's. She could see the bottle of perfume and sample strips in his hand. Sure, he was trying to get them to buy something, but he was so gorgeous. Whatever he was selling, Carolyn Leonard was in the mood to buy.

The off-duty head of the American president's Secret Service detail smiled. She was tall, about five-foot-ten, and very lean. Her red hair was pulled back in a tight ponytail and she looked like a very fit woman.

Roussard bowed his head and smiled at them both. The other agent, Kate Palmer, was shorter, about five-seven, but just as attractive, with a hard, lithe body, long brown hair, and deep green eyes.

"You are easily the most beautiful women I have seen come through the store all day," he said in heavily accented English.

Carolyn Leonard chuckled. "It must be a very slow day."

Roussard smiled. "I am telling you the truth."

"Where are you from?" asked Palmer.

"Italy."

"You don't say," she teased. *"Where* in Italy?"

"San Benedetto del Tronto. It's in the central Marche region on the Adriatic. Do you know it?"

"No," replied Leonard. "But I think I'd like to."

Roussard held up his perfume bottle as if he were demonstrating the newest marvel of technology. "I have to look like I am trying to sell you something. My supervisor has been watching me very closely. He says I flirt too much."

Carolyn laughed again. *"Puh-lease,* that's all part of sales, isn't it?"

"Not when you mean it," replied Roussard.

"Oh, this guy's good," stated Palmer with a smile. "Real good."

"Well, I hate to break it to you," said Carolyn, "But I don't think either of us is in the market for any new perfume, are we?"

Palmer shook her head. "Maybe next time."

Roussard's lips spread into a boyish grin. "At least

please try it. It's quite nice and my supervisor won't be able to say I'm not doing my job."

Carolyn looked at Kate Palmer, shrugged her shoulders, and said, "Why not?"

Roussard handed them the bottle and politely stepped back. The women sprayed the perfume on their wrists, rubbed their necks, and Palmer even sprayed some onto her hair.

"It doesn't have much of a scent," commented Carolyn Leonard.

"That's because it works with your body's own chemistry. Give it a little time and you'll see. It is quite remarkable."

Leonard gave the bottle back as Roussard handed her and Palmer a sample card with the name of the product and a phrase that looked to be Italian.

As the ladies headed out to the parking lot, neither of them had any idea of the horror they had just invited into their lives.

CHAPTER 61

CIA Safe House
Coltons Point, Maryland

The small, unremarkable home sat at the verdant end of Graves Road on St. Patrick's Creek—a small inlet of the Potomac River, less than fifty kilometers from where the Potomac emptied into the Chesapeake.

The cars parked in the home's driveway were equally unremarkable—a smattering of SUVs and pickups, the kind of cars one would expect to see at the weekend home of a general contractor from Baltimore.

Had the neighbors seen any of the men getting out of their vehicles and entering the house, none would have given them a second look. They were trim and of varying heights, their faces bronzed from being in the sun, signs that they were all undoubtedly engaged in the same profession as the home's owner. Had anyone taken any notice of them they would have assumed the men had all come down for the fishing.

The fishing was one of the many reasons that the area around Coltons Point was known as one of the best-kept secrets in southern Maryland. The chamber of commerce slogan made for a wink-wink, nod-nod insider sort of joke among the select few at the CIA who knew about the Coltons Point safe house. If there was anything that the spooks at Langley loved, it was irony.

The six highly skilled men assembled inside the home were known in CIA parlance as an Omega Team. The word Omega was taken from the Greek, which referred to the last and final letter of the Greek alphabet. It also referred to the literal *end* of something. Omega Teams had not been given their name by accident. Theirs was very, very dirty work. Sometimes their missions were overt, but more often than not they were extremely covert and required surgical delicacy.

The team leader unbuckled his leather briefcase and tossed five dossiers onto the dining-room table. He didn't need one for himself. He'd already memorized the contents. "I know many of you are currently standing up other operations," he said, "but effective immediately, this assignment is your one and only concern."

Like most CIA field groups, Omega Teams were composed of highly intelligent and extremely patriotic individuals. One of the team members looked up from the dossier and said, "Are you sure about this?"

"Not that any of you are allowed to repeat this, but this came from DCI Vaile himself."

"But this guy's practically a national hero," said another operative. "It's like asking us to shoot fucking Lassie."

The team leader didn't care for what he was hearing. "What is this, a book club meeting all of a sudden? Nobody asked for your opinions. The subject is a significant threat to national security.

"He was asked repeatedly by the president to stand down and refused. He was then given a timetable within which to turn himself in and he refused again."

"Wait a second. How's President Rutledge involved in this? What's this guy wanted for anyway?" asked another.

"That's none of your business. All you need to know

is that, by not complying with the president's orders, he's putting innocent American lives in jeopardy."

"Bullshit," claimed yet another member. "We've all read his jacket. This guy is one serious tack-driving pipe-hitter. If we're going to go after somebody this experienced, this dangerous, I think we deserve to know what he's really up to. Why won't he comply with the president's order?"

The team leader was in no mood to explain the motivations of their target, or those of the director of Central Intelligence, or those of the president of the United States to his men. "I'm going to say this once and only once, so shut up and listen. All I am going to tell you, and all you need to know, is that both DCI Vaile and the president of the United States have okayed us to take down this target. Our job is to stop Scot Harvath by any means necessary. End of story."

CHAPTER 62

Physically and emotionally, Harvath was wrung out. His nerves had been grated down to stubs and he probably shouldn't have even been in the field. Nonetheless, all he could think about was the Troll. The man had lied to him. There weren't four terrorists who had been released from Gitmo; there had been five. Harvath couldn't wait to get his hands on him.

He'd used the onboard phone to fill Finney and

Parker in on what he'd learned, and they immediately began strategizing. They expected to have several different options to present by the time he returned.

Harvath spent the next several hours going through his own set of scenarios. What little reserves of energy he still had were all but depleted. After the takeoff from refueling in Iceland, his fatigue won out and he fell into a heavy, dark sleep. And with the sleep came his dreams.

It was the same nightmare he'd been having about Tracy, but this time it was worse. He dreamed he was standing on a long rope bridge between two groups of people he cared for, each in imminent danger. He could only save one. But instead of making a choice, he stood paralyzed with fear.

His indecision cost him dearly. He helplessly watched as the members of each group were killed one by one, their deaths gleefully carried out by a sadistic demon bent on extracting every ounce of pain-wracked suffering he could. All the while, Harvath merely stood and watched, unsure of himself and his ability to do anything to stop the holocaust being carried out so savagely in front of him.

It was a rapid ringing of the cabin chimes that tore Harvath from his nightmare. Opening his eyes, he looked out the window and saw that they were over land, though where exactly he had no idea. He raised the handset and punched the button for the cockpit.

"What's going on?" he asked when the copilot answered.

"We've got a major mechanical problem."

"What kind?"

The copilot ignored him and said, "We're about fifty miles out from the airport. Stay seated and make sure your seat belt is tightly fastened." And with that the line went dead.

From the front of the cabin, Harvath heard the bolt of the cockpit door being thrown into place. Maybe it was a legitimate safety precaution, but there was something about it that didn't sit right with him.

Harvath looked at his watch and tried to compute where they were. He had been asleep for a long time.

Protocol dictated that private aircraft stop at the first major city they overflew upon entry into U.S. airspace to clear customs and passport control, but Tom Morgan had been able to pull some strings with people he knew to have those requirements waived for both the Mexico and Jordan trips.

They should have been somewhere over Canada or the Great Lakes, but the terrain beneath them looked more like the East Coast of the United States. Something definitely wasn't right.

The Citation X banked sharply and there was a hurried change in altitude as the private jet raced downward. Whatever was going on, Harvath didn't like it.

He felt the landing gear lower and he cinched his seat belt tighter.

He looked back out the window and a sense of dread welled up from the pit of his stomach as he recognized where they were.

The jet wasn't landing anywhere near Colorado. It was on final approach to Ronald Reagan Washington National Airport in D.C.

Now he knew why the pilots had locked the cockpit door. There was no mechanical problem. Someone had gotten to Tim Finney. Someone knew that Harvath was on this plane and that person was making it land in D.C.

He needed to plan his next move.

A lot would be based upon what kind of law enforcement presence had been sent to meet the plane on the ground.

Harvath sat glued to his window as the Citation X glided in over the runway and then touched down with a gentle bump of its tires. A string of neon fire trucks and two ambulances had been mobilized and were following the jet on a taxiway just beyond the runway.

It wasn't the reception Harvath had expected. There wasn't a police car or an unmarked government sedan in sight. Even so, he remained on guard.

The plane taxied off the runway into a holding area. When the aircraft came to a stop, the emergency vehicles surrounded it and their teams got to work.

Harvath unbuckled his seat belt and moved to the other side of the jet to see what was going on.

As he did, the main cabin door opened and the high-pitched whine of the Citation's Rolls-Royce engines filled the aircraft.

A moment later, several firefighters clambered up the airstairs and entered the cabin. Their walkie-talkies belched with orders being barked back and forth between emergency personnel. It was all just background noise to Harvath. He was focused on the men themselves.

Beneath their Nomex turnout gear, they looked like every other firefighter Harvath had ever met. They were lean and athletic, with serious, hard-set faces that communicated they had a job to do.

The only problem was that they bore the same look as many of the elite military and law enforcement personnel Harvath had met and worked with over his years in both the SEALs and the Secret Service.

Harvath stood up and started moving toward the front of the cabin. That was when he saw it. The second "firefighter" had something pressed up against the back of the man in front of him.

In the reflection from the highly polished cabinetry of the galley, Harvath could make out the unmistakable color and size of a TASER X26 pulsed energy weapon. It was the same device he'd used on Ronaldo Palmera just days before.

Harvath was trapped.

CHAPTER 63

As part of his training years ago, Harvath had taken a hit from the TASER to see what it was like. In a word, it was intense—more intense than anything he had ever experienced. He had no desire to ride the bull again, so now he simply sank to his knees and interlaced his fingers behind his head. His twenty-four hours had evaporated a lot faster than he'd anticipated.

With a knee against his neck and his face pressed against the jet's carpeted cabin floor, Harvath felt the burn of the Flexicuffs as they zipped his wrists up behind his back.

They were being exceptionally rough with him, and their message was clear—*Screw with us and things are going to get much worse.*

A black Yukon Denali was waiting at the bottom of the airstairs. Harvath's feet never even touched the ground.

He was thrown into the backseat and bracketed by two men who slammed their doors in unison. One of them buckled him in as the other told the driver to get moving.

He didn't see the hood until it was placed over his head and everything went black.

It was a long ride. Every minute of sensory deprivation in that impenetrable darkness felt like an hour. When the SUV finally came to a halt, one of

Harvath's minders opened his door and then jerked him from the Denali.

Harvath heard birds and what sounded like a motor of some sort off in the distance. It might have been a lawn mower, but based on the Doppler effect it had produced he guessed it was a boat of some sort. They were probably near the water.

A rough set of hands grabbed hold of him on the other side and he was ushered forward. The smooth pavement under his feet gave way to grass and then to wooden steps.

He was directed up them and made to stop as a door of some sort was opened. The air inside smelled musty, with a faint trace of Pine Sol.

Harvath was steered down a long hallway and stopped in front of another door where his Flexicuffs were removed. The door was then opened and after his wrists were unbound and his hood was yanked off he was shoved inside. Behind him he heard the door close and lock.

At first, all he could see was the color white. Slowly, as his eyes adjusted, he began to make out some blues, as well as the dark color of the distressed-wood floor. A clutch of hand-painted lobsterman buoys were the first objects he could actually focus on. From there, the entire room began to open up.

The décor was straight out of *Coastal Living* magazine—bead-board walls, model ships, pillows created from old nautical flags. While Harvath had envisioned many kinds of cells the president might have him thrown into, none of them had resembled this.

Skirting a small daybed, Harvath walked over to the window. He wasn't surprised that he couldn't open it. What did surprise him was that it appeared to be made out of bullet-resistant glass, about an inch and a half thick. This was definitely no ordinary room.

Harvath figured he was in some sort of safe house. The first agency that popped into his mind as being its likely owner was the CIA, though it could have belonged to any number of others.

Harvath had seen a lot of safe houses in his day, and all things being equal, the quality of the décor in this one suggested the Central Intelligence Agency's involvement over any other group.

The closet was empty, as was the bureau against the far wall. In the nightstand was a Bible with a stamp claiming the Gideons had placed it there, which was obviously someone's idea of a clever joke.

Harvath noted that the model ships throughout the room were named for Ivy League universities. He was definitely in an Agency safe house, but why? Why bring him here?

There were two doors on either side of the room. One led to a bathroom, conspicuously missing the normal hardware such as a shower rod or mirror that could be fashioned into a weapon. Harvath turned on the tap and took several servings of water from a small paper cup before returning to the bedroom.

The other door presumably led to the interior of the house, but it was locked. No big surprise there. Harvath figured that there was at least one, maybe two guards posted on the other side. Knowing the penchant of the CIA for electronic surveillance, he also assumed his room was wired for both sound and video.

With nothing else to do, he removed the Bible from the nightstand and sat down on the bed. A product of the Sacred Heart school system as a boy, Harvath was embarrassed that it had been so long since he had held, much less read, a Bible.

He respectfully leafed through the pages until he arrived at the second book of the Old Testament, Exodus.

The book was broken into six sections, all of which Harvath was familiar with. He read about the Israelites' enslavement and escape from Egypt, the ten plagues bearing especially painful significance for him now.

If the attack on the ski team and its facility in Park City was meant to represent hail and fire, there were six more plagues that were yet to come. He read through them in their reverse order—boils, pestilence, beasts or flies, fleas or lice, frogs, and lastly a river of blood.

While some of them sounded tame by modern standards, Harvath knew the man responsible for all of these attacks, the man he believed to be the fifth terrorist released from Guantanamo, would find an exceptionally deviant and terrifying way to incorporate them into his attacks.

The thought of any more attacks made Harvath's present situation an even more bitter pill to swallow. He had to find some way to get out of here and stop the person who was responsible for all of it.

Placing the Bible atop the nightstand, Harvath rose from the bed. He would take another look around the room. There had to be something here that could aid in his escape. He didn't care if they had him under surveillance or not. Just sitting there doing nothing was not an option.

After checking the closet over thoroughly, he was on his way back into the bathroom when he heard voices outside his door. Looking down he saw the knob slowly begin to turn and he knew that he'd run out of time.

CHAPTER 64

When the door to his room opened, Harvath was surprised to see who was on the other side of it.

Before he could open his mouth, the man raised his TASER and pointed it at Harvath's chest. He threw a pair of handcuffs at him and said, "Your right wrist to the bed frame, now."

When Harvath hesitated, the man yelled, "Now!"

Harvath did as he was told.

With his prisoner secure, the man holstered his weapon, turned to the guard at the door, and nodded.

Once the guard had closed the door and the man with the TASER heard the click of the lock, he threw

Harvath the keys to the handcuffs. "We've only got fif-teen minutes of talk time while the surveillance servers are rebooted."

"What the hell is going on here?" asked Harvath as he removed the handcuff from around his wrist and threw the keys back to Rick Morrell.

Morrell was a CIA paramilitary operative whom Harvath had worked with on several occasions in the past. After a considerably rocky start to their relation-ship, they had developed a professional respect for each other and even a friendship. Harvath didn't know if his being here was a good thing or a bad thing. In the intelligence world, friendships were all too often sub-verted for matters of national security. Harvath hadn't forgotten that President Rutledge wanted him for treason. He'd have to tread very carefully.

"You are in a shitload of trouble. You know that?" replied Morrell.

Harvath *did* know it and he didn't need Rick Morrell or anyone else reminding him of it. "You'd have done the same thing in my situation."

Morrell nodded. "That still doesn't make my job any easier."

Harvath didn't like the sound of that. "Exactly what *is* your job?"

"By order of the president, I have been charged with stopping you from taking any further steps in relation to the attacks on Tracy Hastings, your mother, and the U.S. Ski Team."

"So, the president does believe the ski team attack was by the same person?"

"Yes, he does," said Morrell. "They found a note at the scene matching ones from the other two attacks."

"Then what's the problem?"

"The problem is that the president wants you out of the picture."

"I've got every right to—" began Harvath, but Morrell interrupted him.

"You don't have any rights. Jack Rutledge is the president of the United States. When he tells you to do something, you do it."

"That's not good enough."

"Well, it's going to have to be," said Morrell.

Harvath looked at him with disbelief. "Jesus, you are an asshole. You know that? A minute ago you agreed that you would have done the same thing in my position."

"And I meant it."

"So what's your fucking problem?"

"My problem is that I and the other five members of my Omega Team on the other side of that door have been ordered to take you out if you refuse to cooperate."

The response took Harvath by surprise.

"Dead or alive," said Morrell as he read the expression on Harvath's face.

Harvath had felt betrayed when the president had first turned on him, but now there were no words to describe what he was feeling. "And for an extra twist of the knife, you were chosen to head the hit team up. Should I call you Brutus or is Judas a better fit?"

"Rutledge didn't choose me, Director Vaile did."

"What's the difference? You still accepted the assignment."

"I accepted it all right. The DCI laid out a very compelling case."

"I'm sure he did," replied Harvath, the contempt evident in his voice. "I always liked Vaile, but apparently he never thought that much of me. Hell of a poker player. He had me fooled."

"For the record," said Morrell, "Vaile sucks at cards. And just so you know, he's a decent guy. He's probably one of the best directors the Agency has ever had. He's a patriot who puts our country above everything else, even his own welfare."

"What are you talking about?"

Morrell waved his arm around the room. "He's the reason you've been brought here instead of some federal lockup. He's the reason I'm here heading this team."

"I don't get it," replied Harvath.

"Vaile has a lot of respect for you. While he may not think going head-to-head with the president of the United States is a great career move, he understands why you're doing it. At the same time, he understands why the president is doing what he's doing. The bottom line is that Vaile knows you're not a traitor."

"So then why am I here?" asked Harvath. "Why are we even having this conversation?"

Though all the monitoring devices were supposedly offline, Morrell leaned closer to Harvath, his voice barely above a whisper, though no less intense than it had been, and he said, "Because Director Vaile feels partly responsible for what has happened—Tracy, your mother, the ski team, all of it. He wants you to know why it's going down."

CHAPTER 65

Their time was short, so Morrell spoke quickly. "It is the stated policy of the United States government never to negotiate with terrorists. We all know it's the nation's first and most important commandment in the war on terror—*Thou shalt not negotiate with terrorists.*"

Harvath was well aware of the commandment. "But somebody broke it," he guessed as he thought about the five prisoners released from Guantanamo.

Morrell nodded. "There is an exception to every rule."

"Was the president directly involved in the prisoner release?"

Morrell looked toward the door and then back at Harvath. "Yes."

Harvath had suspected all along that the president had been involved, but now he had confirmation.

"What I am about to tell you," continued Morrell, "stays in this room. Your current status as a fugitive notwithstanding, you are still bound by your oath and the National Security nondisclosure agreements you signed before going to work at both the White House and DHS. Is that clear?"

"Crystal," replied Harvath.

Morrell took a deep breath. "There is only one instance where the United States will break its own rule of not negotiating with terrorists."

In all Harvath's experience he had never seen the First Commandment broken. He couldn't even begin to imagine what would qualify as an exception.

Harvath had seen many horrible things in his career as a counterterrorism operative. A part of him questioned whether he truly wanted to know what would warrant such an exception, but he needed to know why the president was holding him back from protecting the people he cared about. He needed to know why some sick terrorist had been granted blanket immunity to do whatever he wanted to innocent American citizens.

"The exception," said Morrell, "is when a terrorist or terrorist organization has targeted children."

"You mean whoever has been carrying out these attacks targeted kids as well?"

"No. The five released from Guantanamo were still there when the attack in question took place. The group that brokered their release used the attack as leverage to get them out. I know you have been through a lot, but if it's any consolation, the president had absolutely no choice in this."

Harvath wasn't ready to give Rutledge a pass just yet. He needed to hear more and signaled for Morrell to continue.

"Two days before the Gitmo five were released, a school bus filled with children as young as five years old went missing in Charleston, South Carolina. The terrorists threatened to begin killing a child every half hour until their demands were met.

"An immediate news blackout was ordered and federal authorities went into overdrive to find the bus. Satellites were retasked, the FBI's Hostage Rescue Team was activated, and members of Delta Force, SEAL Team Six, SEAL Team Eight, and even elements of the CIA were brought in. This was a direct attack upon our nation, the psychological impact of which could have been extremely severe. The president stopped at nothing.

"To demonstrate how serious they were, the terrorists killed the bus driver and left her behind the wheel of the abandoned bus. When the report came in about the dead driver and the fact that we were no longer looking for a bright yellow school bus, people got even more worried. Either the terrorists had the children at one central location, or worse, the group had been broken up and taken to several different locations.

"Images of the Beslan school massacre in Russia were running rampant through everyone's mind. Everybody knew that trying to take the children back by force could be a horrendous and deadly mistake. If the terrorists were attacked, there was little doubt that they would martyr themselves and take the children with them. There was absolutely no question, the United States' only option was to negotiate.

"Originally, the terrorists wanted all of the prisoners released from Guantanamo. Slowly, the negotiators whittled it down to five and agreed that the president would sign some sort of letter promising, among other things, that all the secret detention facilities the United States was using around the world would be shut down, that prisoners at Gitmo would be provided with better food and medical care and more frequent visits from the Red Cross, that all prisoners would be brought to trial for their alleged crimes, and that these trials would be transparent, with international monitors present to vouch for their legality."

"And the president went for that?" asked Harvath.

"He had no choice. The terrorists had put a gun to his head and they were ramping up to kill their first child. Their leader directed the president to a website where camera phone photos of the child the hostage takers had selected to be the first to die were posted. From what I was told, the photo would have broken your heart. They picked the youngest and cutest of the bunch. The image would have played very, very badly on the news.

"The NSA and several other agencies went to work on the website, while the president huddled with his advisors in the Situation Room. He had a very difficult and potentially historic decision to make.

"And we all know how it ended," responded Harvath.

Morrell held up his hand. "No you don't. It wasn't over, not by a long shot. For the United States, the trouble had only just begun."

CHAPTER 66

Harvath didn't know what to think, or what to feel, for that matter. He'd figured that the president had been motivated to do the right thing for the country and that was certainly what he'd done in this horrible scenario, but it still didn't explain why he'd sidelined him.

He didn't know if Rick Morrell had the answers he was seeking or not, but he knew each piece of information he got would bring him one step closer to solving the puzzle. Harvath knew they didn't have much time left, so he decided to hold his questions and let Morrell finish.

Morrell was obviously concerned with the time as well. He glanced at his watch for the third time and then said, "The secretary of defense suggested to the president that a highly classified tracking program be used to trace the five men once they were released from Guantanamo."

"Via a radioactive isotope," said Harvath, sensing where this was going. "I'm familiar with it."

"The U.S. didn't know who it was negotiating with. And it knew even less about the relationship among the men it was about to free. If they could track the men, it was believed they could locate the organization responsible for the bus hijacking and either bring them to justice or at the very least exact some sort of revenge.

"The only problem was that somehow the other side knew about the blood-spiking program and fully transfused the five detainees in flight. They then used the extracted blood to lead the CIA on a fucked-up chase. The blood wound up in several containers that were tossed in multiple dumpsters and the trunks of several cars.

"The DOD blamed the CIA for losing the men, and the CIA blamed the DOD for hanging their hat on a program that wasn't as ultra-top-secret as they'd thought."

"So the U.S. lost them. I know that much," said Harvath.

"What you don't know is that the terrorists placed a few conditions on the deal they struck with the president."

"Such as what?"

"Such as the men we released were never to be hunted, harmed, or reincarcerated," replied Morrell. "As an insurance policy, the terrorists provided surveillance photos of over a hundred school buses from across the country. The message was clear. If we welshed, they'd be back, and things would be a lot worse the next time. We'd be forced to suffer a gruesome attack against our children and this time there'd be no negotiating."

"That's why the president wanted me sidelined."

Morrell put his hand on his friend's shoulder. "He didn't *want* you sidelined, he had no choice. You've put him in a very difficult position."

"So what? He wouldn't even fill me in on who he supposedly has hunting this guy down."

"Would it have made a difference? Would the president's personnel decisions have convinced you to sit by while this nutjob was targeting your friends and family?"

Harvath didn't know how to answer that question. Finally he said, "Probably not."

"Scot, the president knows you were in Mexico when Palmera was killed."

"How would he know that?"

"The CIA has CCTV footage of you at the airport in Querétaro. They traced the plane you used. They also know who the plane belongs to. That's how we figured out you were on your way back from Amman."

Harvath's heart sank. If he was going down, he certainly didn't want to drag people along with him, especially not decent, patriotic Americans like Tim Finney and Ron Parker. "The guys at Elk Mountain didn't know anything about this."

"You and I both know that's bullshit," replied Morrell. "They're on the CCTV footage with you. The only thing working in your favor is that witnesses claim Palmera ran into the street and was hit by the cab. As far as they're concerned, it was most likely a cartel thing. Whether the terrorists who helped arrange his release from Gitmo believe that is another story."

"Where's that leave us, then?"

"I need to know what happened in Amman. Why were you there? Who did you meet with?"

Harvath shook his head, *no*.

"Scot, listen to me. The Palmera thing can be

made to look like he got mixed up with some bad people from his old life. It's only one death, and while suspicious, it's nothing definitive. Two deaths and we're in big trouble and the shit is most definitely going to hit the fan.

"We have no idea how many school buses these people could potentially target. The only hope we have of avoiding more attacks is to manage this situation from out front. We can't do that unless you give us what we need. What happened in Amman?"

"If the president had been up front about all of this from the start I could have—"

"Scot, what happened?"

"Abdel Salam Najib is dead. His handler too."

"Shit," cursed Morrell.

"What did you expect? What did anybody expect? The lives of the people I care about are at stake here. I couldn't just sit back and do nothing."

Rick Morrell stood up and headed for the door.

"Wait a second!" said Harvath. "That's it? I thought you were going to help me."

"I did help you," said Morrell as he kept walking. "The president said *dead or alive*. You're alive."

Though he was still alive, Harvath realized he'd also been duped into revealing what had happened in Jordan. With two of the detainees dead, there was no way they were going to let him go now.

What he did next was rash, poorly thought out, and just plain stupid, but considering the circumstances he found himself in, it was probably the only move Harvath could make.

CHAPTER 67

Morrell was almost at the door when Harvath slammed his sledgehammer of a fist into the base of the man's skull.

Morrell's knees buckled as he lost consciousness and Harvath eased him gently to the floor. He then glanced down at his watch.

Was Morrell telling the truth about the servers' being offline for fifteen minutes? If he wasn't, the other Omega Team members would be rushing to the room at this very moment. He counted to five. Nothing happened.

Morrell had at least been telling the truth about the cameras, which meant that Harvath now had less than two minutes to get out of the house unseen.

He grabbed his now ex-friend's keys, unholstered his TASER, and rapped twice against the door.

Harvath heard the heavy footfalls of the guard on the other side followed by the sliding of the deadbolt as he unlocked the door. He raised the TASER and prepared to fire.

As the door swung open, the guard exposed himself and Harvath squeezed the trigger. The barbed probes embedded themselves in his chest and he was given the electric bull's ride for five. He fell forward into the room, and after rolling him quickly onto his back, Harvath landed a series of brutal punches to the man's face and head that rendered him unconscious.

He stripped the guard of his .45 caliber Glock, his

keys, a walkie-talkie, and a Benchmade tactical folding knife.

Unlike the TASER Harvath had used in Mexico, this one had a spare cartridge in the grip, and Harvath quickly reloaded the weapon. While these men had been authorized to kill him, they were first and foremost Americans who were doing the job they'd been sent to do. Harvath didn't want to kill any of them if he didn't have to.

Harvath stepped cautiously into the hallway. He could hear voices coming from the main part of the cottage, which made his decision to go in the opposite direction even easier.

As he crept closer to the end of the hallway, he could hear a television set. It was accompanied by an irregular *whirring* sound and an occasional *thwack*. Harvath had no idea what he was hearing until he neared the room and heard a shout.

Peering around the doorway, his hopes for a clean getaway tanked. Two Omega Team members were playing foosball on one of the rattiest-looking tables Harvath had ever seen. Just past them was a doorway that led to the outside world and beyond it, freedom. The one problem was that Harvath had only a single shot remaining in the TASER.

He had to think of something fast. His time was almost up. Sneaking a quick peek around the corner again, he took in as much of the room as possible and seared the image into his brain.

Both of the men were armed, but Harvath had surprise on his side. He could buttonhook into the room with his Glock drawn and tell them to hit the floor, but there was no guarantee that they would comply. If they called his bluff, he'd be in a very difficult position. He had no desire to shoot them, not even to secure his freedom, but he'd do it if he had to. He could kneecap both of them, but the sound of gunfire would bring the other team members and then he'd really be in trouble. Having shot first, he would undoubtedly be targeted as an active threat that needed to be neutralized. Harvath could very well be signing his own death certificate.

The key was getting out with as little noise and drawing as little attention as possible.

Another shout erupted from the foosball game, and Harvath chanced a third look around the corner. Another goal had been scored, and the man who'd been scored upon was readying to serve the ball. The man opposite him had both his hands upon his metal rods ready for action. It was then that Harvath noticed that most of the handles on the ancient table were missing. The two Omega Team members were gripping bare metal.

Harvath waited for the ball to be served. When the man reached for his other bare rod, Harvath raised the TASER sideways, swung fully into the room and squeezed the trigger.

He embedded a probe into each of the men who had their meaty, sweaty hands on the metal poles and let the fifty thousand volts of electricity fly. It was a nasty and unexpected zap, which took the men completely by surprise. Harvath followed up by "drive stunning" the weapon into each of them, completing the circuit and incapacitating the last obstacle that stood in the way of his escape.

Harvath didn't bother trying to knock the men out. He made a beeline for the door and let himself outside as quickly as possible.

Staying below the window line, he crept around to the front of the house and fished Rick Morrell's keys from his pocket. He depressed the remote entry key fob and saw the headlights illuminated on a silver Chevy Tahoe. It would have been a perfect car to make his getaway in except for the fact that it was pinned in at the top of the driveway.

Harvath fished out the other set of keys and repeated the process. A pair of headlights illuminated behind Morrell's SUV, and Harvath whipped out the Benchmade knife he'd taken from the guard outside his room.

After flattening the tires of the other vehicles, he hopped into the guard's pickup truck, slid the key into the ignition, and turned, but nothing happened—not even the sickening *click, click, click* of a shot starter or the whirring noise of an almost dead battery.

There was no way Harvath could escape these guys on foot. Many of them had Special Operations backgrounds and would easily be able to track him. His one hope was the water. As long as they didn't have access to a boat, he might be able to outswim them. All he needed to do was put enough distance between him and them before returning to dry land where he could flag a ride or steal another car.

He was about to hop out of the guard's Ford pickup and make for the water when he discovered the vehicle's antitheft kill switch.

Seconds later, Harvath pulled out of the driveway and headed the truck north toward D.C. and the man he was going to force to give him some answers.

CHAPTER 68

NORTHERN VIRGINIA

Philippe Roussard despised America and Americans for many reasons. He despised them for their gluttony, their sloth, and their arrogance. Most of them had never traveled beyond their own borders and yet they believed themselves to be the center of the world and that their way of life was the only correct and righteous way.

He despised them for what he saw as their empire-building—their constant meddling in the affairs of other nations. He despised them not only for the act, but for the concept of globalization. If America was not stopped, he knew that their poison would continue to ooze and affect every nation on the planet until puss-filled sores of capitalism and democracy erupted everywhere. It was America's greatest failing, the notion that there were only two types of people in this world—Americans and those who wished they were.

As much as he hated America, however, there was much about the actual physical geography of the country that he found quite enchanting. With the vehicle's windows rolled down, Roussard drove through the rural Virginia countryside and admired its beauty.

It often confused Roussard why Allah should have blessed the infidels, in particular America and her Western allies, with such prosperity, abundance, and geographical beauty while He allowed the true believers, his Islamic faithful, to often languish in abhorrent conditions in some of the earth's most desolate locations.

Roussard knew it was wrong to try to discern the mind of Allah, but it was a question he often found himself occupied with. His God was great and He was merciful. In His wisdom He had assigned His people their stations in life so that they might struggle in His name and prove themselves worthy of His acknowledgment. The day of the Muslim people was close at hand. Soon their struggles, their laborious jihad, would bear fruit—ripe, plump, heavy fruit bursting with the sugary sweetness of having vanquished their enemies and having rid the earth of all nonbelievers.

The terrorist recalled a proclamation from a fellow mujahideen who had said that the followers of the Prophet, may peace be upon Him, would not rest until they were dancing upon the roof of the White House itself. The image always made him smile.

He was contemplating whether he would see such a glorious development in his lifetime when the cell phone he had purchased the day before vibrated in his pocket. He had only given the number to one person.

"Yes," said Roussard as he raised the device to his ear.

"I read the update you left for me," said the handler.

"And?"

Though they both switched cell phones after each conversation, the handler was not fond of communicating this way. The Americans and their listening programs could not be underestimated. "I spent significant time crafting the itinerary for your visit. Your changes to it are—"

"Are what?" asked Roussard, angry. He didn't care for the way in which his handler second-guessed everything he did. He was not a child. He knew all too well the risks he was taking.

There was a pause and Roussard knew what his handler was thinking. The mistake had not been made in California—it had been made outside Harvath's home. Tracy Hastings should have been killed. She should be dead right now, not lying in some hospital bed on life support. But she had turned at the very last moment. That accursed dog had yelped, or twitched, or had done something to cause the woman to move her head ever so slightly, so that Roussard's shot had connected, but not where he had intended.

Maybe things were better that way. Maybe the pain would be more intense for Harvath. There were ten plagues in total, and each plague would be visited upon people close to him. He would be made to suffer through their suffering, and then, finally, his life would be taken. It was the ultimate price for what Harvath had done.

"Your changes cause me concern," said the handler.

"All of them," demanded Roussard angrily, "or certain ones in particular?"

"Please. This is not—"

"Answer my question."

The handler's voice remained calm. "The shopping mall was particularly dangerous—too many cameras, too many ways you could have been recorded. You should have stayed with the health club."

Roussard didn't answer.

"But what is done is done," said the handler. "You and I are cut from the same cloth."

Roussard winced at the suggestion

"I will not lie to you," continued the handler. "Giving in to your impulses and deviating from the itinerary, no matter how productive those deviations turn out to be, is dangerous. When you deviate, you venture into unknown territory. Without my guidance, you place not only yourself, but me at great risk."

"If my performance is unsatisfactory, maybe I scrap the plan entirely and finish this my way."

"No," replied the handler, "no more deviations. You must finish your work as agreed. But first, a problem has come up that needs to be dealt with—we have been betrayed."

"Betrayed by whom?"

"The little man your grandfather once used to gather information," replied the handler.

"The Troll?"

The handler, deep in thought, grunted a response.

Roussard was concerned. "How can you be sure?"

"I have my contacts and sources of information. Do you think it was coincidence that you were sent to Harvath's on the same day the Troll sent his gift?"

"I know it wasn't," conceded Roussard.

"Then do not doubt me. The dwarf knows of your release and is actively seeking information about you."

"Do the Americans know what we have planned?"

"I don't think so," said the handler. "Not yet."

"Do you want me to take care of him?"

"I don't like the idea of your having to leave the country before your current visit is complete, but this problem needs to be taken care of before it grows any larger, and you're the only one I can trust to make sure it is taken care of properly."

"He is small and weak. It will be my pleasure."

"You must not underestimate him," admonished the handler. "He is a formidable opponent."

"Where is he now?"

"I am still working on tracking him down."

"He's not in Scotland?" asked Roussard.

"No. I've already had the house and the estate searched. He hasn't been there for some time."

"Let me help you find him."

"No," stated the handler. "Focus on your next target. I will find him myself."

"And then?"

"And then I will decide how he is to be disposed of and you will follow my orders exactly. Is that clear? We are getting very close now. I do not want any more surprises."

Though the bile choked his throat, Roussard kept his anger under control. When this was over, he would deal with his handler.

His voice barely above a whisper, the operative replied, "Yes, it is clear."

CHAPTER 69

Philippe Roussard pulled off the crushed-gravel drive and allowed his vehicle to roll to a quiet stop. From here, the car would be out of sight of any vehicles passing along the main road, as well as from anyone in the small, stone farmhouse about a half mile away.

He gathered the items he'd need from the trunk and proceeded the rest of the way in on foot.

It was actually quite a beautiful day. The sun was bright and only a few thin clouds drifted overhead. Roussard could smell the distinct scent of freshly mown grass from a nearby property.

As he crept through the woods, a variety of birds called out from the treetops above him, but other than that, there were no sounds but his own footfalls to be heard.

At the tree line, he removed the binoculars from

his pack and made himself comfortable. This wasn't anything he needed to rush.

Twenty minutes later, the woman appeared, and snapping at her heels was the dog. He was surprised that she trusted the animal enough not to run off. Harvath had left her with it only a matter of weeks ago, but the accursed dog was still young, nothing more than a puppy, and apparently bonded easily with anyone who paid attention to it.

The woman was older, but not elderly in any sense of the word. She was in her late sixties, tall and attractive, with a face bronzed a deep copper color by the sun. Her steel-gray hair came to her shoulders and she walked her small farm with a haughty self-confidence that Roussard assumed was a prerequisite for anyone who had ever worked for the Federal Bureau of Investigation.

She was tending to her daily chores—gathering eggs from the small henhouse, feeding the chickens, then slicing open a bale and dropping hay into the corral of her two horses.

There were two atrocious potbellied pigs, which only a culture like America's could have ever warmed to as pets, and a clutter of cats that delighted in asserting their dominance over the tiny dog.

As Roussard studied the woman, he found himself thinking of his own mother. It was entirely unprofessional and entirely inappropriate. He was here to do a job and this American woman's similarities, or lack thereof, to his own mother had no bearing on what he needed to do.

The unwelcome distraction edged Roussard into action. He had no desire to sit alone in the woods with his thoughts. It was time.

He would take the woman in the barn. His only concern was the dog, but Roussard believed he had that figured out.

As the woman disappeared around one of the farm's outbuildings, Roussard picked up his backpack and ran.

Ever the pragmatist, he stopped near the small stone house and disabled her vehicle. Should something go wrong, he did not wish to leave her a convenient means of escape.

From the old Volvo station wagon, he then crept to the woman's house. He pressed himself up against the façade, the stones of which, even in the morning's increasing warmth, still felt cool to the touch.

Peering around the corner of the farmhouse, he waited until he could see the woman. When he saw her unwind a long garden hose to clean out the horse trough, Roussard made his move.

He chose not to run for fear of startling the horses. He walked quickly and with purpose, his hand clamped around the butt of the silenced pistol he had withdrawn from his backpack. If the woman noticed him and attempted to cry out, or to flee, he could easily take her even at this distance with a single round.

Once inside the barn, he concealed his pack and made himself ready. There was a gap between the exterior boards where he stood, and it gave him an excellent vantage point from which to observe the woman's approach.

His heart pounded in his chest and he loved the sensation. There was nothing so exciting as lying in wait for one's prey. The adrenaline surged through his bloodstream. Anything else, any other experience of life, was merely a fitful and incomplete dream of reality. To have the power to kill and to take and use that power—that was what life was all about.

Perspiration had begun to form on Roussard's brow. He stood inhumanly still, the beads of sweat slowly trickling together and rolling down his face and neck. *Soon,* he thought to himself. *Soon.*

When the woman appeared again from the corral, the killer's body slipped into a completely different state. Immediately, his breathing slowed. Next his heart rate began to decrease. His field of vision narrowed until all that he could see were the woman and the puppy at her feet. He stood as steady as a granite statue, his muscle fibers tautly spun coils ready to spring forward in sweet release.

When the woman neared, the killer stopped breathing. Nothing else mattered but this. She was almost at the wide open doors. A second later he could see her shadow spilling into the barn.

Finally, she crossed over the threshold and he sprang.

CHAPTER 70

Harvath had dumped the Omega Team member's Ford pickup almost immediately. Once he'd put some good distance between himself and the safe house, he had begun cruising the waterfront homes north of Coltons Point. It didn't take him long to find what he was looking for.

It was a large and obviously expensive house, and Harvath was amazed that it didn't have an alarm system. It was almost comical how little people thought about security once they left the big city behind them.

The keys for the magnificent thirty-six-foot-long Chris Craft Corsair had been hung on a peg in clear sight. While Harvath didn't care for taking things that didn't belong to him, given the circumstances, he wasn't left with much choice.

The Corsair had a fully charged battery, a full tank of fuel, and fired right up. He was "borrowing" a boat with a retail value of over $350,000, and Harvath vowed that its owners would get it back in exactly the same, mint condition it was in now.

He pulled the sleek pleasure craft out into the Potomac, pointed the bow northward, and bumped the throttles all the way forward.

The twin, 420 horsepower Volvo Penta engines growled in response. Like captive lions being set loose from their cages, the throaty engines popped the boat out of the hole and brought it right up on plane.

Harvath rolled up his sleeves and kept his eyes open as gusts of spray frothed up from the sides of the boat. He'd hidden the pickup in the house garage before climbing aboard the Corsair, but there was no telling how close his pursuers were.

The only thing he knew for certain was that even with Rick Morrell at their helm, the Omega Team would stop at nothing, not even killing him, to remove him from the picture.

At the Washington Sailing Marina, Harvath limped in feigning engine trouble and docked the Corsair. The staff left him alone to call his supposed Chris Craft dealer in Maryland, but instead, Harvath dialed a local cab company, and ten minutes later he was being driven the short distance to Reagan National's extended parking lot.

Because the trip to Jordan had been not only personal, but also highly sensitive, he had left his DHS credentials, his government-issued BlackBerry, and his weapon with Ron Parker back at Elk Mountain.

While the taxi waited, Harvath located his black Chevy Trailblazer. From the hitch vault under the rear bumper he retrieved a spare set of keys, a rubber-band-wrapped wad of tens and twenties, a preloaded debit card, and a duplicate driver's license to replace the personal effects Rick Morrell had taken from him when they off-loaded him from Tim Finney's plane.

After exiting the extended parking lot, he paid the cab driver and headed toward D.C. As he drove, he removed one of the throwaway cell phones he kept in his bugout bag and dialed his boss, Gary Lawlor.

"I've been trying to reach you for the last two days," said Lawlor when he answered. "Where the hell are you?"

"Never mind where I am," said Harvath. "I need you to listen."

Lawlor was quiet as Harvath spent the next several minutes filling him in on everything that had happened and everything he had learned since they last spoke.

When he was finished, Lawlor said, "Jesus, Scot, if what you're telling me is true, you've been killing the people the president promised to protect! You're undermining our word and making the president look like a liar. It's only a matter of time before these people decide we've screwed them and they keep their promise about going after more kids."

This was not exactly the kind of support Harvath had been hoping for when he brought his boss up to speed. "Look," he replied, "one of those men released from Gitmo is killing innocent Americans. The president promised to leave them alone based on their past actions, not current ones. But did anyone stop to think that this may be precisely why the terrorists negotiated the deal in the first place? So they could have blanket immunity while they carried out *new* acts of terror?

"Sorry, Gary, it was a bad bargain. I didn't make this mess, but I guess I'm going to be the one to clean it up."

"Good," stated Lawlor. "I want you to nail the son of a bitch."

Harvath could tell by the tone of his voice that he had misread him. Something else had happened. "What's going on?"

"It's Emily."

Harvath didn't need to be given a last name to know who Gary was talking about. Emily Hawkins had been Gary's assistant and right arm while he'd been at the FBI. She'd been like a second mother to Harvath since he'd moved to D.C., and he had left the puppy with her after Tracy had been shot.

"What happened?"

"He got to her. Her and the dog."

Lawlor was not an overly emotional man, and Harvath could tell it was taking everything he had to keep it together. He was completely choked up. "Tell me what happened."

"He was hiding in her barn out near Haymarket. He beat both her and the puppy severely. They've each got multiple broken bones and contusions. He did a real number on them, but that was just for starters. This sick bastard had brought along two body bags, one for an adult and one for a child. He placed her in one and the dog in the other, but before he zipped them up, he tossed in something to keep them company."

Harvath's stomach started to churn. He knew that body bags were nonporous. It was a horrible way to die. Harvath was definitely going to kill this guy. He pulled over to the side of the road and asked, "What did he throw in there?"

"He filled Emily's bag with horseflies. She was bitten over two hundred times."

Horseflies? That didn't make sense. The next plague was supposed to be boils. "Gary, you're sure that's all there was? Just flies?"

"The EMTs that showed up said he put over a thousand fleas in with the puppy."

"So fleas and flies? That's all?"

"No, that's not all. He strung them both upside down from one of the rafters. If Emily's neighbor hadn't shown up when he did, they'd be dead."

"Wait a second," said Harvath. "They're alive? Emily *and* the dog?"

"Yes, but only barely. I'm on my way to the hospital in Manassas now."

"When you get there, make sure the doctor and the vet monitor them both for boils and any sort of plaguelike illness. In fact, you should recommend that they start courses of antibiotics right away. This guy has been combining scenarios from the ten plagues of Egypt. The flies and the fleas were the third and the fourth, or in this guy's case, the seventh and eighth. Just tell them to be on the lookout."

When Lawlor said, "Scot, there's something else I need to tell you," dread seized him.

"Who else?" was all Harvath could manage.

"Carolyn Leonard and Kate Palmer. They were infected with some kind of staphylococcus aureus–bubonic plague hybrid."

The knife had been shoved into Harvath's heart the minute he found Tracy lying in a pool of blood on his doorstep; now it felt as if acid were being poured down the blade. The pain of having it twisted for Emily and the dog was one thing, but with Kate and Carolyn added to the mix, it was almost too much to bear.

"Where did it happen?" he asked.

"At Tysons Galleria," replied Lawlor.

"The shopping center? In public?"

"Some guy was offering perfume samples. We think he had the hybrid aerosolized. Kate gave the Bureau guys a description. Macy's sent over pictures of all their employees, contracted or otherwise, and none of them are a match."

"Are they looking at CCTV footage?"

"The tapes have already been pulled and both Kate and Carolyn are working with sketch artists."

"Will they be okay?" asked Harvath.

"This bug is very fast-acting. They showed symptoms in less than twelve hours, which is pretty much unheard of with either staphylococcus aureus or bubonic plague."

"If I remember my medical training right, staphylococcus aureus causes some pretty nasty boils."

"And can be a real bear to treat because of resistance to most antibiotics," said Lawlor. "The best thing they have going for them is the fact that it was caught early. Even so, the medical people are pretty concerned about how fast-moving it is. They've both been quarantined."

"There's no question in my mind that we're dealing with the same guy," stated Harvath.

"Nor in anyone else's. They found a card in Carolyn Leonard's purse, the kind perfume samples are sprayed onto. It had the name of some bogus perfume and a tagline written in Italian."

"Let me guess," said Harvath. *"That which has been taken in blood, can only be answered in blood?"*

"Exactly," stated Lawlor.

"Does the president know?"

"Yes, he knows."

"And?" asked Harvath.

"And it doesn't change anything. He still expects you to turn yourself in."

"Well, he's going to have to wait until I'm finished."

CHAPTER 71

THE WHITE HOUSE

Jack Rutledge prided himself on his ability to read his people. When Charles Anderson was shown into the residence, the president knew he hadn't arrived bearing good news.

"We've got a problem, sir," said Anderson, confirming the president's suspicions.

Rutledge closed the report he'd been skimming and motioned for his chief of staff to take a seat. "What is it?"

"I just heard from Director Vaile. His team managed to take Harvath into custody."

"That should be good news. What's the problem?"

"Harvath escaped."

"He what?" demanded Rutledge. "How the hell did that happen?"

"It'll all be in the DCI's briefing," replied Anderson, "but there's more."

"How much more?"

The chief of staff lowered his voice. "Before he escaped, Harvath was debriefed about his recent trip to Jordan. Apparently, he was able to lure Abdel Salam Najib out of Syria to Amman."

The president could feel his chest constricting. "Harvath killed him. Didn't he?"

"Yes, sir, he did."

"God damn it!" Rutledge bellowed. "First Palmera and now Najib. When their people realize what's happening they're going to strike back. We need to assemble the National Security Council."

The president had his work cut out for him. He knew there was no way the United States could provide continuous protection for every single school bus in the nation. It wasn't just a logistical nightmare; it would also create widespread panic. American citizens would rightly wonder if school buses weren't safe from terrorists, what was. Would movie theaters be safe? Would shopping malls? How about public transportation? Should they even keep their children in school? Should they even be going in to work?

The specter of terrorism, especially when given

weight and legitimacy by the government, had an amazingly corrosive effect on society. The president had read the classified reports on the impact of the D.C. sniper shootings and had studied the extrapolations of how quickly the U.S. economy would suffer if a similar threat was played out nationwide. After the economic ramifications began to unfold, the societal problems would erupt. If law enforcement couldn't bring the perpetrators to justice, citizens would begin to take matters into their own hands. Hate crimes would spike, and groups who felt they were being persecuted would begin to strike back. If the situation was not addressed quickly and effectively, rioting would ensue. In a word, the situation would devolve into anarchy. The psychological effects of terrorism were absolutely insidious.

The president's chief of staff interrupted his thoughts by saying, "There's also something else we need to talk about."

Rutledge shook his head as if to say *What else could there be?*

"A reporter from the *Baltimore Sun* contacted Geoff Mitchell's office for a statement on a story he's about to run. As you know, being the White House press secretary, Geoff gets asked a lot of wild, conspiracyesque questions, but this reporter has his teeth into something. Geoff's afraid it could get some traction if not put down immediately with a direct repudiation from you."

"What's the story?"

"The reporter is going to claim that you authorized the removal of a John Doe corpse from the Maryland Medical Examiner's Office to dupe the people of Charleston, South Carolina, into believing that their school bus hijacker had been shot and killed."

Rutledge gritted his teeth and grabbed the arms of his chair. "Where the hell did that story come from?"

"At this point, sir, it doesn't much matter. What matters is that it's pretty damaging, and he's going to also allege the White House was complicit in a homicide."

"A homicide? What homicide?"

"According to this guy Sheppard, a Maryland assistant medical examiner and one of his investigators were approached by two men posing as FBI agents who told them to leave the case alone. Shortly thereafter they were killed in a traffic accident."

The president was livid. "Why the hell wasn't I told about this?"

Anderson shrugged his shoulders and said, "I assume you'll have to ask Director Vaile that."

"Get him over here right now," ordered Rutledge. "And after I get to the bottom of this with him, I want to talk to Geoff. We absolutely cannot let that story run."

"Do you still want me to assemble the NSC?"

The president thought about it for a moment and replied. "I want the confirmation on Najib directly from Vaile. Then I'll decide what our next move should be."

The chief of staff nodded and disappeared.

Once he was gone, Rutledge drilled his thumbs into his temples. He could feel a monster migraine coming on. Things were spinning so wildly out of control that they were starting to fly off the track. He didn't want to even think of what might happen next. Deep down, though, he knew that things were going to get much worse before they even had a prayer of getting better.

CHAPTER 72

On Twelfth Street, just south of Logan Circle, Harvath doubled back once more to make sure he wasn't being followed and then crossed the street and entered the bank.

The bank officer was professional and polite. After checking Harvath's ID and signature, she gestured for him to follow her to the vault that contained the safe-deposit boxes.

Harvath produced his key and in a synchronous fashion that he felt certain was designed to impress, the bank officer followed his lead, inserted her key, and turned it at exactly the same moment as if they were about to unleash a nuclear weapon.

Once the box was withdrawn, he was shown to a small, private room where the door was shut behind him and he was left alone.

Harvath lifted the lid off the box and removed the

normal things one would expect to find—stock certificates, bonds, and legal papers. Beneath them was what Harvath had really come for.

As he stared at the items, he felt a strange sense of reluctant contentment for having had the foresight to be prepared for such an event. Actually, who was he kidding? It wasn't foresight. He was just practical. His own government had turned on him repeatedly. What prompted him to keep the stash of items was a keen instinct for survival, plain and simple.

There had been the president's kidnapping years ago, the more recent setup in Iraq with Al Jazeera, and now this. Each time the people he served had left him on the outside looking in. They had branded him a criminal and now, a traitor.

He had always known he was expendable. It was part of the territory, but to lump his family and friends in that category was unacceptable.

Every time he'd been forced to the outside, Harvath had had to muscle his way back in. He'd had to make the powers that be see that he was right and that they were wrong. This time, though, he didn't know if things were that black-and-white. He wasn't going to just sit back while someone stalked the people in his life. And for the first time ever, Harvath thought he might actually burn for what he was doing.

He'd always been about doing the right thing. He had pursued the correct course of action repeatedly throughout his career, often at his own peril, but with the knowledge that as long as he did what he felt was right, he'd be able to look at himself in the mirror and that was all that mattered.

Now, he was confronting something new—two versions of what was right: the president's version and his own. The decision Harvath had to make, though, went much deeper than simply what was right. It was about protecting the people he cared about who had been put in harm's way for no reason other than their love or friendship with him.

In Scot Harvath's mind, there could be no bigger betrayal, no larger disloyalty than to allow these innocents to be harmed. Whatever the cost to himself, he had to stop that from happening.

CHAPTER 73

Harvath gathered the things he needed from his safe-deposit box and left the bank.

As he stepped outside, his eyes rapidly scanned everything—rooftops, parked cars, the people on the street. The president had put an Omega Team on his trail, and Harvath knew that they would use all necessary means to stop him.

The team could be anywhere at this point, and he needed to be prepared for what he would do if they found him.

Harvath made it back to his SUV without incident and headed northwest out of D.C. As he drove, he removed another cell phone from the bag on the backseat and dialed.

He wanted to check on his mother and Tracy, but it was too risky. If the CIA was looking for him, they'd be watching for calls that came in to either of the hospitals. Instead, he dialed the outside access number for his BlackBerry's voicemail system to check for messages.

There were several from Gary Lawlor. Having just spoken with him, Harvath deleted them. The only other message was from Ron Parker. He was urging Harvath to call as soon as possible and left a different number than usual to contact him.

Harvath punched the digits into the phone and waited. The quality of the ringing changed halfway through and it sounded as if the call was being routed. Harvath started to grow uneasy. If the CIA had used Tim Finney's pilots as well as Rick Morrell against him who might be next?

Realizing that any CIA interference would be virtually undetectable, he decided against hanging up. A moment later, Parker answered.

"Are you someplace safe?" he said.

"Safe enough for now," replied Harvath. "Is this line secure?"

"Our mutual fly-fishing friend set it up. As long as we stay away from specifics, I think we'll be okay."

Harvath knew immediately what Parker was talking about. Tom Morgan had set up the communication link and the need to stay away from specifics was because as good as Morgan was, the CIA and NSA were better. If they wanted Harvath bad enough, which apparently they did, the CIA and NSA could have programmed the Echelon eavesdropping system to monitor all calls for certain keywords relating to Harvath and what he was embroiled in.

Therefore, Harvath needed to choose his words very carefully. "Did you know about the change of plans on my trip home?"

"Not until after you had already deplaned. If we had known, we would have told you."

Harvath knew Parker well enough to know that he was telling him the truth. "How'd they find out?"

"They learned about our little trip south of the border. But not until you were already on your way back from overseas. How'd everything work out?"

"It was quite enlightening. Apparently our little buddy has not been completely forthcoming."

"About what?" asked Parker.

"His list was light by one name."

"Do you think it was a mistake?"

Harvath laughed. "Not a chance. He knew what he was doing. We just need to find out why."

There was a long pause before Parker responded. "We need to talk."

Those four words had never meant anything good when uttered to him by a woman, and Harvath felt even less confident about their being anything but a prelude to bad news right now. "What's up?" he asked.

"All of our contracts have been canceled," said Parker.

"*Canceled?* What are you talking about?"

"We received calls from our special clients back east and they all invoked the same cancellation clause. No discussion, no explanation."

Harvath didn't know what to say. The contracts for Site Six and the Sargasso Program were their bread and butter. They represented a tremendous amount of money. "I guess that's the big boys' subtle way of telling you that I'm persona non grata."

"Actually," replied Parker. "It wasn't so subtle. One of the larger dogs in the five-sided kennel called to let us know that all of the contracts could be immediately reinstated."

"If you only agreed to sever all ties with me."

"Pretty much."

Harvath didn't like having put his friends in this position. They'd already done more than enough for him. With the Pentagon offering them a way out, Harvath decided he'd make it easy on them. "Thank your boss for everything and tell him to consider all contacts between us severed."

"You can thank him yourself. He told them all to go to hell."

That was very much like Finney. With all the betrayals Harvath had suffered lately, it was nice to know he still had some real, true friends, which was all the more reason not to let Finney devastate the business he'd worked so hard to build and so loved operating. "He's a charmer. He'll bring them around."

"What about you?"

"I'm going to finish what these people started," said Harvath.

"They can cancel our contracts, but they can't stop us from helping you."

"Yes, they can. The contracts are only the tip of the iceberg. The pressure only gets more intense as your heads get pushed beneath the water. You guys don't want that. You've already helped me a ton and I'm grateful for it."

Parker didn't like being cut out of the loop any more than Harvath. "So we won't actively do anything else unless you ask us. The babysitters will remain in place, though, and that's not an item open for discussion."

Harvath smiled. "I appreciate that." It was good to know that Tracy and his mother would continue to be looked after.

"If you change your mind about additional help," continued Parker, "you've got my number. In the meantime, I've got a couple of housekeeping items for you. They're not much, but they should help sharpen your focus a bit. I'll drop them off shortly."

"Thanks," replied Harvath, who knew that Parker was referring to the internet-based electronic dead drop they had developed in case they needed to communicate while Harvath was away from Elk Mountain. Considering recent developments, he was glad they'd established it.

"Anything else we can do?" asked Parker.

"There is one thing," replied Harvath.

"Name it."

"I need you guys to help me arrange a tee time."

CHAPTER 74

The Congressional Country Club was one of the most exclusive country clubs in the nation. Opened in 1924, its Blue and Gold courses had been later redesigned by Rees Jones, with the Blue course repeatedly named one of the country's hundred best.

The course was a challenging tableau of rolling green hills and tall trees. It embodied the best characteristics of the world's finest courses and was the only thing demanding enough to take James Vaile's mind off the crap that went along with his job as director of the Central Intelligence Agency.

He had a standing Sunday tee time, which he kept even more religiously than Sunday services at Holy Trinity in Georgetown. It was like therapy, and he truly believed it was one of the few things that kept him both sane and civilized in an undoubtedly insane and uncivilized world.

The Congressional Country Club was the playground of Washington's elected aristocracy, and Vaile found it invigorating to be treading the same links that William Howard Taft, Woodrow Wilson, Warren G. Harding, Calvin Coolidge, Herbert Hoover, and Dwight D. Eisenhower had.

The eighteenth hole of the Blue course was normally Vaile's favorite. The view from the tee alone was incredible, as it looked toward the rear of one of the most majestic and imposing clubhouses in the world.

The drive itself took all the concentration Vaile could muster. From the elevated box, it was 190 yards over water. If you were lucky, your ball landed on the peninsula-like green and rolled to the edge of the cup, or better yet straight in.

Today, lady luck was not smiling on the DCI. Still upset over the ass-chewing he'd received from the president and having serious doubts about whether his people would be able to recapture Harvath, Vaile air-mailed his first shot well over the green. He still couldn't believe that Rutledge thought he might have had a hand in the deaths of the Maryland ME and his investigator girlfriend. Though the accident was certainly convenient, neither Vaile nor any of his agents had anything to do with it. The idiot had just blown through a red light.

Even so, the president wanted the reporter from the *Baltimore Sun* taken care of. How the hell Vaile was supposed to do that was anybody's guess, especially as Rutledge had made it crystal clear that no harm was to come to the man.

With two of the five Gitmo terrorists dead, the biggest point of contention between the president and the DCI was what they should do next. Rutledge was all but convinced that a carefully worded Homeland Security directive needed to be sent to all law enforcement agencies about the possibility of an attack on American school buses. Vaile, though, still had his doubts and fell back on many of the same arguments that he had made before.

One thing was certain, there was no way any alert could go out with the threat of the *Baltimore Sun* article looming. It would throw everything that the president did from that point forward into question. His credibility would be severely undermined, and every single terrorism directive that came out of Washington would be second-guessed to death.

Vaile already had the beginnings of a plan in the works and welcomed the opportunity for a little peace and quiet out on the links. Many of his best break-throughs came when he simply quieted his mind and concentrated on his game.

Though the DCI tried valiantly to do just that, his next drive was what was known in golf parlance as an "elephant's ass"—high and stinky. It came up short and rolled down the shaved embankment into a watery grave.

"Except for the distance and the direction," quipped Vaile's golfing buddy, "that was a pretty good shot."

Vaile wasn't in the mood. He tee'd up one more, just to prove that he could put it on the green, which he did. It was his putting, though, that proved to be his final undoing.

It should have been a tap-in, but Vaile ended up four-jacking the hole. He was a man of considerable temper, and it took everything he had not to break his club over his knee. Vaile's chum couldn't decide what he found funnier, three shots off the tee to get to the green, or four putts to get the ball into the hole.

As the man wound up to bust his friend's chops once more, Vaile looked at his watch and informed him that he needed to be on his way. The pair shook hands and Vaile's foul mood notwithstanding, the DCI promised to pick up lunch after their game next week. The CIA director then disappeared toward the clubhouse with his protective detail in tow.

Hitting the locker room, all Vaile wanted to do was take a short steam before heading back to his office in Langley. He prayed to God no one would recognize him, or if they did that they would have the good social grace to leave him the hell alone.

Stripping out of his clothes, Vaile grabbed a towel and headed toward the steam room. His security detail was familiar with his routine and wouldn't expect him to exit the locker room for at least a half hour.

Though he wasn't crazy about his people seeing him naked, the real reason Vaile had them wait for him outside was that he just needed time alone. Being the director of the Central Intelligence Agency was hard enough; being constantly surrounded by bodyguards because so many nutjobs wanted him dead only made it harder. Sometimes, even if it was only for half an hour on Sundays, James Vaile wanted to forget who he was and just be anonymous for a while. And considering the day he was already having, he could use a little escape time more than ever.

Yanking open the door to the steam room, the DCI was greeted with a heavy cloud of thick mist scented with eucalyptus. He grabbed a seat on the lowest tier of the white-tiled benches and listened for the beautiful music of the door clicking shut.

When it did, his body began to relax. For the next few minutes he was completely cut off from the outside world, enveloped in blissful silence.

Vaile leaned back and closed his eyes. He was finally alone.

His mind began to drift, but as soon as it did, his thoughts were interrupted.

"That was one of the ugliest games I've ever seen played in my life," said a voice from one of the benches above him.

Vaile was a well-known figure at the club, and he wasn't surprised that his play had been noticed. Still, he had to fight back the urge to tell the hazy figure sitting above him what he could do with his opinions. Vaile simply wanted to tune everything out.

"This hasn't been one of my best days," he replied, his voice trailing off—a clear signal that he didn't feel like talking.

"You can say that again," replied the man as he leaned forward and cocked his pistol.

CHAPTER 75

Despite the intense heat of the steam room, Vaile's body turned to ice. "Who are you?" he demanded. "What do you want?"

"You'll forgive me, director," said the voice, "if I save us both time and ask the questions."

"My security people are——"

"Not even in the locker room and won't expect to see you for a little while still."

Vaile recognized the man's voice but couldn't place it, at least not right away. "I know you."

Harvath came down off the upper bench and took a seat next to the DCI.

When the curtain of fog parted, Vaile couldn't believe his eyes. "Harvath. Are you crazy? Aren't things bad enough for you? Now you pull a gun on the director of the CIA?"

"First," responded Harvath, "I don't see how things could get much worse for me. And second, I didn't pull a gun on you, I cocked one that wasn't even pointed in your direction."

"I'll make sure to note that subtlety when I report this meeting to the president."

"I know we're in a steam room, but let's not jerk each other off, okay?"

"Listen," replied Vaile, "we both know what this is about. The president was forced to make a deal with the devil and——"

"*And* the people I care about are the ones who are paying for it."

"We had no idea things were going to turn out this way."

Harvath was ready to punch the DCI's lights out. "But now that they have, I don't see anybody doing a hell of a lot to stop it."

"You don't know the first thing about what we're doing," snapped Vaile.

"What do you mean, *we?*"

"The president asked me to put a covert team on the case."

"He assigned a CIA team inside the United States?" asked Harvath. "In addition to the FBI?"

Vaile held up his palms. "The president wanted hefty counterterrorism experience on this and that's what I gave him."

"But they haven't made much progress, have they?"

Vaile didn't bother responding. It was painfully obvious that his people hadn't made much progress.

"Were Morrell and his Omega Team in charge of that too?"

The DCI shook his head. "No. We fielded a separate team. I picked them myself. They're all solid operators with Spec Ops experience, there's just not enough for them to go on."

Harvath shook his head. "And you saved Rick Morrell for the real dirty work so that you could use our friendship against me, didn't you?"

"It was the fastest way to get the information we needed."

"I should have known better."

The DCI took a deep breath and then let it out. "Scot, negotiating with these terrorists was a bad choice, but it was the only choice the president had. We weren't going to let these animals kill American kids. And we're still not. That's why you've got to turn yourself in."

It wasn't an easy call. Harvath didn't want to provoke terrorist attacks on American children, but the fact that Vaile's people hadn't made any progress in catching the person responsible for hunting his loved ones only served to reinforce his decision. "I'm not stopping until I nail this fucker."

"Even if it means you're putting countless American lives on the line?"

Harvath was tempted to tell the DCI what he'd learned from Tammam Al-Tal in Jordan—that his operative, Najib, had been sprung from Gitmo in exchange for Al-Tal relinquishing his contract on Harvath, but at this point he was in no mood to share intelligence with anyone, especially the director of the CIA. Instead he said, "Whoever this guy is, he came looking for me. I didn't start this."

"Either way," replied Vaile, "the president gave his word that we wouldn't go after these men once they were released from Guantanamo."

"One of them has attacked *Americans* on *American* soil. That right there should invalidate any deal the president made. As far as I'm concerned, these five shouldn't be handed a *get out of jail free* card for the rest of their lives."

"I agree with you," said the DCI. "They shouldn't, but there's only one left now."

Harvath didn't understand. "One?"

"You killed Palmera and Najib, and we've recently located two others."

"Which two?" asked Harvath. "Where are they?"

"Morocco and Australia," said Vaile. "They're under surveillance and are very close to being picked up by those countries for engaging in terrorist activity *since* their release from Gitmo. Which leaves—"

"The fifth detainee released that night. The Frenchman."

CHAPTER 76

The DCI nodded. "His name is Philippe Roussard. A sniper by training, he was also known as Juba. Before we caught him, he'd made quite a name for himself in Iraq; over one hundred confirmed kills of American service personnel."

"That's who's killing my friends and family?" responded Harvath, searching his memory banks for the names and coming up empty.

Vaile nodded again.

Harvath's anger was rising once more. "I can't fucking believe this. You know who the hell this guy is and still you're not doing anything to nail his ass to the wall."

Vaile didn't want to get into a pissing match with Harvath, so he changed the subject. "Did you know that I had a nephew who was killed in Iraq?"

"No, I didn't," replied Harvath, trying to get his temper under control. "I'm sorry."

"For obvious reasons, our family and the Marines kept the relationship secret. As it turns out, Roussard was the one who killed him. He had no idea, of course. My nephew was just another infidel crusader to that scumbag; another American notch on his rifle butt.

"Even in death we kept my nephew's relationship to me hidden. The last thing we wanted to do was hand the insurgency such a high-profile victory, especially since Juba, or Roussard, had reached almost mythical status for being untouchable and able to kill anyone he wanted."

".Of course not," said Harvath, sorry for the man's loss, "but at the risk of sounding insensitive, where do I and the people I care about fit into all of this?"

"The name Roussard doesn't ring any bells with you, does it?" asked Vaile.

Harvath shook his head.

"I guess it makes no difference. As long as the president intends to honor his side of the bargain, I have no choice but to bring you in."

"But what if I can get to the people responsible for all of this before you do?"

"Personally," said Vaile as he stood, "I don't think

any of this is about kids, school buses, or conditions at Gitmo. I think somehow it *is* all about you, and I'd like nothing more than for you to hunt down and kill every last one of the people responsible."

There was a long pause in which Harvath sensed there was something else the DCI wanted to say.

A moment later, the man spoke. "But my personal opinions don't really matter much in this case. Professionally, I'm bound to carry out the orders given to me by the president of the United States. I'd recommend you start doing the same, but something tells me we're well beyond the point of that doing any good."

"We are," replied Harvath.

Vaile walked the couple of steps to the steam room door and then, with his hand upon it, turned to look back at Harvath. "In that case, there's something you need to see."

CHAPTER 77

SOMEWHERE OVER THE CARIBBEAN SEA

The flight to Rio should have been restful, but Harvath didn't get a wink of sleep. Vaile had promised to email him Roussard's dossier, but Harvath doubted there'd be much in it of any use.

He still had one slimy little rock to overturn.

Harvath kept thinking about his past in general and one person in particular. Meg Cassidy was the last person he'd been involved with before meeting Tracy.

Brazil was one of those magical places Meg had always wanted to take him to, but Harvath had never been able to find, or never wanted to find, the time to go. As his commercial flight roared south, he thought what an idiot he'd been to lose Meg and how lucky he'd been to find Tracy. If Tracy died, he knew his status as damaged goods would be permanently cast in stone. One was rarely given second chances in life. He'd managed to get his second chance at happiness put on a life support system. It was an ironic metaphor, as his love life had always been in critical condition.

Harvath tried to shake the morbid thoughts, but couldn't. Across the aisle from him was a young, newlywed couple. By the looks of their hand-holding, kissing, and repeated requests for more champagne, they were off to Brazil or points farther afield for their honeymoon.

He hadn't been keeping track of the date at all. Glancing down at his Kobold chronograph, he realized Meg Cassidy's wedding was just days away. He made a mental note to contact Gary to ask him to arrange a special security detail for her, effective immediately. While he and Meg were no longer romantically involved, Harvath still cared deeply for her and wouldn't want to see anything happen to her, especially because of him.

Lawlor had gotten to know Meg very well and

liked her immensely. The president had also grown quite fond of her and visited her summer cottage each year when he vacationed in Lake Geneva, Wisconsin.

Meg had done her country an invaluable service in helping Harvath to track down the heirs to Abu Nidal's terrorist organization several years ago. Lawlor would have no problem getting President Rutledge to agree to assigning her a special detail for the next few days.

That was the window of time Harvath was most worried about. Despite the attack on New York, the last Harvath had heard the president was still planning on attending Meg's wedding. Security would be beyond tight at that point. It was the run-up he was concerned about.

Like Tracy, Meg was an amazing woman. Though it had probably created more than a little friction between her and her fiancé, Meg had sent Harvath an invitation.

When it had arrived, the beautifully engraved note card had hit him like a hammer in the center of his chest. He'd never realized it, but it became apparent at that moment that he still carried a torch for Meg and harbored a hidden desire that things might one day work out between them. Seeing the invitation with her name and that of her fiancé, made him realize that some sort of spontaneous reconciliation cast down from the gods was no longer a possibility.

Not knowing how to reply to the invitation, Harvath simply set it aside and politely changed the subject the one time the president brought it up.

Now, speeding ever closer to Brazil—a country
Meg had been so passionate about having him visit—
Harvath couldn't help but think of her and also of
himself. God, was he really that screwed up? It seemed
like everything he touched turned to dust.

There was a part of Harvath that wondered, just
for a moment, if when the plane landed he should
simply disappear into the wilds of Brazil, never to be
seen again.

CHAPTER 78

RIO DE JANEIRO, BRAZIL

It was in the low seventies when Harvath stepped
off the plane at Rio's Antonio Carlos Jobim
International Airport. His sense of purpose had
returned and his earlier desire to disappear into the
wilds of Brazil faded. He was anxious to get to
work.

Using the false passport he'd removed from his
safe-deposit box in D.C., he cleared customs and
passport control as a German national by the name
of Hans Brauner. The passport was invaluable.
Not only did it allow him to travel without being
tracked by any American intelligence agencies, but
traveling as an EU national allowed him to enter
Brazil without a visa, something he wouldn't have

been able to do had he been traveling on an American passport.

Bypassing the RDE taxi desk, he headed straight to the Rio de Janeiro State Tourism desk and bought a prepaid taxi voucher. The last thing he needed right now was to deal with one of the city's notoriously unscrupulous cab drivers.

After sliding into a cab and giving the driver his destination, Harvath leaned his head back and closed his eyes. He'd been on planes or switching between them for the last eleven hours. He was looking forward to checking into his hotel and getting a shower, as well as a little sleep, but there was work to do first.

The driver took the Linha Vermelha road toward the city. His speeding and lane changing were perfectly choreographed to the local Funk Carioca music pumping out of the boom box taped to his elaborately decorated dashboard.

The American Express office was located beneath the Copacabana Palace Hotel on Avenida Atlântica directly across from the world-famous Copacabana Beach.

Getting out of the cab, Harvath turned his back on the blue-green waters and scantily clad bronzed bodies and headed inside. He used a house phone to contact the American Express office to inquire whether his FedEx package had arrived yet. It had.

After checking in at the front desk and getting his key, he headed down to Amex to retrieve his parcel. He changed a few thousand dollars into

Reais and then returned to the lobby where he asked the concierge to organize a helicopter tour for him.

Up in his room, Harvath tossed the FedEx box onto the bed and dropped his bag near the desk. He walked over to the windows, drew back the sheer curtains, and opened them up. Placing his palms against the sill, he leaned outside.

The view was amazing. The four-kilometer-long beach was covered with people. The salty smell of the ocean poured into the room. Looking at the waves as they crashed upon the beach, Harvath was almost sorry he hadn't brought a bathing suit.

Pulling his head back inside, he crossed to the bathroom and started the shower. After hanging up his clothes, he climbed in and lost all track of time as he let the hot water pound against his body.

Normally, he would have finished his shower by turning the water all the way to cold—a maneuver he found even more refreshing than a cup of espresso—but not today. Today he needed to get caught up on his sleep.

Standing on the soft bathmat, he dried off and then headed for the king-sized bed. He put a *do-not-disturb* on the phone, drew back the sheets, and lay down.

Closing his eyes, he listened to the music of the cars and beachgoers below as he plunged into sleep.

CHAPTER 79

Harvath awoke with a start, and it took him a few moments to realize where he was. He'd been having the nightmare again.

His body was clammy with sweat and his heart was pounding a mile a minute. Though he'd been asleep for several hours, he actually felt worse than when he'd first lain down.

It didn't make a difference. He was awake now and knew that he wouldn't be able to fall back asleep until later on in the evening.

Harvath got back into the shower and this time finished by throwing the water lever all the way to cold.

He shaved and changed into the one clean set of clothes he'd brought along with him. Next he picked up the phone and called down to the concierge. His helicopter tour was all arranged for the next morning, and the helicopter company was even sending a private car to pick him up. Harvath thanked the concierge and after asking directions to the closest pharmacy, he hung up the phone.

The pharmacy wasn't far, and after picking up what he needed for the next day, he returned to his room, opened up the small laptop he'd purchased before leaving D.C., and logged on to the internet. It took him an hour before he was comfortable with the safeguards he'd built to avoid detection. He'd used numerous proxy servers as well as several shareware encryption programs that were actually quite good. If the CIA or anyone else tried to pinpoint his location, they'd have a very hard time.

Harvath logged on to the account he'd given Vaile for this purpose and opened the email. Most of the file had been sterilized, but the highlights were all there. The first things Harvath looked at were the photos of Philippe Roussard.

Harvath was pretty good with names, and he was incredible with faces. Though there was something familiar about the man, Harvath was positive he'd never met him before in his life.

So, if it wasn't Roussard who was out for Harvath, it had to be the people behind him; the people who had gotten him released from Gitmo. He continued to read through the Frenchman's jacket for the next hour, but nothing leaped out at him. As far as Harvath was concerned, there wasn't a single clue in there that could prove useful—other than the actual photos of the man's face.

According to Vaile's email, Carolyn Leonard and Kate Palmer, who were both in very serious condition, had identified Roussard as the man who had offered them the tainted perfume at Tysons Galleria on Saturday. Unfortunately, Emily Hawkins was in no condition to answer any questions at this point, but Harvath already knew that she would ID him too. So would his mother, he realized with a sharp pang, if and when her eyesight returned. In short, having the photos was a start, but a much too slow one.

Harvath logged on to the gmail account he'd established with Ron Parker and Tim Finney and opened the message waiting for him in the draft folder. It started off with a brief recap of everything Parker had already told him, along with a caution not to try to reach either of them on their cell phones as both of them believed they were being monitored. The same went for text messaging or any of their normal email accounts.

There was an intelligence brief from Tom Morgan that backed up what Vaile had said about the Moroccan and Australian terrorists' having been recently put under surveillance in their home countries. Based on the timeline, they could not have been involved in the attacks back in the United States.

Harvath uploaded the pictures of Roussard, as well as the salient details from his dossier, and asked Finney to make sure the security details watching over Tracy and his mother were given copies.

As Parker knew, Harvath would be concerned about contacting the hospitals directly, he provided cell numbers for the men watching his mother and Tracy, if he wanted to safely get updates that way.

After Harvath finished reading the balance of the message, he deleted it and logged off the account. Surfing to one of the multiple VoIP, or Voice over Internet Protocol accounts, he had, Harvath downloaded the necessary software to his computer, plugged in the headset from his BlackBerry, and called his mother's security detail in Southern California.

He spoke briefly with the man who answered,

who assured him the coast was clear before closing the door and handing the phone to Harvath's mother.

They talked for about ten minutes and then Harvath explained to her that he had to go. He promised he'd call her back as soon as he could.

Next, he called Tracy's team. The lead detail agent explained that while Tracy's parents were relatively polite, it was obvious they didn't want them there. Harvath thanked the man for what he and his colleagues were doing. Tracy's parents might not be crazy about all the muscle hanging around the ICU, but if anything happened, they'd be darn glad to have them there.

As Harvath had with the team on the West Coast, he gave the team leader a physical description and a full rundown on Philippe Roussard and told him to expect photographs from Finney and Parker soon.

The guard passed his phone to Tracy's father, Bill. It was an awkward conversation. There was nothing new to report on Tracy's condition. They'd run several more tests, but unless they could wean her off the ventilator, there was no way they could perform an MRI. As it was now, her EEG showed significantly reduced brainwave activity, which the neurology team felt was an indication of permanent brain damage.

The lack of progress didn't surprise Harvath, but it still wasn't what he'd hoped to hear. He spoke briefly with Tracy's mother, Barbara, and then asked if she'd hold the phone up to Tracy's ear for a couple of minutes.

When he was sure the phone was in place, he began speaking. Soon he forgot all about the fatigue that had worked its way into every corner of his body. All he cared about was Tracy and being strong for her. He told her how much he loved her and how much he was looking forward to her getting out of the hospital so that they could pick up where they had left off.

He ran through all the things they were going to do together—the fishing trip to Jackson Hole, Tracy's favorite pastime of seeing the fall colors in New England, and going to Greece, where Harvath couldn't wait to introduce her to the islands of Paros and Antiparos, as well as all his friends.

Finally, Harvath ran out of things to say. Some people might have been ashamed by it, but he and Tracy had realized early on that it was a sign of their compatibility. They were able to enjoy being with each other without saying anything at all.

He told her once more that he loved her and reminded her that she was one of the greatest warriors he knew. She needed to remain strong. She was fighting for her life and she'd make it as long as she remained focused on nothing short of complete and total recovery.

Whether she could hear him, he had no idea. Harvath liked to think she could. He had read enough articles about coma patients to believe that many of them could hear and comprehend what was being said to them. If nothing else, it was a sign of how much he loved and respected her. As long as she was drawing breath, even if it was with the assistance of a machine, he was going to treat her the same way he'd always treated her.

When Tracy's mother took the phone back, Harvath said good night to her and hung up.

Dialing room service, Harvath ordered dinner. Tomorrow was going to be a rough day, and he was going to need every ounce of strength he could muster.

CHAPTER 80

The sleek Mercedes sedan dropped Harvath at the heliport, where a bright blue Colibri EC 120B helicopter was ready and waiting for him.

After a look at the maps he'd pulled and a discussion of what Harvath wanted, the pilot nodded, gave Harvath the thumbs-up, and helped stow his gear.

They buckled themselves in, placed their headsets on, and the pilot fired up the sweeping rotors. Minutes later they were airborne.

He flew them over Corcovado Mountain with the towering statue of Christ, the Cristo Redentor with its enormous outstretched arms. There was something about it that reminded Harvath of Atlas, holding up the earth.

Harvath supposed there were parallels between Christ and Atlas. Judeo-Christian values were one of the few things holding up the modern civilized world against the barbaric hordes of Muslim extremists.

Harvath had to laugh to himself. The term Muslim extremist was starting to wear on him. It was PC-speak, something he loathed in others and absolutely despised in himself. The term was meant to draw a distinction between good Muslims and bad, but as far as he was concerned every single day that good Muslims did absolutely nothing about the atrocities being committed in their name, the line between good Muslim and bad Muslim became even more blurred.

All that was necessary for evil to triumph was for good people to do nothing. Harvath saw it every day, and he was determined that his nation would not be overrun by Islam. The French were already a lost cause and many other nations were following suit by allowing Islamic courts of law, banning historically significant symbols, icons, and pastimes as innocent as coed swimming to appease their rapidly growing and ever more vociferous Muslim minorities. Multiculturalism was bullshit. It was political correctness run amok and it made him sick. If these people wanted things to be exactly as they were in their countries of origin, why didn't they just remain there?

Many of Harvath's opinions may have sounded xenophobic, but he'd earned the right to them. He'd been on the front lines of the war on terror and had seen what the extremists were capable of. Radical Islam was as much about carefully and deliberately applied creativity and ideas as it was about bombs and bullets.

In America, expertly organized cells of so called "moderate Muslims" were waging an ideological jihad, working to undermine everything that the country stood for. They were a patient and determined enemy bent upon turning the nation into the United States of Islam, and many people responsible for protecting America were not paying attention.

Between the tidal wave of illegal immigration and the radical Islamic agenda in America, there were times Harvath felt like weeping for his nation.

They flew over Guanabara Bay and the Pão de Açúcar. The pilot then buzzed both Copacabana and Ipanema beaches before putting the chopper on course for their ultimate destination, the bay of Angra dos Reis forty-five minutes south of Rio by air.

They passed some incredible scenery along the way, most of it coastal villages and thick, lush forests. The ocean sparkled like countless shards of broken glass while enormous superyachts plowed through the water leaving foamy white trails of phosphorescence in their wakes.

It was absolutely pristine and Harvath was developing a keen appreciation for why so many people fell so in love with Brazil.

As they neared the Bay of Angra dos Reis, some forty-odd minutes later, the pilot brought the helicopter so low to the water its skis were almost touching the tops of the waves. Harvath had to look at him twice to make sure he wasn't the same cab driver who had brought him in from the airport the day before.

Like the quick tour upon takeoff of Rio's most scenic sights, this little trick was probably meant as a way for the pilot to endear himself to his clients in order to get an extra-big tip. Harvath didn't care for the man's acrobatics and told him to knock it off. Helicopters drew enough attention as it was.

Sufficiently cowed, the pilot increased his altitude and proceeded as instructed.

From the satellite footage he had studied, Harvath knew that the island the Troll had rented for himself was particularly small. Nevertheless, he wanted to get as close a look at it as he could.

Since an overhead hover was definitely out of the question, Harvath had opted for a straight traverse at a relatively good clip. He'd have to process a lot of information in a short period of time, but it was the only way he could see the island with his own eyes from above without drawing the suspicion of its current inhabitant.

Angra was composed of 365 different islands. The pilot pointed to a tiny speck of land on the near horizon. As they got closer, Harvath studied his map, along with the size and shape of the other islands around the Troll's, and realized the pilot was correct.

He took it from exactly the approach Harvath had asked for. Leaning against the door, Harvath strained to take in as much of it as he could, burning the entire picture into his mind—the main building and its cottages, the helipad, the speedboat at the dock, the shape and layout of the island, all of it.

He'd be coming back tonight, but by then it would be very dark, and the darkness would only contribute to the danger of what he planned to do.

CHAPTER 81

James Vaile's tenure at the CIA had not been marked by a particularly good relationship with the press. The devastating stories about the CIA's secret prisons abroad and how the United States tracked terrorists through their banking habits still weighed heavily on him. And while the stories had come from asinine members of his own agency who put their dislike of the president's policies above their loyalty to their country, all of his attempts to prevent those stories from being run had failed.

He had quickly learned that many newspapers had far more pride in their circulation than they did in their patriotism. That they were hobbling America and empowering her terrorist enemies made absolutely no difference to them. It was no wonder he held out little hope for being able to appeal to Mark Sheppard as an American.

If patriotism couldn't motivate a reporter, sometimes he or she could be swayed by a promise of an exclusive on an even bigger story. But as in the cases of the secret prisons and the terrorist banking programs, Vaile didn't have anything bigger to bargain with. He was going to have to find another way, and he'd have to do it in such a way that the *Baltimore Sun* reporter had no idea that the CIA was involved.

One of the first things Vaile did was to look into the man's background. He'd met very few people in his life who didn't have at least one skeleton in their closet. Unfortunately, though, Sheppard was clean. In fact, he was beyond clean. The man was practically a saint. Outside of a couple of speeding tickets back when he was in college, the reporter hadn't so much as crossed against a light or faked the throw at an unmanned toll both.

Scanning his extracurricular activities, Vaile was further disenchanted as he discovered Sheppard donated a significant portion of his time helping underprivileged children throughout the Metropolitan Baltimore area. He even sat on one organization's board.

Though Vaile didn't want to do it, he quickly realized the only way to dissuade Sheppard from running his story was to threaten to go nuclear on him. If he didn't cooperate, nothing would be left of the man's former life but scorched earth.

A few hours later, once it was confirmed that everything was in place, the DCI picked up his phone and made the call.

The reporter picked up the phone on the first ring. "Mark Sheppard," he sang, coming off a bit too eager. The DCI wondered if the journalist had already cleared space on his desk for his Pulitzer.

Any reporter worth his salt would have a recording device hooked up to his phone, so in addition to making sure his call was untraceable, James Vaile employed a new piece of technology that would

render any recording inaudible when played back. He
also used a modulator to disguise his voice. One could
never be too careful, and what's more, the computerized voice carried with it an added gravitas that often
had a very unsettling affect on the receiving party.
"Mr. Sheppard, we need to talk," he said.

There was a pause as the reporter fiddled around
for his *record* button, and then he said, "Who am I
speaking with?"

"Who I am is not as important as what I have to
say."

"How do I know you're for real then?"

"You called the White House press office for
comment on a story you want to run," said Vaile via
the deep, computerized voice.

"And from what I'm hearing," said Sheppard, "I'm
going to guess that you've called to scare me into
burying it."

"I've called to give you a chance to do the right
thing."

"Really? What would that be?"

"There are serious national security issues at play
here, which you don't understand."

"So as a patriotic American, I should kill the article, right? Forget it. I don't buy it."

Vaile decided to give the man one more chance.
"Mr. Sheppard, the people of Charleston needed closure on that bus hijacking and closure was provided."

The reporter stifled a laugh. "So the U.S. government is now in the business of making crime victims
and their families feel better? Tens of thousands of

crimes go unsolved every year. What makes this one so special?"

"This was a particularly heinous crime against children—" began Vaile before he was interrupted.

"That had national security implications," said Sheppard as his mind put it all together. "Jesus Christ, this wasn't some lone nut job. It was a terrorist act."

CHAPTER 82

A nd you expect me to sit on this?" asked Sheppard.
"Yes," replied Vaile. "Your story would be devastating to the public trust."

This time, the reporter couldn't stifle his laugh. "Well, maybe you should have thought of that before you dreamed this whole thing up."

The DCI was quickly coming to the end of his patience. Before he could say anything, though, Sheppard asked, "Are you going to arrange an accident for me the way you did with Frank Aposhian and Sally Rutherford?"

"For the record, Mr. Sheppard, their deaths *were* an accident. The U.S. government is not in the business of murdering its own citizens."

"Then I have nothing to worry about, do I?"

"That depends on if you're going to cooperate or not."

The reporter had received so many threats over

the years that he didn't spook that easily. "Really? And if I don't?"

"Your story is tentatively entitled 'Invasion of the Body Snatchers'—" began Vaile.

"How the hell do you know that?"

"Shut up and listen," ordered the DCI. "You have it in a password-protected file. The password is *Romero*. Open it."

Sheppard did as he was told. Inside, he saw that a subfolder named *candy cane* had been added. Instinctively, he clicked on it and was greeted by a page of images in thumbnail. He maximized one at random and his breathing stopped.

"You fucking assholes," said the reporter as he realized what they were planning on doing to him. "It'll never work."

"I wouldn't be so sure," said Vaile. "Guilty or not, the stigma of pedophilia is almost impossible to scrub away."

"Good thing I recorded this conversation, then," crowed Sheppard.

Vaile laughed. "I suggest you try to play it back first before you stake your career and the rest of your life on it."

His shockproof bullshit detector was telling him his caller wasn't playing games. "You make me ashamed to be an American," said Sheppard.

"Don't you dare wrap yourself in the flag now," chided the DCI. "You had your chance. We are at war and wars involve secrets. This is about doing the right thing for your country and you passed on it. In spite of that fact, I'm going to give you one more chance."

"What's to stop me from deleting them?" asked Sheppard, sounding determined to remain faithful to his journalistic integrity, but already losing his resolve.

"You can't delete these images. Even if you could, there are more on both your laptop and desktop at home. We also have several convicted pedophiles who are willing to testify to numerous unsavory proclivities of yours. It's a hole so deep you'll never climb out of it.

"The newspaper will be the first to distance itself from you. Your body snatcher story will never see the light of day. You'll be absolutely discredited. Next, your friends will disappear and even your family will start to fade away. And then there are all those children you so nobly mentored. You think anything you ever said or taught them will matter after they all figure out the only reason you were there was to get in their pants? Probably not, but that won't be the end of your problems.

"A conviction on the child porn discovered on your computers and in your house will be a slam dunk. You'll go to prison, and as you're a crime reporter, I don't need to tell you what they do to guys in your situation. Once the rumors get around that you're a pedophile who pled to lesser charges of possession of child porn for a reduced sentence, if you're not killed in the first couple of days, they'll make your life such hell that you'll wish you were dead."

Sheppard had sat through the entire diatribe

stunned. They had him. It was disgusting, but there
was absolutely nothing he could do. His mind raced
for answers, but he knew his only option was capitula-
tion. Finally, he asked, "What do you want me to do?"

Vaile instructed him to gather any and all of the
materials he'd assembled in putting together his story,
including his notes, photographs, and tape recordings,
and bring them in a small duffel bag to an abandoned
warehouse just outside D.C.

Three hours later, the DCI contacted the president and shared with him the good news. After dig-
ging a bit deeper, the reporter from the *Baltimore Sun*
had discovered that his sources were not as reliable as
he had originally thought. Subsequently, he had decided not to pursue his story.

Jack Rutledge was relieved to hear it. That was
one problem down. Now, they needed to refocus all of
their resources on stopping Harvath.

CHAPTER 83

Angra dos Reis, Brazil

Even in the limited moonlight, Harvath's small
boat appeared more to hover than float atop the
amazingly clear water.

He slipped the anchor quietly beneath the surface
and slowly played out the rope. When the boat was

secure, he gave his gear one last check and slipped over the side.

Harvath swam with the confidence of a man who'd spent all of his life near an ocean. His strong, sure strokes propelled him forward through the warm waters of Angra dos Reis Bay.

With a set of night vision goggles and a specially illuminated compass, he navigated his way through the darkness toward the private island known as Algodão.

On the leeward side, he low-crawled out of the water and unclipped from around his waist the rope that he'd used to pull a small dry bag behind him.

From the bag, Harvath removed the 9mm Beretta pistol that he had sent to himself via FedEx priority international shipping.

Harvath checked the weapon and then set it aside as he removed a change of clothes and got dressed. He pulled out a flashlight, his Benchmade Auto Axis folding knife, some Flexicuffs, and a few other items and shoved them into his pockets. He buried his swim gear near a large rock on the beach and checked the remaining contents of his dry bag.

The dogs the Troll kept were one of his biggest concerns. Since rescuing one of them in Gibraltar, he had done a little research on them. Caucasian Ovcharkas were amazing animals—swift, agile, ferocious when need be, and fiercely loyal. It was obvious why they'd been the breed of choice for both the Russian military and the East German border patrol. It was also obvious why the Troll had selected them.

Harvath thought about his own Caucasian

Ovcharka, or rather the poor dog he had asked Emily
Hawkins to take care of while he made up his mind
about what he wanted to do with it. He had a big
problem with keeping a "gift" from a man who'd been
complicit in the slaying of countless Americans,
including one of Scot Harvath's best friends.

To be honest, with Tracy in the hospital and
everything else that had happened, he hadn't really
thought much about the puppy until Gary shared with
him the animal's grisly torture. It was a horrible picture that Harvath forced from his mind. He needed to
focus.

Harvath listened long and hard before slinging the
bag over his shoulder and creeping into the island's
interior. Except for the narrow spits of sand on each
side, the island was nothing but trees and luxuriant
vegetation. The Troll's lair was at the tip of the island,
built outward on stilts above the water.

Harvath had thought hard about how he wanted
to handle the dogs. A tranquilizer gun would have
been the easiest method, but he didn't have one. The
only things he had access to for this trip were those in
his safety-deposit box, as well as a small storage locker
he kept in Alexandria. It wasn't a lot to choose from.

Though he had his Beretta, he didn't have a sound
suppressor for it, and therefore killing the dogs was out
of the question. It would make too much noise. He
had to find another way to incapacitate them. But to
do that, he'd have to isolate them without arousing
suspicion in their master—something easier said than
done.

The dogs were the Troll's own private security force. They never left his side—*except* when they went outside to relieve themselves. That was their moment of greatest vulnerability. And that was when Harvath planned to strike.

Based on satellite imagery he'd studied, Harvath had noticed that the Troll let the animals out a final time around ten o'clock in the evening. It was now just after nine-fifteen, which meant that Harvath had less than forty-five minutes to lay his trap and get himself into position.

Dogs in general, and the Ovcharkas in particular, excelled at night vision and the detection of movement, so it was imperative that Harvath be nowhere near the bait when they came outside.

Opening his dry bag he removed a football-sized object wrapped in paper. He'd had it prepared especially for this situation. It was ten kilograms of freshly ground beef into which Harvath had the butcher in Angra dos Reis grind a kilo of fresh bacon for added irresistibility.

Then, once safely away from shore, Harvath added his own special ingredient, a high-powered laxative from the pharmacy he'd visited in Rio.

Picking his spot now on the narrow trail that led from the Troll's retreat, Harvath divided the meat into two sections and placed them close enough together that the dogs would be able to smell them, but far enough apart so that whichever dog got to the meat first, wouldn't be able to wolf down his portion and then beat his partner to the other.

With the bait set, Harvath stepped into the brush, making sure he stayed downwind as he crept toward the house.

He found a perfect vantage spot among some large boulders near the shoreline. The house glowed with soft lighting and all of its window walls were retracted to let in the evening air. Harvath could hear classical music coming from inside. It was Pachelbel's Canon in D, and he recognized it immediately. It was one of Tracy's favorites. She had it on her iPod and played it on the audio station in his kitchen when she cooked breakfast.

Harvath wondered if she'd been playing it on the morning she was shot.

Drawing his pistol, Harvath pulled back the slide to make sure the weapon was charged and said into the warm night air, "This one will be for you, honey."

CHAPTER 84

Since Harvath hadn't skimped on the drug, it didn't take long for the laxative-laden meat to work its magic. Both dogs began howling almost in unison. The rumbling tearing through their bowels had to have been horrible.

The music was turned off, and Harvath caught his first glimpse of the Troll. It brought the memories of their first encounter in Gibraltar flooding back to him.

The Troll's pure white dogs, which were well over forty-one inches high at the shoulder, towered above the little man. Where the animals had to weigh close to two hundred pounds apiece, the Troll couldn't have weighed more than seventy-five. Harvath placed his height at just under three feet tall. That said, he knew the man's size was absolutely no indication of his cunning.

The Troll opened the front doors of his rustic villa, and the dogs knocked their master out of the way as they tore out of the house. If the Troll had any idea what was wrong with them, he certainly didn't show it. Harvath's guess was that the man had absolutely no idea what was going on. All he knew was that his animals were acting strangely and out of character.

Harvath watched as the Troll followed the dogs outside. It was time.

Stepping out from behind the rocks, Harvath moved quickly up the beach. As he neared the house, he cut around back and hopped a wooden fence that surrounded a lushly planted, open-air bath.

He crossed the fragrant courtyard, and after climbing a small flight of stone steps, entered the house through the wide-open French doors.

Passing through the kitchen area, Harvath dropped a stack of bone-shaped packages on the counter and cupboards and continued in.

Halfway through the living room he noticed a small alcove that must have been used as a reading nook. It had two upholstered chairs, a lamp, and a small side table. Harvath unslung his dry bag, pulled his pistol, and sat down.

To say the Troll was surprised to see him was an understatement. He pulled up short so quickly, he lost his balance. Harvath might have laughed if he hadn't harbored such an intense hatred for the man.

To his credit, the Troll had a very agile mind. Seeing Harvath and his gun, the man summed up the situation very quickly.

"What have you done to my dogs?" he demanded.

"They'll be fine," said Harvath. "It's only temporary."

"You bloody bastard," roared the little man. "How dare you hurt those animals? They have done absolutely nothing to you."

"And I want to keep it that way."

The Troll burned holes into Harvath with his eyes. "So help me. If anything happens to them, I will make it my life's work to see to it that you pay with your very last breath."

His demeanor had switched from agitated, almost panicked, to an icy calm. There was no question that he meant what he said and that he fully believed he could carry out the threat.

"I left two packets in the kitchen," said Harvath, referring to the product known as K-9 Quencher he'd picked up at the same strip mall at which he'd bought his computer before leaving D.C.

"What are they?" asked the Troll, the apprehension obvious in his voice.

"Don't worry. If I'd wanted your dogs dead, they'd be dead. Those packets contain an electrolyte powder specially formulated for rehydrating canines."

"What did you do to them?"

"It's just a laxative. They'll be fine in a few hours. Pour each packet into a bowl of water and leave them outside where the dogs can get to them." As the Troll glared at him, Harvath added, "And make sure you stay where I can see you."

After placing the bowls upon the threshold, the Troll closed the front door, came back to the reading nook, and climbed into the chair next to Harvath. "I knew you'd come for me," he said. "I just didn't think it would be this soon. So this is it, then."

"Maybe," replied Harvath. "It depends on whether you can be of any further use to me."

"So you're not a man of your word after all."

Harvath knew what he was alluding to, but he let the question hang in the air between them.

"You promised I wouldn't be killed," said the Troll in his tainted British accent. His dark hair was cut short and he sported a well-kept beard.

Harvath grinned. "I made that promise to you when I thought you were cooperating with me."

The Troll's eyes shifted. It was an ever-so-subtle tell. Harvath knew he had him. "There should have been another name on that list you gave me. Five men were released from Gitmo that night. Not four."

The Troll smiled. "Agent Harvath, if there's one thing I've learned during my lifetime, it's how to read people, and I can tell that you already know who this fifth person is."

Harvath leaned forward, his face a mask of deadly determination. "If you're such a good reader of people then you should already know that if you do not cooperate, I will kill you with my own bare hands, right here. Do we understand each other?"

If the Troll was intimidated by Harvath's threat, he didn't show it. "It's been a very long day," he said. "Why don't we adjourn to the living room and have a drink?"

When Harvath hesitated, he added, "If you're worried about me trying to poison you, you don't have to join me. I'm quite used to drinking alone."

Either way, Harvath wasn't about to let his guard down. Pointing at the bar with the barrel of his Beretta he said, "Be my guest."

CHAPTER 85

So, Agent Harvath," said the Troll as he scooted up onto the couch with a snifter of Germain-Robin XO and made himself comfortable, "what is it I can do for you?"

Sitting face-to-face with the smug little bastard like this, Harvath's trigger finger began to itch. He was seriously weighing the merits of killing him. If the Troll didn't come up with something of value, he was going to put a bullet in him and toss his body into the bay. "Why did you leave Philippe Roussard's name off the list?" demanded Harvath.

The Troll didn't know what to say. He was angry at himself for underestimating Harvath. He was also angry at Roussard. His foolishness had put the Troll in a very difficult position.

The little man seemed to be a million miles away, so Harvath fired a round into the pillow he was leaning on. "Tick tock."

The booming noise startled the Troll. It was not only extremely aggressive, it was also rude.

Though none of Harvath's behavior should have come as a shock to the Troll, he had felt as if they had developed a partnership of sorts, or at the very least a détente. He felt a professional respect for Harvath, but it was obvious that it was not reciprocated.

Puffing his cheeks full of air, the Troll exhaled and said, "I have not seen or spoken with Roussard in many years."

"So you do know him."

"Yes," replied the Troll. It was hopeless to lie, and he knew it. Harvath held all the cards in his hand—his fortune, his livelihood, even his life.

"When was the last time you saw him?"

"Five, maybe ten years ago. I can't remember exactly."

"But you knew he was one of the five released from Guantanamo," asserted Harvath.

"Yes, I did."

"And yet you purposely left his name off the list

you gave to me. Why? Were you two hoping to kill me before I could stop you? Is that it?" demanded Harvath as he raised his pistol for emphasis.

It was the most logical conclusion for Harvath to come to, but it was absurd. "The last time I saw Philippe, he was nothing more than a very troubled young man."

"Funny how quickly things change."

The Troll thought about laughing it all off, but the pistol pointed at his chest was not particularly amusing. "I have had no contact with him since then."

"So why leave his name off the list?"

"In my line of work, a person collects enemies very quickly. Friends are much harder to come by."

"Roussard is a friend of yours?" asked Harvath.

"You could say that."

Tired of his obfuscation, Harvath put another round through the couch, millimeters from the Troll's left thigh. "My patience is wearing thin."

"My godson," stammered the Troll. "Philippe Roussard is my godson."

"Somebody made *you* a child's godfather?"

"It was more of an honorary title bestowed on me by the family."

"What family?" demanded Harvath as he adjusted his aim and prepared to squeeze the trigger.

A slow smile began to spread across the Troll's face.

"What's so funny?"

"Sometimes," replied the Troll, "the world is an amazingly small place."

CHAPTER 86

It was late, but the president had told his DCI that he would wait up for his assessment. When James Vaile arrived, he was taken upstairs to the residence.

The president was in his private study watching the Chicago White Sox play the Kansas City Royals. It had been a great game that had gone into extra innings.

When the DCI knocked on the study's open door, Jack Rutledge set down his drink, turned off the TV, and waved him in.

"Are you hungry?" asked the president as the CIA chief closed the door behind him and took the empty leather club chair next to him.

"No thank you, sir."

"How about a drink?"

Vaile shook his head and politely declined.

"Okay then," said Rutledge, glad to be getting on with it. "You've had a chance to look at everything. Let's have it."

The DCI withdrew a folder from his briefcase and opened it. "Mark Sheppard is no Woodward or Bernstein in the writing department, but he more than makes up for it in the depth of his research."

Vaile handed a copy of the reporter's article to the president and continued, "The attention this piece would have brought to the *Baltimore Sun* would have sent their circulation through the roof. Based on Sheppard's notes, the paper was looking for ways they could stretch the story into a series of articles. They'd already planned to re-create the car accident, as well as the takedown of the John Doe hijacker in Charleston—fake FBI agents and all.

"We're just lucky this guy Sheppard came looking for a statement a week before he was going to press. Had he come the night before, Geoff Mitchell and the press office wouldn't have been able to put him off while they claimed the White House was looking into it."

"And you never would have had time to get to him," said the president as he finished scanning the article.

"Not the way I needed to," replied Vaile.

"Then we dodged the bullet."

The DCI shook his head. "Right now, Sheppard's editors have to be fuming. This story was the best thing to come along for their paper in years and now it's been torpedoed."

Rutledge had a feeling he knew where this was going. "You think if we put out the alert on the school buses that might trigger the *Sun* into running Sheppard's story anyway?"

"It's always possible. Though we've got all his original source material, they've got the notes they took in their editorial meetings. If they suspect Sheppard killed his story under duress, they might smell blood in the water, decide to reinterview his sources, and run it all without his name on it."

"Then he'd better have been damn convincing when he withdrew it."

Vaile nodded. "He definitely had the proper motivation, that's for sure."

"Yet, you're still opposed to sending out any sort of Homeland Security alert."

"Yes, sir, I am."

The president set the article down on the table. "If an attack does happen, what then? You don't think at that point the *Sun* will repackage the article in a way that's equally damaging?"

"How could they? We're the only ones who know the full story. What they have is only a small piece of the puzzle, and it's a piece we can spin. It'll show we were engaged in a concerted effort, *before* the fact, to bring the terrorists to justice. Harvath's already killed two of them, two more are about to be apprehended in their home countries, and we've got multitudes of agents in the field trying to track down the fifth and final one. I think we should let this play out."

Rutledge admired Vaile's confidence, but unfortunately he wasn't convinced. "If we learned anything from 9/11, it's that hindsight is always 20:20. People will demand to know why, if we knew about a threat to school buses, we didn't put out an alert."

"Because," replied the DCI emphatically, "putting out an alert is an admission of guilt. It would tell our enemies that we believed we had broken our word and that we deserved to be hit, which couldn't be further from the truth."

The president tried to say something in response,

but Vaile held up his hand in order to be allowed to finish. "Rightly or wrongly, our agreement with the terrorists was based on the assumption that the five men released from Gitmo would not use their freedom to strike against us here at home."

"Of course," said Rutledge. "We agreed not to hunt them."

"That's what's been bothering me. The more I look at this, the more I believe the terrorists have had other plans all along."

CHAPTER 87

What kind of other plans?" asked Rutledge.

Vaile looked at him and replied, "Those five men must have been very important for their organization to risk so much to get them released."

"Agreed," said the president, nodding.

"We're also worried that they've remained important enough that their organization will make good on its promise to retaliate for any of their killings."

"I don't see where you're going with this."

"Palmera and Najib are both dead, yet nothing has happened so far. Nothing."

"Well, one was killed in Mexico and the other in Jordan. Maybe their organization doesn't know yet."

The DCI shook his head. "Everyone in the neighborhood knew Palmera, and his death was very public.

Najib was a member of Syrian intelligence and while I have no idea what the Jordanians might have done with his body, Harvath allowed Al-Tal's wife and son to live and they are definitely not going to keep their mouths shut. Word like this travels fast. Their organization knows. And yet I keep coming back to the fact that *nothing* has happened."

The president thought about it a moment. "For all we know, they're putting their people in place as we speak."

"Oh, I think they've done more than that," replied Vaile. "I think they've got one person and he's already been in place."

"Roussard?" asked Rutledge.

The DCI nodded. "If we maintain the reasoning that these five were so important that their organization risked all to spring them from Gitmo and then could be so angered by the deaths of two of them that it would make good on its threat to retaliate, then how could this same organization not know that Roussard was here and not know what he was doing?"

"He could be acting alone. He's obviously got a vendetta against Harvath."

"He might be acting alone in carrying out his attacks, but he's getting a lot of support from somewhere. This kind of operation takes money, intelligence, weapons, forged identification. There's no way, just over six months after being released from Guantanamo, he could pull this off completely alone. His people know what he's doing, and I think this has been their plan from the beginning."

The president was quiet while he thought about this from as many angles as possible. Finally, he said. "It's an interesting theory, but can you prove it? Because you're asking me to risk the lives of tens, hundreds, maybe even thousands of American children on a *theory.*"

"No, sir," answered Vaile. "I can't prove it."

Rutledge rubbed the hairline scar where his right index finger had been reattached, an ever-present reminder of his own gruesome kidnapping several years ago, and said, "Well, there's one thing I can prove. I can prove that these people already hijacked one school bus and killed its driver. Those victims and their families were terrorized and traumatized beyond belief. It made national headlines, and as president, I'm going to do everything in my power to make sure that never happens again.

"So I am going to allow DHS to issue the alert and I'll deal with the *Baltimore Sun* or whomever else I have to deal with if and when they become a problem. In the meantime, I am *ordering* you to find Scot Harvath and stop him. No more excuses. You tell your people to do whatever they need to do to get their job done. And damn it, you remind them that when I said dead or alive, I meant it."

CHAPTER 88

The Troll had dropped a bombshell on Harvath and the impact was intense. Philippe Roussard wasn't the assassin's real name after all. It was the name that had been given to him as a boy to protect him from his family's enemies. His real name was Sabri Khalil al-Banna.

He began to explain who Roussard had been named after, but Harvath held up his hand to stop him. "He was named after his grandfather."

The Troll nodded his head.

There was an acidic gnawing in the pit of Harvath's stomach. Before Osama bin Laden, Sabri Khalil al-Banna had been the world's deadliest and most feared terrorist. His exploits were bloody, ruthless, and the stuff of legends in both the terrorism and counterterrorism worlds.

As was common with Islamic radicals, he was known by many names, the most famous being Abu Nidal. Philippe Roussard was almost a dead ringer for his late grandfather. Now Harvath knew why he had looked so familiar in the material Vaile had sent.

He also knew why he, or more appropriately the people he cared about, were being targeted.

It was payback for a mission he had led several years ago, code-named Operation Phantom. His assignment had been to decapitate a resurgent Abu Nidal terrorist organization. The reins of power had been handed to Nidal's daughter and son, twins who had been born and raised without the knowledge of Western intelligence agencies. Based upon what Harvath was hearing, it seemed something of a family tradition.

"As far as we know, Abu Nidal had only two off-spring."

"Correct," said the Troll, "the son, Hashim, and the daughter, Adara."

Just their names had the power to send a chill down Harvath's spine. They were two of the most vicious terrorists he had ever come across, Adara even more so than her brother, Hashim.

Harvath remembered her all too well. Her hatred for Israel and the West consumed her to such a degree that it poisoned what would have otherwise been ravishing features. She was tall, with high cheekbones and long dark hair. Her eyes, though, were her most striking feature. They were gray to the point of almost being silver, like the color of mercury. But when she was enraged or under stress, they underwent an amazing transformation and turned jet black.

It was in the midst of a hijacking by Adara Nidal and her brother that Harvath had met Meg Cassidy. Together, they had tracked the twins to a vineyard out-side Rome, only to be beaten to the punch by a veteran Israeli intelligence operative named Ari Schoen—a for-mer top-ranking member of the Mossad who had his own axe to grind with the Nidal family.

It had ended very badly. The memories had haunted Harvath for a long time, and he did not care to be reliving them now.

Hashim had appeared like a wraith out of the vineyard and had run right at them with hand grenades in each hand. Harvath prepared himself for the attack, but Hashim ran right past them. He took Schoen and his team completely by surprise. Screaming at the top of his lungs, Hashim jumped into the van just as the door began to close.

Harvath had thrown himself on top of Meg. The grenades detonated and the van exploded into a billowing fireball, taking Schoen, Hashim, and his sister, Adara, along with it.

The horrible smell of gasoline and burnt flesh was one Harvath would never forget.

So now someone from the Nidal family tree was out for blood. The only question was which branch Philippe Roussard represented.

"So whose son is Philippe? Hashim's or Adara's?"

"Adara's," replied the Troll.

"Who's his father?" asked Harvath.

"An Israeli intelligence operative who died before the boy was born."

"Daniel Schoen?" responded Harvath, stunned that the twisted operation had come back to haunt him so. "He was Ari Schoen's son."

Harvath was good. "How did you know that?" asked the Troll.

"I didn't."

"But then—"

"The night Adara was killed," said Harvath, "Schoen confessed to having broken up her relationship with Daniel. He called her a whore and she said something about Daniel wanting to have children with her. But I sensed there was something more—something that she wasn't saying."

"Obviously, there was. She had the child out of wedlock shortly after leaving Oxford where she and Daniel had met. Since the elder Schoen had done such an admirable job of making it look like Daniel wanted nothing further to do with her, Adara raised the boy in secret. She placed him with a French family she had connections with, and they raised him as their own. He wanted for nothing and went to the finest Western schools. But he always knew who he was and where he came from."

"Just like his mother," said Harvath.

Once again, the Troll nodded.

"You still haven't explained your connection. Was it with the Nidals, or the foster family, the Roussards?"

"It was with the Nidals," replied the Troll. "Abu Nidal was one of my earliest clients."

Harvath looked at the dwarf with contempt. "You keep rather distasteful company. Birds of a feather, I suppose."

The Troll took a long sip of his brandy. "Like I said, in my line of work, a person collects enemies very quickly. Friends are much harder to come by. Abu Nidal was one of the best and most loyal friends I ever had. His daughter, Adara, was the second best. Normally, a man like me has to pay for a woman's attention. With Adara things were different."

Harvath had heard some boasts in his time, but this guy was full of shit. "You and Adara Nidal?" he asked.

"A gentleman wouldn't ask such questions," said the Troll as he took another sip of brandy.

From what Harvath knew of her, Adara Nidal was a raving psychopath with unparalleled bloodlust. She was a woman of strange appetites, and the more he thought about it, the more likely it seemed that Adara Nidal and the Troll would be perfect for each other.

At the moment, though, none of that made any difference. Harvath had a killer to catch. "So Adara's son is targeting the people around me because he holds me responsible for his mother's death?"

"It's the only thing I can think of that makes sense," replied the Troll.

"What about tying his attacks to the ten plagues of Egypt? The lamb's blood above my door, the attack on Tracy, my mother, the ski team, the dog, and all the rest of them are tied in to the ten plagues, but in reverse order—ten through one instead of one through ten."

"Hold on a second," said the Troll. "The dog I left for you?"

Harvath nodded.

"What about it?"

Harvath realized that he might have just touched a nerve. "Roussard took great joy in torturing it. He severely beat the puppy and then put it in a body bag infested with fleas. He hung the puppy upside down from a rafter and left it there to die."

The Troll's face flushed with anger.

CHAPTER 89

That dog was an innocent, an absolute innocent!" growled the Troll angrily as he slid off the couch and walked to the bar to refill his glass.

Attributing his increasing loquaciousness to the alcohol, Harvath had no intention of stopping him.

"There's a reason I haven't been in touch with Philippe," said the Troll as he refilled his glass. "He had always been a very disturbed young man."

"How disturbed?" asked Harvath.

"Extremely," he replied as he crossed back over to the couch and climbed up. "There even came a point where the Roussards refused to care for him any longer. Adara had to put him into a very expensive boarding school. But there his problems only got worse."

"What kind of problems?"

"In the beginning, his behavior was marked by a lack of empathy or conscience. He had poor impulse control and exhibited an array of manipulative behaviors. A psychologist the Roussards consulted could not make a specific diagnosis. The boy exhibited both antisocial and narcissistic personality disorders—neither of which was good news.

"To paraphrase the renowned criminal psychiatrist Robert D. Hare, Philippe was a predator who used charm, manipulation, intimidation, and violence to control others and to satisfy his own selfish needs. Lacking in conscience and feeling for others, he cold-bloodedly took whatever he wanted and did whatever he pleased, violating social norms and expectations without the slightest sense of guilt or regret."

Philippe sounded just like his mother, and Harvath wondered if such an abhorrent psychological condition could be inherited.

"The Roussards tried to medicate the boy," continued the Troll, studying the bit of brandy in his snifter, "but he refused to take his pills. When he attacked their youngest daughter with a knife, the Roussards gave Adara an ultimatum."

"Which was?"

"Either she show up within the next twenty-four hours to collect him, or they were going to put him on the next plane to Palestine.

"It was the first in a perceived series of abandonments that undoubtedly contributed to his already precarious mental condition. The boy had always been very conflicted about his Palestinian-Israeli parentage. The use of the plagues, and in reverse order, may be some twisted nod to his father's Jewish heritage."

Now that Harvath's worst fears about the man stalking the people closest to him had been confirmed, he had to focus on how to stop him. "Do you have a way to contact him?"

The Troll shook his head and took another sip of his drink. "Philippe and I had an incident. We never spoke again after that."

"What kind of *incident?*"

"It's not something I like to talk about."

Harvath squinted over the sights of his pistol and began to apply pressure to the trigger. The Troll got the message.

"We had a disagreement. It was over something entirely inconsequential. Any normal person would have forgotten it and moved on, but Phillipe wasn't normal, he was sick.

"He abducted me and held me hostage for two days, during which time I was subjected to torture. It was Adara who finally found me and came to my rescue. She nursed me back to health."

"So why the hell would you want to show any loyalty to a man like that?" inquired Harvath.

"My loyalty wasn't to him," said the Troll, a sad smile playing out on his lips, "but to his mother."

"I want to know something," said Harvath. "I was there the night she died."

"Yes."

"Do you hold me responsible for what happened?"

The Troll was silent. "Does it really matter?" he finally asked.

"Yes, it does."

"I don't know who to blame. Hashim martyred

himself and blew up the van, but he did it to save his sister from an ignoble fate at the hands of Schoen."

"But what about me?" said Harvath.

"You were there. How could I not blame you?" asked the Troll. "I loved her and now she is gone. You were a part of that night, so yes, in part I do blame you."

Harvath watched for any sign that the Troll was not telling him the truth. "Enough to want me dead?"

There was a long pause. Finally the man said, "At one point, I wanted you dead. I wanted everyone involved dead. But I realized that what happened was more of Adara's making than anything else. She was the one ultimately responsible—she and her crazy brother, Hashim. The entire family was destined for tragedy."

"Including Philippe?" probed Harvath.

The Troll's eyes drifted toward the water. There was an odd sound coming from the bay. It sounded like a quickly moving watercraft rhythmically crashing against the waves. The only problem was the bay was perfectly calm. There were no waves tonight.

Harvath noticed it too and looked up just as a blacked-out Bell JetRanger helicopter came into view and began firing into the open living room.

CHAPTER 90

The roar of the large helicopter hovering just above the water outside was eclipsed by the deafening thunder of heavy machine guns emptying themselves into the house.

Harvath grabbed the Troll by the back of his thick neck and forced him to the tile floor as all around them the walls, the furniture, and the fixtures were chewed to a pulp.

Shards of broken glass blanketed the ground, and a fire began in the kitchen. With its wooden construction and thatched roof, Harvath knew the place was going to go up faster than a box of kindling.

Drawing his pistol, he marked in his mind's eye where the chopper had been hovering and readied himself to return fire. But the opportunity never came.

At a pause in the machine-gun rampage, Harvath popped up from the floor with his Beretta poised, only to see the skis of the helicopter as it disappeared overhead.

Despite the ringing in his ears, he could hear the helicopter as it flew over the roof and had a bad feeling about where it was headed—the landing pad.

The JetRanger could carry anywhere from five to seven passengers, which meant that there was no telling how many men were aboard. Harvath had already expended two rounds of ammunition and had only one spare magazine remaining. He didn't like the odds if they got into a protracted firefight. His only hope was to get the drop on whoever was aboard that helicopter.

When Harvath reached down to help the Troll off the floor, he was no longer there. Harvath spun to see the man running for the front door. Harvath caught him right at the reading nook. "We have to get out of here," he shouted as he grabbed the dwarf by his collar.

"Not without the dogs!" he returned.

"There's no time. We have to go now."

"I won't leave them!"

Harvath couldn't believe the Troll would put his life on the line for his dogs. "Now," he said as he spun him in the direction of the dining room and gave him a shove to get going.

Passing the couch, Harvath grabbed his dry bag and slung it over his shoulder.

At the dining-room table the Troll stopped again, this time for his laptop. Frantically, he began pulling the cables from its ports. Before Harvath could say anything, he stated, "We'll want this. Trust me."

Harvath didn't argue. Grabbing the device by its handle, he jerked it off the table, stripping it from its remaining cables, which went whipping off in different directions.

With his other hand, Harvath took hold of the Troll's arm and propelled him forward. They ran to the front of the structure, where the dining room and living room met. Beneath them was the glass floor. Many of its panes had been shattered. Others were pock-

marked and splintered from the waves of machine-gun
fire that had torn up the house.

As Harvath approached the wall of open windows
that led out over the water, the Troll stopped dead in
his tracks. "What are you doing?"

"I'm getting us the hell out of here. Get moving."

The Troll twisted free of his grasp and retreated
backward into the house.

"You're going to get us killed. What the hell is
wrong with you?"

The Troll glanced at the fire engulfing the
kitchen, its flames now high enough to lick at the
roof. As he turned back to Harvath he said, "I can't
swim."

Harvath was about to tell him he had no choice,
when all the lights in the house went out. He knew
that whoever had started the job with that helicopter
was about to storm the house to make sure it was finished.

CHAPTER 91

Hoping the sound of the idling helicopter would
cover their entry into the water, Harvath
wrapped his arm around the dwarf's waist and
jumped.

They swam for as long as Harvath could beneath
the water before coming up for air. The Troll was ter-

rified and sucked in rapid gasps of air when they broke the surface. Harvath spun him onto his back to help keep his head above water and dragged him in a swimmer's carry through the bay.

They swam parallel to the shore as the Troll kept an iron two-handed grip on his waterproof laptop. He was incredibly strong for his size. Had he put up any more of a struggle, Harvath very likely would have had to head butt the man to keep him from drowning them both.

Once they were a safe distance from the house, Harvath changed direction and brought them in to shore. As his feet touched the beach the Troll fell over onto his hands and knees and began retching up the cups of seawater he had swallowed during their short swim.

Harvath ignored him. Removing his dry bag, he pulled out his night vision goggles and powered them up.

As he finished heaving, the Troll wiped his mouth on his soaked shirtsleeve and said, "Where are you going?"

Harvath double-checked his pistol and said, "Back to the house."

"But I've got a speedboat at the dock on the end of the island."

"And they've got a helicopter. Helicopter beats boat every time."

The Troll knew he was right. "So what do we do?" he asked.

Ever since they had escaped from the house, Harvath's mind had been preoccupied with who was behind the attack. Were they here for him or had they come for the Troll?

It seemed highly unlikely that Morrell and his Omega Team had tracked him all the way to Brazil. But even if they had, this kind of assault was complete overkill, even by Morrell's standards.

The more Harvath thought about it, the more he realized that whoever these people were, they had most likely come for the Troll. The little man's list of enemies was long and distinguished. There were any number of governments that would have gladly seen him killed, including America's. And on top of that, the dwarf had worked both for and against some the world's most powerful people and organizations.

The only thing Harvath could count on was that underestimating the attacker would be done at his own peril. "We need to split them up so we can thin them out," he said.

"Split them up how?" asked the Troll.

"Where are the keys to the boat?"

"In a cup holder next to the front passenger seat."

Harvath quickly explained what he wanted him to do. When the Troll nodded, Harvath turned and headed back toward the house.

As he moved, he prayed to God his plan would work.

CHAPTER 92

Harvath ran up the beach to the point where the Troll's house jutted out over the water. It was much closer than Harvath wanted to come, but he had very little choice.

Sliding into the water, he glanced at his Kobold and made a note of how much time he had left.

Pulling the cups of his night vision goggles over his eyes, Harvath swam until he was right beneath the glass floor of the living room. He could hear a chorus of orders being shouted by men's voices up above, but none of them were in English. Every word was in Arabic.

Whoever these men were, they were not here for Harvath. They were here for the Troll. Unfortunately for them, today was going to prove to be a very unlucky day.

Positioning himself with a clear line of fire through several of the broken panes of glass above, Harvath raised his Beretta and waited. When one of the men came into view, it took all of his training not to pull the trigger. Once a second man joined his comrade, Harvath squeezed off two rounds in rapid succession and dropped them both.

He didn't wait to see what the reaction would be. Diving beneath the water's surface, Harvath swam twice as far as he had with the Troll and didn't come up for air until his lungs were seared by a burning thirst for oxygen.

Slowly bringing his head above the waterline, Harvath reappeared a safe distance away and took in deep breaths of air. He watched as the burning house was illuminated by even brighter flashes of gunfire delivered by the two dead men's colleagues through the glass floor at an opponent who had already fled.

Harvath swam for the beach on the far side of the house. Hitting the sand, he wrung the water out of his clothes and made his way toward the main building. The Blackhawk Warrior Wear boots he was wearing had been designed by a former Navy SEAL and were almost completely dry within the first several yards. It was a good thing, as he was going to have to move quickly and the last thing he needed was to be dragging two water-logged cinder blocks around his feet.

Traversing the beach, Harvath made it to the narrow strip of vegetation near the entryway to the house. Lying on his stomach, he used his elbows to pull himself forward. The first thing he noticed when he got within range of the house were the dogs.

They had taken shelter in a culvert beneath a nearby raised outbuilding. Judging from the signs of forced entry, the interior most likely contained the generator used to power the main house.

As Harvath crept forward, he heard the dogs begin to growl. He knew they were in no shape to attack, but the sound was enough to raise the hairs on the back of his neck.

He judged the distance from the main house, which was going to burn the rest of the way to the ground in less than an hour, and decided the dogs would be safe. A large water storage tank with a hose stood nearby.

Leaving the cover of the vegetation, Harvath shot out and quickly unwound the hose. He turned the spigot ever so slightly and then placed the hose near the dogs so they could have access to additional fresh water.

He thought briefly about restarting the generator as a distraction, but all that would have done was call attention to his position. Any psychological advantage would have been very short-lived, and there was not much time left.

Harvath swung around, flanking the house, and got himself into position halfway to the helipad.

He looked down at his watch and observed the final seconds tick away.

Once they did, there was a roar from the other end of the island as the Troll fired up the speedboat and cast away from the dock

Immediately, Harvath saw two men race out of the burning house. They pounded down the footpath, and when they hit the blind curve two meters from his position, he took a breath and pulled the trigger of his weapon twice in rapid succession.

Two cracks erupted from his Beretta and the men were felled, each by a perfect head shot.

Harvath scrambled from his hiding spot and pulled their bodies off the trail into the underbrush. They were carrying 9mm silenced Ukrainian Goblin submachine guns.

Harvath pulled a Goblin from one of the dead men, along with two spare magazines, and rushed toward the house. He had no idea whether the others could have heard his shots over the roar of the fire, but when the helicopter failed to lift off, the remaining men on the ground were going to get suspicious.

Taking up a position directly opposite the front door, Harvath waited. And waited. The house was almost completely engulfed in flames. *Had there only been four men in the assault team and had he killed them all?*

It didn't seem likely, but neither did it seem as if anyone would have remained in the burning house. The heat had to be unbearable. All told, there weren't that many rooms to search.

Harvath held his position, the Goblin chambered and ready to fire. Minutes passed.

He was about to creep closer to the house to have a look inside when he heard movement behind him. He spun just in time to see two guns shoved into his face.

CHAPTER 93

I t's you," said one of the men in perfect English. As he spoke his gun drew back and Harvath focused beyond its barrel. It was almost like staring into the face of a young Abu Nidal, his eyes dark and full of hate. Harvath recognized Philippe Roussard instantly.

There was an awkward moment of silence on the killer's part as he tried to figure out what was going on. Harvath could almost hear the gears of his twisted brain grinding against each other.

"Where is the dwarf?" Roussard finally demanded as the other man stripped Harvath of his weapons and stood back. "We know he's not in the boat. It's out there doing circles in the bay."

"Fuck you," said Harvath, his body seething with rage. The man he'd been hunting was standing right above him and there was nothing he could do. Harvath had never felt so helpless in his life.

"So you know who I am," Roussard replied with a smile before he struck Harvath across the jaw with the butt of his weapon. "I will ask you again. Where is he?"

Harvath turned his face back up to him and replied, "And I will tell you again, *fuck* you."

Once more, the enigmatic smile spread across Roussard's face and with it came another butt stroke. "Your tolerance of pain is nowhere near as great as my desire *and* ability to administer it. Now, where *is* the Troll?"

Harvath's head felt as if a million red-hot spikes were being pounded into it. "Umm," he replied, his vision slightly dimmed. "Oh, I remember, fuck you!"

Roussard drew back his weapon for another go and then suddenly thought better of it. Placing the muzzle against Harvath's forehead he whispered, "I'm only concerned with the Troll. Tell me where he is and I'll let you live."

"You're in no position to negotiate anything."

"Funny," said Roussard. "I thought I was the one holding the gun."

"For all the Marines you killed in Iraq," replied Harvath, "as well as everything you have done to the people I love and care about, I am going to watch you die."

The smile returned to Roussard's face. "Revenge is indeed a noble motive. A pity that it won't be possible for you."

Roussard snugged the weapon up against his shoulder and prepared to fire. "You see, the only one of us who's going to die here today is you."

Harvath's eyes darted left and then right looking for a rock, a branch, anything he could use against his captors. There was nothing. On top of that, neither of the two men was standing close enough so that he could sweep their legs out from under them. He had absolutely no options.

Harvath looked Roussard in the face and was about to speak when the killer's finger tightened around his trigger and Harvath saw a blinding flash of light.

CHAPTER 94

The white phosphorous flare lodged in the chest of Roussard's accomplice and lit him up like a lighthouse beacon.

When Harvath's vision returned, he saw the Troll

waddling toward him, a spent flare gun dangling in his hand.

The accomplice was dead. His smoking body lay on the ground several feet away. Harvath looked around for Roussard, but couldn't find him.

The moment he stood up, his legs threatened to give out beneath him. The blows to his head had been worse than he'd thought.

"Slowly, slowly," cautioned the Troll as he ran up to Harvath to help steady him.

"Where's Roussard?"

"He took off toward the helipad."

"Why didn't you stop him?" Harvath demanded as he reached for the dead man's submachine gun and his two extra clips.

"*Stop him?* I did stop him . . . from *killing* you. You ungrateful arsehole."

Harvath was on the footpath, running for the helipad, before the Troll even finished his sentence. The sounds of the spinning helicopter rotors were growing in intensity. It was already lifting off.

By the time Harvath got to the pad, the chopper had already cleared the trees and was heading out over the water. Harvath tore through the forest to the beach on the other side of the island.

When he got there, he raised the Goblin and opened fire. He saw at least two rounds connect near the tail rotor, but not seriously enough to bring the aircraft down or force it back for a landing. Harvath blew through his other two magazines even though he knew the helicopter was at the very far end of his range, if not already beyond it.

With the Troll's house fully ablaze, help would be coming soon. They needed to be gone before anyone got there.

Harvath left the beach and threaded his way back through the forest. When he got back to the charred body of Roussard's henchman, the Troll was gone, as were the rest of his weapons, including Harvath's Beretta.

He heard a noise near the generator shack and quietly crept forward to investigate.

The Troll was on his hands and knees, the weapons stacked along with Harvath's dry bag next to him.

"Did you get him?" asked the Troll without turning around.

"No," replied Harvath as he pointed the empty automatic weapon at him.

"I only had one shot, you know," continued the Troll. "I shot the man closest to me, and even then I was afraid I was going to miss."

"I want you to move three steps to your right, away from those weapons."

"These?" said the Troll as he gestured to the pile and stood up to face Harvath. "I collected them for you. Consider it a thank-you for running the hose for the dogs."

"Just step away."

The Troll did as he was told.

As Harvath moved in to collect the items, the dwarf grinned and said, "You don't trust me, do you?"

Harvath half-laughed as he checked to make sure a round was chambered in his Beretta and then placed the other items into his dry bag.

"It's not my fault the man I shot wasn't Roussard. All you tall people look alike from behind."

"All the more reason I'll be sure never to turn my back on you," replied Harvath as he picked up the bag and slung it over his shoulder.

"Why did you lie to Roussard?" asked the Troll, changing the subject. "If you'd told him where I was, you might have saved your own life."

"Roussard was going to kill me either way. I didn't tell him where you were because I've got a thing about not helping bad people get ahead in life."

"Touché."

"By the way," asked Harvath, "why'd you come back? You were supposed to tie off the boat's steering wheel, send it out into the bay, and wait for me."

"When I didn't hear the helicopter take off, I figured you'd been successful in the first part of your plan, but I still had a few reservations about the rest of it."

"I suppose I should be glad."

"No," answered the Troll, "just grateful. If only a little bit."

Harvath didn't know how he felt about owing his life to such a man, so to avoid thinking about it he took his turn at changing the subject. "What made you take the flare gun?"

The Troll looked at Harvath and replied, "In life, even the smallest advantage is better than no advantage at all."

CHAPTER 95

Instead of going north toward Rio, they headed south along the coast to Paraty, a small eighteenth-century Portuguese fishing village. Set against the forested slopes of the Serra do Mar, Paraty looked out over a bay of hundreds of uninhabited islands. It was similar to Angra dos Reis, but lore low-key.

Residents and visitors alike were more discreet here, preferring to own or rent a refurbished fisherman's cottage or one of the town's diminutive terracotta-roofed villas. It was completely different from the jet-set style of Angra, and that suited Harvath just fine.

He swam back out to his boat and returned to the island to pick up the Troll as well as his two dogs, Argos and Draco. It was a colossal pain in the ass, but the Troll had refused to leave without them.

They beached the boat a mile outside town, and Harvath hiked back to secure transportation for them. There were plenty of cars to choose from—most of their owners having left them in one of two public parking areas specifically set aside for island dwellers who had no need of their vehicles until they drove back home to Rio.

Harvath chose the first one he saw, a white Toyota Sequoia SUV with tinted windows.

When they arrived in Paraty, it was still dark. They

purchased more water for the dogs and some food for themselves at an all-night gas station and then parked along a quiet agricultural road to eat and rest. But first, Harvath had a question. "Why would Roussard want to kill you?"

"I've been wondering about that too," said the Troll as he sank his spoon into a Styrofoam cup of thick bean and sausage stew known as *feijoada*. "For some reason, he's been keeping tabs on me. He used me to find you and now that he knows I'm helping you try to stop him, he wants me dead. It's the only thing that makes sense."

The man was right. It was the only explanation that made sense. The Troll was good at covering his trail, but he wasn't exactly perfect. If he had been, Tom Morgan and his people at Sargasso never would have been able to track him down.

"My friends call me Nicholas," said the Troll after a long silence.

Harvath was in no mood to cozy up with him and ignored the remark as he unwrapped his sandwich.

The Troll was undeterred. "It's a nickname of sorts. I've always been fond of children, and Saint Nicholas is their patron saint."

"As well as the patron saint of prostitutes, robbers, and thieves."

The Troll smiled. "Strangely appropriate for a boy who grew up in a brothel, wouldn't you say?"

This guy is a real chatterbox, thought Harvath as he went to work on his food.

"How about you?" asked the Troll. "How is it you only spell Scot with one T?"

Harvath took a swig of his water. He knew he was going to have to say something. "My mother chose the spelling," he said, setting the water down. "My middle name is Thomas and she didn't like the way it looked to have three Ts all run together when my name was written out. So, she lopped off one of the Ts."

"I am sorry for what Roussard did to her."

"If it's all the same to you," replied Harvath, "I'd rather not discuss my personal life with you."

The Troll put up his hands in defeat. "Of course. I understand. No one can blame you for feeling that way. The people you care about have been through an incredible amount."

"That's putting it mildly," Harvath grunted.

"You don't like me very much, do you, Mr. Harvath?"

Harvath slammed his water bottle down, spooking his passenger and raising the ire of the dogs in the back, who started growling.

Looking into the rearview mirror, Harvath ordered the dogs to be quiet and they immediately fell silent.

Turning back to the Troll, Harvath said, "One of my best friends was killed in New York because of you. Running off Roussard with that flare gun isn't going to make us even."

The Troll was quiet for several moments. The entire time, Harvath's eyes drilled into him. Finally, he spoke. "I know there is nothing I can say or do to bring your friend back to you. If it's any consolation, Al Qaeda still would have hit Manhattan, even without the intelligence I provided them."

"New York never would have been a target if it wasn't for your intelligence," snapped Harvath.

"That's not true. The individual in your government who sold me that information was offering it to the highest bidder. I just happened to have the most readily available checkbook. If it hadn't been me, some other broker would have purchased it, and the information would have still found its way to Al Qaeda."

"And you think that makes what you did okay?"

"No," said the Troll. "It doesn't. I want you to know it's not easy to live with."

Harvath glared at him. "Thousands of Americans died in an attack worse than 9/11 and you find your role in that difficult to live with. Well, I'm glad to know you at least have a subtle pang of conscience."

"And you expect me to believe that you've never done anything you are ashamed of?"

"Believe what you want," replied Harvath. "My conscience is clear."

"Every single time you pulled a trigger, you knew the person on the receiving end deserved to die? You did it for America. Mom and apple pie, so to speak. Right? Never questioned if what you were doing was the right thing. Never questioned if maybe your superiors had made a mistake. You were simply following orders."

Harvath held the steering wheel in a death grip. "Let's get something straight. The only reason you are sitting next to me and still breathing is that I think you still can be useful."

They spent the rest of their time in silence. Harvath's thoughts were occupied with stopping Roussard, while the Troll's were occupied with the thought that his fate was now inexorably entwined with Harvath's. Roussard wouldn't stop stalking either of them until they were dead, or the terrorist himself had been killed. Like it or not, the Troll understood that he and Harvath now shared a very dangerous enemy. He also understood that Harvath represented his best chance of neutralizing Roussard, permanently.

The stakes at this point were well beyond getting his money and data back. His life, in more ways than one, was in Harvath's hands.

When the shops and businesses finally opened the next morning, Harvath used his Brauner alias to rent a small, walled villa overlooking the ocean outside town. The less attention they drew to themselves, the better.

When Harvath returned from purchasing supplies, he found the Troll in the grassy courtyard playing fetch with the dogs.

As Harvath approached, one of the two dogs began growling. The other trotted over and dropped the stick he'd been playing with at Harvath's feet. The animal then sat obediently down and waited to see what Harvath would do.

"I think Argos remembers you," said the Troll as he came across the courtyard. Nodding at the box Harvath was carrying, he asked, "Do you need any help unloading?"

"Yeah," he replied, tilting his head toward the road. "There's a bunch of stuff still in the truck."

As the Troll headed for the vehicle, Draco followed, but Argos remained right where he was.

Once they were out of sight, Harvath sighed, balanced the box in his left arm, and bent over to pick up the stick.

CHAPTER 96

The villa Harvath had selected was outfitted with all the creature comforts: high-speed internet, plasma television with satellite hookup, an impressive stereo system, and a kitchen worthy of a master chef.

The Troll was standing near the stereo with his laptop as Harvath put the rest of the groceries away.

"Do you mind?" he asked. "I like to play music when I cook."

Harvath shrugged and continued to unpack the bags and boxes as the Troll connected his laptop to the stereo and uploaded one of his digital playlists.

"Since you went to the store," announced the Troll as he shoved his way past Harvath into the kitchen, "the least I can do is cook lunch."

"You don't have to do that," replied Harvath.

"Yes, I do," he said as he took a stepladder from the broom closet and dragged it over to the sink, where he washed his hands. "Done with a focused mind, cooking can be a Zenlike experience. I find it helps relax me. Besides, I don't get to cook for other people that often."

Pulling a Brahma beer from its six-pack, the Troll held it out as a peace offering.

Harvath needed the beer more than the little man knew and reached out and accepted the bottle. He found a church key, popped the top, and sat down on a bar stool at the kitchen island. His mind was racing. He needed to check in on his mom and Tracy. He also needed to check in on Kate Palmer and Carolyn Leonard, as well as Emily Hawkins and the dog. *Jesus,* he thought. It was no wonder he felt he needed a drink before getting into all that.

He took a long pull. It tasted good. Cold, the way beer was supposed to be. It was a small pleasure, but one of the very few he'd allowed himself in a long while. The monastic life did not agree with him.

As the Troll's music began playing, he removed the wafer-thin stereo remote from his pocket and punched up the volume. "Cooking is all about the ingredients," he remarked. "Even the music."

Harvath shook his head. *What an eccentric,* he thought to himself as he took another sip of beer. The liquid was halfway down his throat when he realized what they were listening to. "Is this Bootsy Collins?"

"Yes. The song is called 'Rubber Duckie.' Why?"

"Just curious," replied Harvath, who owned the *Ahh . . . The Name Is Bootsy, Baby!* album, from whence "Rubber Duckie" came, on vinyl *and* CD.

"What?" asked the Troll, a dish towel over his left shoulder and a chopping knife in his right hand as he prepared lunch. "You don't think a guy like me can appreciate classic American funk music?"

Harvath held up his hands in mock self-defense. "I just don't meet a lot of people who are into Pachelbel *and* funk."

"Good music is good music, and when it comes to funk, Bootsy is one of the best. In fact, without Bootsy and his brother Catfish, there'd be no funk music at all. At least not like we know it today. James Brown never could have become the Godfather of Soul without the Pacesetters shaping his sound. And don't even get me started on what they did for George Clinton and Funkadelic."

Harvath was impressed. "I'll drink to that," he said, raising his beer. There was a lot more to the Troll than met the eye.

It was like watching a magician. Harvath considered himself a good cook, but he was far outside the Troll's league. The little man had taken a small amount of fish, a little bit of bread, and a few other ingredients and had created an amazing fish soup with bread and rouille.

As Harvath cleared the table, he picked up the remote and muted the music. "Something is still bothering me about all of this," he said. "In all your dealings with Adara Nidal, you never asked her what her son was up to?"

The Troll pushed himself back from the table and dabbed at the corner of his mouth with his napkin. "Out of courtesy, of course I asked. She wasn't very forthcoming when it came to matters regarding Philippe. I think she was extremely disappointed in him. She would say things like, *He's working for the cause,* or, *He continues to show great promise as one of Allah's most noble soldiers.*"

"Which was all bullshit, right?" stated Harvath as he set their dishes near the sink and turned around. "I mean, she never struck me as a devout Muslim. She drank and did a whole bunch of other stuff I think Allah would have frowned on."

The Troll laughed. "Despite the many habits she had developed to better blend into Western society, I feel she was still a true mujahideen at heart."

Harvath pulled another beer from the fridge and sat back down at the table with the opener. "So who's running Roussard then? He didn't spring himself from Gitmo. With Hashim and Adara dead, the Abu Nidal organization effectively fell apart. It wasn't a many-headed hydra like Al Qaeda. We cut off two heads and the monster died."

"Or so your intelligence told you."

"Do you know something different?"

"No," said the Troll as he got up to make coffee. "Everything I have seen is in line with your assessment."

"So then Roussard became a free agent. Somebody had to have picked him up. The question is who?"

The Troll slid the stepladder over to the stove and climbed up. "If we knew what kind of leverage was used to get the U.S. to release Philippe and his four fellow prisoners from Guantanamo, maybe we could begin to piece together who he was working for. But we don't have that, and without it, I really don't think we have very much to go on."

Harvath hated to admit it, but the Troll was right.

He also hated to admit that the only way to get around the impasse he now saw himself at was to share a secret of enormous national security importance with a direct enemy of the United States.

CHAPTER 97

This time, Harvath really had committed treason. There was no doubt about it. The only saving grace would be if something of greater value came of it.

It couldn't be something of greater value to himself. It had to be something of greater value to his country. Failing that, Harvath very well could have just betrayed everything he stood for.

He searched the Troll's face, but there was nothing there. "This plot doesn't sound familiar to you in any way? Adara or the Abu Nidal organization never mentioned anything like this to you?"

"By targeting children, the plot sounds very much like what happened in Beslan. In fact, I'd say hijacking the school bus was an improvement. It's a lot easier to capture a school bus than a school."

"But what about Adara? Did she or her people ever mention something like this?"

"I didn't talk tactics with her," replied the Troll. "At least, not often. I deal in the realm of information. That is my stock-in-trade. If Adara or her deceased father's organization had any plans for an attack like this she would have known better than to talk to me about it. She knew me well enough to know that I would be against it."

"That's right. I forgot," said Harvath. "Saint Nicholas."

"In the world we live in, bad things happen every day. Innocent people are killed. Sometimes these innocents are children. I believe in America you call it collateral damage. But to specifically target children is reprehensible. Whoever conceived of this attack should be strung up by his balls."

Harvath couldn't argue. But his agreement with the Troll's position didn't bring him any closer to finding out who was behind Philippe Roussard and what else they had planned.

He sat there for a long time in silence, thinking, until the Troll said, "I've been trying to find a connection, outside of ideology, between Philippe and the other men who were released with him. Maybe that was a mistake."

"How so?"

"Maybe there is no connection. Maybe the other four were simply decoys. Like when multiple versions of your president's helicopter lift off at the same time and go in different directions."

Harvath hadn't thought of that. "I started with Ronaldo Palmera because he was close, proximity-wise."

"It doesn't matter who you started with. We've been looking for a connection between the five released from Gitmo and I don't think there is one. I think this has been about Philippe from the beginning, and lumping him in with four others was a smoke screen."

Harvath was with him that far. "Okay, so let's say the other four don't matter for our immediate purposes. We still know nothing about who's behind Roussard."

"Not yet at least."

"I don't follow you."

The Troll looked at Harvath and smiled. "The one thing we can agree on is that someone is helping Philippe. Whoever that person—"

"Or organization," added Harvath.

"Or organization is, they've obviously got it out for you and they sent Philippe to stop me from helping you."

"Agreed."

"Then let's break this down into the smallest, most logical bits of data we can," replied the Troll. He was the puzzle master and completely in his element now. "Most likely, Philippe had neither the contacts nor the resources to mount that attack on me. Someone had to play matchmaker and paymaster for him."

"And he used Arabic-speaking talent," added Harvath.

"Which narrows down the pool of operators in South America considerably."

"Unless they were shipped here specifically for this job."

The Troll nodded. "It's possible. But a lot went into this. Someone had to secure the weapons, the helicopter, and a willing pilot. Most likely surveillance was conducted. Even if the muscle came from outside, someone had to help them locally, and it had to be someone Philippe's people had a relationship with and could trust."

Harvath watched him as he listened.

"There's one other thing," said the Troll. "The most important thing of all."

"What's that?"

"The money," he replied. "This would have been pretty expensive. They couldn't have just walked into the country carrying that kind of cash. The Brazilians are very serious about money laundering and illicit activities. This would have required—"

"Banks," interrupted Harvath.

The Troll nodded again.

"Do you think there's a way to track backward via the money flow?"

Pressing his fingers into a steeple, the Troll thought about it. "If we knew what group or individual

Philippe used locally to facilitate everything here, I think I could."

"What would you need?" said Harvath, careful not to let his enthusiasm show in his voice.

"Two things. First, it takes money to find money. I'd need cash and a lot of it. You'd have to unfreeze a substantial sum. I'm going to have to go to market to get the facilitator's name and background info. To get that information quickly we're going to have to pay a premium. Antennae will go up among the brokers we're going to approach. They're going to smell blood in the water and will wonder if they can sell the information someplace else for more. We have to be able to offer so much right off the bat that they'll be afraid to jerk us around and shop the intel."

"What's the second thing?" asked Harvath.

"Once we're on the trail we're going to have to move fast. I'm going to need a lot more computing power than I have now."

"How *much* more?"

The Troll looked at him and replied, "Do you have any friends at the NSA or CIA who owe you a favor?"

CHAPTER 98

Harvath had friends at both the NSA and the CIA. In fact, he'd even recently taken a steam bath with the CIA's director at his country club. But something told him that reaching out to anyone for help at either agency at this point would only make his problems worse.

By having the Troll define his computing needs a little bit better, Harvath realized the NSA and CIA weren't the only government agencies with the capacity that would satisfy him. There were others, one of them being the National Geospatial Intelligence Agency, or NGA.

Formerly known as the National Imagery and Mapping Agency, the NGA was a major intelligence and combat support subsidiary of the Department of Defense. They also had serious computer power at their disposal and just happened to be the current employers of a friend of Harvath's named Kevin McCauliff.

McCauliff and Harvath were members of an informal group of federal employees who trained together every year for the annual Washington, D.C., Marine Corps Marathon.

McCauliff had been instrumental in helping Harvath during the Fourth of July terrorist attacks on Manhattan and had received a special commendation from the president himself. It was something he was very proud of. Though he'd broken many internal

NGA rules and more than a few laws in the process, he would have done it all again in a heartbeat, no questions asked.

Since McCauliff had helped him with sensitive assignments in the past, Harvath hoped he'd be able to count on him again.

It took the Troll two days and twice as much money as he'd anticipated to get the information he was looking for. But in the end, it was worth it. Brazil was a relatively small country, and he not only discovered who had assisted Roussard locally, but he also assembled a loose idea of how they washed and had moved their money.

At that point it was Harvath's turn, and he decided to call Kevin.

"Are you out of your fucking mind?" asked McCauliff when Harvath got him on the phone. "No way."

"Kevin, I wouldn't ask you if it wasn't important," said Harvath.

"Of course you wouldn't. Losing my job for helping you is one thing, losing my life when I'm found guilty of treason is something completely different. Sorry, but we are done with this conversation."

Harvath tried to calm him down. "Kevin, come on."

"No, *you* come on," he replied. "You're asking me to turn over control of DOD computers to a figure renowned for stealing intelligence from government organizations."

"So firewall off any sensitive areas."

"Am I talking to myself here? These are *D-O-D* computers. *All* their areas are sensitive. It's one thing to ask me to pull imagery, Scot, but it's another thing entirely to ask me to open up the door and give you an all-access pass . . ."

"I'm not asking you for an all-access pass. I just need enough capacity to—"

"To launch a denial-of-service attack from U.S. government computers on several banking networks so you can more effectively hack your way inside."

That was the crux of the request right there, and Harvath couldn't blame McCauliff for his reluctance. Everything he'd asked the NGA operative to do for him in the past paled in comparison to this. McCauliff was going to need a bigger reason than just their friendship to put his career and possibly more on the line.

Harvath decided to fill him in on what had happened.

When he was finished, there was silence from the other end of the line. McCauliff had no idea Harvath had been through so much since the New York City attacks. "If the banks found out where the attacks came from, the fallout for the U.S. would be beyond radioactive," he said.

Harvath had been expecting this answer, and the Troll had made extensive notes for him on what he wanted to do. "What if there was a way this could be done without a trail leading back to the U.S.?" asked Harvath.

"What do you have in mind?"

Harvath explained their plan as McCauliff listened.

"On the surface," the NGA operative replied, "it makes sense. It's probably even doable that way, but there's still one wild card that kills the deal."

"The Troll," said Harvath despondently.

"Exactly," replied McCauliff. "I'm not saying you would ever intentionally do your country harm, but this could be the mother of all Trojan Horses and I am not going to be the dumb son of a bitch remembered for having swung open the gates so it could be wheeled inside."

Harvath couldn't argue with McCauliff's reasoning. Allowing the Troll access to those computers was akin to handing a professional mugger a loaded gun and sending him into a dimly lit parking garage full of bejeweled society matrons. You couldn't trust either of them to be on their best behavior.

Though McCauliff felt for Harvath's predicament and genuinely wanted to help, boosting an enemy of the United States over the government's firewall was out of the question.

The image, though, gave Harvath an idea. "What if we leave the Troll out of this?" he asked.

McCauliff laughed. "And I'm supposed to feign idiocy when I get questioned? I know you're with him right now. If I even open up one socket for you, it's the same as opening it for him."

"But what if you didn't open anything for either of us?" asked Harvath.

"Who would I be opening things for? If it's not

you, and not the Troll, who are you going to get to carry out this hack?"

Harvath paused for a minute and then replied, "You."

"Me?" replied McCauliff. "Now I know you're nuts."

McCauliff disliked the idea of carrying out a hack against a host of financial institutions just as much as allowing Harvath and the Troll inside the DOD network to run the operation themselves. Either way he looked at it, there was no upside.

It wasn't that McCauliff couldn't do it. His talents at breaching complicated networks weren't in question. The problem was that he actually enjoyed his job. He liked the NGA. He liked his bosses and he liked the people he worked with. This time, Harvath was simply asking for too much.

The list of things that could happen to McCauliff if he got caught was just too long. He wanted to help Harvath out, but he couldn't find a way to do it without putting himself in serious jeopardy.

Harvath must have known exactly what he was thinking because he said, "I'm sending you an email," and moments later, there was a chime as something arrived in Kevin McCauliff's inbox.

The email was from Harvath's official DHS account and provided the NGA operative with the one thing he needed to strip away his reservations and come to Scot Harvath's aid—plausible deniability.

In the email, Harvath stated that he was working under direct orders from President Jack Rutledge and that McCauliff's assistance, as it had been in the New

York City attacks, was necessary in a matter of urgent national security.

Harvath specifically noted that McCauliff's discretion was of paramount importance and that he was not to inform his superiors or anyone else that he worked with about what he was doing. The email assured him that the president was well aware of McCauliff's role and was appreciative of his undertaking any and all tasks that might be assigned to him by Harvath.

Plain and simple, it was an insurance policy. As soon as McCauliff finished reading it, he printed out two copies. One he locked in his upper desk drawer and the other he placed in an envelope, which he addressed to himself at home.

The content of the email was bullshit and Kevin McCauliff knew it, but he liked Harvath a lot and wanted to help him. The last time he'd broken the rules, and the law, for Harvath he'd received a commendation from the president for his efforts.

McCauliff figured that if this time his bacon landed in the fire, the right attorney could probably use the email from Harvath to save him from getting fried.

That, of course, presupposed his getting caught, which was something Kevin McCauliff didn't plan on letting happen.

"So are you in?" asked Harvath.

"Seeing as how I've been informed that this is a direct request from the president of the United States," replied McCauliff, "how can I say no?"

CHAPTER 99

Technically, the bar on the outskirts of Virginia Beach, Virginia, had no name—at least none that could be seen on the outside of the ramshackle structure or on any illuminated signs rising from its dirt parking lot. Like its clientele, this was the kind of place that didn't want to draw attention to itself.

To the initiated, it was known as the Bucket of Blood, or simply "the Bucket." How it got the nickname was anyone's guess. The low profile had been designed to keep out persons who didn't belong there, be they townies or tourists. The Bucket was a bar for warriors, period.

Specifically, the bar served the local men and women of the United States Navy's Special Operations community, but its doors were open to any Spec Ops community personnel regardless of which branch of the military they served in.

The Bucket was also a popular watering hole with another group who were every bit the warrior—the off-duty members of the Virginia Beach PD.

It was open seven days a week, and there really was no such thing as a bad night to visit the Bucket. In spite of its somewhat narrow membership focus, it was packed with regulars at the time.

As it was owned, managed, and run by Andre Dall'au and Kevin Dockery, two retired members of SEAL Team Two, the Bucket was considered the Team's de facto home away from home.

As far as décor, the usual tavern trappings of neon beer signs and liquor-company-sponsored pieces of swag were abundant, but what made the Bucket unique were the items contributed by its customers.

Like the Venetian doge who commanded the merchants of Venice to bring back treasures to enhance the city's basilica, Dall'au and Dockery made it clear that they expected their patrons to bring back items from missions abroad that would help contribute to the glory of the Bucket.

The challenge was so taken to heart that the Bucket had become a mini museum, displaying souvenirs from operations all around the world. From the radio Saddam Hussein had been listening to when he was captured, to the knife Navy SEAL Neil Roberts had used in Afghanistan once he'd run out of ammo and hand grenades. The Bucket's collection was extraordinary.

In fact, the proprietors had put the director of the Navy SEAL museum on retainer to help record and catalog all of the pieces. The mini museum had quite a reputation and was the envy of the nation's most prestigious war colleges.

Because it was a SEAL establishment, a lot of the

items were heavily slanted in that direction. On one wall was a mural from former UDT Frogman Pete "The Pirate" Carolan, of SEALs in action from Vietnam through the present bringing freedom to the far reaches of the globe.

One corner was reserved as a place of deep respect. A UDT/vest, swimmer's mask, and MK3 dive knife on a guard belt stood behind a small round table with a sailor's cap, place setting, and empty chair standing in memory of fallen comrades. On the wall were photos of every SEAL killed in action since the beginning of the War on Terror.

Elsewhere, an Iraqi bayonet, an Afghan AK-47, and movie posters from *Navy SEALs* and *The Rock* kept company alongside a life-sized Creature from the Black Lagoon and a full color photo of Zarqawi after the bomb had been dropped on his head.

There was a collection of paper money from the Philippines, multiple Middle Eastern countries, Africa, South America, and everywhere else the SEALs had been deployed over the years.

Next to that were pictures from the Apollo Space Program with the UDT Frogmen who were used to recover astronauts after they splashed down into the ocean.

Both the men's and ladies' restrooms were adorned with Navy recruiting posters, and above the Bucket's main doorway, visible only as customers exited, was the motto, "The Only Easy Day Was Yesterday."

The Bucket's latest acquisition was something that

was bittersweet for Dockery and Dall'au to put on display. It had arrived via DHL from Colorado and it took reading Scot Harvath's letter to understand what they were looking at.

Two of the men tortured and killed in Afghanistan by Ronaldo Palmera had been Bucket customers. Though the proprietors of the Bucket would have much preferred to have Palmera's pickled head on display, a photo of him lying dead in a Mexican street along with the TASER used to help put him there and his hideous boots were the next best things.

As a former member of SEAL Team Two, Harvath had been a longtime supporter of the Bucket. The items he contributed to the bar's museum were legendary. Dockery and Dall'au had often joked that if he kept it up at the current pace, they'd need to build a wing and name it after him.

Outside, in the Bucket's parking lot, Philippe Roussard closed his eyes and took a deep breath. He felt the familiar sensation radiating from the farthest points of his body. It was the indescribable excitement that he'd once heard referred to as "the quickening."

His reverie, though, was short-lived. The scent from the Vicks VapoRub swabbed beneath his nose was almost as bad as the odor rising from the bags of fertilizer stacked behind him. He thanked Allah that he'd stopped noticing the fumes from the fifty-five-gallon drums of diesel fuel and reminded himself that it would all be over soon.

Climbing out of the RV, he closed the door and locked it. He walked around to the rear and smiled at the *Save water, shower with a SEAL* sticker he'd affixed to the bumper. There was one remembering MIAs and one that read *My RV Loves Iraqi Gas.* Anyone who doubted that Philippe Roussard's RV belonged in the parking lot of the Bucket of Blood probably would have changed his mind upon seeing his bumper stickers.

Not that it mattered much. Roussard didn't plan on being there for too long. In fact, he had just pulled a newly acquired motorbike off the platform attached to the rear of the RV when he was approached by two off-duty Virginia Beach PD officers. Though they weren't in uniform, they had a distinct law enforcement bearing about them that convinced Roussard they were cops.

"Hey, you can't park that thing here," said the taller of the two.

Reflexively, Roussard's hand began to reach for the 9mm Glock hidden beneath his jacket, but he stopped himself.

"Especially not when it smells like that," replied his female partner. "When was the last time you emptied the holding tank on that thing?"

"It's been a while," said Roussard as he forced a smile.

"I'm just kidding you," said the male cop as he pointed at the motorbike. "That's a nice Kawasaki you got there."

"Thank you."

"You're living the dream, aren't you? Nothing but you and the slab. Boy if the guys from BUDs could see you now, eh?"

Roussard politely nodded his head and pulled the motorbike the rest of the way from its carrier platform.

"You haven't been drinking, have you?" asked the female officer as Roussard removed a set of keys from his front pocket.

"Not at all," he replied. "I just have a few errands to run. I'll be back soon."

There was something about this guy she didn't like. Sure, he was well-built and good-looking, but those characteristics alone didn't make a SEAL. "Doc sure is generous when it comes to you guys parking your rigs here."

"He sure is," said Roussard, beginning to sense that something might be wrong.

"How long you staying?" the woman asked.

"What difference does it make," asked her partner. "You interested in this guy or something?"

"Maybe," the female officer replied. Turning back to Roussard, she asked, "So are you going to be around for a couple of days?"

"No," said Roussard. "I have to leave tomorrow."

The woman looked disappointed. "Too bad."

"Don't mind her," replied her partner. "When you come back, we'll be inside. We'll buy you a beer."

Climbing onto the motorcycle, Roussard said, "Sounds good."

With the bike started, he slipped on his helmet and was about to pull away when the woman placed her hand on his handlebars and said, "What's your purge procedure?"

"Excuse me?" he responded, anxious to get going.

"Your *purge procedure,*" the female officer responded.

Roussard's mind raced for an appropriate answer to the question. He had no idea what the woman was talking about. The way she was touching his handlebars, it had to have something to do with the motorcycle. Having been taught that the simplest lie was always the best, Roussard admitted his ignorance. "I've only had this thing about a week. I'm still learning its ins and outs."

The female Virginia Beach PD officer smiled and stepped away from the motorbike.

As Roussard drove away, her partner asked, "What the hell was that all about? *Purge procedure?* You don't really know anything about motorcycles, do you?"

"No, but I know something about SEALs, and that guy wasn't one. If he was, he'd have known what I was talking about."

"C'mon," replied the other cop. "You're off-duty. Give it a rest."

The woman looked at him. "That guy didn't bother you at all?"

"I was in the Army. And judging from his bumper stickers he was or is a squid, so of course he bothers me, but as a resident of Virginia Beach, I've learned to live with them."

The woman shook her head. "What about him parking his van here? Dockery hates RVs. He and Dall'au never let anyone park here overnight. If you're dumb enough to get shit-faced in their joint, you'd better have come with a plan to get yourself *and* your car the hell outta here."

"So what?"

"So something isn't right."

The woman's partner shook his head. "I'm going inside to get a beer."

"Well, while you're there," she said, "find Doc and tell him to come outside. I want to talk with him."

"And in the meantime what are you going to be doing?"

Pulling a lockpick set from her coat pocket, the female officer replied, "I'm just going to take a little look around."

CHAPTER 100

Though Kevin McCauliff was emboldened by the email Harvath had sent him, he still had qualms about carrying out the hack in the light of day. He decided to do it that night when there was lighter traffic on their servers, as well as fewer personnel around who might stumble on to what he was doing and begin asking questions.

The Troll had done the hardest work of all, narrowing in on who had set up the operation in Brazil. He'd even gone so far as to provide a list of banks and a date range as well as an approximate amount of money that McCauliff should be looking for.

It wasn't easy by any stretch, but the NGA operative eventually found it. The payments had been broken up and wired through a series of intermediary banks in Malta, the Caymans, and the Isle of Man, but they all had one thing in common. Each payment could be traced back to a single account number at Wegelin & Company, the oldest private bank in Switzerland.

That was as far as McCauliff got. Wherever Wegelin & Company kept its records, they weren't on any of their servers, at least not any that could be accessed from outside. McCauliff tried every trick he knew to no avail. Whoever these people were Harvath was hunting, they were extremely careful about covering their tracks. Extremely careful, but not perfect. It was nearly impossible to move large sums of money without leaving some sort of trail.

The only problem for Harvath at this point was that the trail dead-ended at Wegelin & Company, the archetype for Swiss banking discretion. If he wanted answers, he was going to have to go to Wegelin & Company directly.

Harvath thanked McCauliff for the information and logged off their call. Removing the ear bud from his ear, he turned to the Troll and shared with him the news that the funds had been traced back to a bank outside Zurich called Wegelin & Company.

The minute the name was out of his mouth, a pall fell across the Troll's face and he held up his index finger.

His stubby fingers rattled across his laptop. When

he found what he was looking for, he recited a string of numbers. They were a perfect match for the account McCauliff had just identified.

"How did you know that?" asked Harvath.

The Troll ran his hand through his short, dark hair and replied, "I'm the one who set up the account."

"You?"

"Yes, *me*. But it gets worse. Plain and simple, Abu Nidal was nothing more than a terrorist. Despite his father's success as a businessman, he didn't know anything about banking or protecting his assets."

"So you handled his money?" asked Harvath.

"No. Not for his organization. He had people for that. Nidal asked me to do something different. He wanted this to be *off the books*, as it were. He didn't want it tied to the FRC. If anything ever happened to him, he wanted to make sure this layer of protection was in place."

"Protection for whom?"

The Troll looked at Harvath and said, "His daughter, Adara. It was set up to be her private, personal account."

Over four thousand miles away, an analyst at the National Security Agency had just tagged and compressed the audio file he was working on.

Picking up his phone, he dialed a cell phone number. It was the second time in twenty-four hours he'd called the anonymous man on the other end.

When the voice of his contact came on, the analyst said, "You wanted to know if Scot Harvath made any further attempts to speak with Kevin McCauliff, the analyst at the NGA?"

"Go ahead," replied the voice.

"He just hung up with him less than three minutes ago."

"Did you get a fix on Harvath's location?"

"No," said the NSA man, "but based on his conversation, I think I may know where he's headed."

CHAPTER 101

SOMEWHERE OVER THE ATLANTIC

As he raced back toward the States, Harvath was consumed by conflicting emotions. Shortly after speaking with Kevin McCauliff, he'd contacted Ron Parker to ask for a favor, only to be filled in on the failed plot at the Bucket of Blood.

Though the police hadn't apprehended the suspect yet, based upon the description of the man they were looking for, he was a dead ringer for Philippe Roussard. The Bucket of Blood was a SEAL Team Two hangout, Harvath was a former SEAL, the SEALs were often referred to as frogmen, and the next-to-last plague had to do with frogs. It was enough to cement for Harvath that the Bucket had been Roussard's target.

Thanks to two sharp Virginia PD officers, the killer had been prevented from carrying out his attack.

Score one for the good guys, even if it was the first time they had managed to put anything up on the board.

Roussard had gotten sloppy, and Harvath wondered if maybe the killer was getting tired.

That said, Harvath was pretty tired himself. It had taken him a full day to set everything up, and even though he'd had a couple of down days in Brazil before that, he hadn't gotten any significant rest. He'd slept with one eye open the entire time. The Troll was someone he'd never be able to fully trust, and having to sit and wait while he plied his seamy trade in search of Roussard's Brazilian connection had almost driven him crazy.

When the info about the Wegelin & Company account came, he was happy to make plans for Switzerland. But the email about the attempted attack on the Bucket changed all of that. Harvath couldn't be in two places at once. Roussard had returned to America, and Harvath knew his only chance of stopping him before his last and final plague was to return there too.

But, actually, maybe there was a way he could be in two places at once.

The Troll had gladly arranged for Harvath's jet. Not only did he need him to remove the threat of Philippe Roussard, but if he wanted to live, he also needed Harvath to see him as an ally.

For his part, Harvath was driven by the same two things since the beginning—a desire to prevent anything further from happening to the people he cared about, and a desire to make Philippe Roussard and whoever was behind him pay for what they had done.

Before leaving Brazil, Harvath had contacted an old friend in Switzerland. It seemed ironic that with Meg Cassidy's wedding only days away, he was now turning for help to one of the other good women he had pushed out of his life.

Claudia Mueller was a lead investigator for the Swiss Federal Attorney's Office and had helped him rescue the president when he'd been kidnapped and secretly held in her country. Harvath had enlisted her assistance on one other occasion, a dangerous assignment that had involved not only Claudia, but the man who was now her husband, Horst Schroeder—a police special tactical unit leader from Bern.

Before she could act on Harvath's latest request, there were a series of things she needed from him, not the least of which was a video statement from the Troll, complete with all the information regarding Abu Nidal and the bank account he had established for his daughter at Wegelin & Company. If what Harvath was telling her was true, and she had every reason to believe it was, this was something she wanted to secure a warrant for and do by the book.

In spite of what everyone thought about the Swiss banking system, the world had changed since 9/11, even for them. They had no desire to help terrorists launder or hide money. Claudia felt confident that she could secure the proper paperwork to compel the bank to give her the information that Harvath needed. The only part she couldn't guarantee was how long it would take. It could be a matter of hours, or depending on the judge, it could be a matter of weeks.

Considering that lives were at stake, she hoped it would be the former.

Before hanging up, Claudia had joked that this was the first time Harvath had ever asked her for a favor that didn't involve putting her life in danger. While getting a Swiss bank to part with its records wasn't exactly easy, it was definitely easier than having somebody shoot at you.

The joke had made Harvath smile. Claudia was a good woman. She also knew him well enough not to be surprised when he told her there was a second favor he needed, and that it was going to be slightly more dangerous than her trip to the bank.

With the majority of the Swiss operation entrusted to Claudia and a small percentage to the Troll, Harvath had proceeded to a private airport outside São Paulo to meet his plane.

The entire time, he was wrestling with a very bad feeling as he put together a picture of who might be behind Philippe Roussard. Of course, there was the very real possibility that Roussard had access to his mother's account at Wegelin & Company, but that wouldn't explain who had gotten him out of Gitmo. There was more to this. There was someone else involved.

The Troll had been thinking the exact same thing, but their shared conclusion was impossible. Harvath had been there the night Adara Nidal was killed, and he had seen her die.

CHAPTER 102

Though Harvath was traveling on his German passport as Hans Brauner and could go anywhere in the world he wanted, he had been marked a traitor, which made him a man without a country, and what was worse, he had absolutely no idea where he should be going.

In Roussard's twisted countdown, the Bucket of Blood might have been meant for the final two plagues, but Harvath doubted it. He had a very bad feeling there was still one attack to go, and that it would represent the plague in which the waters were turned to blood.

Harvath tried to run through all of the people he knew who lived on or near water. He had grown up in California, spent a significant amount of time in the Navy, and lived on the East Coast for the last several years; the list was long. It was so long, in fact, that Harvath couldn't keep track of all the names inside his head and had to find a pen and paper to write them all down.

It was a hopeless task. There was no telling where Roussard was going to strike next. The U.S. Ski Team facility in Park City and the Bucket of Blood in Virginia Beach were almost as random as Carolyn Leonard, Kate Palmer, Emily Hawkins, and his dog. They were all significant to him, but they were not people or places he would ever have anticipated being attacked.

After the jet had made its descent into Houston's Intercontinental Airport and Harvath had made his way through passport control and customs, he proceeded to the private aviation business center.

The first thing he did, after building his layers of proxy servers, was to plug in his ear bud and make hospital calls. Finney's security teams were still in place and Harvath spoke with their captains. Ron Parker had updated each of them on the failed attack in Virginia Beach.

As a precaution, the team watching Harvath's mother had her moved to another room, which didn't face the street. From a car bomb perspective, Tracy was already protected.

Harvath spoke with her father, who told him that they had run additional tests and the results weren't good. The new EEG suggested further decreased brain activity, and they had been attempting to wean her off the ventilator without any luck. Tracy was still not able to breathe on her own. There was a double downside to that, as not only could she not breathe on her own, but as long as she was on a ventilator there was still no way to conduct a full MRI to look for the exact cause of her coma and the true extent of the damage.

There was a tone of fatalism in Bill Hastings's voice that Harvath didn't like. "This is not what Tracy would have wanted," he said. "All these tubes and wires. The ventilator. Remember Terri Schiavo?" Bill asked. "We had talked about her once, and Tracy told us she would never want to live like that."

Bill and Barbara Hastings were Tracy's parents and

her next of kin, so that gave them the power to make medical decisions on Tracy's behalf, but it sounded as if they were considering throwing in the towel.

As long as Tracy was alive, there was still hope that she might pull through, and Harvath told them so.

Bill Hastings was not as optimistic. "If you'd spoken to the doctors, Scot. The neurologists. If you'd heard what they had to say, you might feel differently."

The man didn't have to say it. Harvath knew he and his wife were seriously considering removing their daughter from life support. He asked them not to do anything until he could come back and be there. It seemed like a reasonable request. Though he and Tracy hadn't been together long, their relationship was intensely close and committed.

The elder Hastings's response took Harvath completely off-guard. "Scot, you're a good man. We know you cared for Tracy, but Barbara and I feel this is a family decision."

Cared? They were talking about her as if she were already dead. Immediately, Harvath knew what he had to do. He'd find a way to get into the hospital without being apprehended. He had to. He had to be with Tracy and more important, he needed to speak with Tracy's father, man-to-man.

Harvath was ready to alert his pilots to file a flight plan for D.C. when an email appeared in his gmail account that changed everything.

CHAPTER 103

Claudia had found a judge with a real thing against terrorists who used Swiss bank accounts to fund their actions. The judge moved quickly, granting Claudia everything she asked for.

Attached to the email was a transaction history for the Wegelin & Company account. Harvath scanned through it, paying close attention to activity that had taken place subsequent to the night Adara Nidal was supposedly killed. One of the first things he noticed was a series of payments to something called the Dei Glicini e Ulivella in Florence.

Harvath did a Google search and discovered that Dei Glicini e Ulivella was an exclusive private hospital. It had an elite plastic surgery team billed as "one of the best" in Europe. Among their many specialties was the treatment of severe burn victims, including reconstructive surgery, rehabilitation, and recuperation.

He didn't know how she had done it, but Adara Nidal had somehow survived. She had not only managed to get away from the scene of the explosion, but she had also managed to get to someone inside the Italian law enforcement apparatus to sign off on one of the charred corpses from the scene as being hers. It was an elaborate vanishing act, but she had done it. Harvath didn't want to believe it, but the proof was right in front of his face, and he had learned a long time ago not to underestimate any of the terrorists he went up against.

Skipping ahead to the most recent transactions, he came to something even more troubling. Shortly before each of the attacks, money had been transferred to a nearby bank. Harvath scanned the list and ticked off the dates and locations of all the attacks so far—Bank of America in Washington, D.C.; California Bank & Trust in San Diego; Wells Fargo Bank in Salt Lake City, Utah; Washington Mutual Bank in McLean, Virginia; Chase Bank in Hillsboro, Virginia; First Coastal Bank in Virginia Beach, Virginia; and finally, U.S. Bank in Lake Geneva, Wisconsin.

As the pilots were filing their flight plan and readying the plane for takeoff, Harvath contacted Ron Parker and gave him instructions to overnight the items he'd left at Elk Mountain to the Abbey Resort in Fontana, Wisconsin.

After Parker took down the information, he asked Harvath how much longer Finney's jet and its two pilots had to remain in Zurich. Finney had an important guest for whom he needed the plane and its crew.

Harvath told Parker to thank Finney again on his behalf and to assure him that he wouldn't need it too much longer.

It had all been part of that second favor he'd asked Claudia for. When Kevin McCauliff had sent Harvath a follow-up email from outside the NGA with additional details he'd pulled about Wegelin & Company's being the source of the money routed to Brazil, he'd included a warning. Though he couldn't prove it, he had a sense that both his phone and his work computer were being monitored and suggested Harvath be on his guard.

From that email, Harvath had devised a plan of how to be in two places at once and how to make it work to his advantage.

His country club chat with Jim Vaile, the director of the Central Intelligence, notwithstanding, he had no illusions about what would happen to him the next time Morrell and his team caught up with him.

At best, they'd take him back into custody, and if that happened, Harvath knew Morrell's men would see to it that he didn't escape. And at worst, one of Morrell's people would put a bullet in him.

Either would remove him from the game and give Roussard an open field to finish his rampage. Harvath couldn't let that happen. As far as he could see, he was the only chance the people in his life had. The president was mired in gridlock and regardless of his promises to the contrary, wasn't capable of stopping Roussard.

Morrell and his people were good, and Harvath was tired of looking over his shoulder for them. They needed to be drawn off-guard and taken out of play. That was why Harvath had gotten Tim Finney to send his empty jet to Zurich.

Harvath knew the FAA would be monitoring the jet's flight plans. After Kevin McCauliff's word of caution it seemed like the only way to go. If Morrell and his team knew about the Wegelin & Company account, and if they saw Finney's jet heading for Zurich, it might be enough to make them believe Harvath was on it.

To make the bait even more attractive, Harvath had Claudia register him at a Zurich hotel under one of his DHS aliases, and the Troll established an electronic credit card trail around the city that would all but confirm his presence. While his professional aliases were in no way public knowledge, he was confident that Morrell and his people would be looking for him to pop on the grid with one of them. It was exactly what he would do in their place.

The idea was to lure Morrell and his team to the hotel where Claudia's husband, Horst, and his tactical team would be waiting to take them into custody.

Claudia had assured him that under Switzerland's rigid antiterrorism laws, if any of Morrell's men were carrying weapons of any kind, she could hold them for quite some time before actually filing any charges. The only hitch was that she had to catch them first.

CHAPTER 104

CAMP PEARY, VIRGINIA

Rick Morrell didn't like any of it. It had fallen right into his lap. It was too sloppy, especially for a guy like Harvath, and that's why he decided to pull the plug.

Standing his team down, he put up with all their bullshit complaints as he had them unload the plane and stack their gear back in the two trucks they had used to drive out to the CIA's private airstrip.

"I still don't get it," said Mike Raymond as they passed the final checkpoint and headed toward the highway. "It's almost like you don't want to catch this guy."

"If that's what you believe then you are just as stupid as Harvath thinks you are," replied Morrell.

"What are you talking about?"

"I'm talking about Harvath completely disappearing from the grid. Nobody sees him, nobody hears from him, and then suddenly, *whammo,* he pops back up."

"Correction," stated Raymond. "Suddenly he gets *in contact* with someone the NSA *already* has under surveillance. That's how we got our lead."

Morrell looked at his subordinate and realized he was going to have to connect the rest of the dots for him. "And it doesn't bother you that McCauliff started back-scrubbing all of his data trails and had the DOD do a pickup sweep on all his phone lines? He might not have known when he was talking to Harvath that someone was peeping on him, but he figured it out pretty fast."

"You're paranoid. Even if McCauliff did know about it, it didn't change the nature of the intel he gave Harvath."

"Meaning?" asked Morrell.

"Meaning Harvath has been off the grid because he went to ground. It wasn't until he got something actionable that he popped back up."

"And the fact that he popped back up using one of his known DHS aliases and a credit card doesn't bother you?"

Mike Raymond shrugged his shoulders. "Switzerland is fucking expensive. Show me one hotel that doesn't expect you to present a credit card upon check-in."

"How about a hostel?" offered Morrell. "Or a *Gästezimmer* in a private house? He could use a campground. He could even pick up some unwitting woman and shack up at her place. This is tradecraft 101."

"Sure, maybe, but—"

"He knows we're watching his buddy Finney's aircraft," said Morrell, plowing on, "yet he'd use it anyway to go to Zurich? I don't buy it. It's too good a trail."

"So just like that you pull the plug?"

"Listen, Harvath's problem has always been that he thinks he's smarter than everyone else. You read his jacket yourself."

"We all read his jacket, but what if Harvath set this all up because he knew you'd react this way."

Morrell smiled. "He's smart, but he's not that smart."

Raymond shook his head. "Either way, it probably doesn't make much difference. Even if he was in Zurich, he's already got a head start on us. We could make the trip only to discover he's already long gone."

"That's also one of the reasons I changed my mind."

"But what if you're wrong?"

"And Harvath really is in Zurich?" asked Morrell.

Raymond nodded.

"If Finney's plane wasn't a decoy and Harvath was dumb enough to use it, we can still track it. Let's wait and see what happens."

"What about the hotel Harvath supposedly registered at?"

"I've already got that covered."

"Are you going to use an agency person from our embassy over there?" asked Raymond.

"No. The DCI was very clear. This needs to be kept absolutely quiet. I've got a friend; an ex-DOJ guy who retired and moved over to Copenhagen. He can go in and check things out for us."

"You mean that book dealer? Malone?"

"Yeah, he owes me a favor. He can be in Zurich in a few hours," replied Morrell.

"And you trust him?"

"Completely. He's a smart guy. He knows what he's doing."

Raymond looked at Morrell. "And what if Malone calls and says Harvath really is in Zurich?"

Morrell scoffed. "We'll jump off that bridge when we come to it. Personally, I think we've got a much better chance of Harvath turning up here in the States than we do overseas."

"I hope you're right."

"Trust me," replied Morrell. "When it comes to Harvath, I know exactly what I'm talking about."

CHAPTER 105

Known as the "Hamptons of the Midwest," Geneva Lake and the handful of resort towns and villages that surrounded its crystal-clear, spring-fed waters were a vacationer's paradise. There was boating, sailing, swimming, hiking, fishing, shopping, and amazing golf.

Thirty-six holes plus lunch was what Harvath offered his pilots when he booked them into the Abbey Resort along with himself and asked if he could have use of their rental car in exchange.

The pilots were more than happy to comply. While they had an okay per diem, the sitting around and waiting for a client part of their jobs was normally the worst part. They didn't always get to stay in a resort of the Abbey's caliber and get thirty-six holes of golf and lunch to boot.

The arrangement worked out well for Harvath too. He didn't want to let anyone know where he was, and if he used his real ID or credit cards, anyone who was looking for him would instantly know where he was. And as useful as the Hans Brauner alias was, it didn't come with a driving permit.

Of course Harvath could have stolen a car, but in such a small community that was something he would have done only if he were desperate.

Meg's wedding and reception were the day after tomorrow and were to be held at the Lake Geneva Country Club. The club, or LGCC as it was commonly called, sat on the southeastern shore of the lake. It was an idyllic setting for a wedding.

What Harvath couldn't figure out, though, was how Roussard was going to spin the last plague and cause the waters to run red with blood. With the president in attendance, security was going to be beyond tight. In fact, no matter how badly Harvath wanted to go take a look at LGCC and the security the Secret Service had put in place, he knew it was pointless. He'd been a presidential advance team leader. The club would be locked up tighter than Fort Knox.

Even coming in via the water was out of the question. As boring a job as it was standing guard over a location in advance of a presidential visit, the local, state, and federal law enforcement officers who would be there right now would be taking their jobs very seriously. No one ever wanted to have something happen to the president, especially on their watch. Harvath knew that firsthand, and he knew it the hard way, because it had happened to him once.

The more Harvath had thought about it, the more targeting Meg's wedding made sense. Roussard would get a lot of bang for his buck. Not only could he gain international fame and notoriety for the attack, but the killer could also harm additional people who were very significant to Harvath. There had to be something Harvath could do to stop him.

But first, he had to understand what his play was

for Lake Geneva and Meg's wedding. Did he have
access to extra muscle? And just as important, as this
was the final plague and seemed to involve the president as well, would his mother, Adara, show?

With payments recently made from her account
in Switzerland to the private burn treatment hospital
in Italy, Harvath doubted it. If Adara were up to it, she
would have been the one hunting him, not her son.
Harvath and Adara would have their final dance soon
enough, but before that, he needed to stop Roussard
once and for all.

The basic questions of *what, why, where, when,* and
how ran through Harvath's mind as he tried to fit the
pieces together.

The *what* was the attack itself. The *why* was something Harvath had tried to understand but couldn't, at
least not one hundred percent. Adara Nidal wanted
revenge for Harvath's thwarting her plans to ignite a
Muslim holy war with Israel, and she was using her
son to exact that revenge. That was the best Harvath
could make of it.

The *where* was the Lake Geneva Country Club
and the *when* was sometime during Meg's wedding or
reception. Her nuptials were set to be one of the social
events of the year. Her guest list undoubtedly read like
a *Who's Who* of Chicago elite. The wealthy, the beautiful, and the powerful would all be there. On top of
that, both the mayor of Chicago and the president of
the United States would be in attendance. If it was
successful, Roussard's attack would make headlines and
be felt around the world.

Harvath had four out of five criteria for stopping Roussard's attack figured out. He had the what, a good chunk of the why, as well as the where and when. All he needed now was to uncover the *how*.

CHAPTER 106

It was a perfect evening. The temperature was in the low seventies, all of the stars were out, and a light breeze was blowing in off the lake.

Meg Cassidy's friend and next-door neighbor, Jean Stevens, had opened all her doors and windows. This wasn't the kind of night you wasted by sealing yourself up in your cottage and running the air-conditioner.

They had been blessed with an amazing Indian summer. There was no telling how much longer it would last and Jean Stevens intended to squeeze every last ounce of enjoyment out of the season before she returned to the Chicago suburbs and another interminable Chicago winter.

Refilling her glass with sailboat-shaped ice cubes, she poured herself another vodka and tonic. As she turned to walk back out onto her porch, she got the scare of her life.

Before she could scream, the figure standing in front of her placed his hand over her mouth.

Cautioning her not to make a sound, the man

turned out the lights and led her to one of the chairs at her breakfast table.

"What the hell are you doing?" she asked as Harvath removed his hand from her mouth and let her sit down. "You almost gave me a heart attack."

"Surprise," answered Harvath as he pulled out a chair for himself and sat down.

"*Surprise* is right. What are you doing here? Meg told me you never RSVPed for the wedding. She had no idea if you were coming or not. It's rather poor form not to respond, you know, especially when Meg was big enough to invite you. Just because you two didn't work out is no reason not to be courteous. Wait a second," she said as she paused. "Where are my manners? Come here and give me a hug."

Harvath stood and gave her a hug. Jean hadn't changed a bit. Meg had always referred to her as Auntie Mame meets Lily Pulitzer. She was a warm and endearing character. It was obvious why she and Meg had become such close friends. To know Jean Stevens was to love her.

"So are you here to convince Meg to drop that jackass she's marrying and run away with you?"

"Todd's not that bad, Jean," replied Harvath.

"The hell he isn't," said Stevens as she got up to fix Harvath a drink. "He's manipulative, controlling, overbearing—"

"And he's also the man she picked to spend the rest of her life with," stated Harvath as he held up his hand and waved Jean back from the bar.

"Then you're not here to convince her to marry you instead," she replied flatly as she retook her seat.

"I'm afraid not."

"That's too bad; you two were good together."

"I need you to do me a favor, please," said Harvath, changing the subject.

"You just name it, honey," replied Jean. Her bangled wrist jangled as she patted him on his knee.

Harvath removed an envelope from his pocket. "I need you to give this to her."

Jean Stevens arched her left eyebrow. "I'm sensing the possibility of some eleventh-hour fireworks here," she said with a smile. Reaching for the cordless phone behind her, she added, "Why don't I just call her? I'm sure she's tearing her hair out with all the last-minute details, but I think she could find a minute or two to come over and say hello. Seeing you, maybe she'd come to her senses."

Harvath put his hand on top of hers and lowered the phone to the table. "This is complicated."

"Most things in life are, honey. Listen, I'll make daiquiris and you two can talk. I don't even have to be here. I can take a walk if you'd like. It would probably be better if you two were alone anyway."

Harvath couldn't help but smile. He'd never met anyone who'd meant well more than Jean. "By complicated, I mean professionally, Jean. Not personally. I shouldn't be here."

"If you're worried about Todd—"

This time Harvath laughed. "No, I'm not worried about Todd, believe me."

"Cloak-and-dagger stuff, huh?" she replied with a conspiratorial wink.

"Kind of. Listen, no one can know I'm here. Meg doesn't know yet and this has to be kept very quiet. Can I trust you?"

"Honey, nobody keeps a secret like me. My lips are sealed," she said, accepting the envelope. "Consider it done. Now, how about something to eat?"

"I'm sorry," replied Harvath as he stood. "I can't stay."

"Well, as long as we're both single, how about being my date for the rehearsal dinner tomorrow night? It should be pretty swanky. We're getting picked up on the dock at five-thirty for a little cocktail cruise and then it's off to the club for dinner."

"I have to say no to that too," replied Harvath, shaking his head.

Jean stared at him. "Honey, can I ask you a question?"

Harvath had already pressed his luck by coming within thirty yards of Meg's place and the Secret Service detail assigned to watch her. "Okay," he conceded, "one question."

"Are you happy? I mean *honestly* happy."

The question was quintessential, get-right-down-to-it Jean Stevens, but it still took him by surprise. "What do you mean?"

"What do you think I mean? It's a simple question. Are you happy?"

"I guess it would depend on how you define happy," said Harvath, anxious to get moving and also maybe a bit uncomfortable with how the woman he was standing in front of had always had such an uncanny ability to read people.

"Being happy boils down to three things. Something to do. Someone to love. And something to look forward to."

She said nothing more. As her words hung in the air, she studied him. He and Meg *had* been good together. Harvath was a great guy and reminded Jean a lot of her husband, strong, good-looking, and exceedingly kind to the people he cared about. It was a damn shame that things hadn't worked out between him and Meg.

Harvath stood there for several moments, the uncomfortable silence growing between them. Finally, he bent over and kissed her on the cheek. "Thank you for getting my note to Meg," he said, and then he was gone.

CHAPTER 107

Philippe Roussard stood on the end of his private pier and looked out across the darkened lake. Closing his eyes, he felt the breeze as it moved around him. From somewhere off in the distance, he heard a chorus of sailboat halyards clanking against aluminum masts as the craft bobbed up and down at their moorings.

Roussard had spoken with his handler again, and again the conversation had ended badly. They had argued about the botched attack on the bar in Virginia Beach. His handler blamed him for its failure, because he was the one who had changed the plan at the very last minute. The RV was overkill, as was the amount of diesel fuel and fertilizer. Roussard should have stuck with the pickup truck with a lesser amount contained within its enclosed bed. Had he proceeded as instructed, everything would have been successful.

The pair was also still at odds over how the last plague attack would be carried out, as well as how Scot Harvath should be killed afterward.

Roussard was tired of arguing. He was in the field and he would make the decisions as he saw fit. He had a means to get out of the country once his work was done and he also had enough money at this point to finish the job. The incessant bickering was counterproductive.

The simple truth was that they were strangers to each other. Too much time had passed, and blood alone was not enough to bridge the gap between them.

Roussard opened his eyes and lit another cigarette. He knew he was going to do exactly what he wanted. The last attack would be dramatic. It would be chilling in its audacity and a fitting finale to all that had preceded it.

He took a long drag and thought about where he would go when it was all over. In his day-to-day existence in Iraq and then during his absolutely hopeless incarceration at Guantanamo, he had never thought much beyond the next hour, much less the next day, week, month, or even year, but that was beginning to change inside him. He could see a value in preparing for the future, in setting goals for oneself.

He had tasted real field work and he liked it. He did not fear capture, although he was smart enough to realize that his days in America were numbered. He needed to be leaving soon, but not before his crowning achievement.

Raising the night vision binoculars to his eyes, he took one final look at his target and then walked up the dock and retired to his rented cottage. It was time to get some sleep. Tomorrow would be a very busy day.

CHAPTER 108

Though asking Gary Lawlor to arrange for a special security detail for Meg had been the right thing to do, it only made Harvath's job harder.

He needed to talk to Meg face-to-face, and meeting her in broad daylight was out of the question. She'd have too hard a time shaking the detail.

Losing them at night, after they already thought she'd turned in, was something Meg could pull off.

Harvath sat in the back of Gordy's Boathouse, one of Fontana's most popular waterfront bars, and looked at his watch for a fifth time. He tried to compute how long it should have taken for Jean Stevens to get his note to Meg and then for Meg to get out of her house and walk the old Indian footpath along the lakeshore to Gordy's.

The bar was crowded with the young, the wealthy, and the good-looking who made Lake Geneva their summer playground. A DJ spun records while bright strobes of colored light knifed across the dance floor.

As Harvath watched, he remembered the good times he and Meg had had here. He was still watching the crowds of people dancing when he felt a hand, a man's hand, fall upon his shoulder.

He'd been looking for Meg, and while he'd noticed the man's approach in his peripheral vision, he hadn't paid him much attention. To be honest, he wasn't that remarkable. It wasn't until Meg's fiancé, Todd Kirkland, actually touched him that Harvath realized who he was.

"We need to talk," said Kirkland.

"About what?" asked Harvath, though he knew why the man was there.

Meg's fiancé held up the note Harvath had given to Jean Stevens and said, "This."

They moved away from the dance floor to the front of the bar where they found a freshly vacated table and sat down.

"You want to tell me what this is all about?" asked Kirkland, waving the note in Harvath's face.

Harvath ignored him as a waitress approached.

Picking up the table's empty wineglasses and handing them to her, he asked the waitress to please bring them two beers.

The minute she walked away, Kirkland was back at it. "Who the hell do you think you are? You think you can just . . ."

As much as Harvath had tried to take the high road with Jean Stevens, she'd been right. Kirkland was a jackass. He was arrogant and rude, which no doubt stemmed from a deep sense of insecurity. Harvath didn't know what the guy had to be insecure about.

He made a shitload of money as a commodities trader and his looks weren't all that bad, especially after he supposedly had gotten his nose, eyes, ears, and chin done by one of the best plastic surgeons in Chicago.

Despite his faults, Meg had found something in him that she loved. If he was indeed manipulative, controlling, and overbearing, that was Meg's problem. Nobody was forcing her to marry him.

Nobody had forced Harvath to sabotage his relationship with her either, and as he sat across the table from the man she was going to marry in less than forty-eight hours, he couldn't help but wonder what it was she saw in him.

"You're going to explain this letter to me right now," asserted Kirkland, drawing Harvath's mind back to the matter at hand. "What the hell are you trying to do?"

"Nobody's trying to do anything, Todd," said Harvath calmly.

"My ass you're not," he responded. "This is all about you. You're in cahoots with that crazy bitch who lives next door, aren't you? She's always asking Meg questions about you, especially when I'm around and—"

"Todd, Jean Stevens and I aren't in cahoots together in anything."

"Really? Then how'd she end up with this letter for Meg? Keep in mind that it's kind of hard to deny you sent it when you were sitting exactly where the letter said you'd be."

"I'm not denying anything. I needed to talk to Meg," replied Harvath.

"And you couldn't do it over the phone?"

The waitress had returned and Harvath waited for her to set their beers down before answering Kirkland. "No. I need to speak to Meg in person."

"About what? The fact that you still have feelings for her? If that's the case, I can tell you with absolute certainty that she is one hundred and ten percent over you, pal."

Harvath hated when people called him pal, especially ignorant assholes who not only were most certainly not his pal, but also didn't know what the fuck they were talking about. "I'm assuming Meg doesn't know about my note?" said Harvath, trying to keep the conversation on an even keel.

"No, and she's not going to, as far as I'm concerned."

Harvath hated the high road. He took a long sip of beer and tried to maintain his composure. Finally, he said, "I have reason to believe that Meg is in danger."

"Which is why you had the Secret Service assigned to protect her, isn't it?"

"Yes, but—"

"*Yes,* my ass," spat Kirkland. "You just did it to flex your muscle, and I'm pretty goddamn sick of it. Every time I turn around I've gotta be reminded of you. It stops right here, right now."

Harvath had to tell himself to ease up on the grip he had around his beer glass before he broke it. "Don't turn this into a pissing match with me, Todd. This is a serious threat."

"So why aren't you talking to the Secret Service about it, then?"

The man did have a point, and Harvath hated to concede it to him. "Because we don't yet know the exact nature of the threat."

"*We?* Who's we? DHS? FBI? CIA?"

When Harvath didn't answer, Kirkland responded, "See, I didn't think so. This is all about you. *You* and Meg—at least in your mind. But I've got news for you. There is no you and Meg, not anymore. It's over. So stay the fuck away from us," he added as he rose and pushed his chair in.

Harvath pushed the chair back out with his foot for Kirkland to sit back down. "Don't be such an ass. I'm here because a credible threat exists. This guy is serious and he's going to be gunning for your wedding."

Meg's fiancé wasn't interested in sitting. "Something tells me that with the president attending our wedding, if there was a real *credible* threat you'd be working with the Secret Service to stop it, not trying to meet up with my wife in the middle of the night at some bar."

Kirkland fished a twenty-dollar bill out of his wallet and threw it on the table. "And just for the record, the only reason Meg sent you an invitation to our wedding was that she wanted to show you she had moved on with her life. Maybe you should think about doing the same."

CHAPTER 109

Todd Kirkland climbed back into his Bentley Azure feeling pretty damn good about himself. He'd longed to tell off that prick Harvath once and for all and he'd done it. A huge weight had been lifted from his shoulders.

Dropping the Azure's top, he adjusted the rearview mirror and smiled at himself.

Harvath had been the one thing about his wedding day that had really bothered him. He'd argued repeatedly with Meg about her reasons for inviting him, but none of that mattered now. Based upon the look on Harvath's face when he'd told him off, Kirkland doubted he'd have the balls to show up at the ceremony. With Harvath out of the picture, he could focus on enjoying the rest of the weekend and the rest of his life with Meg Cassidy. After all, he'd won. He had Meg and Harvath didn't. That's what it all boiled down to.

Kirkland pulled out of the parking lot and turned on to south Lake Shore Drive for the quick jaunt back to Meg's cottage. As he was thinking about how good he had it, he felt something eating away at him. He tried to push it from his mind, but it refused to go away. *What if Harvath was telling the truth?*

Kirkland never really knew what Harvath did for a living other than that he was employed by DHS and that Meg couldn't talk about it. It was one of those secrets that she shared with her ex-beau that really burned him up. Could there be a threat the Secret Service wasn't aware of? Could Meg be in greater danger than anyone knew?

As he reached the turn-off for Meg's cottage, Todd Kirkland decided it would be in everybody's best interest if he had a little chat with the Secret Service agents who were standing guard outside.

An hour and a half later, Rick Morrell's cell phone rang. After taking down all the information, he alerted the members of his Omega Team. They'd located Harvath. He was in Wisconsin.

CHAPTER 110

When the FedEx truck pulled beneath the Abbey Resort's porte cochere, Harvath was ready and waiting for it.

Presenting his Hans Brauner ID, he signed for his package and gave the valet the ticket for the pilots' rental car.

Powering up the onboard navigation system, he entered the address for U.S. Bank in Lake Geneva and got on the road.

He removed his Heckler & Koch USP compact tactical pistol, his Benchmade knife, his BlackBerry as well as his DHS credentials and two spare clips of ammunition Ron Parker had thrown in out of courtesy and then tossed the empty FedEx box into the backseat. As he drove, he asked himself what the hell he had been thinking when he had attempted to set up a rendezvous with Meg.

What could he possibly have achieved? Was he hoping that she would call off her wedding? Or was he hoping that somehow she would speak with the president on his behalf and everything would be made all right?

As the answers raced through his mind he knew none of them were correct. What he had wanted to do was to warn her.

Harvath wanted to give Meg the chance that Tracy, his mother, and all of Roussard's other victims hadn't had. But it was more than that. Looking deeply into himself, Harvath discovered that what he wanted more than anything else was to alleviate the guilt he was feeling that he still had not been able to stop Roussard. If anything happened to Meg, at least he would have known he had warned her. What bull-shit.

No matter what he did or didn't tell Meg Cassidy, if anything happened to her, it would fall squarely upon his shoulders, and he knew his guilt would be just as great as the guilt he carried over what had hap-pened to Tracy Hastings.

He was the only person at this point who could stop Roussard.

That said, it didn't mean the Secret Service shouldn't be aware of what he had discovered. Todd Kirkland had been right about that, and Harvath had contacted Gary Lawlor and had filled him in.

Gary would see to it that the Secret Service was informed, but Harvath knew there was only so much they could do with the information.

Harvath emailed Lawlor the full dossier he had on Philippe Roussard, including the photographs. He trusted his boss to scan it and pass along all of the per-tinent details. The Secret Service would make sure all of their agents were carrying Roussard's photos.

The Secret Service in turn would ask their local and state law enforcement contacts to be on the look-out for him. But that's where it would end. If any of them happened across Roussard, it would most likely not be until it was too late.

The cops had gotten lucky with Roussard in Virginia Beach. Harvath doubted it would happen again.

CHAPTER 111

The Lake Geneva branch of U.S. Bank was located on the east side of the lake in the town of Lake Geneva near the intersection of Geneva and Center streets.

Carrying a plain manila envelope, Harvath entered the bank, presented his DHS creds to one of the loan officers, and asked to speak with the branch manager.

He was shown into a private office, where an attractive woman in her late forties stood and introduced herself as Peggy Evans.

"How can we be of service to the Department of Homeland Security?" she asked once her visitor was seated and she had finished looking at his ID.

Harvath reached into his envelope and pulled out the pictures of Philippe Roussard he'd printed at his hotel's business center. "Do you recognize this man?" he said as he handed them to Evans.

The woman studied them for a few minutes and then asked, "What is this in regard to?"

"The man in those photos is a wanted terrorist. We have records indicating that he received funds via wire transfer at this bank two days ago."

"Are you suggesting the bank has done something wrong? Because I can assure you that—"

Harvath held up his hand and shook his head. "Not at all. We're just trying to gather as much information as we can about him."

"Do you have any specific information about the transaction?"

Harvath handed her copies of what Claudia had emailed him from the Wegelin & Company bank in Switzerland.

Evans studied the records, then picked up her phone and dialed an extension. "Arty, will you come in here, please?"

Moments later, a heavyset Hispanic man in his early thirties knocked and entered the office. "You wanted to see me?"

"Yes, I did," said Evans as she introduced the man to Harvath. "Arturo Ramirez, this is Agent Scot Harvath from the Department of Homeland Security. He has a few questions he'd like to ask about a customer we had in the bank two days ago."

Harvath rose and shook the man's hand.

"Arturo handles all the wires," the woman continued. "He also never forgets a face. Do you, Arty?"

Ramirez smiled politely at his manager and accepted the series of photographs. "Yes, I remember him," he said after studying the pictures. "Peter Boesiger was his name, I believe. Nice guy. Swiss."

"Interesting," replied Harvath, as he pulled a pen from his pocket. "How do you know he was Swiss?"

"He used a Swiss passport for ID. I assumed that meant he was from Switzerland. He spoke with an accent too."

"Did you make a copy of his passport, by any chance?"

"Of course," said Ramirez. "It's standard bank procedure."

"May I see the copy, please?"

Ramirez looked at Evans, who nodded.

He disappeared from the office and returned several minutes later with a photocopy of Roussard's Boesiger passport.

"Is there anything else you can tell me about him?" asked Harvath.

Ramirez looked at him. "Like what?"

"Did he have anyone else with him?"

"No," answered the portly teller. "He came in by himself."

"How about his vehicle? Did you notice what he was driving?"

Ramirez shook his head *no*. "Didn't see it."

"Did he make small talk with you at all? Did he mention where he was staying, anything like that?"

"Not that I can remember."

At this rate, Harvath was quickly coming to the end of possible questions he could ask.

Then Ramirez said, "Wait a second. He asked me for directions. It was an address for a real estate office. It was near here, but I can't remember which one. We talked about walking versus driving there. I told him that if he was already parked, he'd probably be better off walking it than trying to find a new spot once he got there."

Having remembered the crucial piece of information, Ramirez's broad face was cleaved with a wide grin.

As Harvath accepted a phone book from the bank manager, he wondered how many real estate offices there could be in a resort town like Lake Geneva.

CHAPTER 112

When Rick Morrell and the members of his Omega Team arrived in the village of Fontana, they split into two squads and, posing as FBI agents, interviewed Todd Kirkland and Jean Stevens simultaneously.

Neither of them was able to provide any concrete leads to Scot Harvath's whereabouts. Next, they visited the bar and restaurant where Harvath had been the night before, Gordy's Boathouse. While the waitress remembered serving Harvath once Morrell had shown her his picture, she hadn't spoken with him other than to take his order.

With only a handful of hotels in the village, Morrell and his team got to work trying to figure out where Harvath was staying. They started with the hotel in closest proximity to Gordy's Boathouse, the Abbey Resort.

Very quickly, the resort looked like it was going to
be a bust. There was no one registered under the name
of Scot Harvath, or any of his known aliases. None of
the front desk staff recognized his photograph. It was
the same with the bell staff.

Morrell and one of his men were on their way
back to the car when they passed the valet stand and
handed Harvath's picture around.

"Yeah, I know that guy," one of the valets said. "I
brought his car up to him this morning."

"You're sure?"

"Positive."

Morrell whipped out his cell phone and text mes-
saged the rest of his team to come back from the other
hotels they were investigating. They'd found where
Harvath was staying.

With the valet's recognition of Harvath, Morrell
and his men began the slow process of piecing together where Harvath was in the hotel.

First, they sifted through the morning's vehicle
claim checks. Once they weeded out the ones the
valet was certain hadn't belonged to Harvath—two
Porsches, an Audi, and a new Mercedes convertible—
they took the rest inside.

With the help of the front desk manager, they
were able to ascertain which checks belonged to guest
rooms with guests who had checked in within the last
twenty-four hours. Morrell doubted Harvath had been
here longer than that.

The only guest to have checked in within the
last twenty-four hours and to have had his vehicle

go out first thing that morning was a man named Nick Zucker, registered in room 324. Having already established himself as an FBI agent pursuing a fugitive from justice, Morrell asked the front desk manager for a passkey.

The manager made up a keycard, and no sooner had he handed it to Morrell than he and his men moved quickly out of the lobby.

There was a housekeeping trolley at the end of the hallway, and flashing his badge, Morrell conscripted a young housekeeper. Outside 324, Morrell and his people took up positions on either side of the door, and he nodded for the housekeeper to knock.

She gave a loud rap, calling out, "Housekeeping."

When no one answered, Morrell waved her away, slid his own keycard into the lock and opened the door.

He and his men swept inside, but the room was empty. They found a small toiletry kit in the bathroom with prescription medications labeled for a Nick Zucker from a pharmacy in Phoenix and a pilot's uniform hanging in the closet that couldn't possibly fit Harvath.

A small overnight bag contained a change of clothes, a worn paperback thriller, and a Sudoku workbook. Inside the workbook were several pictures of a man and his family, one of which showed him in his pilot's uniform next to a plane with his teenaged daughter and son.

They'd made a mistake. Scot Harvath was not posing as Nick Zucker. Morrell had his men put everything back the way they'd found it.

They were halfway down the hallway when the front desk manager appeared and held up two additional keycards.

"I did a little more looking," he stated when he reached Morrell. "Zucker checked in with another man named Burdic. According to their registration cards, they both work for the same aviation company. There was a third man who checked in at the same time; his name is Hans Brauner. He told the clerk last night that he would be paying for their rooms and also arranged for golf and lunch for them today."

Burdic's room was as useless as Zucker's, and the one belonging to the supposed Hans Brauner had nothing. Morrell, however, knew they had zeroed in on Harvath.

Instead of having the desk clerk from the previous night come in to work to ID Harvath's photo, they simply emailed it to him. Over the phone, he confirmed that the photo belonged to the man registered as Brauner who had shown up with the two pilots.

So now Morrell not only knew the alias Harvath was using, he also knew how Harvath was getting around, both in the air and on the ground. Through his contact at Langley, Morrell had credit reports pulled for Zucker, Burdic, and Brauner.

He wasn't surprised that nothing came back for Brauner. Zucker and Burdic, though, were another story. Among the run-of-the-mill crap one would expect to find—mortgage payments, department store charges, and so forth—was a particularly serendipitous find. Zucker had rented a car at the airport yesterday.

Not only was the car from a national chain, but Morrell also knew that they used a GPS tracking system in their vehicles as part of something known as "fleet management." It was beginning to look as if Harvath might not be that hard to catch after all.

CHAPTER 113

As it turned out, there were eight real estate offices in downtown Lake Geneva, and each employed a multitude of agents. The proverbial needle in a haystack analogy didn't even come close to what Harvath was facing.

It took him all morning and well into the afternoon to make his way through the offices and to track down the realtors who might have had contact with Roussard/Boesiger in the last two days.

He'd come up empty in all of the offices except one, Leif Realty, which had a sign in its window saying it was closed for the day and would reopen tomorrow. Harvath had left multiple messages on the Leif Realty voicemail system and finally managed to get the owner's cell phone number from another realtor in a nearby office.

It was almost four o'clock when Leif Realty's owner, Nancy Erikson, called him back and told him she could meet him at her office in fifteen minutes.

When Harvath arrived, Erikson unlocked the front door and let him inside.

The office was small and had been decorated to look like the interior of a lakeside cottage.

"Being able to close for a personal day, especially at the end of the season, is one of the perks of owning your own business," she said as she powered up a Tassimo "cup-at-a-time" coffee machine.

She rattled off a list of hot beverages she could make, all of which Harvath politely declined. Erikson was his last lead, and he was eager to find out what she knew about the man he was hunting.

"He set up everything almost exclusively via email," said Erikson as she pulled a file from the stack on her desk. "I'd say over seventy-five percent of our business happens through our website these days. You almost don't need a realtor," she added with a chuckle.

"Can you tell me about the house Boesiger rented?" asked Harvath.

The woman slid a flyer from the file and handed it to him.

"Nice place," said Harvath as he studied the pictures. It was a large home right on the water. "Seems like a lot of house for one person."

"I thought that too, but that's the way a lot of Europeans are. They live such cramped existences over there that when they go on vacation they really want some breathing room."

Harvath doubted that was what was motivating Roussard. He'd picked this house for another reason.

"Can you show me where specifically on the lake the property is located?"

Erikson rolled her chair over to the bookcase and returned with a large book about Lake Geneva. She opened it to the center and unfolded a large map. Her finger hovered over the lake's north shore until it came down with a *plop* and she stated, "The house is right about there."

She spun the book around on her desk so Harvath could see where the property was located.

Lake Geneva was the second deepest lake in Wisconsin. It was 7.6 miles long, but only 2.1 miles across at its widest point. One of the possibilities that Harvath was quietly considering was that Roussard had selected the house because it provided an unobstructed line of sight to his target. A missile or RPG attack was not something Harvath was willing to rule out, especially when he knew it was one of the Secret Service's worst nightmares and something that was all but impossible to defend against.

As soon as Harvath located the Lake Geneva Country Club along the lake's south shore, he ruled out his line-of-sight rationale. He compared the location of Roussard's rental to Meg Cassidy's cottage as well as the estate of Rodger Cummings, the president's college roommate, with whom Rutledge always stayed when he visited Lake Geneva. Neither of them fit the bill either. Whatever kind of an attack Roussard was planning, he wasn't going to launch it from where he was now.

Turning back to the flyer, Harvath asked, "Do you have any other photos of the property?"

"We've got a couple more on our website," said Erikson as she booted up her computer. When she had clicked through to the page for the house Roussard had taken, she turned the monitor so Harvath could see for himself.

"Can you click on the virtual tour, please?" said Harvath after she had scrolled through all the static images.

Erikson was halfway through the second 360-degree virtual tour when Harvath ordered her to stop. "Back up," he said.

The realtor dragged her mouse, slowly moving the image back the way it had come. Finally, Harvath said, "Right there. Stop."

The camera had been set on a manicured lawn that led down to the water. It provided a perfect view of the home's short pier and the view beyond. What Harvath was interested in wasn't the view, though. It was the hull of a sleek powerboat that sat beneath a striped awning in the pier's sole boat slip.

"Oh, that," replied Erikson, rolling her eyes. "That boat almost cost me the deal."

"What do you mean?" asked Harvath.

"When Mr. Boesiger arrived, I had to explain to him that it had developed a problem with its fuel line and had to be taken in to the shop. The home's owners offered a very generous discount on his rental rate but he didn't care about the discount, he wanted the boat and was very angry that it wasn't available.

"I know the family who owns the Cobalt dealership in Fontana. They agreed to lease me one of their best boats so Mr. Boesiger could have a comparable watercraft for the duration of his vacation."

Harvath couldn't believe his good fortune. "And how long is that supposed to be for?"

"Mr. Boesiger is paid through Sunday, but when we were trying to arrange a new boat for him he said he didn't care when it came as long as he had it by today."

CHAPTER 114

As Harvath left Leif Realty, he knew he had uncovered a major part of how Philippe Roussard planned on carrying out his attack. It was going to come from the water.

Scenes of a USS *Cole*–style ramming attack briefly flashed through Harvath's mind, but he discounted them. Roussard did not strike him as suicidal, and when it came to the Lake Geneva Country Club, there was nothing to ram. The club was perched high at the water's edge and almost impossible to get significantly close to because of a series of wooden piers and boat slips.

There was a chance that Roussard could pack his boat full of explosives and try to leave it in one of the slips closest to the clubhouse, but it would be next to impossible for the craft to avoid Secret Service scrutiny. Well before the president had arrived they would have checked each boat over completely and matched it with its rightful owner, upon whom a thorough background investigation would have already been completed along with background checks of all the other members of the club.

Harvath backed out of his parking space and followed the directions Nancy Erikson had given him for the rental property. As he drove, he gave play to every conceivable scenario that might involve Meg's wedding and Roussard's access to a high-powered speedboat.

The SEAL team that accompanied the president whenever he visited marine environments would be on, under, and all around the water during the wedding. In addition, there would be numerous support craft keeping boaters a good distance away from the area. A straight kamikaze-style run by Roussard would certainly fail.

Reaching Highway 50, Harvath turned left and headed west, parallel to the lake's north shore. There had to be something he wasn't seeing; something about the boat, but he couldn't figure out what it was.

With a hard perimeter established around the country club, the only way it could be breached was with an attack that, once launched, couldn't be stopped. Again, Harvath returned to the idea of a projectile of some sort, along the lines of a Stinger missile or an RPG.

Consulting his map, Harvath noticed that he was coming up on the turnoff for Roussard's lakefront rental. When he saw the road sign, he eased off the gas and applied his turn signal.

Moments later, he was driving down a paved lane

shaded by a canopy of tall oaks that had been planted at equal intervals along both sides of the road.

As Harvath drove, he focused on what lay ahead of him. Most important, he focused on the need to keep Roussard alive until he uncovered what the man had planned.

For all Harvath knew, the boat might have nothing to do with Roussard's attack and everything to do with his getaway. He couldn't close his mind off to any options.

As Harvath followed a gentle bend in the road, he was unable to see the dark SUV that had just turned off the highway behind him.

CHAPTER 115

About a half mile before Roussard's, Harvath came upon a small home undergoing extensive renovation. As it was nearing five o'clock, all the construction workers had gone. He pulled into the gravel drive and parked. He'd cover the rest of the distance on foot.

Roussard's rental property was bordered on three sides by thick wood. Harvath decided to approach from the far side, opposite the road.

He moved as quickly as he could without making too much noise. Nothing moved save for a cloud of gnats that seemed to follow him every step of the way.

At the edge of the woods, Harvath stopped. From where he sat, he could make out the entire rear and one side of the French château–style home.

Roussard had registered a Lincoln Mark VII with the real estate office, but the driveway was empty.

There were no interior lights and none of the windows were open. Only the hum of the air-conditioning unit hinted at the possibility of human life inside. It was time to make his move.

Maneuvering through the woods to a spot nearest the garage, Harvath located the side door off the garage and removed the set of keys the realtor had given him from his pocket.

Crouching low, he pulled his H&K, counted to three, and made a break for it.

He moved fast, making sure his approach wouldn't be seen from any of the windows. At the door, he slid the key into the lock and opened it slowly.

The first thing he noticed was Roussard's Lincoln. Harvath walked over and placed his hand on the hood to see if it had been driven recently. It hadn't.

Skirting a collection of brightly colored beach toys, he headed for a short flight of steps and the door that led into the house. He didn't expect it to be locked and it wasn't. Roussard was like most people who trusted the overhead garage door to be a sufficient line of defense.

The air inside the home was much cooler than that in the garage. It washed over Harvath as he slipped inside and silently shut the door behind him. He was in a mudroom area just off the kitchen.

He stood for what felt like an eternity and quieted his breathing to focus solely on listening. His ears strained for any sound that would tell him where in the house Roussard might be, but no such sound came.

Tightening his grip on his pistol, Harvath began to systematically clear the structure. He moved with practiced efficiency as he swept into each room with his H&K at the ready.

Room after room was empty. There was no sign of Roussard anywhere on the first floor. Reaching a grand staircase, Harvath took the carpeted steps two at a time as he raced upward, eager to confront Roussard and end the chase that had begun the moment Tracy had been shot.

Harvath buttonhooked into each bedroom, checking closets, bathrooms, and under beds. Nothing, no sign of Roussard anywhere.

Harvath reached the master bedroom and finally began to see evidence that Roussard had actually been staying in the house. The bed was unmade and the bathroom sink and shower were slightly wet. As recently as that morning, Roussard had been there, but the walk-in closet was empty, not a suitcase, backpack, or bag to be seen anywhere. Roussard was already prepared to disappear, but it didn't make any sense, the wedding wasn't until tomorrow. *Why pack up your clothes, your toiletries, and everything else a day early?*

Looking out the French doors that led to the master bedroom's private balcony, Harvath had an unimpeded view of the lake. His eyes were immediately drawn to the pier and the conspicuous absence of the Cobalt speedboat Nancy Erikson had arranged for Roussard.

A bad feeling was growing in the pit of Harvath's stomach.

He backtracked the way he'd come, rechecking everything along the way. When he got to the garage, he opened the driver's-side door of Roussard's Lincoln and popped the trunk.

Smiling back at him was a bright blue Kiva duffel. "Gotcha," said Harvath.

But after opening it and sifting through all its mundane contents, he realized he hadn't gotten anything. Clothes, toiletries, it was all run-of-the-mill stuff. Not only was there nothing incriminating inside the bag, there was nothing at all pointing to what Roussard was planning to do.

Harvath slammed the trunk closed and was about to go back inside when he noticed a large plastic garbage can by the garage door.

He ran to it and threw back the lid. At the bottom was a white garbage bag. Harvath pulled it out and took it back inside the house.

Clearing off the dining-room table, he ripped open the bag and emptied its contents. Illuminated by the shafts of waning afternoon light, he picked through the few bits and pieces of trash that had accumulated over Roussard's short stay.

There were empty mineral water bottles, microwavable entrée packages, ashes, butts, and a couple of empty packs of Gitanes. Mixed in among every-

thing was a brochure for the grand yachts of the Lake
Geneva Cruise Line company.

Harvath took a dish towel and wiped the brochure
clean. Rental homes the world over were filled with
local magazines, as well as brochures on sights and
things to do. It was no surprise that the owners of this
house would have done the same for their renters. But
what was it about this brochure that warranted Roussard's throwing it out?

Harvath rapidly flipped through the pages, trying
to discern its significance. It wasn't until he neared the
end that he noticed a dog-eared page, and his heart
stopped cold in his chest.

The text at the top read "The Grand Yacht *Polaris*
was built in 1898 for Otto Young, one of the first mil-
lionaires on Geneva Lake. Experience the luxurious
lifestyle of this time period while surrounded by the
original mahogany and brass aboard the *Polaris*. Her
deck is open to the lake breeze and the cabin area
contains a beautiful brass-top bar. Perfect for private
tours, or treat your guests to a one-of-a-kind cocktail
party."

Harvath had been wrong. Roussard's target wasn't
Meg's wedding, *it was her rehearsal dinner.*

As he dropped the brochure on the table he heard
the distinct sound of a hammer being cocked behind
him. It was followed by Rick Morrell's voice from the
other side of the kitchen saying, "Don't move, Scot.
Don't even breathe."

CHAPTER 116

A million and one things sped through Harvath's mind, chief among them being, *How the hell had they found him?*

Harvath knew that any attempt to negotiate with Morrell would be futile. He didn't care how close he was to nailing Roussard and he wouldn't care that Roussard was at this very moment about to carry out another attack. Morrell's sole purpose was to put a hood over Harvath's head and throw him into a dark hole for a long time.

If there was one thing that Harvath knew about life, it was that it was all about timing, and Morrell's just plain sucked.

Without warning, Harvath dropped to the floor and out of sight of Rick Morrell and his men. As he scrambled on his hands and knees into the living room, the dining area erupted in a hail of silenced weapons fire. Morrell's marching orders were clear— Harvath was to be taken dead or alive.

The front door exploded inward and Harvath fired a volley of booming rounds into the frame, which scattered an additional contingent of Morrell's men and sent them scurrying for cover outside.

Firing several more rounds as he ran, Harvath made it to the grand staircase and charged up the steps. Reaching the master bedroom, he could hear men pounding up the stairs behind him.

There was no time to slow them down by barricading the door. Harvath needed to maintain his lead.

Racing through the bedroom, he shut the doors to the walk-in closet and the bathroom and let himself out the French doors onto the small balcony.

Checking first for any signs of Morrell's men on the ground below, Harvath hopped up onto the stone balustrade and pulled himself onto the steeply sloped roof.

The slate tiles were almost impossible to get traction on. Harvath's feet kept slipping as he moved his way down the roofline. His goal was to drop onto the garage and from there to the ground where he could make his way back into the woods. However, it didn't turn out exactly the way he had planned.

Ten feet away from the garage, Harvath's foot caught a loose tile and he lost his balance—this time for good.

He went down hard, hitting the edge of the roof before being launched into the open air. Harvath tried to right himself, but he was traveling at too great a rate of speed.

He landed hard on his left side, the force of the impact crushing the air from his lungs. Despite the thick bed of landscaping mulch, had he landed on his head, his neck would have snapped like a matchstick. Though Harvath didn't feel very lucky at the moment he was, *extremely*.

Even though his brain was scrambled from the fall and he couldn't breathe, he knew on a primal level that he needed to get moving or he was going to be dead.

He sucked in huge gulps of air, trying to saturate his lungs with oxygen. As his chest heaved, he caught sight of his pistol lying in the dirt several feet away.

He scrambled toward it, and as his fingers closed around the slide, he felt the air returning to his lungs.

Getting to his feet, Harvath made sure to remain below the window line as he ran toward the garage. When he got there, he pulled up short, flattening his back against the cool stone wall. Raising his H&K to chest height, he risked a quick peek around the corner.

Two of Morrell's men were already on the ground looking for him, and one was headed his way. In a word, Harvath was *fucked*.

CHAPTER 117

The only chance Harvath had of escape was to draw Morrell and his men off his trail, and to do that, he was going to need to take one of them out of commission.

Planting his feet, Harvath crouched and gripped his pistol by the barrel, turning the butt outward. All of this would be so much easier if he were willing to kill Morrell and his team, but that was still off the table.

He quieted his breathing and listened. He knew the man was just around the corner, no more than a few feet away, yet he couldn't hear anything.

Harvath's legs burned and sweat was breaking out on his forehead. He was like a coiled spring that had been wound too tight. He wasn't going to be able to hold this position much longer.

Suddenly, there was a flash of color as one of Morrell's men did a hasty peek around the corner of the garage. That was when Harvath sprang.

Grabbing the man's submachine gun with his left hand and pulling him off-balance, Harvath slammed the butt of his pistol into the man's temple hard enough to make him see stars, lots of them.

Instantly, his knees buckled, and Harvath yanked him the rest of the way around the corner to his side of the house.

Keeping his own pistol trained on him, Harvath took the man's MP5, as well as a spare magazine, and slung it over his shoulder. The man carried a .40 caliber Glock in a paddle holster at his hip, and Harvath helped himself to that too.

In the man's ear was a Secret Service–style ear bud. Harvath checked his collar and found a microphone, which was connected to a small, Midland walkie-talkie on his belt.

"I'm going to give you one chance," whispered Harvath. "Tell your team I'm in the woods, north of the house headed for the road. Got it?"

"Fuck you," spat the man, his head still reeling.

Transitioning to the silenced MP5, Harvath jammed the weapon into the man's groin. "He's in the woods, north of the house and headed for the road," repeated Harvath. "Do it, or I'll blow your balls off."

With his eyes glaring at Harvath, the man nodded.

Harvath reached over and activated the microphone.

Wincing in pain, the man stammered, "This is McCourt. Harvath's in the woods north of the house. He's headed for the road."

Releasing the *transmit* button, Harvath pulled the submachine gun out of the man's crotch and cracked him across the side of the head, knocking him unconscious.

He waited until he heard Morrell's people go crashing through the brush at the north end of the property and then made his break for the waterfront.

As he ran, his mind replayed what Jean Stevens had said about the rehearsal dinner. *We're getting picked up on the dock at five-thirty for a cocktail cruise and then it's off to the club for dinner.*

Harvath looked at his Kobold. It was already five-thirty-three.

No longer caring that his cell phone could allow the CIA to pinpoint his location, Harvath pulled his BlackBerry from his pocket and turned it on. As soon as it registered a signal, he dialed Meg's cell phone. He was immediately dumped into her voice-mail and realized that the phone must have been turned off.

The only other person he knew on the boat was Jean Stevens, but he had no idea if she even carried a cell phone, much less what her number was.

Harvath contemplated calling the Secret Service, so they could alert the agents on Meg's detail, but working his way through the chain of command would take too much time.

He was the only person who could possibly stop Roussard, but to do that, he needed a way to get to the other side of the lake.

Arriving at the shore path, Harvath stopped. He could go either right or left, but whichever direction he chose it needed to have a pier in close proximity with a fast boat. If he chose wrong, Meg Cassidy, as well as her Secret Service detail and all of her guests, were going to die.

Harvath ran out to the end of Roussard's dock to get a better view. East of his location for at least a thousand yards was nothing but shoreline, while less than two hundred yards to the west were a handful of short piers like the one he was standing on. Several of them had boats, and one even had a family that was loading theirs with food and wine as they prepared to go out for an evening cruise.

Harvath pulled his creds from his pocket and spun, ready to ID himself to the boat's owners as he ran for their dock, but was instead greeted by the sight of Rick Morrell's silenced MP5 pointed right at his head.

CHAPTER 118

You were always too smart for your own good," said Morrell, his gun trained on Harvath. "Where's McCourt?"

"Sleeping it off behind the garage," replied Harvath. "Listen, Rick—"

Morrell held up his hand. "My guys wanted to grab you in downtown Lake Geneva when you were heading for your car, but I said no. It was too public. Now I've got one man down and the rest of my team on a wild-goose chase. This is going to end right here before anybody else gets hurt."

Harvath started walking toward him. "We don't have time for this."

Morrell responded by painting a racing stripe with his MP5 right up the dock, stopping only inches from Harvath's feet. "Stop right there and drop all your weapons, right now," he commanded.

"Roussard is on his way to kill Meg Cassidy."

"Roussard's not my problem. Now drop your weapons."

"He killed Vaile's nephew, for Christ's sake. You'll be a hero at the Agency for bagging him. Jesus, Rick. You know Meg. You know better than anybody else what she risked when she agreed to come on that assignment with us. I don't care what anybody has told you, you can't let some shitbag terrorist kill her."

"It doesn't matter. I'm not authorized to—"

"Fuck *authorized*. This is about us—all of us who were part of that operation to hunt down Abu Nidal's kids. Do you know who Roussard is?"

Morrell shook his head. "I don't think it would make any diff—"

"He's Adara Nidal's son, Rick," replied Harvath, cutting Morrell off again. "This whole thing is about revenge. Payback for whatever twisted thing they think I did to her. And it's why he saved Meg for last."

A flood of images sped through Morrell's mind. He remembered all too well the mission to take down Adara and her brother that he and Harvath has been assigned to years ago.

"All that matters," continued Harvath, "is that we stop Roussard. After that, I'll put the cuffs on myself, but we've got to get the hell out of here."

Morrell lowered his weapon and said, "How?"

CHAPTER 119

The twenty-nine-foot-long Cobalt speedboat his realtor had provided was more than up to the task Roussard had set for it.

Affixing the commercial-grade tripod to the deck in the rear seating area had proven to be a little more time-consuming than he had anticipated, but it wasn't anything he couldn't handle. The specially milled joining plates provided a perfect mount for the weapon.

Originally, Roussard had thought he'd have to wait until the very last moment to seat it, but then he witnessed the family a few docks over returning home from an evening of waterskiing and tubing. The next morning, he purchased a similar oversized neoprene-covered "ski tube" and found that it concealed the tripod-mounted weapon perfectly.

The 20mm M61A2 Vulcan was an electrically fired, six-barreled Gatling-style gun that could spit out over six thousand rounds per minute. Not only would Meg Cassidy and all of her guests be ripped to shreds before they knew what had happened, but so would all the bystanders on the shore behind them. The *Polaris* itself would also be so badly damaged that it would very likely catch fire and sink.

There was no doubt that the waters of Lake Geneva would run red with blood, the fulfillment of Roussard's final plague.

His body coursed with adrenaline as he bobbed silently in the water a safe distance away. Through his binoculars, he watched as the last of Meg Cassidy's tardy guests were loaded aboard the oblong pleasure steamer moored at the end of her pier. It was only a matter of minutes now.

Roussard had picked the perfect spot for the attack. The bar at the Abbey Springs Yacht Club would be loaded with early-bird customers, as would its restaurant and the terrace outside. Beneath the terrace, the Yacht Club's beach would be populated with families barbecuing, as well as beachgoers who had not yet called it a day.

The scene both on the *Polaris* and behind on the grounds of Abbey Springs would be nothing short of horrific. Roussard shook with anticipation.

Peering through his binoculars once again, he watched as the last of Meg Cassidy's passengers boarded and the crew began to untie the lines.

The water was calm and there was little wind to upset the boat's orientation and equilibrium. It was a perfect night for the type of killing Philippe Roussard was about to do. He smiled as he reflected on how proud his mother would be. He almost didn't want it to end, but of course it had to. And after tonight, he had only one last name to check off his list. After tonight, he would finally begin to hunt Scot Harvath.

Three sharp blasts of the *Polaris*'s steam whistle signaled its departure from the pier. Roussard reached down and turned the key, firing up the citron-yellow Cobalt's engines.

He had already piloted the route several times during the day. As the *Polaris* passed the subdivision before Abbey Springs known as the Harvard Club, Roussard would uncover the Vulcan and move in for the kill. By the time he reached Meg Cassidy and her guests, they would be parallel with the Yacht Club and the fun could begin.

As he watched the *Polaris* cruise past a small spit of land that jutted out into the lake, which he'd learned from his maps was called Rainbow Point, he could hear laughter and the tinkling of glasses accompanied by jazz music.

The passengers of the *Polaris* were blissfully

unaware of what was about to happen, and Roussard's sense of power soared. Nudging his throttles forward, he picked up speed.

He took in the positions of the other boats around him, noting that the lake looked no different than it had over the last two days. The small number of law enforcement boats the lake did have were actively tied up at the Lake Geneva Country Club, preparing for the president's attendance at a wedding that would never happen. In essence, Roussard's getaway was all but guaranteed. And if any do-gooder was stupid enough to give him chase after the attack, he would have more than enough ammunition left to blow him right out of the water.

Seeing the *Polaris* approaching the Harvard Club, Roussard peered beneath the ski tube to make sure the weapon was "hot" and ready to fire.

Satisfied that everything was exactly as he wanted it, he straightened up and focused on the target.

As the steamship neared the Harvard Club, Roussard bumped the throttles farther forward and began to pick up speed again.

When the *Polaris* pulled even with the Harvard Club's swim pier, Roussard threw the ski tube overboard and pushed the Cobalt's throttles all the way forward.

It took only a moment for the speedboat to pop out of the hole, and once the craft was on plane, it accelerated like a jet off an aircraft carrier.

He'd already opened the boat all the way up earlier in the day, but the sensation was nothing like what he was feeling now. He rose from his seat, feeling his body become one with the craft. With the Vulcan, the three of them combined to create the perfect killing machine.

Roussard watched as the distance between him and his unknowing victims aboard the slow-moving *Polaris* narrowed.

As he got within a thousand meters of the steamship he began to count down in bite-sized chunks. Seven hundred meters. Six hundred meters. Five hundred.

He wanted to shout the attack cry of his ancestors as his boat ripped through the water and he closed in on the final several hundred meters. Already he could see passengers on the *Polaris* taking notice. At first their faces reflected bewilderment and then terror as they realized what was happening and comprehended that they were powerless to stop it.

He was within a hundred meters of where he needed to bring the boat to a stop so that he could man the Vulcan. Seventy-five. Now fifty meters!

As Roussard cut back the throttles, the engines failed to quiet. Instead they roared and grew louder.

It took the killer but a fraction of a second to comprehend what was happening, and by then it was too late.

CHAPTER 120

The hull of the bright-red Cigarette boat sliced right through Roussard's Cobalt. At the moment he realized what had happened, the deed was done. Roussard was barely able to throw his hands up in front of his face before impact.

Passengers aboard the *Polaris* began screaming as soon as they saw that the low-slung Cigarette boat was doing nothing to avert an impending collision with the bright-yellow Cobalt.

The sound of the impact was sickening. Fiberglass was ripped apart and rent asunder as the Cigarette plowed right through its victim and kept going, grazing the stern of the *Polaris*.

The Cigarette finally stopped when it ran aground halfway up the rolling hill that met the thin strip of rock, sand, and grass that composed the Harvard Club's shorefront.

The first thing Harvath heard as he came to were the terrified screams from the *Polaris*. Blood was dripping into his right eye, and he raised his hand to his forehead and felt a gash several inches long. Looking to his left, he couldn't find Morrell and assumed he'd been ejected.

Smoke was pouring from the engine compartment. Harvath cut the engines and the wildly spinning props soon fell silent. Stumbling from the boat, he looked for Morrell and found him lying near a rock wall over thirty feet away. He was barely conscious, and Harvath knew better than to move him. He told Morrell to stay still and that he'd be back with help soon.

What he didn't share with him was that he had something else he had to do first.

Off the end of the Harvard Club boat pier, Harvath could see the two halves of Roussard's boat upturned and bobbing just above the waterline. Ignoring the splitting pain from his head, Harvath took off running down the pier, launching himself at the end of it in a flying leap over the water.

When he plunged beneath the surface, he opened his eyes and began looking for Roussard. He stayed down as long as he could, until he had no choice but to come up again for air. Circling the wreckage in search of the terrorist, he ignored the burning sensation of spilled gasoline that was pouring into his wound.

He was about to submerge himself again when he heard coughing from about seventy-five yards away. It had come from a fleet of moored sailboats. Swimming as quietly as he could, Harvath made for the sound.

From Fontana, the village air raid siren was calling the police, volunteer fire, and rescue workers to duty.

Unobserved, he moved closer to the sailboat, and then, taking a deep breath, Harvath slipped once more beneath the surface of the water.

When he got beneath the sailboat's heavy, fixed keel he looked up and saw a pair of legs feebly treading water. Sliding his Benchmade from where it was

clipped in his pocket, Harvath depressed its lone button and the blade swung up and locked into place.

Like a great white shark circling its prey, Harvath
made a loop beneath Roussard and headed upward,
quietly breaking the surface behind him.

The man must have sensed Harvath's presence,
because all of a sudden he spun, his eyes wide with
fear. Blood was running from his nose as well as
both of his ears. When he coughed, great gobs of it
came out, and as Harvath positioned himself for the
kill, he noticed that one of Roussard's eyeballs must
have become detached, as it remained stationary and
didn't track the way the other one did.

There was no mercy in Harvath's heart for this
terrorist, this killer of innocent men and women.
Roussard was beyond rehabilitation, and Harvath
knew the greatest gift he could give the American
taxpayers was to prevent Roussard from ever standing
trial and living out the next twenty years on appeal
after appeal in some prison somewhere.

Harvath swung the knife with one fluid slash, and
its blade tore through the soft flesh of Roussard's
throat. *That which has been taken in blood, can only be
answered in blood,* he thought to himself.

Watching him die, Harvath began to realize that
he'd made a mistake. The blade was so razor-sharp that
Roussard probably hadn't even felt it. Bleeding to
death was too good for him. Harvath wanted him to
be filled with terror as he died, just as so many of his
victims had.

Quickly swimming around behind him, Harvath

placed both of his hands upon Roussard's shoulders and pushed him beneath the surface of the water.

The man struggled violently for almost a minute. Then his body fell quiet and Harvath knew he was dead.

CHAPTER 121

Harvath remained at the scene with Rick Morrell until an ambulance arrived. Though the CIA operative insisted he'd be fine, the EMTs put him in a cervical collar, placed him on a backboard, and transported him to the hospital for evaluation. Once Morrell was gone, Harvath made his way back down to the water.

The *Polaris* had docked at the end of the Abbey Springs boat pier, and when Todd Kirkland saw Harvath making his way to where all the passengers were gathered, he thought for sure he was coming for him. But he wasn't. Nor was he coming for Meg. Instead he spoke briefly with Meg's two Secret Service agents and then took Jean Stevens by the hand and led her away.

After walking back along the lake path to her cottage to pick up extra clothes and her car, Jean drove Harvath to the Abbey Resort. Still soaking wet, he walked straight past the gaping-mouthed stares of the front desk staff to his room.

He called the pilots and told them to be ready to move in five minutes, then quickly changed into the clothes Jean Stevens had given him. As she drove them to the airport, Harvath informed Zucker and Burdic that they were flying to D.C. His one hope was that he would make it there before Tracy's parents could remove her from life support.

When the plane touched down it was raining. Through the rain-soaked windows of his cab, he could see by the light of the D.C. streetlights that the leaves were already beginning to turn color. Summer was officially over.

Tracy's night nurse, Laverna, was the first one to notice him when he stepped into the ICU. "I tried to call you. Didn't you get any of my messages?" she asked.

Harvath shook his head. "I've been out of pocket for a few days. How's Tracy?"

The nurse gripped his arm. "Her parents took her off the ventilator this afternoon."

The tide of emotion that welled up inside him was overwhelming, and he was too exhausted to try to fight it. He could not believe that Bill and Barbara Hastings had done it. They could have at least waited for him to return. Tears formed at the corners of his eyes and he did nothing to try to hide them.

"She's strong," stated the nurse, "she's a fighter."

Harvath couldn't understand what she was saying. He was too exhausted. He just stared at her blankly.

"She's still alive."

Harvath turned and moved quickly away from the nurse's station.

When he entered Tracy's room, her parents looked up from where they were sitting. Neither of them knew what to say.

Ignoring them, Harvath walked to the other side of the bed and picked up Tracy's hand. He gave it a squeeze and said, "It's me, honey. It's Scot. I'm here now."

There was a movement, and at first Harvath thought he was imagining it. Then it happened again. It was weak, but Tracy had squeezed his hand. She knew he was there.

At that moment, everything came flooding out of him. He buried his head in her hair and as she squeezed his hand again he began to cry.

CHAPTER 122

JERUSALEM

Tracking down the puppeteer pulling Philippe Roussard's strings began with a visit to Dei Glicini e Ulivella, the exclusive private hospital in Florence where payments from Roussard's mother's Wegelin & Company account had been made.

Harvath didn't know what to expect. Part of him thought he might find a badly burned Adara Nidal sitting up in her hospital bed waiting for him, her silver eyes unmistakable behind a mask of charred flesh.

What he discovered was that the payments weren't for Adara Nidal. Instead, they were for a male patient with a name Harvath had never heard before and who had recently up and left.

All Harvath's suppositions had been wrong. Adara was not the person behind Roussard's release from Gitmo and his subsequent attacks within the United States. It was somebody else—a man with a false name who had simply vanished.

The first person who entered Harvath's mind was Hashim, Adara's brother and Philippe's uncle. But when the hospital administrator finished touring Harvath through the patient's abandoned room and showed him into his office, Harvath realized how wrong he'd been in assuming Adara or her brother were behind the monster that had been Philippe Roussard. Sitting on the credenza behind the administrator's desk was something that pointed to another person—someone far more complex, far more twisted, who had a reach long enough to fake his own death, even for a second time.

When asked about it, the administrator claimed it had been a gift from the patient whom Harvath was looking for. It was all the identification Harvath needed.

Harvath's taxi cab pulled up in front of an old, four-story building in Jerusalem's popular Ben Yehuda district. The storefront was composed of two large windows crammed full of antique furniture, paintings, and fixtures. The gilded sign above the entryway read

Thames & Cherwell Antiques, followed by translations in Hebrew and Arabic.

A small brass bell above the door announced Harvath's arrival.

The dimly lit store was still packed with tapestries, furniture, and no end of faded bric-a-brac. It had been preserved exactly as it was on his first visit here years before.

He neared a narrow mahogany door and pulled it toward him to reveal a small, wood-paneled elevator. Pressing a button inside, he watched as the door closed and he felt the elevator rise.

When it arrived on the uppermost floor, the door opened onto a long hallway, its floor covered by an intricately patterned Oriental runner. The walls were painted a deep forest green and were lined with framed prints of fox hunting, fly-fishing, and crumbling abbeys.

As Harvath walked forward, he remembered the infrared sensors placed every few feet and guessed that there still were pressure-sensitive plates beneath the runner. Ari Schoen was one man who took his security very seriously.

At the end of the hall, Harvath found himself in a large room, more dimly lit than the shop downstairs. It was paneled from floor to ceiling, like the elevator, with a rich, deeply colored wood. With its fireplace, billiards table, and overstuffed leather chairs, it felt more like a British gentleman's club than the upper-floor office of a shop in West Jerusalem.

Sitting up in a mechanical hospital bed near a pair

of heavy silk draperies drawn tight against the windows was the man himself.

"I knew one of you would eventually come," said Schoen as Harvath stepped into the room. He was even more hideously deformed than before, his nonexistent lips barely able to shape the words emanating from his charred hole of a mouth. "I assume Philippe is dead."

Harvath nodded.

"How did you know it was me?" asked Schoen.

"Adara's bank account at Wegelin."

"The payments to the clinic," mused Schoen as medical instruments clicked and buzzed around him. "I think you're lying, Agent Harvath. That was a completely clean alias I was registered under. There was nothing to tie anything back to me. It had never been used before and hasn't been used since."

"It wasn't the alias, it was your whiskey," Harvath said, pointing at the antique globe that hid Schoen's bar beneath its hinged lid. "The 1963 Black Bowmore. 'Black as pitch,' you once told me. You must have thought very highly of the hospital's director to have given him such an expensive present."

Schoen raised his hand to brush the thought away as if it was nothing. "You are more intelligent than I gave you credit for."

"Tell me about the other men you had released from Guantanamo. What was their connection to you?"

"There was no connection," said Schoen with a laugh. "That was the point. They were background noise that Philippe could be lost in. They were randomly selected to keep anyone in your government's intelligence services who might come investigating, guessing."

"And the plot with the children?"

"An unfortunate, but extremely effective motivator. When I discovered I had a grandson, I reached out to him, but our relationship was understandably strained. He wanted very little to do with me, but somewhere inside him he understood that we were the only family each other had.

"When he was captured and taken to Gitmo, I decided I would do anything to get him back."

Slowly, all of the madness was beginning to make sense. "I want the names of your people who kidnapped and killed the school bus driver. I also want to know all of the other bus routes you had targeted."

Schoen looked at him for a moment and then said, "The school bus we hijacked in South Carolina was the only one. There are no others. The photos of other buses were ploys to gain your government's acquiescence, nothing more."

His face was a mass of twitches and spasms, which made him nearly impossible to read. "How do I know you're not lying?" asked Harvath.

"You don't," replied Schoen. "Only time will tell."

"What about the names of the operatives who hijacked the bus?"

"I will take them to my grave," said the man.

Harvath wasn't surprised, but that would be for

someone else to take up. He had other questions at this point. Glancing at the silver-framed photographs positioned on an adjacent console table, he asked, "So why me? Why *my* family and the people I care about?"

"Because Philippe wanted the man responsible for his mother's death."

"Which was his uncle, Hashim."

"But his uncle was dead," said Schoen. "The very idea of your being responsible for it all filled him with rage. Rage is a very powerful emotion. If a man has enough of it he loses his self-control. And when a man loses his self-control he is much more susceptible to the control of another."

"So you pinned it on me," responded Harvath.

"As I said. It was nothing personal."

Harvath looked at him. "What was in all of this for you?"

Schoen sat up from his bed and spat, "Revenge!"

CHAPTER 123

Revenge against whom?" demanded Harvath. "Against me?"

"No," hissed Schoen. "Against Philippe's mother."

"For what? The first time a Nidal blew you up, or the second?"

"It was for taking my son away from me," he replied as he sank back into his bed.

"But Adara Nidal was dead," said Harvath who was beginning to wonder if Roussard's warped psychopathology was a condition inherited not from his mother, but rather from his paternal grandfather.

"It made no difference to me. Stealing her son from her and turning him to my cause would have been the ultimate act of revenge."

"How could you expect an Arab, a Palestinian Arab at that, to renounce Islam and pick up the Israeli cause?"

"You forget that after my Daniel died I studied everything I could about Abu Nidal, his organization, and most important, his family. I knew more about them than they even knew about themselves. Philippe lacked a masculine role model."

"And that was going to be you?" said Harvath facetiously.

"Half of my blood, my Daniel's blood, ran through his body. He was half Israeli and I believed I could appeal to that side of him. But before he would listen to anything I had to say—"

"He wanted me dead," stated Harvath, finishing Schoen's sentence for him.

"Precisely. But he didn't only want you dead. He wanted you to suffer. He wanted you to feel the pain he had felt at losing his mother. I knew I could use this incredible rage to draw him closer to me."

"And the plagues and running them in reverse order?"

Schoen was wheezing, and stopped for a moment to catch his breath. Finally he said, "The plagues were a tribute to his mother, who devoted her career as a terrorist to igniting a true holy war against Israel. Her attacks were often tinged with Jewish symbolism.

"As for running the plagues in reverse, you must already comprehend what a disturbed individual Philippe was. In his mind, the first plague was the most shocking and dramatic, so he ran the plagues backward, conducting himself as God's opposite, the devil, if you will, who was saving his favorite plague for last."

"And you thought you could reprogram this monster?" said Harvath.

"For a while, yes. If I could convince him to follow my orders, I would not only have beaten Adara, but in a small way, I would have regained my son. But I realized eventually that he was out of control and likely would have come after me. Which is why I left the hospital in Italy and returned here."

The man was absolutely pitiful, and Harvath shook his head and turned to walk away.

"Where are you going?" demanded Schoen.

"Home," replied Harvath, who hoped to never gaze upon Ari Schoen's hideous face again.

Schoen laughed. "You don't even have the courage to pull out your gun and shoot me."

"Why should I?" replied Harvath as he turned back to face him. "As far as I'm concerned, a bullet is too good for you. And as for courage, if you had any you would have already shot yourself. The worst thing I can do for you is to wish you a long life and walk right out that door."

And that was exactly what Harvath did.

★ ★ ★

As he exited the shop he noticed a black SUV with heavily tinted windows parked across the street. It was strangely out of place.

Reaching beneath his jacket, Harvath's hand hovered just above the butt of his pistol.

The SUV's rear window rolled partway down and in the sea of black, there was suddenly a flash of white. It belonged to a long white nose and was followed by a pair of dark eyes and two long white ears.

Harvath crossed the street and held his hand up for the dog to smell. As he scratched Argos behind his ear, the SUV's window rolled the rest of the way down.

"Did you have a nice visit?" asked the Troll, who was sitting inside between his two Caucasian Ovcharkas.

"Hello, Nicholas," replied Harvath. "Why am I not surprised to see you here?"

"We have unfinished business between us."

Harvath removed his hand from the dog's head and said, "No we don't. I made good on my promise to you. You cooperated and I didn't kill you."

"I want my data and the rest of my money back," responded the Troll. "*All* of it."

The man had balls, big ones. "And I want my friend Bob and the other Americans killed in New York back," stated Harvath. "*All* of them."

The Troll leaned back and conceded. "Touché." Slowly, the little man's eyes drifted up to the apartment above the antique store. "What about Schoen?" he asked. "Did you kill him?"

Harvath shook his head. "No, I didn't."

"After everything he did to you. Why not?"

Harvath thought about it for a moment and then replied, "Death would have been too good for him."

"Really?" stated the Troll, raising an eyebrow. "I'm surprised you feel that way."

"If you could see what he's been reduced to," said Harvath, "you'd understand. Life is a much crueler punishment for Schoen. He's already been blown up on two occasions."

The Troll withdrew a small beige box, extended its antenna, and depressing its lone red button replied, "Then maybe the third time's the charm."

The explosion blew the windows out of the top-floor apartment and shook the entire block. Shards of broken glass and flaming debris rained down onto the street.

Harvath picked himself up off the ground just in time to see the Troll's SUV recede into the distance.

CHAPTER 124

Harvath had refused all the president's invitations to come and meet with him at the White House.

Though the charges of treason against him had been dropped, Rutledge still wanted to have a serious heart-to-heart so that they could put the past behind them and move forward.

To his credit, Harvath was smart enough not to deny the president's requests outright. Since Tracy's release from the hospital, she had been living at his place. He told everyone that taking care of both her and his recovering puppy kept him busy around the clock.

The president knew Harvath was lying, but let it go. Harvath had been through a lot. He'd been thrown under the proverbial bus, and not only had the president not helped him out from under, but he had ordered him to stay there while the bus's tires rolled right over him.

Rutledge didn't blame Harvath for not wanting to see him, but enough was enough. The president called Gary Lawlor and told him in no uncertain terms that he wanted Harvath standing in front of his desk inside the Oval Office by the end of the day or it was going to be Lawlor's ass on the line.

Ever the good soldier, Lawlor had his assistant clear the rest of his day, and he went to drag Scot in to meet with the president.

When he arrived at Bishop's Gate, he didn't see Harvath's car and figured he had gone out to pick up groceries or medications for Tracy or the dog, which they had named Bullet, after their mutual friend, Bullet Bob, who had been killed during the attacks on New York City.

Lawlor parked his car and walked up the front steps. Looking down at the threshold, he wondered for the umpteenth time what it must have been like for Harvath to come down and find Tracy lying there in a

pool of blood. It was a horrible image, and he tried to
shake it from his mind as he raised the heavy iron
knocker and let it slam against the thick wooden door.

As he waited, he thought how ironic it was that
Harvath should live in a former church. The man had
become a devout penitent to the people whom Roussard had harmed. He visited his mother repeatedly in
California, and as her eyesight began to return, he
made sure she had the best of care once she was ready
to come home. He visited both Carolyn Leonard and
Kate Palmer at their hospital in D.C. as often as he
could and kept their rooms filled with fresh flowers
until they were well enough to be discharged. After
that, he bombarded them with more flowers and basket upon basket of food. No matter what anyone said
to him, Harvath wouldn't stop. This was his self-
imposed penance, and until the guilt was lifted from
his soul there was no stopping him.

When it became known that Kevin McCauliff
had used the NGA's DOD computers on Harvath's
behalf, the young analyst was brought up on discipline
charges. Harvath called in every favor ever owed him
and pulled every string imaginable to have the charges
dropped and for McCauliff to be honorably discharged from his position at the NGA. Tim Finney
and Ron Parker offered McCauliff a job at Sargasso
the very next day.

Lawlor knocked on the heavy door once more,
but no one answered. There wasn't even the sound of
Bullet's barking, which was a given lately.

Having been told where Harvath kept his spare

key, Lawlor retrieved it and opened the front door.

"Hello?" he shouted as he poked his head inside. "Anybody home?"

Lawlor waited, but there was no response. Coming the rest of the way inside, he closed the door behind him.

He walked into the kitchen first and found that everything had been cleaned and put away. Normally, it was a chaotic jumble of pots, pans, dishes, and glasses as Scot and Tracy moved from one culinary undertaking to the next. Something definitely wasn't right.

Opening the fridge to help himself to a beer, Lawlor found it completely empty. None of this was making any sense.

He strolled out of the kitchen and into the large area that functioned as Harvath's living room. Everything here had been straightened and put in its place as well.

Suddenly, Lawlor noticed something on the stone mantelpiece above the fireplace. Walking over, he found Harvath's BlackBerry and his DHS credentials. Next to them was a crisp piece of Tracy's stationery folded in half.

Opening it, he read a simple two-word message that had been written in Harvath's hand.

Gone fishing.

ACKNOWLEDGMENTS

My beautiful wife, **Trish**, made it clear that in this book I should thank my readers first. She's right, of course (she's always right, I've learned), but there's part of me that wonders what kind of husband I would be if I didn't thank her first. On more nights than I can count, Trish came home from her own demanding career only to gladly feed and bathe our little ones so I could keep on writing. Thank you, honey. I love you more than you will ever know.

Having snuck in that thank-you to my wife, I want to now thank you, **the readers**. It has been a pleasure meeting you on tour and at book festivals and writing conferences across the country. It is because you recommend me to your friends, family, neighbors, and co-workers that my career is growing. I continue to be humbled and appreciative of your support.

Without the fabulous **bookstores** and the **Atria/ Pocket sales staff**, you wouldn't be holding this in your hands right now. I am extremely grateful to all the people who have worked so hard to build me as an author and who strive to make every book bigger than the last. It is a team effort, and along with the **Pocket/ Atria art and production departments**, I couldn't hope to be aligned with more creative, intelligent, or nicer people in the publishing business.

I dedicated this book to **Scott F. Hill, Ph.D.**, for many reasons. His knowledge of the thriller genre is broader and deeper than that of any human being I have ever met. He continues to be an excellent sounding board and a great friend to brainstorm with. More than that, Scott is a model patriot who has dedicated his life to improving the lives of our veterans. People like him make me proud to call myself an American.

I have a pool of gentlemen and one lady who have definitely been there, done that, and have the T-shirt to prove it. I like to refer to them as my sharpshooters, and they work hard to make sure I get things right. When I don't, it's my fault, not theirs. In no particular order, these exceptional patriots are **Rodney Cox**, **Chuck Fretwell**, **Steve Hoffa**, **Chad Norberg**, and **Steven C. Bronson**. To this list I am honored to also welcome and thank **Cynthia Longo** and **Ronald Moore**.

My Sun Valley crew was right there with the latest in political and federal law enforcement issues. My sincere thanks, as always, go out to **Gary Penrith**, **Frank Gallagher**, **Tom Baker**, **Daryl Mills**, and **Terry Mangan**.

Anyone who has been to the annual gathering in Sun Valley knows how much we all appreciate the folks at TASER International. In particular, I want to thank my good pal **Steve Tuttle** for all of his help with this book. All of the good guys who deploy with TASER products know how exceptional they are and that they absolutely save lives. Thanks, Steve.

Ronaldo Palmera is a slime bag of the highest order who was based upon a real terrorist. In no way should he be confused with my delightful father-in-law, **Ronald Palmer**. Ron's vast experience south of the border was the inspiration for all things Mexican in this novel, and his insight and guidance was, as always, very much appreciated.

Patrick Doak and **David Vennett** have remained my steadfast guides through the wilds of Washington politics. I couldn't write what I write without them and I wouldn't have near as much fun when I visit D.C. Thank you, gentlemen.

Bart Berry of Aquarius Training Systems can always come up with just the right thing to help me with my novel. He is both my cousin and climbing instructor, and while I didn't need much climbing help with this book, like Ron, he also has significant experience south of the border, and I thank him for his input.

As always, if it flies, eats sushi, or speaks German, I will absolutely not write about it without running it by **Richard and Anne Levy**, as well as our dear friend **Alice**.

Tom and Geri Whowell once again provided invaluable assistance with my manuscript. From what I understand, "Scot Harvath" is now a password at both Fontana, Wisconsin's Gordy's Boat House bar and restaurant as well as the Cobalt boat dealership. How much of a discount it gets you, I have no idea, but I plan to find out this summer. I'll know that I've really arrived when they decide to name a drink after me.

Tom Gosse is one of the neatest people I know. As a funeral director, he provided me with some invaluable information for this book. His brother-in-law Patrick Ahern is a great friend, and I am sure the fact that I killed off Pat's character in my first book but let Gosse live in this one will be a source of good-natured grief I will have to live with for some time.

I have some other good friends who are out there kicking ass and taking hyphenated names on a daily basis. No matter where they are or what they are doing, they are willing to answer my questions. True to their reputations as "quiet professionals," they asked that I not recognize them by name here. You all know who you are, and I thank you.

I also need to thank **Mark**, **Ellen**, and everyone else at **La Rue Tactical** down in Texas for their kindness to me and their unwavering support of our elite warriors in the field.

My two greatest assets, advocates, and allies are my magnificent agent, **Heide Lange**, and my superb editor, **Emily Bestler**. Their contributions to my career are immeasurable, and I know for a fact that neither of them will ever grasp how important they are to me. Thank you.

Two more ladies in the pantheon of publishing who are invaluable to me are my publishers, **Louise Burke** and **Judith Curr**. It is through their tireless efforts that my career is where it is, and I thank them.

Jack Romanos and **Carolyn Reidy** often operate behind the scenes without much thanks from their authors. Each year I learn a little bit more about the book business, and as I do, my appreciation for what they do, in particular for my career, grows. Thank you for everything.

With the passing of James Brown, **David Brown** has inherited the mantle of the hardest-working man in show business. On the eighth day God created publicists, but they were not all created equal. David Brown was created head and shoulders above the rest. From the Top of the Rock to the Pig & Whistle, thanks for everything, David.

Alex Canon, **Laura Stern**, and **Sarah Branham** continue to be incredibly helpful day in and day out. This small mention here hardly comes close to thanking them for everything they do for me.

Ernest Hemingway once said that to be a good writer you need to be possessed of a shockproof bullshit detector. I think the same attribute is necessary for a good lawyer, especially one in Hollywood. I'm extremely fortunate in that I don't have a good lawyer, I have a *great* one. **Scott Schwimer** is hands down the best entertainment attorney in the industry. He has also become one of my best friends, and for that I am doubly blessed.

SIMON & SCHUSTER AND
POCKET BOOKS UK
PROUDLY PRESENT

THE LAST PATRIOT

The next thrilling novel
by Brad Thor

Turn the page for a preview of
The Last Patriot . . .

PROLOGUE

Andrew Salam stepped out from behind the bronze statue of Thomas Jefferson and asked, "Are you alone?"

Twenty-three-year-old Nura Khalifa nodded.

Her thick, dark hair spilled over her shoulders, stopping just above her breasts. Beneath her thin jacket, he could make out the curves of her body, the narrowness of her waist. For a moment, he believed he could even smell her perfume, though it was more likely the scent of cherry blossoms blown by a faint breeze across the tidal basin. He shouldn't be meeting her at night and alone like this. It was a mistake.

Actually, the mistake was allowing his lust for her to cloud his judgment. Salam knew better. She was a gorgeous, desirable woman, but she was also his asset. He had recruited her and he was responsible for the tenor of their relationship. No matter how perfect he thought they could be for each other, no matter how badly he wanted to feel, just once, her lips and that body pressed against his as he buried his nose in the nape of her neck and drank in the smell of her, he couldn't crumble. FBI agents controlled their emotions, not the other way around.

Shutting out his desire, Andrew Salam remained professional. "Why did you contact me?"

"Because I needed to see you," said Nura as she moved toward him.

He thought about holding out his hand to stop her. He was afraid he wouldn't be able to control himself if she got any closer. Then he saw the tears that stained her face and, without thinking, opened up his arms.

Nura came to him and he pulled her into his chest. As she sobbed, his head fell to the crown of her head and he allowed his face to brush against her hair. He was playing with fire.

As quickly as he had allowed her to come to him, he knew it was wrong and he gently pushed her away until he was holding her by both shoulders at arm's length. "What happened?"

"My uncle's the target," she stammered.

Salam was stunned. "Are you sure?"

"I think they've already hired the assassin."

"Hold on, Nura. People just don't go out and hire assassins," began Salam, but she interrupted him.

"They said the threat has grown too great and it needs to be dealt with, now."

Salam bent down so he could look into her eyes. "Did they mention your uncle by name?"

"No, but they didn't have to. I *know* he's the target."

"How do you know?"

"They've been asking lots of questions about him and what he's working on. Andrew, we have to do something. We have to find him and warn him. *Please*."

"We will," said Salam as he looked around. "I promise. But first, I need to know everything you've heard, no matter how small."

Nura was trembling.

"How did you get here?" he asked as he removed his coat and draped it over her shoulders.

"I took the Metro, why?"

Though the couple had the memorial all to themselves at this time of night, Salam was uncomfortable about being out in the open. He had a strange feeling that they were being watched. "I'd feel better if we went someplace else. My car is parked nearby. Are you up to taking a walk?"

Nura nodded and Salam put his arm around her as they exited the statue chamber.

While they walked, Nura began to fill him in on what she had learned.

Salam listened, but his mind was drifting.

Had he been paying attention to more than just how good she felt pressed up against him, he might have had time to react to the two men who sprung from the shadows.

CHAPTER 1

The Italian Centre for Photoreproduction, Binding, and Restoration of State Archives, also known as the CFLR, was located in an unassuming postmodern office building three blocks from the Tiber River at 14 Via Costanza Baudana Vaccolini. It boasted one of the world's leading archival preservation facilities as well as a young deputy assistant director named Alessandro Lombardi, who was eager to begin his evening.

"Dottore, mi scusi," said Lombardi.

Dr. Marwan Khalifa, a distinguished Koranic scholar in his early sixties with a handsome face and neatly trimmed beard, looked up from the desk he was working at. "Yes, Alessandro?"

The Italian adopted his most charming smile and asked, "Tonight, we finish early?"

Dr. Khalifa laughed and set down his pen. "You have *another* date this evening?"

Lombardi approached and showed the visiting scholar a picture on his mobile phone.

"What happened to the blond woman?"

Lombardi shrugged. "That was last week."

Khalifa picked his pen back up. "I suppose I can be done in an hour."

"An *hour*?" exclaimed Lombardi as he pressed his hands together in mock prayer. "Dottore, if I don't leave now, all of the good tables outside will be gone. Please. When the weather is this nice, Italians are not allowed to work late. It's state policy."

Khalifa knew better. No matter what the weather, there were always people working late in the CFLR building—maybe not in the Research and Preservation department, but there was almost always a light burning somewhere. "If you want to leave your keys, I'll lock up the office when I go."

"And my time card?" asked Lombardi, pressing his luck.

"You get paid for the time you work, my friend."

"*Va bene,*" replied the young man as he fished a set of keys for the department from his pocket and set them on the desk. "I'll see you in the morning."

"Have fun," said Khalifa.

Lombardi flashed him the smile once more and then made his way toward the exit, turning off any unnecessary lights along his way.

Dr. Khalifa's desk was a large drafting-style table, illuminated by two adjustable lamps. His time as well as Lombardi's was being paid for by the Yemeni Antiquities Authority.

In 1972, workers in Yemen had made a startling discovery. Restoring the aging Great Mosque at Sana'a, said to have been one of the first architectural projects of Islam commissioned by the Prophet Mohammed himself, the workers uncovered a hidden loft between the mosque's inner and outer roofs. Inside the loft was a mound of parchments and pages of Arabic texts that at some point had been secreted away, and were now melded together through centuries of exposure to rain and dampness. In archeological circles, such a discovery was referred to as a "paper grave."

Cursory examinations suggested that what the grave contained were tens of thousands of fragments from at least a thousand early parchment codices of the Koran.

Access to the full breadth of the find had never been allowed. Bits and pieces had been made available to a handful of scholars over the years, but out of respect for the sanctity of the documents, no one had ever been permitted to study the entire discovery. No one, that is, until Dr. Marwan Khalifa.

Khalifa was one of the world's preeminent Koranic scholars and had spent the majority of his professional career building relationships with the Yemeni Antiquities Authority and politely petitioning it to allow him to review the find. Finally, there was a changing of the guard and the new president of the Antiquities Authority, a significantly younger and more progressive man, invited Khalifa to study the entirety of what the workers at Sana'a had uncovered.

It didn't take long for Khalifa to realize the magnitude of the find.

As Yemen didn't have the proper facilities to preserve and study the fragments and as the Yemeni government was absolutely opposed to Khalifa's taking the items back to the United States, an arrangement was made for the complete contents of the grave to be transferred to the CFLR in Rome, where they could be preserved and studied before being returned to Yemen.

With the blessing of the new Antiquities Authority president, Khalifa oversaw the entire process, including the technical side, which included such things as edge detection, document degradation, global and adaptive thresholding, color clustering, and image processing.

His anticipation grew as each scrap was preserved and he was able to begin assembling the pieces of the puzzle. A significant percentage of the parchments dated back to the seventh and eighth centuries—Islam's first two centuries. Khalifa was handling pieces of the earliest Korans known to mankind.

A billion-and-a-half Muslims worldwide believed that the Koran they worshiped today was the perfect, inviolate word of God—an *exact* word-for-word, perfect copy of the original book as it exists in Paradise and just as it was transmitted, without a single error, by Allah to the Prophet Mohammed through the Angel Gabriel.

As a textual historian, Khalifa was fascinated by the inconsistencies. As a moderate Muslim who loved his religion, but believed deeply that it was in need of reform, he was overjoyed. The fact that he had found, and was continuing to find, aberrations that differed from Islamic dogma meant that the case could finally be made for the Koran to be reexamined in a historical framework.

He had always believed that the Koran had been written by man, not God. If such a thing could be proven, Muslims around the world would be able to reexamine their faith with a modern, twenty-first-century perspective, rather than the outdated, unenlightened perspective of seventh-century Arabia. And now it seemed that he had just the proof he needed.

It was such a powerful discovery that Khalifa could barely sleep at night. It dovetailed so well with another project his colleague Anthony Nichols was working on back in America, that he felt as if Allah himself was steering his research, that this was His divine will.

All Khalifa could think about when he wasn't at work was getting back to the CFLR facility each day to further investigate the fragments.

Though on evenings like this Khalifa missed Lombardi's companionship as well as his expertise with the technical equipment, the truth was that he hardly noticed when the young Italian was gone. In fact, he was often so engrossed that he barely noticed Lombardi even when he was standing at the desk right in front of him.

Turning to the voluminous collection of information he had stored on his rugged Toughbook laptop, Khalifa pulled up one of the thirty-two thousand images the CFLR had already digitally archived. While he could have crossed the room and retrieved the fragment itself, he often found it unnecessary, as accessing the digital images was much easier.

Khalifa was working on lining up six slivers of text written in the Hijazzi script, when a shadow fell across his drafting table. "What did you forget this time, Alessandro?" the scholar asked without looking up.

"I didn't forget anything," responded a deep, unfamiliar voice. "It is you who have forgotten."

Dr. Khalifa looked up and saw a man in a long, black soutane with a white collar. It was a common sight throughout Rome, particularly near the Vatican. But, even though the CFLR did do a certain amount of work with the Holy See, Khalifa had never seen a priest inside the building. "Who are you?"

"That's not important," replied the priest as he moved closer. "I would rather discuss your faith."

"You must be confused, Father," said Khalifa as he sat up in his chair. "I'm not a Catholic. I'm Muslim."

"I know," said the priest softly. "That's why I'm here."

In an explosion of black cloth, the priest was suddenly behind Khalifa. One of his large, rough hands cupped the scholar's chin while the other gripped the side of his head.

With a powerful snap, the priest broke the scholar's neck.

He stood there for a moment, the corpse clutched tightly, almost lovingly to his chest, then stepped back and let go.

Khalifa's head slammed against the table before coming to rest beneath it.

The priest dragged the body across the floor and positioned it at the bottom of a set of stairs which led up to a small archival library. From there, it took only moments to set the fire.

Two hours later, having showered and changed, the assassin sat in his hotel room and studied Khalifa's laptop. Connecting to a remote server, he had the Koranic scholar's password program cracked within fifteen minutes. From there, one e-mail confirmed everything he needed to know.

> *Marwan,*
>
> *Finally, good news! It appears we have located the book. A dealer named René Bertrand is bringing it to market in Paris at the Antiquarian Book Fair. I will be meeting him there to negotiate the purchase. As you know, my funding is limited, but I have faith that barring an all-out bidding war, the book will be ours!*
>
> *As planned, I will see you next Monday at 9:00 a.m. in the Middle Eastern Reading Room of the Library of Congress—although now we'll have the book and can begin deciphering the location of the final revelation!*
>
> *Anthony*

The assassin had had Khalifa under surveillance long enough to know who the sender was and what he was referring to. It was a parallel and potentially more damaging project, which up until this point had appeared stalled. Obviously, things had changed—and not for the better.

The assassin shut down the laptop and spent the next several hours pondering the implication of what he had learned. He then started formulating a plan. When all of the angles had been considered and tested in his mind, he reactivated the computer.

Attaching the relevant e-mails between Khalifa and Anthony Nichols, he composed his report and delivered his assessment to his superiors.

Their response came back twenty minutes later, hidden in the draft folder of the e-mail account they shared. The assassin had been cleared for the Paris operation.

At the end of the message, his superiors instructed that funds would be transferred to Paris and all necessary arrangements would be made. They then congratulated him on his success in Rome.

The assassin deleted the message from the draft folder and logged off. After reciting his prayers, he disconnected his phone and hung the Do Not Disturb sign on his door. He would be leaving early in the morning and needed to rest.

The next several days were going to be very busy. His superiors were in agreement that the Prophet Mohammed's lost revelation needed to stay lost—forever.

CHAPTER 2

Thirty-seven-year-old American Scot Harvath studied the amazing woman sitting at the café table next to him. Her blond hair had grown back and came to just below her ears.

"We need to make a decision," she said.

There it was—the topic he'd been trying to avoid since killing the man who had shot her nine months ago.

"I just want to make sure that you're fully—" he began, his voice trailing off.

"Recovered?" she asked, finishing his sentence for him.

Harvath nodded.

"Scot, this stopped being about my recovery the minute we left the United States. I'm fine. Not one hundred percent, but as close as I'm probably going to get."

"You don't know that for sure."

Tracy Hastings smiled. Prior to being targeted by an assassin bent on revenge against Harvath, Tracy had been a Naval Explosive Ordinance Disposal technician who had lost one of her luminescent, pale blue eyes when an IED she was defusing detonated prematurely. Though her face had undergone significant scarring, the plastic surgeons had done a remarkable job of minimizing the visible damage.

Hastings had always been in great shape, but after the accident she had thrown herself into her fitness routine. She had the most perfectly sculpted body of any woman Harvath had ever known. Self-conscious about her disfigurement and the pale blue eye given to her by her surgeons as a replacement, Tracy had been fond of joking that she had both a body to die for and the face to protect it.

It was a joke that Harvath had worked hard to wean from her repertoire. She was the most beautiful woman he had ever met, and slowly his hard work had paid off. The closer they grew and the safer Tracy felt with him, the less her self-deprecating humor seemed necessary.

The same could be said for Harvath. Ten years Tracy's senior, he had used sarcasm largely to keep the world at bay. Now, he used it to make her laugh.

With his handsome, rugged face, sandy brown hair, bright blue eyes, and muscular five-foot-ten frame, they made a striking couple.

"You want to know what I think?" she asked. "I think this is more about your recovery than mine. And that's okay."

Harvath started to object, but Tracy put her hand atop his and said, "We need to put what happened behind us and get on with our lives."

They had been together less than a year, but she knew him better than anyone ever had. She knew he'd never be happy living an ordinary life. So much of who he was and how he saw himself came from what he did. He needed to get back to it, even if that meant her nudging him toward it.

Harvath slid his hand out from under hers. He couldn't put what had happened behind him. No matter how hard he tried, he couldn't shake the picture of finding Tracy in a pool of blood with a bullet in the back of her head, or the memory of the president who had stood in his way while the person responsible continued to target those closest to Harvath. A couple of friends suggested that maybe he was suffering from PTSD, but in the words of an Army colonel he once cross-trained with, Harvath didn't get PTSD, he *gave* it.

"We can't be gypsies forever," Tracy insisted.

"Our lives have been on hold long enough. We need to get back to the real world, and you need to think about going back to work."

"There's about as much chance of me going back to work for Jack Rutledge as there is of me going to work for a terrorist organization. I'm done," he said.

A Navy SEAL who had joined the president's Secret Service detail in an effort to help improve the White House's ability to stave off and respond to terrorist attacks, Harvath had grown to become the president's number one covert counterterrorism operative and was exceptional at what he did.

So exceptional, in fact, that the president had created a top-secret antiterrorism effort known as the Apex Project specifically for him. Its goal was to level the playing field with international terrorists who sought to strike Americans and American interests at home and abroad. That goal was achieved through one simple mandate—as long as the terrorists refused to play by any rules, Harvath wouldn't be expected to either.

The Apex Project was buried in a little-known branch of DHS known as the Office of International Investigative Assistance, or OIIA for short. The OIIA's overt mission was to assist foreign police, military, and intelligence agencies in helping to prevent terrorist attacks. In that sense, Harvath's mission was in step with the official OIIA mandate. In reality, he was a very secretive dog of war enlisted post–9/11 to be unleashed by the president upon the enemies of the United States anywhere, anytime, with anything he needed to get the job done.

But that part of Harvath's life was over. It had taken him years to realize that his counterterrorism career was incompatible with what he really wanted—a family and someone to come home to; someone to share his life with.

Starting relationships had never been his problem. It was keeping them going that he never could get right. Tracy Hastings was the best thing to ever happen to him and he had no intention of letting her go. For the first time in he couldn't remember how long, Scot Harvath was truly happy.

"We don't have to go back right away," said Tracy, interrupting his thoughts. "We can wait until November, after the elections. There'll be Christmas and then the inauguration in January. Unless the constitution has been rewritten and Rutledge is elected to a third term, you'll be dealing with a completely new president."

Harvath was about to respond when he

looked out across the street and noticed a well-dressed Arab man remove a "Slim Jim" from beneath his blazer.

Popping the lock on a faded blue Peugeot, the man climbed in, shut the door and disappeared beneath the window line.

He didn't know why, but something inside Harvath told him this was more than just a car theft.

POCKET
BOOKS

Takedown
Brad Thor

After years without a terrorist attack on American soil,
one group has picked the 4th July weekend to pull out all the
stops. In a perfectly executed attack, all the bridges and
tunnels leading into and out of Manhattan are destroyed just
as thousands of commuters begin their holiday exodus.

With domestic efforts focused on search and rescue,
a deadly team of highly trained foreign soldiers methodically
makes its way through the city with the sole aim of locating
one of their own – a man so powerful America will do
anything to keep him hidden.

Scot Harvath is now the nation's only hope. Fighting his
way through the burning streets of Manhattan, he must
mount his own operation to track down a man the US
government refuses to admit even exists.

'Brad Thor will kidnap even the most demanding readers,
deprive them of sleep, and convert them into instant
devotees' DAN BROWN

ISBN: 978-1-4165-2238-6
PRICE £6.99

**POCKET
BOOKS**

Blowback
Brad Thor

**A weapon designed to decimate the Roman Empire
has just become the No 1 threat to the USA!**

After three summers of record-breaking heat across Europe,
one steadily melting Alpine glacier has given up an ancient
secret – a secret which could thrust civilization back into the
Dark Ages. Now this ultimate weapon has fallen into the
hands of terrorists determined to rid the Middle East of
Western infidels, and the US president has no choice but to
call on Navy SEAL turned covert counterterrorism agent,
Scot Harvath, to pull out all the stops to prevent a
catastrophe of terrifying proportions.

From Cyprus, London and Paris to Italy, Switzerland and
Saudi Arabia, Harvath faces a supercharged race
against the clock to stop one of the greatest
evils ever to face the western world.

'The action is non-stop' KYLE MILLS

ISBN: 978-1-4165-2237-9
PRICE £6.99

**POCKET
BOOKS**

This book and other **Brad Thor** titles are available
from your local bookshop or can be ordered
direct from the publisher.

978-1-4165-2238-6	Takedown	£6.99
978-1-4165-2237-9	Blowback	£6.99
978-0-7434-3678-6	State of the Union	£6.99
978-0-7434-3676-2	Path of the Assassin	£6.99
978-0-7434-3674-8	The Lions of Lucerne	£6.99

Please send cheque or postal order for the value of the book,
free postage and packing within the UK, to
SIMON & SCHUSTER CASH SALES
PO Box 29, Douglas Isle of Man, IM99 1BQ
Tel: 01624 677237, Fax: 01624 670923
Email: bookshop@enterprise.net
www.bookpost.co.uk

Please allow 14 days for delivery. Prices and availability
subject to change without notice.